Praise for beloved romance author Betty Neels

"Neels is especially good at painting her scenes with choice words, and this adds to the charm of the story."
—*USATODAY.com's Happy Ever After* blog on *Tulips for Augusta*

"Betty Neels surpasses herself with an excellent storyline, a hearty conflict and pleasing characters."
—*RT Book Reviews* on *The Right Kind of Girl*

"Once again Betty Neels delights readers with a sweet tale in which love conquers all."
—*RT Book Reviews* on *Fate Takes a Hand*

"One of the first Harlequin authors I remember reading. I was completely enthralled by the exotic locales…. Her books will always be some of my favorites to re-read."
—*Goodreads* reviewer on *A Valentine for Daisy*

"I just love Betty Neels!… If you like a good old-fashioned romance…you can't go wrong with this author."
—*Goodreads* reviewer on *Caroline's Waterloo*

Romance readers around the world were sad to note the passing of **Betty Neels** in June 2001. Her career spanned thirty years, and she continued to write into her ninetieth year. To her millions of fans, Betty epitomized the romance writer, and yet she began writing almost by accident. She had retired from nursing, but her inquiring mind still sought stimulation. Her new career was born when she heard a lady in her local library bemoaning the lack of good romance novels. Betty's first book, *Sister Peters in Amsterdam*, was published in 1969, and she eventually completed 134 books. Her novels offer a reassuring warmth that was very much a part of her own personality. She was a wonderful writer, and she is greatly missed. Her spirit and genuine talent live on in all her stories.

BETTY NEELS

Tangled Autumn
& The Edge of Winter

H HARLEQUIN® SPECIAL RELEASE

ISBN-13: 978-1-335-04505-8

Tangled Autumn & The Edge of Winter

Copyright © 2018 by Harlequin Books S.A.

The publisher acknowledges the copyright holder
of the individual works as follows:

Tangled Autumn
Copyright © 1971 by Betty Neels

The Edge of Winter
Copyright © 1976 by Betty Neels

Recycling programs
for this product may
not exist in your area.

This edition published by arrangement with Harlequin Books S.A.

For questions and comments about the quality of this book,
please contact us at CustomerService@Harlequin.com.

® and TM are trademarks of Harlequin Enterprises Limited or its
corporate affiliates. Trademarks indicated with ® are registered in the
United States Patent and Trademark Office, the Canadian Intellectual
Property Office and in other countries.

Printed in U.S.A.

www.Harlequin.com

CONTENTS

TANGLED AUTUMN

Chapter 1

The rain fell, soundless and gentle, veiling the dimming heather and all the rusts and reds and brown of the autumn countryside, and almost blotting out the distant mountains while it in no way detracted from their beauty. This view was not, however, shared by Miss Sappha Devenish, sitting behind the wheel of her red Mini. She had been halfway up a moderately steep hill when the little car had coughed, spluttered, hesitated and then continued its climb, only to come to a halt again. The road was a narrow one, the Mini had stopped squarely on its crown, and its driver, calculating her chances of steering it into the side, decided against it. The country was fairly open ahead of her—anyone coming down the hill would see her in ample time to pull up, and anything climbing behind her would be, of necessity, travelling slowly. Besides, she had no mind to

ruin her expensive suit and still more expensive shoes—
someone would be bound to pass one way or the other,
sooner or later. It seemed as though it would be later,
she had been watching the rain for more than an hour,
and now turned to study the map on the seat beside her.

She had left the main road at Torridon and had
passed through Inver Alligin, which according to her
reckoning meant that she was a bare five miles from her
destination. She glanced at her watch—it was already
four o'clock, and her thoughts dwelt longingly on tea,
though it was her own fault that she wasn't going to get
it. She should have filled up at that last petrol station,
but she had been in a hurry to arrive at her journey's
end and she had thought that she could just do it. Foolish, and all the more so after her well-planned, effortless
two-day trip from London—almost six hundred miles.
Well, she had wanted to get as far away from Andrew
as possible—the hospital too; it looked as though she
had achieved her purpose, for the countryside she was
now in was indeed far away.

She had jumped at the chance her uncle had offered
her to go as nurse to a patient of his staying in this remote district of the Western Highlands, but now, suddenly, she wondered if she had been wise. Viewed from
faraway London, and with the bitter aftertaste of her
break-up with Andrew still to be borne, it had seemed
a splendid idea, but now, surrounded by distant mountains and an unfamiliar countryside made sombre by
the rain, she wasn't so sure. She stared glumly out of the
car's windows, beset by the feeling that she shouldn't
have come; a feeling that was heightened by the nag-
ging suspicion that she would probably be homesick for
the ward she had left behind her at Greggs'.

She had been Sister of Women's Surgical for only a year—she had been a fool to give it up; any other girl, less soft and silly than herself, would have put a bold face on things and stuck it out. She sighed, aware that however reasonable this argument sounded, she would remain soft and silly, although in the last few weeks she had succeeded in acquiring a cool impersonal shell to cover it. She interrupted her thoughts to consider the sound of a car coming up the hill, travelling rather faster than she thought either possible or wise. She turned in her seat and craned her neck to peer out of the rain-washed rear window. It was a Land Rover, coming towards her with a fine burst of speed which took no account of the possibility of there being other traffic. It came to a halt only a foot or so from her rear wheels and its driver did not immediately get out; when he did, his movements were irritatingly unhurried. He was a very tall man with broad shoulders, wearing, she observed, a shabby duffle coat and corduroy trousers stuffed into rubber boots—a farmer, she decided, then felt uncertain of this as he approached and she was able to take stock of him, for he didn't look like a farmer at all, not with that dark fierce face, haughty and hawk-nosed above a straight mouth; dark hair brushed back from a wide forehead and a pair of winged eyebrows, so arched and thick that they gave him the look of a satyr.

She wound down the window, feeling nervous and just a little silly—justifiably so, as it turned out, for he said without preamble:

'Of all the fool places to stop—I might have known it was a woman.' He had a deep voice with the hint of an accent and he spoke without haste and apparently without temper, which for some reason caused her own to rise.

'I'm out of petrol!' she snapped, and could have bitten out her tongue the next instant, for he said at once:

'Naturally.' His dark eyes studied her person in leisurely fashion. 'A stranger, of course—no one in these parts travels without a spare can, let alone allows the tank to run dry. You could have got to the side of the road, though.'

Sappha lifted her chin. Even though she was aware that she had been careless, she didn't much care for the way he was pointing the fact out to her.

'It's raining,' her glance went involuntarily to her shoes—hardly made for a muddy road in the more remote parts of the Scottish Highlands. His gaze followed hers and his rather stern mouth curved for an instant. He said with perfunctory kindness:

'I don't suppose that you realised that tweeds'—his gaze flickered over her beautifully cut suit, obviously he didn't mean that kind of tweed—'and thick boots are—er—more suitable at this time of year.' He gave her an enquiring look. 'But perhaps you're only passing through? If you are, I should warn you that the road ends at Dialach.'

She stared at him, her brown eyes smouldering. 'I know—I have a map. I'm going to Dialach.'

He received this sparse information with an expressionless face, although she was aware of the glint in his eye as he straightened up, saying: 'In that case, I'll put some petrol in your tank—unless you would like a tow?'

Sappha felt the stirrings of temper again and quelled them. After all, he was being helpful even though he appeared to find it tiresome.

'No thanks,' she said politely. 'I'll be OK, if I could just have the petrol,' and watched while he fetched a can and filled her tank. When he had finished he came back to stare at her through the window once more, and she asked: 'How much did you put in?' and reached for her handbag. 'I'd like to pay...' to be interrupted brusquely by his 'My dear good girl!' uttered in such a tone of mocking arrogance that she coloured faintly and snatched her hand away from her handbag as though it was red hot, and when he made no further attempt at conversation, she said awkwardly: 'Well, thank you very much,' and switched on her engine, praying that she would make a smooth start. Anything else under those dark mocking eyes would be the last straw, but to her relief the Mini pulled away without a hitch, gathering a little speed as it breasted the hill, and at the corner, between the dripping birch trees Sappha looked in the car mirror—the man was still standing in the middle of the road watching her.

She forgot about him in the next instant, allowing the little car to run steadily while she took her fill of the scene before her. Below and a little to her left she could see Dialach tucked cosily into the trees which lined the loch. It was a small place, with its houses crowded together around the tiny harbour and a scattering of larger houses on the hill behind it. There was a causeway on the left of the town, running out across the rain-smoothed water of the loch to a little island that supported a huddle of dwellings. Sappha, straining to see them clearly through the rain, concluded that they and the causeway were in ruins, and turned her attention to the church, its square grey tower standing in Dialach's centre. Her patient was a guest at the Manse, her uncle had said, so presumably if she made for the church it would be the quickest way of getting there.

She allowed the car to dawdle to a halt and sat, no longer looking at her destination below her, but straight ahead at nothing at all, a little pucker of unhappiness between her beautiful brown eyes. Despite the despondency of her expression, she was an extremely pretty girl, with an oval face framed by naturally dark curling hair, which although confined in a french pleat, had escaped in soft tendrils on either side of her cheeks. Her nose was straight and a little on the short side, and her mouth, released from its present downward droop, was soft and mobile. Her good looks were offset by the clothes she wore—well cut and fashionable, although not excessively so, and her hands, free of her driving gloves, were nicely shaped and beautifully kept. She leaned her rather determined chin on them now, thinking about her new job. When her Uncle John had offered it to her she had accepted without thought. To stay in London in the same hospital as Andrew was unthinkable—it offered a means of escape from an untenable position. She had given a sympathetic Matron her notice, and after a month in which she had learned to hide her real feelings under a cool, impersonal manner she hadn't realised she possessed; she was free. She thought wearily back over the last few months, wondering where she had gone wrong— if, indeed, she had been at fault.

She and Andrew had been engaged for several months, and although the actual date of the wedding had never been discussed, everyone had taken it for granted that it would be soon. She ignored the first spiteful whispers about him; she was sensible enough to know that in a hospital the size of Greggs', there would always be someone ready to start rumours of that sort, and when they had persisted, she had even joked about them with Andrew, because Staff Nurse Beatty, although possessed of a lush blonde beauty, was hardly his type. He had laughed with her and agreed with an apparent sincerity which had made it all the harder to bear when she had come across them in a deserted Outpatients Department. Their embrace had been so close and so long that she had gone away without them even noticing…she had waited two terrible days for him to tell her about it, during which time it had become common knowledge throughout the hospital, and when he did, making out that it had been no more than a momentary impulse on his part and certainly the same on the part of Beatty, she had swallowed her pride and forgiven him, turning a stubbornly deaf ear to her friends' guarded hints, and a still more stubborn ear to her mother's thinly veiled warnings. She had known Andrew for more than a year; they loved each other and she trusted him… She shifted a little behind the wheel and laughed ruefully; at least she was wiser now—it would be a long time before she trusted any man again.

She hadn't believed the Sister from Men's Medical when that young lady had told her, with tact and kindness, that Andrew and Beatty had been seen time and again together in various places by various people—it seemed that London, for all its size, wasn't big enough… She had hotly denied it, because Andrew had told her that he was attending a series of post-graduate lectures, but in the end she had been forced to believe it, for she had seen them together coming out of Wheeler's one evening as she was on her way back to Greggs' after visiting her mother, who was staying with friends in Cum-

berland Terrace. She had got off the bus to cut through
the complexity of small streets to reach the hospital
and came face to face with them. This time she didn't
wait for Andrew to come to her; she waylaid him on the
way to Outpatients the next morning and with almost
no words at all had handed him back his ring and then
gone straight to Matron's office and resigned.

It was her mother who had enlisted the help of Uncle
John without telling Sappha that she had done so, and
in any case, Sappha couldn't have cared less what she
did. She took the job he offered her so providentially
and here she was. She sighed, switched on the engine
and drove down the winding road to Dialach.

The Manse was easy to find, for it stood foursquare
beside the church; a solid roomy house surrounded by
a pleasant garden in which the autumn flowers and
trees made a splash of colour even on such a grey day
as this. Sappha drove up its neat short drive and had
barely turned off the engine before the front door was
opened and the minister appeared on his doorstep. He
was a friend of her uncle's, but she hadn't expected quite
such a warm welcome—it acted like a tonic upon her
downcast spirits, she resolutely tucked her own troubles
away in the back of her mind and greeted him with a
quiet friendliness of her own which lighted up her face
to a quite breathtaking loveliness.

'You're tired and chilly, I daresay, my dear Miss Devenish,' said Mr MacFee. 'My wife has tea waiting for
you, and presently, when you are rested, you may like
to go and see our district nurse, Miss Perch, so that she
may tell you everything there is to know about Baroness van Duyren.'

He had drawn her across the hall as he spoke and now

opened a door into a pleasant room with comfortable shabby furniture and a blazing log fire. Sappha, feeling that she was being treated more as a patient than a nurse, allowed herself to be led across the room to where Mrs MacFee was standing, to be greeted by a kindness at least the equal of the minister's, and then bustled into a chair and told to undo her coat and stretch her feet to the fire. She barely had the time to do this before she was being plied with tea and hot buttered toast, while her kind host and hostess talked with gentle inconsequence of the weather, her Uncle John, the excessive rainfall and the delicate flavour of the quince preserve she had been pressed to try on a scone. It wasn't until she had followed the scone with a teacake and that with a slice of rich fruit cake that she was allowed to enquire about her patient, 'for', as she pointed out, 'Uncle John has told me a great deal about the case, and I know he will be down to see her next week, but of course he hasn't much idea of the nursing routine.'

Mrs MacFee smiled comfortably. 'Indeed one would scarcely expect him to, but you'll find Miss Perch most helpful and your patient very co-operative. She and I are old friends, of course—your uncle will have told you that already. We went to school together—Switzerland, you know and we still see a good deal of each other. She and her husband used to come every year to visit us, usually with their children. She has a family of six…' Mrs MacFee, who was childless, paused to sigh. 'After his death she continued to come, but now of course all the children are married, save for the eldest and the youngest.' She paused for breath, beaming kindly at Sappha, who had conjured up a picture of a desicated spinster wearing glasses following Mother wherever she chose to go…she hoped that she was going to like the Baroness.

It had stopped raining by the time she had convinced the minister and his wife that she was sufficiently rested and refreshed to visit Miss Perch. Mr MacFee went with her to the Manse door and pointed out the way she should go—a not very arduous walk as it turned out, for the district nurse lived in the end cottage in the little street behind the harbour, a bare three minutes' walk away. Sappha knocked on the stout door, looking around her as she did so. The harbour was indeed small, and the causeway, now that she was near enough to see it properly, was nothing but a crumbling mass of rocks and stone and wood with here and there rough steps connecting its uneven surface—she wondered if it was still used, and as if in answer to her question she glimpsed smoke rising from the muddle of buildings on the island to which it led.

She turned from their contemplation as the door opened and she saw with pleased surprise that Nurse Perch was a girl of her own age, small, blonde and blue-eyed, who grinned engagingly and said 'Hullo, do come in,' as she put out a friendly hand which Sappha took with quite obvious signs of relief. 'I expected you'd be a tough old battleaxe,' she burst out, 'but don't ask me why.'

Miss Perch giggled. 'And I thought you'd be some high and mighty Ward Sister for ever reminding me of the size and importance of your ward.' They laughed in unison and as they went inside, Sappha said:

'My name's Sappha.'

'Mine's Gloria.'

The sitting room was charmingly odd, for it had been

furnished largely by the better-off members of the community, but as most of the inhabitants had contributed something, there was a delightful hotch-potch of Victoriana; handsome rugs, two armchairs with rather startling covers, a modern and very efficient-looking desk crammed into one corner, and a variety of cushions of every conceivable size and shape. The walls supported a remarkable collection of pictures, dominated by 'The Stag at Bay' over the fireplace, on either side of which were two dim sepia-tinted photographs of elderly ladies in the heavily laden hats of a past era, and they in turn were flanked by 'When did you last see your Father?' on the one side and a cross-stitch text framed repulsively in plush and bearing the words 'Flee from the Wrath to come' on the other.

Sappha allowed her fascinated gaze to take in these samples of art before turning her attention to the third wall, which held, surprisingly, a delicate watercolour of the harbour and a pair of coloured prints each depicting a gauze-swathed young woman in the act of encouraging—or possibly repelling—the advances of a young man in a tricorne hat. Sappha was still trying to decide which it could be when her hostess spoke. 'Shattering, isn't it? The first day I was here I swore I'd have the whole lot down, but this place was furnished by practically everyone who lives here and if I moved a single picture I'd hurt someone's feelings.' She made a face and Sappha laughed.

'I've never seen anything like it,' she admitted, 'though I love the watercolour.'

Gloria coloured faintly and looked pleased. 'Oh, do you? Actually I did it myself.' She grinned cheerfully and went on, 'Come and sit down and I'll tell you all about Baroness van Duyren. I'm so glad you've come to take over—I mean I've got my hands full and after all she is a private patient. Mr Devenish is your uncle, isn't he? He comes out most weeks, but anything trifling he leaves to me or Dr MacInroy.'

She said this name in such a way that Sappha was constrained to ask:

'Is he nice—Dr MacInroy, I mean?'

'Well, he's—we're engaged—that's why I came here, to be a bit nearer him until we marry, but of course we don't see a great deal of each other; when I'm free he's usually up to his neck in measles or something and when he's got a day off I'm delivering babies.' She sighed. 'All the same, it's nice here, the people are dears and the countryside is heavenly.' She eyed Sappha's rather townish clothes with a little doubt not unmixed with envy. 'Do you like the country?'

Sappha, to whom any part of the world would have been preferable to London at that time, replied that yes, she thought she would love it.

'It'll be a bit different from the bright lights of London,' Gloria warned.

'Yes,' Sappha agreed, 'but I—I wanted a change.' She frowned. 'Just for a few months, you know.'

Gloria's eyes slid discreetly to Sappha's ringless hands resting on her lap. She said airily: 'Well, that's all right, and it's good fun here too. There's always something going on here—whist drives and play-readings and dances, and when you can't think of anything else to do you can always come here, you know. I don't lock the door, only on my days off, and I'll show you where I keep the key so's you can just walk in.'

Sappha thanked her warmly. 'I've got a little car,' she said. 'I thought I'd get out and about when I can get off.'

'Walking's better,' said Gloria. 'Now, shall we go

over the notes and charts and so on? I've got them ready and a rough routine, though I expect you'll change that to suit yourself. I don't know when you'll get your day off, but I'll pop up and do the necessary when you do...'

'Is she nice—the Baroness? She sounded a bit...' Sappha left the sentence in mid air, but all Gloria said was, 'Well, I'll leave you to form your own opinion— she's Dutch, you knew that, I expect? But her English is as good as yours or mine. She comes to stay with the MacFees at least once a year. She's fifty-four and has six children—the youngest is sixteen and the eldest thirty-ish. Lashings of money, though they've had so much for so long that you hardly notice it, if you see what I mean.'

Sappha nodded. 'It's a month since she had parathyroid osteodystrophy done, isn't it? Uncle John was rather pleased with the op—he said it was a nasty tumour. Funny no one found it sooner...'

'Well, it's a rare condition, isn't it? And the signs and symptoms are a bit like rheumatoid arthritis, aren't they? It was her son—the one who's a doctor—who suspected a tumour on a gland. He'd been away for several months, though, and she was already over here on holiday when he joined her, and he got your uncle to see her. He caught her just in time I fancy, and as it is, the poor dear has mild renal failure and to crown everything she fell down the first day she was got out of bed after the op and fractured an arm and a leg—the bones were already a bit softened because of the lack of calcium and the tumble did the rest. Still, she's not the sort to give in and she's on the mend, we hope, but dreadfully depressed at times, poor dear. You can see why she needs a private nurse.' She paused and looked at Sappha. 'Are you sorry you came?'

Sappha said slowly, 'No, it's quite a challenge, isn't it? I think I shall like it.' She got to her feet. 'I should go back. Mrs MacFee said something about me seeing the Baroness before suppertime and I ought to run over these notes first. Is there anything else I should know? Drugs and so forth?'

They bent their heads over the charts and prescriptions and TPR sheets, and presently, promising to ring up her new friend if she found herself in difficulties, Sappha made her way back to the Manse.

Her patient had a large room on the first floor, and the small room leading out of it had been turned into a very comfortable bedroom for herself. She took off her outdoor things, tidied her hair and was led by Mrs MacFee into the Baroness's room. Her first reaction was one of surprise; her patient wasn't at all what she had imagined her to be. Sappha, who had a lively imagination, had conjured up a middle-aged heavily built woman with iron grey hair and a commanding manner. What she saw was a small, extremely pretty woman, whose hair was so fair that the silver in it was hard to see, and whose face, though woefully thin and colourless, was lighted by the sweetest of smiles. She was sitting very erect against her bed pillows and despite the plastered right arm and the bed cradle, managed to look as though she were dressed for a party. Mrs MacFee made the introductions, remarking: 'Now I shall leave you two to get to know each other. Supper won't be until half past seven, and perhaps if…' she paused and looked at Sappha. 'My dear,' she said, 'I'm not sure what I should call you. Sister—or Nurse or Miss Devenish. I know you're a hospital Sister, so perhaps…'

Sappha said at once: 'I'd like it if you would call me

Sappha. Sister is a bit stiff, isn't it?' She looked at her patient. 'Baroness van Duyren may wish to call me something else—'

'Indeed no,' said the little lady vigorously. 'We're going to be seeing a great deal of each other for the next few weeks, aren't we? I'd like to call you Sappha if I may.'

This important point having been settled to everyone's satisfaction, Mrs MacFee went away and Sappha pulled a chair up to the bed. 'I've some marvellously clear instructions from Miss Perch,' she said, 'but as she has never been here all day I thought we might fill in some of the gaps between us and then I'll bring you your supper and perhaps you would tell me what you would like to do until bedtime.'

The day's routine was discussed at some length and minor points such as time off and free days for Sappha were settled too. It was at the end of this discussion that the Baroness said: 'You wear very pretty clothes, my dear, if you don't mind my saying so. I'm afraid you'll not have many opportunities to go out here, though Ida did tell me that you have a car of your own. How clever of you to drive—I must confess that I have no idea as to what is under the bonnet. Did you not find the journey from London very tiring?'

'No,' said Sappha. 'I stopped overnight on the way up and the roads are good except for the last twenty miles or so. I was stupid enough to run out of petrol coming up the hill from Inver Alligin, but some man came along in a Land Rover and filled the tank for me.' She looked annoyed as she spoke, remembering the dark stranger who had been so coolly critical of her and her clothes.

'Dear me,' observed the Baroness, 'he seems to have vexed you in some way. Do tell.'

'He looked like the Demon King—you never saw such eyebrows,' said Sappha with ill-humour. 'He—he said that he might have known it was a woman…and he didn't like my clothes. I think he was laughing at me.'

She was interrupted by a tap on the door and the man she was talking about came in, this time impeccably dressed in tweeds and exquisitely polished shoes. He seemed a great deal larger at close quarters and his eyes looked quite black. Sappha sat staring at him, the picture of consternation, her lower lip caught between her teeth, her eyes round with surprise. A surprise not shared by her patient, who looked from Sappha's face to that of her son's and said, so softly that neither of them caught her words: 'Enter the Demon King—how very interesting life has suddenly become!'

Chapter 2

The Baroness shook out a lace ruffle, raised her voice and said pleasantly: 'There you are, Rolf—how nice,' and turned to smile at Sappha. 'This is my son, Rolf, my dear—he's on a short visit from Holland—just to see how I am, you know.' She gave Sappha just enough time to murmur politely before she went on: 'Rolf, this is Miss Sappha Devenish who has come to nurse me back on to my feet again—all the way from London too. I daresay you remember, dear—I did mention...' Her voice took on a vague note. 'I believe you have already met...'

Sappha had gone a delectable pink. She said baldly: 'Yes, we have, I was just telling you.' She glanced across at the man standing so quietly in the doorway, her brown eyes snapping because she suspected that behind the politeness of his expression he was laughing at her. He walked across the room without saying anything at all, kissed his mother, said in a voice deeper than Sappha had remembered: 'Yes, Mother, I remember very well,' and turned to shake Sappha's hand. At close quarters he seemed very large indeed and handsome in a dark sort of way. He enquired gravely how she did and when she looked at him she could see that his eyes were alive with laughter. He said: 'I hope you will enjoy staying here, it is—er—a little quiet.'

He allowed his gaze to sweep over her well-turned-out person so that she made haste to say with a touch of haughtiness: 'I shall be wearing uniform,' and was instantly furious with herself for saying anything so stupid, for his mouth curved in a faint smile and the peculiar eyebrows lifted. 'Of course,' he said mildly, 'what could have made you suppose I should expect anything else?' He sat down carefully on the end of his mother's bed. 'Tell me, did you have a good journey? Which way did you come?'

'The M1—from London, you know.' Her voice had an edge to it. 'And at Inverness I got on to the A832, through Garve and Achnasheen and Torridon—it was a good road all the way, excepting for the last few miles.'

'Ah, yes.' She was sure he was laughing at her again. 'There are very few roads around here—just the one to Torridon. You will enjoy the walking, I have no doubt.' His voice was silky and she had her mouth open to answer him back, but he went on smoothly: 'Am I interrupting something? Would you prefer me to come back later?' Which was so obviously a polite way of asking her to leave that she got to her feet at once with a remark that she would unpack.

She found her way down to the kitchen presently to

fetch her patient's supper, having disposed of her clothes and changed into a crisp white uniform and perched her Greggs' cap upon her nicely arranged hair. It was a spotted muslin trifle, goffered, edged with lace and rather fetching. Mrs MacFee, helping in the preparation of the invalid's supper, complimented Sappha upon it. 'Such a refreshing change, my dear, after some of these odd styles—not,' she added hastily, 'but what you looked charming when you arrived.' She set a steaming pipkin of soup carefully upon the tray and added its lid.

'Now, dear, if you wouldn't mind taking this up. I don't feel that I should be telling you what to do, really I don't, but I'm sure you will find your way around in no time at all, and then you must do as you think best for your patient. I expect Dr van Duyren is with her now?'

Sappha said, 'Yes,' and cast around for something else to say about him. She could, of course, have mentioned that they had already met, she could even have passed a remark about his satyr's eyebrows, but Mrs MacFee might find that a little odd. Instead she asked: 'Does he stay here? I mean when comes to see his mother?'

'Oh, yes. Of course he's been coming here ever since he was a very small boy—Mr MacFee thinks of him as a son—he comes and goes as he likes and he knows everyone for miles around. He keeps a Land Rover here and many's the time he's gone to some outlying croft when there has been an accident or a baby arriving too soon and we couldn't get Hamish MacInroy.' She paused for breath. 'They're good friends, anyway.'

Sappha, cutting toast into neat squares, agreed that it sounded most convenient, while the unbidden thought that Andrew—a great stickler for etiquette—would never have countenanced casual help from a colleague crossed her mind. Presumably it was a different kettle of fish in these remote parts. She picked up her tray and went upstairs to find that her patient was alone and looking rather downcast, so when she had arranged everything so that the Baroness could manage with her one hand, she said: 'I want to write up your charts—do you mind if I sit here and do them while you have your soup?'

Her patient lifted her spoon. 'Would you?' she asked eagerly. 'A new face is so refreshing.' She spooned another mouthful. 'You were quite right, Sappha—Rolf does look like a demon king—it's extraordinary that I have never noticed it before.'

Sappha put down her charts. 'I must apologise, Baroness. I should never have said that—I had no intention…'

Her companion nibbled toast. 'Why should you be sorry?' she asked. 'I expect he was wearing some dreadful clothes and muddy boots and probably he hadn't shaved. I believe he went out very early this morning—a broken leg near Ben Eighe and he would have to walk part of the way you know—it was off the road. Hamish was out on a baby case and one really can't leave a person lying with a broken leg, can one?'

Sappha said dryly: 'No, that would be rather unkind,' and her patient nodded before continuing: 'Really, I hardly recognise him sometimes. At home, of course, he looks exactly like a doctor.' She waved a hand in an expressive gesture, 'and naturally, being the eldest, he tends to throw his weight around—is that the right expression?'

Sappha smiled. 'Yes, though perhaps it's a little severe.'

'Not nearly as severe as Rolf when he's annoyed,' retorted his mother with spirit.

'All the same,' commented Sappha, 'you must be very glad of his support.'

'Oh, I am, child, I am. My husband died when Rolf was twenty-five, and Antonia—the youngest—was only nine. The others are married now, which means that Rolf has more leisure, though he always has time for Tonia—they're so fond of each other.' She smiled a little wistfully. 'She is such a dear child and I do miss her. She's at school and I had hoped that she would be able to come over for a day or so—it's so long to Christmas, but anyway, I shall be home before then.'

Sappha took the empty soup bowl. 'Good gracious, yes,' she said bracingly, 'but surely she could fly over for a weekend? There's an airfield at Inverness...' She stood deep in thought. 'We could at least make a few enquiries.'

'That would be lovely, but I believe Rolf thinks that it would be unsettling for Tonia—she has her studies...'

'Oh, pooh,' said Sappha inelegantly, 'she can do some extra homework to make up for it—shall I talk to Dr van Duyren and see if he will change his mind?' She was on her way to the door and didn't see the Baroness's face which held an expression of mischief mixed with anticipation.

When Sappha returned after a few minutes with a fricassée of chicken and an egg custard, and having placed these delicacies before her, poured a glass of wine and put it within her reach, her patient said: 'What a great deal of work I am going to give you, Sappha.'

'Indeed you won't—in hospital I ran around all day

except when I had to sit at a desk and fill in forms and answer the telephone.'

The Baroness speared a morsel of chicken and asked: 'Will you not be bored just with me to look after?'

'Not in the least.' Sappha spoke with a conviction which wasn't quite genuine, for she had her private doubts on the subject; not only would her working day be far less exacting, her private life was going to be very different too. No more going out on her evenings off duty to the theatre or dinner and dancing or to the cinema. She tried to remember where she had seen the last cinema on the way to Dialach. Probably one had to go back to Inverness, or at least Achnasheen or Garve. Her speculations were brought to an abrupt end by the realisation that even if she were in London there would have been no theatres or cinema or dinners—not with Andrew, at any rate. She said rather abruptly: 'I'll fetch your coffee,' and when she got back her patient had finished her supper and was lying back against her pillows, deep in thought, she roused herself, however, to say pensively: 'Of course, you'll have our Gloria—she's about your age. Such a pretty girl—I expect you know that she's engaged to Hamish—a dear boy, your uncle thinks very highly of him.' She watched Sappha pour the coffee and then obediently swallowed the pills she was offered. 'Loathsome things,' she muttered crossly, and Sappha laughed and said encouragingly:

'Yes, but think how much worse everything would be if you didn't have them.'

'Since no one has told me what they are or why I am taking them, how can I possibly agree with you?' her patient wanted to know, and then on the same breath and with a suddenness which took Sappha by surprise:

'Why are you not married or at least engaged? You're a pretty girl, young—twenty-three or four?—intelligent and well dressed.' And when Sappha didn't reply: 'Perhaps I shouldn't have asked. Forgive me, I didn't mean to be rude, I'm just a curious old woman.'

Sappha managed a smile, 'You're not old, nor are you rude. I'll tell you one day, but just for now I'd rather not talk about it.'

She went downstairs, outwardly calm, but inwardly a little ruffled. She had, after all, come several hundred miles in order to be free from just such questions as the Baroness had asked.

Mrs MacFee was in the sitting room, sitting before the fire, and Mr MacFee was standing in the window, engaged in conversation with Dr van Duyren. They paused as she went in, however, and came over to the fire.

'You two have met, I understand,' remarked Mr MacFee cheerfully. 'Well, now you can sit down for a few minutes and get better acquainted.'

'Just as though,' thought Sappha crossly, 'we can't wait to tell each other how pleased we are to meet again.' She sat down, accepted a glass of sherry and was instantly affronted by the manner in which Dr van Duyren walked as far away from her as possible, saying: 'Oh, we shall have time enough for that, I imagine. I'm sure Nurse would prefer to rest a little.'

She gave him an open-mouthed, indignant look while Mrs MacFee observed: 'Why, of course—such a long journey—how thoughtless we are. You must be worn out, my dear, although I must say that in that uniform you look so fresh and efficient.'

Sappha, murmuring politely, looked up and caught

Dr van Duyren's dark gaze bent upon her and it was obvious that he was laughing. She lifted her rather determined chin, nettled at his lack of interest coupled with his implication that she was a useless creature who needed a rest, or worse, that she looked as though she needed one. And calling her 'Nurse' too, she hadn't been called that for eighteen months or more.

Reading her thoughts with an uncanny accuracy, he said smoothly:

'Forgive me—I have been guilty of demoting you. You were a Ward Sister, weren't you?' He looked apologetic, although she was sure he wasn't, and when he continued: 'I shouldn't have any idea what to call Gloria,' the remark somehow made things seem worse because it reminded Sappha that she was a stranger in a small community where apparently everyone knew everyone else. She wondered rather wistfully if they would accept her, and then, catching his eyes on her again, unsmiling now, decided that it didn't matter in the least.

She treated him with a cool politeness throughout supper and when that meal was over, asked him if he would spare her a few minutes as she had something to discuss with him, to which he replied that he would be delighted although she saw that he was a little surprised too, if his eyebrows were anything to go by.

Mr MacFee had urged them to make use of his study; a small dark room, cluttered with old copies of the *Statesman* and some dusty volumes which looked like encyclopaedias and probably were. It was furnished with a large desk upon which were laid paper, pens and a great deal of blotting paper—her host's sermon, waiting to be written, thought Sappha as she preceded her companion into the room and took a remarkably uncomfortable chair pushed up against the wall. The doctor had the good sense to rest his bulk against the desk, from which he regarded her without speaking.

She folded her hands tidily in her lap and said austerely: 'I should be glad of your co-operation, Doctor,' and watched the eyebrows arch once more.

'So soon? I am amazed—I thought that that would be the last thing you would wish.' He sounded mildly amused.

Sappha suppressed a desire to answer him back, knowing that it would get her nowhere. She closed her pretty mouth on the words which bubbled to her lips and was silent for so long that he enquired, still very mild: 'You wanted me to co-operate, I believe. How?'

'Your mother is anxious to see your sister—Antonia—she feels that you wouldn't approve because of her studies. Surely it could be arranged for her to come over by air, even for a day or so?'

He said coldly: 'Antonia's schooling is important. She is doing very well—probably she will go on to a university.'

'Oh, fiddle,' said Sappha rudely and quite out of patience. 'Surely she can do some extra homework or something—your mother's peace of mind is much more important.' She shot him a sharp glance. 'Your sister will probably marry before she even gets to university.'

His cold voice became icy. 'Probably, but as you yourself are aware there is many a slip between the cup and the lip when it comes to marriage.'

Sappha sat very still, staring at him. She had gone rather white even though she appeared quite composed. She hadn't realised that the man standing in front of her would know about her and Andrew, but of course Uncle

John would have told him. She felt humiliation, so bitter that she could taste it, well up within her. She took
her lovely eyes from his face and focused them on the
wall above his head, and said quietly: 'We are discussing your mother, I believe,' and heard his voice, won-
derfully kind and gentle saying: 'I beg your pardon, that
was unforgivable of me. I am afraid I have no excuse,
only the unsatisfactory one of always having my own
way with my family and taking it for granted that no
one will gainsay me.'

He crossed the space between them and caught her
by the shoulders so that she came to her feet, willy-nilly.
'Forgive me—if you will, I'll arrange for Tonia to come
over whenever you say.'

Sappha studied his face; his eyes, now that she saw
them so close, weren't black at all but brown, and at that
moment they looked warm and friendly. She said uncertainly: 'I say pretty breastly things myself sometimes—
and I forgive you without the bribery—or is it blackmail?'

'Whichever you like, I'll take the blame for both.'
He smiled at her so that his face changed completely
and just for a second she caught a glimpse of someone
quite different, but only a glimpse, not enough to stop
her saying: 'It's rather difficult to put into words, but I
think we should understand that...' she paused so as to
get it quite right, 'some people don't get on very well—
I think perhaps we are all like that.'

'Ah,' he said blandly, 'mutual dislike and so forth—
is that what you mean? It has been known. Well, in that
case, we must conceal our true feelings for each other
under the guise of good fellowship, mustn't we?' He
walked a little away from her. 'That shouldn't be too
difficult, for I go back to Holland tomorrow and you

will have plenty of time to practise a friendly approach before I return. Now, shall we go back to the drawing room? I usually spend half an hour with Mother at this time if you have no objection. I'll be gone early tomorrow morning, so you won't need to strain your friendly approach.'

It wasn't until they had parted with outward goodwill and she was sitting with the MacFees that she came to the conclusion that he had been laughing silently when he had made that last remark.

Sappha had expected to spend a wretched night; leaving London had been a wrench, and the peace and quiet she had anticipated in the Highlands had been strangely ruffled by her meeting with Dr van Duyren. She went to bed prepared to lie awake, and promptly slept, to awaken only when Meg, the little daily maid, came in with her morning tea.

'It's a fine bright day, Miss,' she observed as she drew the curtains, revealing a glimpse of the sea and the rugged coastline beyond the rooftops. 'The Baron left with the sun on him.'

Sappha sat up, tossed her hair over her shoulders and yawned. 'Baron who?' she enquired, not quite awake.

Meg turned a surprised face towards her. 'Why, miss, the Baron, ye ken, though maybe ye call him the doctor, but here in the village he gets his rightful title.'

Sappha sipped her tea. 'Oh, Dr van Duyren, the Baroness's son.'

Meg nodded. 'The Baron,' she stated simply. 'Breakfast is at half past eight, I was to tell you.' She went away, leaving Sappha to ponder this titbit of information. She had never met a baron before; she supposed, after due thought, that he was very like a baron should be—the very name conjured up a swashbuckling, high-handed gentleman, for ever shouting down his inferiors and being charming when it suited him. She got up and dressed rapidly, reminding herself the while of everything about him that annoyed her.

Her patient was awake after a good night and very ready to talk while Sappha performed the few necessary tasks prior to bringing up her breakfast. Her son, she told Sappha, had left at first light to board a plane at Inverness and she wasn't at all sure how long it would be before he would be coming again, for as well as running a practice with his two partners, he lectured in Groningen.

'Ah, yes—somewhere in the north of Holland, then,' said Sappha, shaking down the thermometer, and was taken back when the Baroness said touchily: 'Not North Holland—our home is in Dokkum, which is in Friesland. Groningen, of course, is not.'

Sappha begged her pardon, made a mental note to have a look at an atlas when she got downstairs, and besought her patient to open her mouth.

Uncle John came later that morning and spent a long time examining his patient, and a still longer time talking to Sappha about her. He was pleased with the results of the operation he had performed; the tumour had been removed before it could do lasting damage and the bones were hardening once more with the increased calcium, moreover the renal failure was improving at a heartening rate, but he warned Sappha of the depression which was bound to attack the Baroness from time to time—the aftermath of her rare disease. 'But we'll pull her through, I have no doubt,' he said cheerfully, then asked without pause: 'I suppose Rolf has gone?'

Sappha gave her uncle a level look. 'You mean Dr van Duyren—or should I say Baron van Duyren?'

He returned her look with an innocent one of his own. 'My dear, how should I know? Everyone around here calls him Rolf—the people in the town address him as Baron, I believe, but I hardly think he would expect you to address him as such. Don't you like him?'

Sappha pinkened faintly. She said crossly: 'How ever should I know, Uncle John? I've hardly spoken to him.' She picked up a batch of forms and went on in a businesslike way: 'Shall I fill these in for you to sign? I expect you're taking them with you.'

Dr McInroy arrived just as her uncle was preparing to leave. He was a sturdy man in his early thirties, of middle height, and with good features and bright blue eyes. After he had greeted the specialist, he turned to Sappha with a warm smile, saying: 'Miss Devenish— I've heard all about you from Gloria and I'm delighted to welcome you to Dialach.' He sounded so genuinely pleased to meet her that Sappha found herself smiling widely as she shook hands, but even as she did so, she had a fleeting recollection of her meeting with Dr van Duyren, who hadn't greeted her at all...but there was no time to indulge her own thoughts; the two doctors began to discuss their patient, and as they seemed to take it for granted that she should stay with them, she concentrated upon the subject in hand, so when she was drawn into their conversation from time to time she was able to join in in a manner which caused Dr MacInroy to look at her with something like respect and remark:

'You know a great deal about osteitis fibrosa cystica— have you seen one before? It's a rare condition.'

Sappha shook her head. 'No, never, that's why I read

up all I could about it before I came—I picked a few brains too.' They all laughed and presently she left them to return to her patient.

The Baroness was lying back in bed looking bored. As well she might, thought Sappha, with only one leg and one arm available. She bustled around with an exaggerated cheerfulness getting ready to bedbath her patient, and presently, while she was doing this, asked: 'What else do you do—other than reading?'

'Oh, crosswords—there's nothing else with one hand...' The Baroness spoke listlessly and Sappha made haste to say: 'Uncle John is delighted with your progress—he wants you to do a few exercises each day, so that when your arm comes out of plaster it will be fairly strong. I'm going to get you out of bed and into a chair by the window—there's a lovely view. I suppose you don't paint?'

Her patient looked surprised and faintly interested. 'Yes, I used to—how did you know?'

'I didn't—but I was thinking if we could get hold of some paints and a canvas or some paper, you could amuse yourself.'

The Baroness lifted eyebrows which reminded Sappha of her son. 'With one hand?' she enquired.

'Why not? If I arrange everything within reach— we can find some way of keeping the paper steady, and I shall be on hand for a good deal of the day—would you like to try?'

She had been wrapping her patient in a dressing gown as she spoke; now she pulled the chair alongside the bed and lifted the Baroness in her strong young arms into it and trundled her over to the window.

'I'll get you some coffee and while you're drinking it I'll see if Mrs MacFee can help about the paints.'

Mrs MacFee, when appealed to, not only produced an elderly paintbox of her own but a sketching pad as well and spent half an hour with her friend discussing the best view to start on; while Sappha busied herself making the bed and tidying the room; with such success that Sappha was able to leave the two ladies together after lunch and take an hour or two off duty. She went first to the post office to send a hastily written letter to her mother and then explored the little town and its harbour. The day, which had started off in sunshine, had become overcast and windy, so that the waves beat against the lonely shore; only in the harbour was the water smooth although it looked cold enough.

She was on her way back when she met Gloria, who fell into step beside her saying: 'There you are—how nice. No good me asking you to come in for tea, I'm afraid—I'm just off to see a patient.' She waved vaguely in the direction of the causeway and Sappha asked: 'Where? You're pointing out to sea.'

'Well, she is in a way,' said Gloria cheerfully. 'At least, I have to be rowed over because the causeway's in ruins—there's a baby due any time now and a good thing it's not later in the year, for there's a terrific current and if it's stormy the boat can't make it—the locals think nothing of scrambling over the causeway when the weather's bad, but I'm no mountain goat—even they hesitate a bit unless it's daylight.'

'Who lives there?' asked Sappha, interested.

'The family MacTadd—father's a fisherman and there are Mum, Gran and a clutch of children. There's a plan to rehouse them, but there's nothing suitable for them at the moment, and besides, they don't want to go. They've patched up the croft very nicely, though there's no H and C and no electricity either. Hamish has tried to persuade Mrs MacTadd to go to hospital, but she absolutely refuses, so all we can do is to keep a sharp eye open and pray for fine weather.' She grinned cheerfully. 'I'm going down here—Mr MacTadd will be waiting for me—let me know when you've fixed your days off and I'll pop up and see to the Baroness for you. Bye.' She turned away and then paused to say over her shoulder: 'I've fixed Saturday for mine, so don't have that.'

Sappha took her day off on Friday; during the four days she had been at the Manse she had got the routine nicely settled, and in any case, she didn't go until she had got her patient up for the day, arranged with Gloria for that young lady to call in after lunch and arranged with Mrs MacFee that the Baroness shouldn't be left too long alone in case she moped. She then set out with the Mini. The weather was good; she suspected that before many weeks as the autumn settled into winter, she would have to spend her free day in Dialach—it seemed a good idea to explore as far afield as possible while she could. She took the road to Ullapool, where, Gloria had informed her, there was a rather delightful shop selling local handicrafts and tweeds. Besides, she intended to visit the garden at Inverewe—it wasn't the best time of year to do so, but various of her friends in London had urged her on no account to miss it.

She thought briefly of Dr van Duyren as she drove to Torridon—his mother, beyond mentioning that he had got home safely and was very busy, had offered no further information, although she had been voluble enough about Antonia, who, from all accounts, was not only very pretty but a little spoiled and wilful as well. Sappha stopped for a late cup of coffee at the Loch Maree Hotel, feeling breathless from the magnificent scenery she had just passed through, and eager for more. The day was going to be too short. She decided to press on to Ullapool, have lunch there, take a quick look around the town and then visit Inverewe on her way back. Even so, by the time she had reached Ullapool she knew that she would have to return, not once, but several times if she were to take her fill of the scenery.

She lunched at the Caledonian Hotel, and for the first time since she had arrived in Scotland, felt almost happy. She supposed it was the magnificent country through which she had been driving which somehow had the power to make London and its pleasures seem a little unreal. She spent a pleasant half hour looking round the little town, quiet now after its summer season, but she was anxious not to miss the gardens and sped back through the forest land, resisting the urge to stop and gaze at the mountains around her. Next time, she promised herself, going downhill fast towards Gruinard, and then up the other side to Inverewe gardens.

They were lovely even though there was only an aftermath of summer's glory in the flower beds. She left reluctantly, promising herself that she would pay another visit in some distant summer, and stopped for tea in Aultbea, and then, pleasantly tired, took the road back to Dialach. It had been a successful day, made more successful by the friendly people she had met wherever she had stopped and the openly admiring glances of the young man in the deerstalker cap who had entered the hotel while she was having lunch, and had at once engaged her in conversation while he ate his own meal at a nearby table. It was only after they had parted in mutual friendliness that she felt a twinge of regret that they weren't likely to meet again, for as far as she could see, there weren't many men of her own age in Dialach—Dr MacInroy couldn't be counted, of course, for he was Gloria's anyway, and the Baron, with his peculiar eyebrows and bossy ways, certainly had no place in her thoughts. She spent several minutes convincing herself of this as she changed back into uniform and went to seek out her patient. And felt instantly contrite when she saw her; the Baroness was in bed—Gloria had seen to that before she had left at teatime—and turned a listless tear-stained face to Sappha as she went in; it took a few minutes of patient comforting on her part before she could induce her patient to speak. 'I—I h-hope you h-had a lovely d-day,' she sobbed, 'and this is s-so s-silly, because I d-don't know why I'm c-crying,' and then contradicted herself by adding: 'Rolf s-said he would t-telephone and he hasn't.'

'Perhaps he's been too busy,' said Sappha, who felt strongly that the telephone was a modern blessing which had its drawbacks. How many times had she sat by the wretched instrument in London waiting for Andrew to ring, and all the while… She jerked her thoughts back to her patient; it was really too bad of the tiresome man, he should have squeezed in a call whatever he was doing. 'He'll telephone later,' she said with a conviction she didn't feel, 'and don't worry about being a bit tearful, Baroness—remember what Uncle John said; that you were bound to feel depressed for no reason at all. I'm going to wash your face and tidy your hair, and after supper we'll play that game of draughts we never had.'

The evening was cheerful after all—with the fire alight in the old-fashioned grate and the chintz curtains drawn, the room looked cosy and inviting. Sappha ate a hasty supper and went back upstairs and true to her promise got out the draughts board and allowed the Baroness to beat her soundly before giving her her sleeping pill and tucking her up for the night. She had only just got downstairs to say goodnight to the MacFees when the telephone rang and Mr MacFee, who answered it, said:

'It's for you, Sappha,' he smiled a little, 'a man.'

She could feel her heart pounding in her chest as she crossed the room. It could be Andrew, miraculously in love with her again, telephoning to say so because he couldn't wait to write it. She picked up the receiver and said Hullo in a voice which shook with excitement.

But it wasn't Andrew, although it was a man—a man with strange eyebrows who had laughed at her and thought her clothes were silly, and who had forgotten to telephone his mother. His deep voice came lazily over the wire: 'Oh, dear, I'm not the right one, am I?' he asked outrageously. 'How's Mother?'

She choked back disappointment, furious with him and with herself.

'She's been waiting for you to ring up,' she said sharply. 'She was upset...'

'I'm sorry. I imagine you've given her her sleeping pill by now, that's why I thought I'd better speak to you first.'

'Well, it's no good, she's asleep.' Sappha spoke with some thing of a snap.

'You sound like a love-starved spinster with no looks and no prospects.' He was laughing, and forgetful of the

MacFees, sitting across the room politely not listening, she burst out: 'How dare you!'

'I'll dare anything if I have a mind to,' he said coolly, 'and just for the record, you'll never starve for lack of love, my good girl, and your prospects are about as good as they can be.'

Sappha drew a deep breath, let it out noisily and said helplessly:

'Well!' She was prevented from saying anything else because he went on at once: 'I'm sorry I couldn't telephone earlier—circumstances prevented it. I'll ring in the morning—you can tell her that if she wakes. I hadn't forgotten, it was quite impossible.'

She said: 'Very well' in a stiff little voice and he went on as though she hadn't spoken. 'I've arranged for Tonia to come over with me. It's most inconvenient, but I don't dare face you without her. That will be a week on Thursday. Goodbye.'

He rang off before she had time to open her mouth. She put down the receiver slowly and went back to the MacFees and repeated what he had said, but with a good deal of it expurgated, so that her mild version didn't tally in the least with the heated retorts she had given. This quite escaped her, and the MacFees, beyond a mild comment on the pleasure of seeing Rolf and Antonia again, didn't mention it.

Later on, in bed, Sappha went over all that he had said. She hadn't understood his remarks about her not starving for love and having good prospects and she thought about it for a long time, getting more and more frustrated because it didn't make sense, finally she said out loud: 'Oh, he's crazy,' then turned over and went determinedly to sleep. The following days passed quietly enough and the boredom which she had half expected to settle upon her after a week or so, didn't materialise. Instead, she began to find the days not quite long enough. The Baroness had taken heart again; Rolf had telephoned her several times and she was full of excitement at seeing Antonia so soon. She had never asked Sappha if she had spoken to Rolf about her daughter's visit, nor did she do so now beyond making a comment upon his kindness and understanding. Sappha, asked to agree with her patient upon her son's excellent qualities, agreed woodenly, remembering what he had said—she wondered if she would ever forget his words even though she had forgiven them. She pummelled the pillow she was shaking up with unnecessary vigour—he was one of the most unpleasant men she had ever met.

She had her day off on Wednesday and took the Mini in the other direction down to Balmarca, so that she might see the hills of Skye across the Kyle of Lochalsh. She had lunch at the hotel there and then went on to look at Eilean Donan Castle on the edge of Loch Duich. She followed on down the steep road to get a good view of the Kintail Mountains, but they were fast disappearing in heavy clouds, so she found a place to turn the car and started back home. She had promised to have tea with Gloria anyway, and it was already getting on for four o'clock.

Gloria wasn't home, but Sappha let herself in, poked up the fire, put on the kettle and then went to fetch the cake she had brought from the baker's. The cottage had a small rather cluttered kitchen, gay with gingham curtains and a collection of copper pans which Sappha coveted. She pottered around, rather enjoying herself so that she found herself reflecting, while cutting bread for the toast, that life in Dialach was so pleasant that the idea of going back to London seemed quite laughable. A fortunate thing, in the circumstances, because that was the last place she wanted to be in—probably by now Andrew had married that beastly little blonde...

She frowned and sighed at the thought, so that Gloria, coming in at that moment, exclaimed: 'Good lord, Sappha, what's eating you? You look ferocious—sadly ferocious—or do I mean ferociously sad? What's the matter?'

Sappha speared bread on to a toasting fork. 'Hullo—nothing, really.'

Gloria cast her hat on one chair, her coat on another and her case on the table. 'Not bored, are you?'

'No, on the contrary—I was just thinking how bored I should be in London.'

'Well, even if you were,' said Gloria, making the tea, 'you won't be after tomorrow. Rolf and Antonia will be here, you can't be bored when they're around. What do you think of Rolf?'

Sappha buttered toast. 'Well, I don't really know him—I mean we only talked a little.'

Gloria laughed. 'But he's not the kind of man you need to talk to—don't tell me he didn't make an impression on you, or you'll be the first woman under ninety who hasn't been bowled over.'

The two of them sat down by the fire in the little sitting room and bit into their toast. 'If you want to know,' said Sappha, her mouth full, 'I found him rude, bossy—and he laughs behind his face.'

Gloria stared at her over her tea cup. 'I haven't asked you yet, but it's obvious to anyone with eyes in their heads that you came up here to get away from something or someone—a man, I suspect. It's hardly fair to colour your impression of Rolf by your own experience.' She put down her cup and held out a friendly hand. 'That was a beastly thing to say—I'm sorry. I know how I'd feel if Hamish...'

'I daresay you're right,' conceded Sappha, privately thinking her all wrong. 'Now tell me, what are you going to do with your day off?'

'Inverness—with Hamish. He's coming for me about nine and we won't be back until the late evening. There's nothing to worry about in the village; old Mrs Mac-Gower is off her penicillin injections and Mrs MacTadd is OK. She should go another three weeks—the babe's a transverse lie, but there's time enough for it to right itself—Hamish has turned it twice already. Are you a midwife? You are?—good, just in case I'm not about when Mrs MacTadd starts, I shall warn them to come for you.' She had spoken jokingly and Sappha replied in kind, and Rolf's name wasn't mentioned again for the rest of Sappha's visit. Before she went home though, Gloria said with a laugh: 'I'm going to show you where everything is kept in the surgery, Sappha, so that if ever there is an emergency you could cope.'

So Sappha was invited to see where the key was hidden and where the midwifery bag was housed, and the gas and air apparatus, even the blood taking and giving sets—'For,' said Gloria, 'we just have to be prepared for everything—and by the way, there's a litre of O blood, Rhesus positive, in the fridge—Hamish brought it with him today in case Mrs MacTadd does the dirty on us.' She went with her guest to the door. 'Do you want anything from Inverness?'

Sappha considered. 'No, I don't think so, thanks. I

thought I'd drive over on my next day off and do some shopping, but there's nothing urgent.'

She said goodbye and drove the short distance to the Manse, where she put the car in the little lean-to at the back of the house which the minister had put at her disposal, and ran indoors. The house was warm and quiet; the faint murmur of voices from the drawing room told her that Mr and Mrs MacFee were enjoying their usual evening chat together; she forbore from joining them, for she suspected that it was probably the only hour in the day when they could be reasonably sure of being uninterrupted, but went on upstairs, to pause at the Baroness's door undecided whether to go and see her first or wait until she had taken off her outdoor things. She decided to go in; probably the Baroness was feeling lonely. She opened the door and poked her pretty head round it.

The Baroness was not lonely at all; she had company— a very pretty blonde girl curled up beside her on the bed, and the Baron, crouching on the floor, tinkering with a portable TV set. He came to his feet in a surprisingly agile manner for so large a man and said: 'Hullo—had a nice day?'

Sappha said yes, thank you, a trifle breathless with surprise and some other sensation which, if she hadn't disliked him so much, she would have admitted was pleasure. The Baroness beamed at her. 'Sappha, isn't this a lovely surprise? Rolf brought Tonia a day sooner and he's brought a TV for me too…come and meet my daughter.'

Antonia had left the bed and had pranced over to Sappha. She really was extraordinarily pretty with great blue eyes and dimples, her hair was straight and thick and corn-coloured, cut in a fringe across her forehead.

She put out a hand, remarking disarmingly: 'You're far too pretty to be a nurse. I don't believe you're much older than I am—I'm sixteen.'

Rolf said lazily from the floor: 'Antonia, you mustn't ask Nurse how old she is—she might not want me to know.'

'Stuff,' said his sister inelegantly. 'You make her sound like some old bag in her thirties—just because you're thirty-two yourself...' She turned her lively little face to Sappha. 'Tell me later,' she invited, and bounced back to make herself comfortable by her mother once more as that lady said indulgently: 'Tonia, you're not to talk to Sappha like that—you hardly know her.'

'Oh, yes, Mama, I do, you know. Sometimes you meet someone and it's as if you've known them all your life.' She appealed to her brother. 'Rolf, people do feel like that, don't they?'

He looked up briefly, but not at her. His dark eyes dwelt for a few seconds on Sappha, who felt herself turning slowly red under them. But all he said was: 'Oh, yes, of course, only it's more satisfactory if they both feel the same way at the same time.'

'There, you see?' Antonia addressed the room at large and smiled widely at Sappha. 'I know we're going to be friends.' She studied Sappha's heightened colour and went on with devastating candour: 'You've gone very red—it makes you prettier than ever. Rolf...'

He didn't look up and his voice was bland. 'I'm sure Nurse wants to take off her coat.' And Sappha cast him a look of relief mingled with the vexed thought that he had called her nurse again. She said primly:

'I'll be back with your supper presently, Baroness,' and went away.

Hours later, sitting up in bed thinking about the evening, Sappha had to admit that she had enjoyed herself. Antonia had lent a sparkle to the conversation, and so too, surprisingly had Rolf. He was certainly very fond of his sister and she, for her part, was equally devoted to him, and although it was apparent that she could twist him round her little finger, it was also quite clear that she had a wholesome respect for him too. Sappha smiled to herself, thinking about her; she was spoilt and a little wilful but so good-natured and sunny-tempered that she doubted if anyone, even her eldest brother, could be annoyed with her for more than a couple of seconds at a time. And, reflected Sappha, she had been instantly obedient to the suggestion that it was her mother's bedtime, and afterwards, sitting on the end of Sappha's bed while the latter rearranged her hair, she had asked some remarkably sensible questions about her mother's illness and when Sappha had hesitated to answer them, said: 'I know a great deal about it already—Rolf said it would be better for me and for Mother if I did. And of course he's right. He always is,' she added simply.

Sappha thought it wise to say nothing to this; quite obviously, the Baron ruled his family with a rod of iron, albeit a well camouflaged one. She found herself speculating upon the poor girl he would coerce into marrying him and felt fiercely sorry for her. She could imagine what it would be like—'Half a dozen children,' she muttered to herself, thumping her pillows. 'The woman's place is in the home, and all that, however luxurious that home might be.' She had a sudden vivid mental picture of the Baron sitting at the head of a table lined with little barons and baronesses, all with miniature satyr's eyebrows and herself at the end. She pulled herself up short, hastily substituting this ridiculous idea with the interesting question as to what a baron's children were called, but before she could go deeply into the matter she was disturbed by her patient's voice from the bedroom next door, asking if she might have another sleeping tablet because one hadn't seemed to be enough. Sappha got out of bed, her unruly thoughts forgotten. She said soothingly: 'It's only because you've had such an exciting evening—you have been to sleep and you'll soon drop off again. I'll read to you, shall I? Are you quite comfy?'

She made a few deft movements amongst the pillows and bedclothes.

'There, not a wrinkle in sight. Close your eyes—I'll go on with *Jane Eyre*.'

She read for several minutes until the Baroness interrupted her to say:

'What an arrogant man he was—but of course he loved Jane, and she loved him. Was the man you loved—still do perhaps, Sappha—arrogant?'

Sappha looked up from her reading. Her dressing gown was a soft pink, a perfect contrast to the dark hair hanging around her shoulders. She smelled faintly of Roger and Gallet's Violet soap and she looked as pretty as the proverbial picture. Her patient, studying her closely, thought it a great shame that there was no one other than herself to see her.

Sappha said in a wooden voice: 'No, not arrogant. It was just that he found someone else—blonde and sexy and willing to give him what I wouldn't—I'm old-fashioned about marriage...'

'Me too,' said the Baroness briskly, 'and you would be surprised at the number of men who want an old-fashioned girl for a wife—a girl who will love them and run their home with pride. And children—men want children.' She waved her plastered arm in the air. 'It's no good me telling you that you will get over it and meet another man—there aren't any other men at the moment are there? And you're sure that you will never get over him, aren't you?'

She took another look at Sappha, and it was a pity that Sappha, instead of looking at her companion, was looking backwards over the last few disastrous months, for the Baroness's pretty face wore the look of someone who had just had a brilliant idea. She did, in fact, look very like her young daughter when that young daughter was plotting mischief. There was a little pause until Sappha said quietly: 'Shall I go on reading?'

The Baroness yawned daintily. 'I do believe I begin to feel sleepy again, dear. Would it be too much trouble if I asked you to fetch me just a little warm milk?'

Sappha padded downstairs and presently, with the milk in her hand, went back again through the quiet old house, to stop in the bedroom doorway at the sight of Rolf, still dressed, lounging over the end of his mother's bed. He said nothing at all, but his gaze swept Sappha from head to foot. It was the Baroness who said in her soft voice:

'Sappha, Rolf heard us talking and came to see if anything was the matter.' She smiled at them in turn, giving her son a bright glance which dared him to imagine otherwise. He stared back at her, his eyes snapping with laughter. 'And now that I see you are in such excellent hands, I'll leave you to settle, dear Mother.'

He bent and kissed her, said a brief goodnight to

Sappha without apparently seeing her, and went back to his room.

The Baroness accepted her milk with the blameless air of a good child.

'You poor girl,' she said contritely, 'I've kept you from your bed, but I'm sure that I shall sleep very well now.' She finished the milk, allowed Sappha to settle her once more, said goodnight in a grateful voice and closed her eyes, leaving Sappha to go back to bed, but not at once to sleep. It was a pity that her patient had asked her those questions—answering them had made Andrew very clear in her mind once more, and she wanted so much to forget him.

Chapter 3

There was no sign of the Baron the next morning. Sappha busied herself with her patient, helped and sometimes hindered by the well-meaning efforts of Antonia, who, after lunch, declared her intention of sitting with her parent while Sappha went for a walk.

Sappha, who was feeling moody and restless, felt more inclined to sit and brood in her room, but she had some letters to post; she would go down to the post office and take a look at the sea at the same time, so she put on her raincoat and tied a scarf over her hair and went out into the rather wild afternoon. It was raining; not very hard, but the wind was boisterous and the mountains behind the little town stood head and shoulders in dark cloud. She walked around the harbour, shivering a little because the wind was keen as well as strong, eyeing the angry waves beyond the harbour's mouth, they were battering the causeway too. A solitary fishing boat was battling its way in and she stopped to watch it, thankful that she wasn't called upon to leave dry land.

It was after she had been to the post office and was on her way back to the Manse that she came face to face with Andrew. She stopped short, her eyes like saucers, her mouth, bulging with a wedge of the toffee she had purchased along with the stamps, slightly open. Andrew however didn't look in the least surprised, nor for that matter did he look awkward or ashamed of himself, but then, some small detached part of her mind reminded her, Andrew never did. But this thought was swamped by the rush of excitement inside her, emotion caught her by the throat so that, what with her heart in her mouth as well as the lump of toffee, she was quite unable to speak.

Andrew, unhindered by either the one or the other of these encumbrances, stopped in front of her and said with all his well-remembered charm, 'Sappha—darling, how marvellous to see you again! I had a couple of free days—it seemed a good chance to come and look you up.'

Sappha, once more in control of both her breath and the toffee, gave him what she hoped was a cool, unflustered look. She said:

'Oh, indeed. How did you know that I was here?'

'I wormed it out of old Mother Martin.' Mother Martin was Home Sister at Greggs' and a notorious passer-on of gossip. Andrew's good-looking face broke into a smile as he caught one of Sappha's hands in his. 'I thought you would be glad to see me—you are, aren't you, Sappha?'

She caught her breath. Of course she was glad, she

was on the point of saying so when she felt the weight
of a great arm on her shoulders and heard the Baron's
voice, mildly, amused, say: 'Hullo, Sappha, taking an
hour or two off?' She felt the arm tighten. 'Andrew
Glover, isn't it? Thought you'd show up—the landlord
of the pub at Torridon mentioned on the telephone that
you were heading this way. My name's van Duyren,
by the way.'

Sappha watched Andrew's face as he tried to make
up his mind how to treat the Baron, who, she noted, was
looking ruffianly enough in a thick sweater and terrible
old trousers stuffed into rubber boots—he was swinging a string of fish in one hand too. She choked down
a sudden desire to laugh because Andrew had no idea
who the Baron was and the Baron had equally no intention of telling him. She looked sideways up into his dark
face, changing the toffee lump from one cheek to the
other as she did so, a childish action which caused him
to blink rapidly while the nostrils of his commanding
nose quivered ever so slightly. He said carelessly: 'Why
not take the afternoon off, Sappha—or for that matter,
the rest of the day? Antonia and Mrs MacFee will cope.'

Sappha frowned. For one thing Andrew had said
nothing about taking her out—he'd had no time—and
for another, it made her sound too eager. She was eager,
she told herself, but Andrew mustn't know that. She
said icily: 'How kind of you, Doctor, but I've had my
off-duty for today and I see no reason for giving myself any more.' And went pink under his mocking gaze.
It was maddening that he should spoil this unexpected
meeting with Andrew—it could have been something
exciting and even more than that, though Andrew, at the

moment, didn't appear to be exactly carried away... He said now: 'Are you a doctor—I had no idea...'

The Baron waved the fish and said mildly: 'Oh, I've a practice—a small country town in Friesland.'

Andrew smiled with a hint of patronage. 'Oh, a GP.' He was contemptuous and faintly pitying. 'I've rooms in Wimpole Street—consultant you know—a nice little private practice.'

'You are to be congratulated upon your success.' The Baron's voice was silky, and Sapphia stirred uneasily under his confining arm, remembering dimly that the Baroness or someone had mentioned that he lectured in Groningen and hadn't she said something about examining? With feminine unfairness she was instantly up in arms against him—he was taking the mickey out of Andrew. She said positively: 'I really must go—there are things to do.'

If she had hoped to get rid of the Baron she was sadly mistaken, for he remarked immediately: 'We'll all go. Come up to the Manse for tea, my dear fellow—Mrs MacFee will love to see a new face and you and Sappha can sort out her time off.'

He turned up the lane leading to the Manse, and Sappha perforce turned with him. Andrew fell into step beside her. 'A pity you can't manage today,' he remarked smoothly. 'What about tomorrow—afternoon or evening perhaps, old girl?'

Sappha quivered with temper; not only had she been called old girl, her free time was being discussed and arranged for her without so much as a by your leave. She opened her mouth to say so, but the Baron spoke first.

'Of course, tomorrow, why not? And I must insist that you take both the afternoon and evening, Sappha.

It's not quite the weather for a drive, but there are some splendid walks—I can lend you a pair of boots—' he flung a friendly aside to Andrew. 'I suppose you're at the pub here. They make you very comfortable and Mrs MacGregor is a good cook—she'll turn out an excellent dinner for the pair of you.'

'I'm not sure—' began Sappha looking at the Baron with frustrated rage, to be met with a look of such limpid friendliness that she was struck dumb; if she hadn't been prepared to think the worst of him, she could have supposed that he was trying to make things as easy as possible for her and Andrew.

They turned in at the Manse gate and walked slowly up the short drive to the front door, and any idea Sappha may have had about keeping Andrew's visit from her patient's ears was scotched by the Baron, who paused and waved at the Baroness's window. Sappha felt sure that even if she didn't happen to be looking out at that moment, Antonia would have seen them. She excused herself in the hall and flew upstairs to change back into uniform. It was foolish, but she felt better able to cope with the situation once she had clasped the silver buckled belt round her slim waist and tucked her hair tidily under her cap.

The Baroness and Antonia were sitting by the window when she went in and although Antonia said nothing, Sappha gained the strong impression that this was because she had been told not to. The Baroness turned her still beautiful eyes upon Sappha and asked merely: 'A pleasant walk, I hope, dear?' Sappha, repeating her impressions of the sea and relaying the little bits of gossip she had gleaned from the post office, wondered why her patient didn't ask about Andrew, for it was obvious from their faces that they had seen him. She hadn't long to wait to find out, however, for very soon the Baroness told Antonia to go down to tea and tell Mrs MacFee that Sappha would be down directly, and that young lady had barely closed the door when her mother said:

'So he came after you, Sappha. I hope he doesn't intend to take you back with him—not,' she added earnestly, 'that I should dream of stopping you.'

Sappha paused in the clearing up of the bed table in preparation for the tea tray. She said a little wildly: 'But he hasn't asked me. I don't even know why he's here—I've had no chance…we'd only just met when Dr van Duyren joined us.' She added bitterly: 'He insisted on bringing Andrew back for tea and he's kindly arranged for me to be free tomorrow afternoon and evening.'

Her patient seemed to miss the sarcasm in her attendant's voice, for she said kindly: 'Now, isn't that nice? How thoughtful of Rolf. I expect they took to each other at once.'

Sappha, who had her own opinion about this, muttered: 'Oh, well—they're both doctors,' and remembered the Baron's modest admission to being a GP.

'Exactly what does Dr van Duyren do?' she asked.

The Baroness closed her eyes the better to think. 'Let me see now—he has a large practice in Dokkum, but of course he has two partners, then he has consultant's chambers in Groningen as well as being a professor at the Medical School—he has a teaching round and so on and he's an examiner—he specialises in stomachs and I never have understood why, my dear.'

Sappha said weakly: 'He's busy.'

'Too busy,' agreed his mother, 'I sometimes think. But he seems to like it, though I have warned him that

if he's not careful he'll have neither the time nor the inclination to marry. When he does, of course, his wife
will come before everything else,' she sighed, 'just as
I did with his father.' Two tears rolled down her cheeks
and Sappha hurried across to her to put her arms around
her and say: 'There, there—and how proud you must
be to remember that, and I've no doubt that you were
worth every second of his time.'

This remark induced the Baroness to give a watery
smile. 'Oh, yes indeed I was—and the children too,'
she added, 'Rolf's very like him.'

Sappha straightened up. There was no accounting for
tastes, she told herself crossly, and after all the Baroness
was his mother. She was on her way to the door when
the Baroness observed: 'Well, I daresay your young
man will tell you why he came when you see him tomorrow. I must say he has a great deal of patience after
coming all this way.'

Sappha had thought so too, but it wasn't very nice
to be reminded of it by someone else. But it was a long
way, surely Andrew hadn't driven hundreds of miles
just to say hullo. Besides, there was still the question
of Staff Nurse Beatty. Sappha said tonelessly: 'I'll get
your tea, Baroness.'

She put off going down to her own tea for as long as
possible, so that by the time she went into the sitting
room everyone was having second cups and Andrew
was explaining at some length just how important it
was to have the right sort of practice. He was forced to
break off while Sappha was told to sit down and asked
if there was enough milk in her tea and was the toast
really hot still; she sensed his annoyance at being interrupted even across the room. He had nodded briefly at

her when she went in, but it was the Baron who had got up and pushed her gently into his own chair and then, taking no further notice of her, gone over to sit by Andrew, to listen, apparently tonguetied with admiration, to that gentleman's dissertation upon his brilliant future. Sappha munched morosely at a scone and drank her tea, watching Andrew. He was enjoying himself—he had an audience who appeared to be interested in him, even though he wasn't in the least interested in them. She glanced round the room; Mrs MacFee was listening with a charmingly attentive air, so was the minister, Antonia was gazing at him with rapt attention—and so to was the Baron, too rapt, thought Sappha. He looked up and caught her staring at him and returned it with one of his own, a long searching look which ended in a faint smile.

She dressed with care for her meeting with Andrew— a fine wool dress in a warm shade of pink with a high neckline and full sleeves gathered into bands and then ruffled over her hands. She covered it with her raincoat and tied a matching scarf over her hair. Andrew said that they would go for a run before tea and then sit in Mrs MacGregor's parlour until dinner was ready for them. There were things, he had said, which had to be discussed. She pondered this remark while she was putting on her good shoes—a reckless act, she knew, seeing that the weather was worsening every minute, but she wanted to look nice for him.

When she was dressed, however, she sat down on the bed, reluctant to go, even though he had said he would call for her at two o'clock, and it was already past that hour. It worried her that she didn't feel happier or more excited than she was. Perhaps it was the shock of seeing

Andrew again which made her so curiously apathetic about the afternoon's outing. She got up and went to the Baroness's room to say goodbye and found that lady straining to see out of the window from her chair. She looked round as Sappha went in and said:

'He's just come, dear—he seems a very smart man, I hope you'll have a lovely time. Antonia is very taken with him, you know, not that that signifies anything— I daresay you will come back with a ring on your finger once more.'

Sappha said slowly: 'I don't know. I think I'd want to wait this time. I—I have to be sure.' She picked up a pillow and put it where it belonged. 'You're sure you can manage? I feel it's all wrong leaving you alone— Gloria isn't here either…'

'Nonsense,' said the Baroness comfortably, 'Antonia is dying to play nurse; you've put out my pills, my exercises are done, and Rolf will be in, I daresay, to make sure everything is all right.'

Sappha said goodbye and went downstairs to where Andrew was waiting, talking amusingly to Mrs MacFee. He smiled at Sappha as she joined them and said casually: 'Hullo there,' looking so completely at ease that she felt a small prick of annoyance because he was so sure of her. After all, it had been he who had let her down even though he had come back to her.

The afternoon wasn't an unqualified success. Andrew was a good driver and he handled his car—a Jaguar— well, but as Sappha pointed out, the wind was now almost gale force and the rain was developing from a thick drizzle to a steady downpour. It seemed foolish to take the road through Shieldaig and Kishorn just so that they might see the heights of Skye from Auchtertyre; in any case, Sappha pointed out reasonably, in such weather there would be nothing to see. To all of which Andrew replied with a laugh. 'Nonsense,' he said, 'we can talk as we go and worry about the scenery when we get there.'

But talking was impossible. At first it hadn't been too bad going down into Torridon, for there was shelter from the forests which lined most of the narrow road and later on the newly constructed road towards Shieldaig, but then the road reverted to its former width, winding up and down the hills so that Andrew had to pay attention to his driving. At Loch Kishorn Sappha suggested that they could probably see Skye from there, but Andrew said sharply: 'What's come over you, Sappha? Don't you want a chance to see the country? We'll go on to Auchtertyre—it's not much further. We'll go there for tea and talk.'

Naturally there was no Skye to be seen, but Andrew at least seemed to have derived some satisfaction from reaching his goal, if only for the reason that he would be able to tell the Baron about it later. They stopped for tea in Lochcarron, and although the hotel was empty the tea was delicious. Despite herself, Sappha relaxed and began to enjoy herself, Andrew could be an amusing companion and he was making great efforts to please her. They had almost finished tea when he said: 'Sappha, you must know why I came to this outlandish spot...darling, I'm lost without you.'

'What about Beatty?' Sappha asked in a cool little voice which disguised the warm glow of excitement at being wanted again. She gave him a level look. 'Did she find someone else?'

She watched Andrew grow red. 'It was mutual— we weren't suited. I suppose I was a fool.' He caught her hand on the table and held it tightly. 'Listen, darling, come back with me. Leave this awful godforsaken place, you don't belong here. We could have such fun together.'

She stared at him across the table. It was lovely to be wanted; to be missed—London might be fun and perhaps he loved her very much to have come so far to say so. The uneasy thought that he hadn't said so crossed her mind. She withdrew her hand gently and said:

'Look, Andrew, don't expect me to answer you now. I must have time to think about it.' She saw the faint annoyance on his face.

'My dear girl, what on earth do you have to think about? I'm doing you a favour—giving you a chance to escape.'

Sappha said quietly: 'But I like it in Dialach. I didn't think I should, but I do—and I can't leave my patient just like that, where are they going to get another nurse at a moment's notice? My patient has been very ill and she will need care for weeks yet.'

He shrugged his shoulders. 'Good lord, Sappha, stop being such a do-gooder. They'll rub along, and she's got that brigand who calls himself a doctor, hasn't she?'

Sappha put down her cup with a hand which shook a little. 'That's a beastly thing to say. He doesn't look in the least like a brigand.' She felt guilty saying it, for had she not likened him to a brigand herself? She hurried on: 'He's good to her—he comes over from Holland every week or so and he helps the local doctor when he's needed…'

Andrew was laughing at her. 'More fool he. Are you a fan of his? Or perhaps you've fallen a victim to his charm?'

'Neither,' she snapped. 'I—I don't like him, but that's no reason to be spiteful, and I won't leave until another nurse is found to replace me.'

He smiled. 'We'll not argue about that now. We'll go back and make ourselves comfortable round Mrs Mac-Gregor's fire and I'll guarantee to make you change your mind.'

He gave her a look which sent the colour into her face but left her bewilderingly unexcited. She followed him out to the car in silence, puzzled at her lack of response. Three months ago she would have flown into his arms and now she felt herself moving away from the touch of his shoulder in the car. But he didn't notice this nor her silence; he was talking about his future and how much money he intended to make, and not once did he mention her...

The journey back was tricky. The wind, now a gale, buffeted the car, while the rain, coming down in good earnest, made the windscreen-wipers useless. Even on a fine dry day the road needed care, and although Andrew was a good driver, he wasn't a patient one. Sappha was glad when they skidded to a halt before the small brightly lighted inn. Inside it was warm and cheerful and a table had been laid for them in the little parlour behind the bar, and two comfortable chairs drawn up before the fire. Sappha took off her raincoat and scarf and hung them tidily behind the door, then followed Mrs MacGregor up the narrow staircase to one of the bedrooms so that she might tidy herself. The room was spotlessly clean and rather cold; its little window over-looked the houses lining the harbour, and she stood for a moment watching the boiling sea. There was a light twinkling at the end of the causeway and she wondered if Mrs MacTadd was all right. She wondered about Gloria and Hamish too; they surely wouldn't be driving back in such weather, probably they would wait until the storm had quietened down or the morning light made the journey easier; listening to the wind howling outside, she didn't blame them.

They had finished their sherry and Mrs MacGregor was in the act of placing two plates of steaming soup on the table when she was almost knocked over by a boy who darted in from the bar. He was so wet that the water ran in little rivulets down his arms and legs and formed pools on the matting, but even while Mrs MacGregor was scolding him he had pushed past her and handed Sappha a sheet of paper wrapped carefully in a scrap of plastic. She put down her glass and said in surprise:

'For me? Are you sure?'

The boy nodded, 'Aye, miss,' and when she said: 'Well, take off your wet coat while I read it,' surprised her by saying: 'Nay, I'll not,' and looked so beseechingly at her that she took the paper out of its sopping wrappings and began to read.

'Sappha, Mrs MacTadd has jumped the gun. A shoulder presenting and well jammed. I'll have to do a Caesar. Go to Gloria's and fetch her midwifery bag, the gas and air, blood giving and taking sets and the vacoliter of blood in the fridge. Keep the boy with you, he'll bring you back. Ask Glover if he'll give a hand.' It was signed R.v.D.

She looked up from it to find Andrew's eyes on her. He said irritably:

'Give the boy something and let's get on with our meal.'

Sappha folded the paper carefully. 'No, we can't do

that. Listen, Andrew.' Almost before she had finished explaining he exclaimed: 'But you're not going, Sappha. The man must be mad. Why can't he send the woman to hospital? He's only a GP anyway.'

She answered him patiently. 'How? There's no ambulance in the village—how could she be brought over the causeway or put in a boat on a night like this, and then be driven miles?' She added stubbornly: 'He's perfectly able to deal with it himself if he must.' As she spoke she was astonished to find that she believed what she was saying.

She went to the door and took down her raincoat and started to put it on; Andrew strode across the little room and caught hold of her.

'Sappha, you're not to go. Let him manage as best he can.' His voice held a faint sneer.

'He wants your help,' she reminded him as she evaded his hand and tied on her head-scarf. Andrew flung away and went to sit in one of the chairs. 'I have no intention of going. I don't even know that the fellow's a doctor—after all, he's a foreigner, supposing the woman were to die—my reputation—I have myself to consider.'

Sappha turned away without a word. It was funny to think that if this hadn't happened she might have decided to go back to London, if not immediately, then in a short time, not because Andrew had wanted her to, but for some vague reason of her own which lurked somewhere at the back of her mind, and there was too much on that at the moment for her to give it a second thought. She had to help Rolf, of that she was certain. Not looking at Andrew she said, 'Come along,' to the boy and pausing only long enough to ask Mrs Mac-

Gregor to send a message to the Manse, she followed
the boy out into the storm.

Gloria's house was close by but it was dark and she
had no torch; it took precious minutes while she blun-
dered round searching for the key. Inside, she went
straight to the surgery key's hiding place and opened
its door. As she collected what she needed she sent up a
little prayer of thankfulness that Gloria had shown her
where everything was kept. Before she locked the door
again she possessed herself of Gloria's torch, a solid
rubber affair with a vast beam, scribbled a brief note
to leave on the sitting room table and went over to the
boy, standing patiently by the door. She gave him the
torch and said worriedly: 'You poor lad, you're soaked!'
She touched his wringing sleeve. 'What's your name?'

'Ian. Are ye ready?'

She nodded. 'Will you take this bag, Ian—I can manage the rest.'

She had got wet coming from Mrs MacGregor's,
but when they were out in the lane again, she realised
that that had been only a preliminary. Ian crossed over
the narrow street, turned down behind the post office
and so to the harbour, where the full force of the gale
met them with a wall of wind and blinding rain. It was
only then that Sappha saw that Ian was heading for the
causeway beyond the harbour. She clutched him by the
arm and shouted against the wind: 'We're not going
over the causeway?'

She heard his answering 'Aye' before he started off
again, quickening his pace as she struggled to keep up
with him, her bags and bundles banging against her legs
as she went. It was like a nightmare; but if this was a

nightmare, she had no words for the causeway when they reached it.

For the first few yards it wasn't too bad, for although its stones were broken and uneven, there was some foothold, but then she was confronted by half a dozen crumbling steps, covered in seaweed and lashed by spray. She looked at them and said simply: 'I can't, Ian. I'm afraid.' He made a small grunting sound which sounded sympathetic, then:

'Ma'll die,' was all he said. There was only one answer to that; Sappha put a sodden and completely ruined shoe on the bottom step.

'Will you go first,' she asked, 'and I'll pass you the bags—I must have one hand free.'

She scrambled up somehow, helped by Ian, who put the bags carefully down and came back to help her. It was a mercy that it was so dark, she decided as she landed on her hands and knees, for if she were to see where she was she would probably scream the place down. In obedience to Ian's shouted advice she ducked to avoid the full force of the wind and the rain, trying to keep her balance while she clutched the two bags and the precious vacoliter in wet hands. But now, by straining her eyes, she could see a light ahead and she said involuntarily, her voice snatched by the wind: 'Oh, it's too good to be true!' as indeed it was, for half a dozen staggered steps further Ian stopped and shone the torch on more steps, leading down this time, but not only did they lead down, they sagged sideways as well and in one place her horrified eyes saw that there was almost no step at all.

Ian said something in Gaelic and disappeared to negotiate the impossible with comparative ease, for he

was back very shortly to take the bags from her and
scramble down again. It was when he came back for
the second time and said: 'Come, miss,' that Sappha
whispered: 'But I can't—really I can't.' No one heard
her, of course, and she went on standing there, unable
to move for fright and cold. It was only seconds later
that another, more powerful torch spotlighted her feet
and she heard the Baron bellow: 'Stay where you are
and hang on to that blood!'

Even in her terror Sappha's mind registered the fact
that he seemed far more worried about the blood than
about her, but she was beyond caring and almost beyond movement, although her hand tightened obediently around the vacoliter. The next moment he was
balanced on the step below her, prising the precious
bottle from her stiff fingers, to go again before she
could make a sound, but he was back in a moment, his
voice close in her ear to shatter her eardrums above the
roar of the wind.

'Turn round—go on, I've got you safe enough—and
do as you're told.'

She did as she was told, muttering uselessly into
the gale:

'That's right, bully me, you fiend!' She felt the tears
streaming down her face and didn't care; she was already so wet, no one would notice. She felt the Baron's
large firm hands clamped on either side of her waist,
but it was only after he said: 'Let go—let go, damn it!'
that she took her hands from the stone at the top of the
steps to clutch frantically at thin air.

'Stop flapping like a wet hen,' besought the Baron—
above the gale's scream she heard him laugh. 'Lean
back against me.' Which she did; it was like leaning

against a tree-trunk, solid and safe and strong and when his calm voice ordered, 'Stretch your left leg down and put your weight on it,' she did so without hesitation. 'Now the right,' came his voice once more. She could feel that she was balanced on a narrow slipery ledge tilting sharply to one side, spray from the sea soaked her legs, the wind tore at her hair—it had whipped her scarf away long since. When the Baron said 'Jump,' she closed her eyes against the awful, noisy dark and jumped, his hands still firm on her waist, and when he shouted 'Good girl!' she felt a warm glow despite her shivering body.

'Two more steps,' he said, 'easy ones.' She could feel their sliminess under her feet and screamed as one foot slipped, unaware that she had screamed his name, but his hands still held her fast; she felt rough grass and boulders under her feet as he caught her by the arm and hurried her the few yards to the croft. Ian was already there, the equipment stacked tidily against one wall. Inside, it was very warm, with a driftwood fire sending sparks up the chimney and a good deal of smoke into the room as well. There were oil lamps on the table and the mantelpiece, and as they entered an old lady came through an inner door carrying another lamp in her hand. The Baron spoke urgently to her in a language Sappha couldn't understand, then turned to her.

'We'll have to be quick before she starts haemorrhaging again.'

Sappha started to unbutton her raincoat with cold shaking fingers, but she made clumsy work of it, so that he came across the little room and did it for her, stripping the soaking garment off her and throwing it into a corner of the room, revealing her dress—her lovely pink woollen dress, plastered to her body, its collar shapeless, the pretty ruffles torn and filthy with bits of seaweed sticking to them. The Baron caught her by the arm, remarking cheerfully: 'A write-off, isn't it? So it won't matter if I do this.' He caught the tattered ruffles and ripped one sleeve up to the elbow and rolled it up tidily, then did exactly the same with the other while she watched with speechless fascination.

'Your hair,' he said briskly, and took the slender suede belt she wore and went behind her, gathered her hair into it and tied it securely.

'Next room,' he said, still brisk, and swept her before him, pausing only to hand her the midwifery bag and pick up the remainder of the clutter himself. The room Sappha entered was small but well lighted by reason of the lamps ranged on the little shelf over the fireplace and the chest in one corner. The patient lay in the big iron bedstead pushed up against one wall; there was a large wooden table in the middle of the room covered with a sheet, and a stand with a basin and several jugs of steaming water upon it. The Baron went past her to the bed and bent over his patient, saying over his shoulder: 'We'll get that blood into her as soon as possible, but first we will get ready to operate.'

Sappha found herself saying meekly: 'Yes, Doctor,' as though she were quite in the habit of preparing for a Caesarean section in a stuffy little room without so much as a cold water tap. She went to open the first of the bags and caught sight of herself in the mirror on the wall. At any other time she would have stared incredulously and then burst out laughing at her ludicrous reflection, but now she scarcely paused, but began setting out the sterile packs with the same careful precision she would have used in the operating theatre in Greggs'.

She was a practical girl as well as a good nurse—the small table under the mirror would do excellently for the instruments—she cleaned its top lavishly with Savlon, draped it in a dressing towel, and laid the packs upon it. The baby's cot was already in the room, she took the tiny blanket from the midwifery bag and wrapped it around the old-fashioned hot water bottle already in the cot, then opened the blood giving set, put it neatly, still in its sterile wrappers, beside the instruments, and said, with commendable coolness:

'We shall want at least two buckets or bowls and something in which to put the swabs—they'll have to be checked,' and the Baron bending over his patient, took his stethoscope out of one ear and shouted through the half open door into the other room. Presently the old woman came in with two buckets, a baby's bath and a small wash-tub. Rolf looked up briefly. 'There you are—take your choice,' he remarked. 'Are you ready your end?'

Sappha said yes, she was, and wondered why she could feel so calm about it all—perhaps it was because he was so matter-of-fact about everything and so quietly certain; indeed, he was no longer a brigand, nor, for that matter, a bossy baron, but a man in complete command of an awkward situation. She trusted him completely and was quite prepared to do anything he might ask of her.

She tied herself into the gown she had taken from one of the packs, put on a mask and watched him while he lifted Mrs MacTadd on to the table and covered her with a blanket. Mrs MacTadd, Sappha saw with concern, was unconscious, she wondered what the Baron intended to do about an anaesthetic. As though in answer to her thought, he observed:

'I've got my case here—I'll give her a spinal—but the blood first.'

He went to scrub his hands and then over to the little table Sappha had prepared and she went to the chest and picked up the vacoliter. As she turned round to give it to him, it slipped through her fingers. She stood for a frozen eternity staring at him, the bottle in splinters at her feet while its precious contents oozed gently in all directions, waiting for him to utter the blistering words she undoubtedly deserved. But all he said was: 'I hope you're O group, Rhesus positive.' He didn't sound in the least angry; she had never heard his voice so mild, and when she nodded wordlessly, he said, still mildly: 'Then it's our lucky day, isn't it? Jump on the bed, there's a good girl, and I'll take a pint or so off you.'

She did as she was told, hardly noticing the old woman, who, in answer to another of the Baron's unintelligible shouts, came in to clean up the mess. 'Clever of you to bring the blood donor set,' he remarked cheerfully. 'Can you bear the needle straight in without a local? It'll save time.'

Sappha stared down at his head bowed over her arm. 'Yes, of course I can bear it,' she said in a shamed little voice, 'and don't call me clever.' She choked a little on the word and added: 'I'm sorry.' It sounded inadequate, and perhaps it was, for he merely looked up briefly, said: 'Now,' and slipped the needle into the inner side of her elbow where the vein showed blue. But then he said very kindly: 'If you hadn't come our patient and

the baby might very well have been dead by morning—
that cancels out any dropped bottles.'

Sappha continued to stare while the elusive thoughts
she had buried so firmly under the emergencies of the
evening suddenly became very clear indeed. She knew
now why she ought to go back to London—and soon.
She had fallen in love with Rolf and since she had been
fool enough to pick on someone who didn't care for her
at all, the quicker she went away the better. The sensible
half of her brain approved of this while the other half,
which was ruled by her heart, deplored it. She curbed
a desire to stretch out her free hand and touch his dark
hair and reminded herself sternly where she was.

'Clench your fist, Sappha,' Rolf bade her, and
shouted to the old woman again, who poked her head
round the door and withdrew it again, while Sappha,
for the sake of saying something because she could no
longer stay silent with her thoughts, asked: 'Why don't
you speak English?'

'She wouldn't understand—some of the older people
here speak only the Gaelic.'

'Oh—and you speak it too.'

'After a fashion. I've been coming here for years,
you know—it's like a second home.' He tightened the
blood pressure armband above her elbow and presently
loosened it. 'Mrs MacTadd will bring you some tea and
some bread and butter, you'll stay here and have it while
I'm getting this into our patient.'

Sappha looked lovingly at the back of his downbent
head. 'You won't be able to manage,' she said positively.
'This isn't like theatre or even a hospital ward.'

'I shall manage. You'll do as I say. I shall need you

presently and I don't want you fainting all over everything. Feel all right?'

'Yes, thank you. Have you ever done this thing before?'

'Taken blood? Oh, yes, a few hundred times, I should imagine.'

'I mean operating like this—with no mod cons.'

'Yes—never a Caesarean though. An appendix or so and an amputation, and Hamish and I did a bad hernia together—on an old shepherd who had never been to hospital in his life, in any case it was too late to move him.'

He whipped out the needle and she didn't even notice. 'Did they all recover?' she wanted to know.

He laughed a little. 'Of course. People who live close to nature nearly always do—they have faith and trust.' He looked up at her, his eyes twinkling. 'Alas! My poor ego.'

'I didn't mean—' began Sappha. 'That is, I think you could do anything.'

He nodded without conceit, and they didn't talk any more after that. She ate her bread and butter and drank the dark sweet tea and watched him working. He was quick, but his movements were so economical that he gave the impression that there was no haste. Presently he said without looking up: 'OK. Will you clean yourself up? I shall want some help with the spinal.'

It was amazing how smoothly the operation went. Sappha who had been used to half a dozen persons at least in the theatre for a Caesarean section, discovered that, with a little forethought and ingenuity, it was quite possible to manage with two. It was by no means ideal, of course, but once the sterile packs were opened and the sutures had been put ready and the swabs counted out, she was able to scrub up while she listened to Rolf's instructions. She was to remain sterile until they had the baby; longer if possible, so that she could hold the forceps while he tied off, because time mattered now, more than anything else. It helped that Mrs MacTadd was still unconscious, although it was possible that she would regain consciousness before long now that she had had some blood, but Rolf had explained to her hours before what he might have to do; even if she came round before the end of operation she would know what was happening.

'The baby was a little girl. They'll be glad—they've got three boys,' said the Baron as he laid the small wriggling creature on the sterile sheet and turned back to his patient.

Half an hour later, Sappha was making up the bed while the doctor mounted guard over his now conscious patient and the baby. The room looked terrible; it would take hours to clear up, but that didn't matter in the least, because they had got the baby and the mother was safe too. Sappha made the bedclothes into a neat pack, said: 'Ready when you are,' and went to pick up the baby while Rolf lifted Mrs MacTadd carefully into her bed. She was still far from well, but at least she was alive and likely to remain so. She smiled tiredly at Sappha as she tucked her in and gave her the baby and lay quietly while they put up a saline drip; drank the tea she was offered and stayed awake just long enough for her husband to creep in. He kissed her white cheek and she said contentedly: 'It's a lassie,' and smiled again before she was at once asleep.

Mr MacTadd crept out again and returned soft-footed with more tea and an offer to clear up the mess, but Sappha thanked him warmly and said no, she'd do it in a brace of shakes herself, swallowed the rest of her tea and got to her feet. It was, incredibly, just nine o'clock. She looked across at the doctor, sitting on a small folding stool which didn't look as though it would bear his weight. He appeared lost in thought, but looked up immediately as she moved.

'A half-hour pulse chart, I think, don't you? I'll give her some Pethedine when she rouses; we'll get her to hospital as soon as we can, but it's impossible for the moment. You'll have to stay the night, you know that?'

Sappha shuddered, then said with spirit: 'Nothing would induce me to go back over that awful causeway again.'

'Well, we'll have to see about that,' he remarked placidly. 'In the meantime you can sleep here. I would have suggested that you stripped off those wet clothes, but I imagine that they have dried on you by now.'

Sappha nodded and took off her gown to reveal a dress that was a ruin; probably everything underneath it was as well, she thought gloomily; her shoes looked as though she had been walking in them continuously for months on end, and when she put a hand up to her hair, he said mildly: 'Leave it—it's beyond all hope—luckily there's no one to see.' She was getting over this remark when he asked: 'What happened to Glover?'

She was going round the room, bundling the dressing towels and sheets into a tidy heap. She paused with her back to him and strove to make her voice matter-of-fact. 'He—he didn't want to intrude—I mean, it wasn't his case.'

'It wasn't mine either,' Rolf said blandly, and when she turned round to face him she saw that he was wearing his satyr's face. 'I'm sorry,' she said miserably, 'I did ask him.'

The Baron put down his cup and strolled towards her, his face quite normal again. He said kindly: 'It's not your fault and you have nothing to be sorry for.'

She whispered: 'Oh, yes—the blood,' and he waved a hand airily.

'I daresay yours did her a great deal more good,' he smiled so that her heart turned over. 'Thank you for coming, Sappha.'

She had become completely enchanted by the smile. She stood before him trying out several answers and discarding them. One couldn't say 'Delighted,' or 'Don't mention it,' or even, 'It was nothing.' She finally came out with: 'Oh, well…'

He had come very close; before she realised what he was going to do he had bent and kissed her on one cheek. If she had had any latent doubts as to her feelings for him—which she hadn't—they would have been tossed into oblivion, and if a casual kiss on the cheek had the power to make her heart thud against her ribs as it was thudding now, how would she feel if the kiss were not so casual?

It was best not to think about it. She moved back a little and said matter-of-factly: 'I'll have your gown, shall I? If I put everything to soak in cold water, it shouldn't be too bad…'

He made a small sound which might have been a chuckle, divested himself of the garment and said: 'I'll get the water, shall I?'

Sappha made short work of the clearing up, after all for, contrary to her expectations, the Baron proved a willing helper. As good as a nurse, she thought, watching him scrubbing instruments and wishing the night would go on for ever. All the same when he remarked that he couldn't understand why any girl in her senses wanted to do such work for the pleasure of it she answered coolly enough that they liked it anyway and then, 'Do you suppose Dr MacInroy and Gloria will come over here tonight?'

He threw the last of the cleaned instruments on the table and dragged his thick sweater on over his shirt. 'No—not unless they're out of their wits.'

'How did you know—about Mrs MacTadd, I mean?'

'Ian came for me.' He went over to the bed and took his patient's pulse and looked at the chart Sappha had written up between her bouts of cleaning. He said offhand: 'Have you finished? Go and lie down on that folding contraption in the corner, it looks uncomfortable, but you should be able to get some sleep.'

'And what about you?' demanded Sappha. 'You can't sit up all night.'

His voice was cool. 'Certainly I can.'

'Then I shall too.' And wished she hadn't said it when he replied:

'Oh, come now, isn't that carrying good fellowship a little too far?'

It was unanswerable. If she said: 'But I've discovered I love you since I said that,' he would probably give one of his great gusts of laughter, or would look like a satyr and say nothing at all. She went and lay down and after a minute ventured to ask: 'You will call me if you need me?'

He said irritably: 'Of course. I intend calling you at four o'clock anyway so that you can take over until morning.' His voice held a note of finality so that she thought it prudent to say nothing more, so she pulled the blanket up to her chin and closed her eyes.

She awoke to the feel of his hand on her shoulder and his voice saying quietly: 'Here's some tea—it will clear your wits.'

Thus encouraged, she swallowed the strong, hot brew, got up and went to look at Mrs MacTadd, who was sleeping, as was the baby.

'I gave her Pethedine just before two o'clock,' Rolf explained. 'She will probably sleep until six—the baby too. There's a bottle with some sterile water keeping warm by the fire—if she yells give her some, unless Mum wakes up as well—and keep an eye on that dressing.' He gave her the rest of his instructions, said: 'Call me at seven will you?' then went and stretched himself on the little bed and was at once asleep.

Sappha called him exactly at seven, but before then she had seen to the baby and washed Mrs MacTadd and given her some tea. It was surprising how well the patient looked and how serenely she accepted the situation. Sappha left her lying back on her pillows, still pale but cheerful, while she went to rouse the Baron. He was still asleep and she paused to study his face. It looked remote and austere and very handsome, rather like a crusader knight reclining in perpetuity on some ancient tomb; she wondered how she could ever have found him unattractive. When his eyes flew open she gave a gasp and jumped so violently that he asked coldly: 'Do I scare you as much as all that?' and without waiting for her answer, got up and went straight to his patient, and presently, after drinking the tea she had got for him, he went into the other room, presumably to speak to Mr MacTadd. She heard the door open and shut and

after a few minutes he came back to inform her that
the weather had settled nicely and he had no doubt that
Hamish and Gloria would be with them within the hour.

'But it's only seven o'clock,' Sappha protested.

He said reasonably: 'It's only sixty miles or so and
Hamish knows the road—my guess is they left around
six. Provided the road is clear they'll be here by eight.'

Chapter 4

Rolf was right, it was barely eight o'clock and Sappha was recording Mrs MacTadd's pulse when she heard the door open once more and Gloria and Hamish came in. Hamish and the Baron exchanged laconic hullos and began, with the calmness of men who knew what they were about, to discuss the case. Gloria, however, went at once to look at Mrs MacTadd, firing questions at Sappha as she did so. 'And how did you get here?' she wanted to know finally.

Sappha shuddered. 'Over that awful causeway—it was pitch dark, and a good thing too or I should never have made it.' She added apprehensively: 'I've just begun to wonder how I shall get back—it will be so much worse because now I can see…'

The two men were talking by the fire; now Hamish said over his shoulder: 'No need to worry, lass, you'll do fine in the boat.'

'Shall I?' enquired Sappha faintly, wondering if she was expected to take the oars herself—perhaps the wretched thing would have an outboard motor, which as far as she was concerned would be even worse. But she was given no time to brood over this problem; the Baron asked her to give her report to Gloria as the latter would be staying until Hamish could get an ambulance organised. Hospital was undoubtedly the best place for Mrs MacTadd—she needed another blood transfusion and some antibiotics to combat the shortcomings of an operation performed in a room there had been no time even to dust. The two men fell to discussing ways and means while Sappha gave details concerning the patient with unhurried calmness. When she had finished, Gloria said:

'OK, and thanks a lot—I never thought when I showed you the surgery that you would have to make use of it.' She eyed Sappha cautiously. 'I heard about your broken date from Mrs MacGregor—she was on the lookout for us—I'm sorry, Sappha, it was rotten bad luck.' She added with engaging frankness: 'You look awful, though if it's any consolation to you, you're the only girl I've met who could still look eye-catching in that deplorable dress—it must have been pretty.'

Sappha nodded. 'I'll have to throw it away,' she remarked, not really minding. She would go to Inverness on her next day off and buy something to take its place. She checked Mrs MacTadd's pulse once more and the Baron said 'Ready? We're going back with Hamish.' He fetched her raincoat and buttoned her into it with the air of a patient man who hadn't much time to spare. As they went out he said to Gloria: 'I'll be back.' He had already talked to Mrs MacTadd, his voice quiet and reassuring, then waited while Sappha said her own goodbyes and then followed her outside into the early morning. The clouds had melted away leaving a pallid sky which wasn't warmed by the thin sunshine, the sea looked mountainous to her anxious eyes, but as neither of the men seemed in the least perturbed, she said nothing, but walked between them to where Ian and Mr MacTadd were holding a small rowing dinghy, and got in when she was bidden to, averting her gaze from the causeway, which, in daylight and at close quarters, looked too awful for words. The equipment was stowed away and she sat silently while the two men got in, half expecting the little boat to sink like a stone under their combined and not inconsiderable weights. It did no such thing, however, and they disposed themselves with the careless unconcern of men who had lived with boats since childhood. It seemed the Baron was to do the rowing; she sat facing him as he sent the craft through the still rough water, looking more of a ruffian than ever, for he lacked a shave. She supposed it was the want of sleep that had made his already formidable nose look even more formidable; his brows were drawn together, his eyes half closed against the spray; he looked tired and fierce with it. All the same he plied the oars with the same vigour that a man who had had a good night's rest and a hearty breakfast might have displayed. He looked at her unexpectedly with a gleam of mockery so that she reddened and put a self-conscious hand up to her hair which the wind had whipped into a tangle, ad the red deepened as his mouth widened into a smile and he said in a voice so soft she could barely hear it: 'What does it matter what you look like?' He bent to his oars once more, leaving her to guess, without much success, at what he meant. Dr MacInroy's voice roused her.

'Ye'll have the vacoliter by ye, lassie?'

Sappha half turned to look at him, moving gingerly because the boat was bucketing about on the choppy water. She said woodenly:

'No, I—I smashed it. I'm sorry.'

'Ah, weel, it was no night to walk the causeway— not to mind.'

She kept her head turned away from the Baron, who was grinning at her.

'It wasn't on the causeway—I can't think why not,' she amended bitterly. 'If I'd known what it was going to be like… I smashed it, for no reason at all, just as Dr van Duyren was ready to give it.'

She turned round again and looked steadily at the tiny jetty they were fast approaching.

'Did ye now?' commented the Scottish doctor. 'Yet I obsairved that Mrs MacTadd had received an infusion of some sort.'

Sappha didn't answer. It was the Baron who answered for her. 'Indeed she did, Hamish—a pint or so of pure English blood from our Miss Devenish here— it served its purpose very well. Here we are,' he added, and Hamish jumped out to secure the boat while the Baron shipped his oars in a businesslike manner, then stood up, stretched hugely, and plucked Sappha from her seat and set her tidily on her feet upon the jetty. She found herself between them, arm-in-arm, walking through the little lane to the inn. 'We left the car there,' Hamish explained, 'and I told Mrs MacGregor to be on the look-out for us—she'll no doubt have a pot of tea ready.'

She had indeed, as well as a plate of bread and butter and anything else they might fancy. She fussed around them, clucking like a small motherly hen over Sappha's deplorable state.

'That bonnie dress—and the shoes! Ruined—and there, I almost forgot!' She drew a letter from under her apron. 'Your young man—he left an hour since, he asked me to give ye this wee letter.'

Sappha said thank you, took it from her kind hostess and pushed it into her raincoat pocket. She had forgotten all about Andrew; he seemed like someone from another world. She wasn't in the least interested in what he might have to say. She frowned and looking up, found the Baron's eyes on her, but this time they held no gleam of laughter; he said gently: 'He's got his work like the rest of us—he'll be back.' His voice changed; he said briskly: 'Talking of work, how about getting this stuff back to Gloria's place?'

She cast him a grateful look because his remark had made everything normal again. 'I'll see to that,' she said almost cheerfully, 'if you wouldn't mind telling your mother that I'll be back within the hour.'

Rolf got to his feet and as though she had never spoken, said:

'Hamish, be a good chap and let them know at the Manse, will you?'

'I said me,' said Sappha with a regrettable lack of grammar.

He gave her a smile with a hint of mockery in it. 'So you did,' he observed, his voice all silk. 'Are you ready?'

They said goodbye to Hamish and Mrs MacGregor and walked up the street to Gloria's cottage, where the

Baron retrieved the front door key from its hiding place
with the air of one who had done so many times before.
Inside he said briefly: 'You deal with the midwifery
bag, I'll see to the rest.'

They worked silently, passing each other on their way
to various drawers and cupboards and being carefully
polite about taking turns at the sink. Sappha filled with
a longing to hear his voice, began several tentative con-
versations, which he squashed with polite blandness,
and she reminded herself sadly that when they had first
met she had made no secret of her dislike of him and
now it seemed he had accepted that fact easily enough,
she thought ruefully, since he didn't seem to like her
overmuch in his turn.

He finished a few minutes before her and strolled
into the sitting room and when she followed him in to
make a list of what they had done for Gloria's benefit,
she found him standing in front of 'The Stag at Bay'.

'A revolting picture,' he observed as she began to
write. 'I have begged Gloria to throw it away, or at least
hang it in some obscure corner, but she's anxious not
to hurt the donor's feelings.'

'You don't like stags?'

He turned to look at her, his eyebrows arched. 'Like
them? Of course I like them, but I abhor blood sports.
Why do you look so surprised?'

She fidgeted a little under his bright enquiring gaze.
'Oh do I? Well, actually, you look as though you might
enjoy hunting—things.'

His eyebrows met in a frown and his eyes narrowed.
'And what brought you to that conclusion?' His voice
was bland.

Sappha hesitated. She thought that he might have

been amused even though her remark had been a silly one, but he was obviously annoyed and she would have to answer him—she knew him well enough by now to know that he liked answers to his questions.

'You look like a—a baron,' she said, feeling foolish, and picked up her pen again and without looking at him, finished her list. If he had liked her, even just a little, he might have laughed; as it was, she wasn't surprised when he said coldly without a trace of humour: 'A bold, bad baron, I presume, Miss Devenish.'

She stood up. 'Yes—since you ask, Dr van Duyren.' And went to the door—but he hadn't quite finished with her. 'You haven't read your letter, you must be longing to do so.'

His voice held the faint familiar mockery which could annoy her so much, so that her voice was sharp. 'I'll read it in my room, when I'm alone,' she said and went through the door and waited while he put the key back and then walked silently beside him through the streets to the Manse. They parted in the hall without a word.

She didn't see him again until midday, by which time she had bathed, changed into uniform, taken in her patient's breakfast and eaten her own before continuing with the usual morning routine, all against a lively background of comment and questions from everyone in the house, with the exception of the Baron; he, having breakfasted and bathed, had left the house again, presumably to assist in getting Mrs MacTadd safely into the ambulance Sappha had seen roll past the Manse during the course of the morning. An hour later, it passed again, going hospitalwards, but there was no sign of Dr van Duyren—perhaps he had travelled with it. Sappha turned away from the window and went on making the Baroness's bed, unaware of the forlorn look upon her face. When the Baroness, who had been looking at her thoughtfully, remarked:

'I've often wondered what Rolf is like to work with—do tell, Sappha,' she paused in her work, glad of the opportunity of talking about him.

'He's super—he doesn't flap, you see, and he knows what he's doing without being cocksure; he didn't let me flap either, and I wanted to once or twice,' she added honestly.

Her patient nodded. 'He sounds quite human,' she observed with an air of surprise so that Sappha felt compelled to say: 'Oh, but he is. He was sweet to Mrs MacTadd and her family, just as though he were in the habit of doing Caesars in bedrooms and thought nothing of it. I don't think any of them realised…he's not easily deterred from doing what he intends to do, I think.'

His mother smiled. 'No, my dear. He is also in the habit of getting what he wants, whether it's the successful treatment of his patients or the conquest of some pretty girl.'

She spoke lightly and Sappha made an equally light reply which cost her quite an effort. 'I can quite believe that, and,' she added thoughtfully, 'if all Dutch girls are as pretty as Antonia, he must be kept quite busy with his conquests.'

The Baroness didn't answer this, merely remarking that Antonia was a Friesian, not Dutch, and that Friesian girls on the whole were good-looking but rather big. 'Not like you, Sappha, for you are quite a small woman, are you not, though you are what we used to call very nicely covered.'

'What is very nicely covered, Mother?' enquired the Baron's voice from the open door. 'May I come in? I see you're in your chair.' He nodded to Sappha, kissed his parent and sat down beside her, to spend the next five minutes or so answering her questions about Mrs MacTadd, who was now safely stowed in hospital. 'And now answer my question, my dear,' he said mildly. The Baroness looked vague. 'Something was nicely covered,' he prompted. She smiled. 'Of course, dear, now I remember—Sappha…'

He turned his head and stared across the room and Sappha said hastily:

'I'll go and get your lunch, Baroness,' and whisked down the stairs at a fine speed, forgetting to shut the door as she went. It was too bad of the Baroness, although probably she hadn't quite realised—she was sometimes a little vague. Sappha messed about in the kitchen, getting in everyone's way, until the minister poked his head round the door and asked her to go to the study because her uncle was on the telephone.

And so he was, with the Baron listening to him, sitting on Mr MacFee's desk, swinging one long leg. As she went in he said:

'Here she is now, sir. Hold on.' He gave her a brief smile. 'Mr Devenish is coming to see Mother—he wants to know if tomorrow suits you.' Sappha nodded and he said: 'Yes, that's fine—you want to speak to her?'

It seemed that Uncle John did. The Baron held out the receiver and moved along the desk to make room for her, and when she hesitated, put out a long arm and scooped her up to sit beside him, and as he kept his arm around her and it was impossible to get down again without an undignified struggle, she had per-

force to stay where she was while she answered Uncle
John's questions about his patient. These satisfactorily
dealt with, he went on: 'Are you happy, Sappha? Not
too lonely after London, I hope—I expect you find it
very quiet.'

She thought of the previous night. 'I find plenty to
do,' she said at length. 'I like the village and the people.'
Her uncle gave a non-committal grunt, wished her goodbye and rang off, and the Baron moved his arm so that
she was able to get off the desk and walk with dignity to
the door. But before she was quite there he said: 'Don't
go—I have something to say to you.' His voice, though
polite, had a ring of authority so that she stopped, albeit
reluctantly, and turned to face him. He had got to his feet
and was standing with his hands in the pockets of his
well-cut tweed suit. He was shaved and well-groomed
and she hardly recognised him for the man who had been
with her at Mrs MacTadd's; perhaps circumstances had
made him seem more approachable—now he seemed
remote and when he spoke his voice was impersonal.

'I talked to your uncle before you came in—I told
him about last night.'

She said quickly: 'Oh—not about Andrew?' For how
could she explain to Uncle John that she no longer cared
twopence for Andrew, when only ten days ago he had
been instrumental in sending her hundreds of miles
away to this job because her heart was broken…

The Baron's voice was very quiet. 'No, not about Andrew. What do you take me for, Sappha?' He looked at
her so haughtily that she hastily begged his pardon, but
he went on as though she hadn't spoken.

'He agrees with me that I should reimburse you for
the—er—clothes which were ruined last night. I will

give you a cheque for a suitable amount and you will be good enough to accept it.'

Sappha had gone a brilliant and highly becoming pink during this high handed speech. She said wrathfully: 'I'll do no such thing! I went of my own free will and I'm not in the habit of accepting money from—from...'

'Barons?' he supplied nastily, and went on to enrage her still more. 'My dear good woman, aren't you being a little melodramatic? We're living in enlightened times now, you know. I am not bribing you, nor am I expecting any return for my money; I am in your debt, and I am not in the habit of being in debt to anyone.'

'I couldn't care less about your habits,' said Sappha very crossly. 'If you give me any money, I shall tear it up—I'm well able to afford to clothe myself without any help from you.'

He took a few steps towards her and she saw that he looked as ill-tempered as she felt, and suddenly wished that they didn't need to quarrel. How strange it was that she could argue with him so fiercely and yet love him so much. Unexpected tears filled her brown eyes and ran down her cheeks and she took her handkerchief from her uniform pocket, blew her pretty nose prosaically and mopped her face, took a steadying breath and said: 'I'm sorry, I didn't know I was going to cry.' She gave him a defiant look and found that he was staring at her with such intensity that she caught her breath and hiccupped.

He said evenly: 'If you hope to get your own way by crying, Sappha, I should warn you that you're in for a disappointment. If necessary I shall buy a dress and shoes and personally put them on you.'

She sniffed: 'You wouldn't dare.' He smiled, not at

all nicely, so that he looked like a satyr; she saw that of course he would dare. She blew her nose again to give herself time to think, then:

'I shall ask Uncle John's advice,' she said, and watched his dark face break into another smile; there was a hint of patient mockery in it this time so that she felt like a child who had tried to get the better of a grown-up and hadn't. Uncle John was no use at all. He had arrived early and had undertaken an exhaustive examination of his patient with Sappha in attendance. Afterwards they had gone into the study where he had outlined the Baroness's further treatment. 'Very satisfactory,' he remarked. 'There had been a tendency to depression before you came, but it seems to me that our patient has a new interest in life—you have no idea what it is, I suppose, Sappha?'

She thought. 'No, Uncle, unless it's Antonia's visit. It's made home seem nearer, I fancy, and of course she can speak her own language.'

'H'm—I daresay that may have something to do with it. I think we might discontinue the intramuscular gluconate and give calcium lactate by mouth. And now the elbow—I think that next week the plaster might come off. You've been exercising her fingers and wrist and shoulder, haven't you? Yes, well, I feel we could safely remove the splint. I'll get MacCombie to come over and have a look. As for the leg—she's been sitting out for several weeks, hasn't she? There's nothing much we can do there for several weeks. That disposes of the orthopaedic side of things, doesn't it? MacCombie may want an X-ray, but that's up to him. I'll have those specimens tested and let you know the results; they should be greatly improved, I fancy. On the whole, I think we have made considerable headway, don't you?' He smiled at Sappha. 'And so you've settled down here, Sappha?'

'Oh, very well, Uncle John. How long is the Baroness likely to be here?'

He gave her a questioning look. 'Well, it's hard to say. If this improvement is maintained I see no reason why she shouldn't go home in say, a month's time—probably less. She won't be able to bear any weight on that leg, but that is of no consequence; there's plenty of domestic help, I believe. Why do you ask? Nothing to do with last night's little adventure, I hope?'

'No—Yes, it is in a way. I didn't mind going to help in the least—why should I? There wasn't anyone else.' She told him about the ruined dress and shoes and Dr van Duyren's insistence that she should accept new ones at his expense. When she had finished she waited, a little breathless, for her uncle to speak.

'Well, my dear, aren't you making a mountain out of a molehill? Why shouldn't you accept replacements of the things which were spoilt while helping Rolf? I find nothing unusual in it at all, it seems to me to be a matter of common sense.'

He took off his old-fashioned glasses and gave her a keen look. 'Perhaps you and Rolf don't—er—quite hit it off and I appreciate that at the present time you tend to despise and dislike all men, but you mustn't allow that to blind you to good sense. Rolf is a very sound man and the fact that you dislike him—probably he dislikes you too, my dear—could make no difference to his doing whatever he feels is the right thing. I suggest you defer to his judgment.'

So she went back to her patient, and as the Baroness, naturally enough, wanted to talk about her bright-

ening future, she was unable to give her own concerns
any thought at all, and at lunch, to which Uncle John
stayed, neither he nor the Baron made any reference to
the preceding night's activities. The conversation was a
rather lofty one about droving and old military roads in
and around the Highlands, and as Sappha knew nothing
at all about the subject she had to sit and listen with as
much interest as she could muster, and was even forced
from time to time to give her attention to the Baron,
who, with a kindly patience which made her grit her
teeth, brought to her notice the more interesting points
of their talk.

She didn't see him again for the rest of that day. She
had said goodbye to Uncle John after lunch, made sure
that her patient was comfortable, and then, leaving her
to be entertained for an hour by Antonia, went to her
room. The weather was still bad; there seemed no point
in going out, so she curled up in the old-fashioned armchair and switched on the electric fire. They had sat a
long time over lunch and there was only an hour or so
before she would have to fetch the Baroness's tea. It
hardly seemed worthwhile writing letters. She sat up
with a jerk, remembering Andrew's letter, still in her
pocket. She drew it out and turned it over in her hand,
then presently got up, fetched an envelope of her own,
addressed it to him, put his unopened letter inside and
sealed it. Perhaps he would understand from that that
she wanted nothing more to do with him.

She stamped it and then sat on her bed, debating
whether to take it to the post office or not; there was,
after all, no great hurry. She laid it on her beside table
and went back to her chair, kicked off her shoes, took
off her cap, and curled up once more. It was an excel-

lent opportunity to think; after all, she would have to make some plans for the future sooner or later, but the future, when she thought about it, seemed vague and unimportant and it didn't seem to matter what she thought about anyway, because it was immediately blotted out by the Baron's face. She wondered where he had gone; she supposed that he had a great number of friends and acquaintances living round and about—probably had gone to visit one of them. Her overtired mind conjured up a variety of charming women, all young, beautiful and ready to fall into the Baron's embrace. The thought was so disquieting that she got up and went over to the window for distraction, but her eyes lighted on the rain-washed isthmus where she had spent the night with him and her action did no good at all. She went back to her chair again, telling herself sternly that probably her feelings for him were merely the result of her unhappy affair with Andrew—'caught on the rebound', it was called. Probably in a few weeks' time when she left the Baroness and was once more working in some hospital or other she would laugh… The tears trickled down her cheeks at the thought of it.

The sun was out the next morning and the Baroness remarked upon it with such gaiety that Sappha said cheerfully:

'You are better, Baroness. I'm so glad Antonia came to see you—it's done you the world of good.' She smiled at her patient, hoping that she might tell her how long Antonia and Rolf were staying, but the little lady merely said: 'Yes, I feel marvellous. Mr Devenish said something about Mr MacCombie coming to see me. It would be so nice to have my arm back… I really think I could eat some breakfast this morning, Sappha, and do you suppose the post has come?'

Sappha glanced at her watch. 'It's a bit early, but I'll go and see.' She remembered her letter to Andrew; the post-man would take it with him if she asked. She fetched it and ran downstairs and into the kitchen to find the Baron standing at the open back door, drinking tea. The sight of him took her breath, but apparently he had no such sensation on seeing her, for he said casually: 'Hullo, you're early, aren't you?'

'Well, it's a nice day and your mother is feeling so well she wants a proper breakfast—and her post.' Her eye fell on the little pile on the table and he said at once:

'There's nothing for you—Mother's are underneath.' He put his cup down. 'I'm going to the post office, do you want anything?'

Sappha had handed him the letter to Andrew before she had thought about it. He read the envelope deliberately and gave her a pensive, considering stare; she thought he was going to speak, but instead he turned on his heel and went through the open door. She watched him walk unhurriedly down the kitchen garden path until he turned the corner of the house and she couldn't see him any more. Now he would suppose her to be still in love with Andrew—not, she told herself bitterly, that that would make a ha'porth of difference; Rolf treated her with tolerant amusement most of the time and didn't scruple to be nasty when he chose; she might just as well have been cross-eyed and spotty for all the attention he paid her.

He was away all that day too, although when she came back from her afternoon walk, it was to hear that he had spent an hour with his mother. He quite obviously wished to avoid her, and Sappha, who had been popular all her life and never lacked for friends of both sexes, felt puzzled and hurt and finally, angry. Well, she thought defiantly, two can play at that game. Only it was a pity that she had no chance to play it, for next day he took Antonia to visit the laird, who was, it transpired, Antonia's godfather, and the following day was Sunday. Sappha, standing at the Baroness's window, watched the members of the minister's household cross the short stretch of garden between the Manse and the church. Everyone went, Mr MacFee leading the way with Antonia, and Rolf, darkly handsome and exceedingly well turned out, escorting Mrs MacFee. Meg and the postman, who was the odd job man around the Manse, brought up the rear.

'What is Antonia wearing?' asked the Baroness from her bed. 'She's just started buying her own clothes, you know, and some of them aren't quite…she has a hat, I hope?' she queried anxiously.

Sappha, with her eyes on the Baron's broad back, said: 'Yes—a very pretty one—green felt, I think.'

'Ah yes, good. And Rolf, is he there?'

Sappha replied slowly: 'Yes' and turned away from the window. 'He's with Mrs MacFee.'

'A pity you couldn't go too, dear. I feel such a nuisance…'

Sappha started to arrange cushions in the armchair. 'Nonsense, Baroness, I'm used to working on Sundays—besides, I shall go to church this evening, I expect. Mrs MacFee said she would love to sit with you for a little while.'

Which was what she did, leaving not only Mrs MacFee with her patient but Antonia and Rolf as well.

He had barely spoken to her all day and then only a few polite remarks, and Antonia, who had spent half an hour in Sappha's room that afternoon, trying on her hats and looking at her clothes, gave the opinion that her brother had something on his mind. 'A girl, probably,' she said airily, 'though they don't usually have such an effect on him. He's quite forgotten to be bossy and when I asked him if we could stay another day or so he just said "Why not?" I mean, it just isn't like him; he rules me with a rod of iron, you know.'

Sappha laughed. 'Tonia, what a thing to say! I think you have just about everything you want.'

Antonia turned from the mirror where she was trying on the smart little hat Sappha intended to wear to church. 'Yes, I do,' she agreed with engaging frankness, 'but Rolf is very strict—far worse than a father—he says I'm much too impulsive. He won't even let me go out on a date, only if there are several of us, and then he has to know who they are.' She pouted, looking like a discontented kitten. 'We're rich, you see, and Papa left me a great deal of money as well, and Rolf says there are plenty of young men around who would like to get their hands on it.' She gave an exaggerated sigh. 'I suppose he'll make me marry some stuffy man he approves of.'

'I don't imagine your brother numbers stuffy people among his friends for a start, and I'm sure he's far too fond of you to want you to be unhappy. There are quite a lot of wolves around, Tonia.'

Antonia eyed her thoughtfully. 'You sound just like Rolf. Your boy-friend's pretty super, Sappha. I like the way he laughs, and he liked me, didn't he? I could fall for him in a big way, but of course I wouldn't be so mean.'

'No, I'm sure you wouldn't,' said Sappha hastily,

'but there's plenty of time to meet someone like him. I know you're an old maid of sixteen, but there's still hope.' They laughed together and Antonia said: 'I do like you, Sappha—I wish you were in the family. What a pity you don't like Rolf, and he doesn't exactly swoon over you, does he?'

Sappha managed a laugh. 'I'm only here on a job for a few weeks, you know, so likes and dislikes don't matter very much. I shouldn't arrange my future too carefully if I were you—and now go away do, you scheming creature, and leave me to write my letters in peace!'

But she had written no letters at all, only sat thinking about Rolf. Somehow the news that he was rich made everything seem even more hopeless than it already was. What was it Antonia had said? 'He doesn't exactly swoon over you.'

Monday morning was fine, which was perhaps why the Baroness was in such a hurry to be bathed and got up into her chair. She did her exercises with none of the little pauses for a chat which she usually indulged in; she even knew immediately what she wanted to do with her morning. Sappha was adjusting the bed's counterpane to a nicety when the door opened and Antonia and Rolf came in together. They wished their parent a good morning and Antonia pulled up a chair to sit by her mother while Rolf strolled over to the bed, to lean over its high brass end.

'How long will you be?' he enquired mildly.

Sappha gave the pristine bedcover a final pat. 'How long will I be?' she reiterated foolishly, her voice sounding a little quavery because when he came upon her suddenly like this it did something to her breath.

He said patiently: 'Yes—how long will you be?

You've finished here, I imagine. Can you change in half an hour? I want to get away by half past eleven.'

'Away? Where to?'

'Inverness—to get your dress and shoes. As we arranged,' he added wickledly, his dark eyes snapping. He grinned at her cheerfully, just as though they were friends of long standing instead of two people who had barely exchanged half a dozen sentences in the last couple of days. She ignored the grin. 'I don't wish...' she began in what she hoped was a severe voice, only to be interrupted by her patient.

'Such a splendid idea of Rolf's, dear. You see, they're going home tomorrow, and if you go today, I shall have Antonia for company—such a lovely day for a drive too.'

Sappha looked at the Baron, who was, she noted, suitably dressed for an outing and as usual on these occasions, well tailored and well groomed, but today, despite the impeccably cut tweeds and the handmade shoes, he wore the distinct air of a brigand. He said softly: 'It's no good, Sappha, you see I've made up my mind.'

Sappha's fine eyes flashed. She had made up her mind too—not to go. It was therefore all the more astonishing when she heard herself say meekly: 'Very well, I'll come.'

Rolf straightened up. 'Good. You can shop while I collect Mr MacCombie. I'm bringing him back to see Mother—Tonia and I can drop him off in Inverness as we go tomorrow.'

For some reason Sappha found this piece of information depressing. While she changed she was forced to admit to herself that she had actually supposed that the Baron had asked her to accompany him to Inverness because he had wanted to, but this was obviously not so—it was merely convenient that way. She ground her splendid teeth together as she surveyed herself in the old-fashioned mirror in the wardrobe door. She looked nice, even in her own critical eyes. Her tweed suit was oatmeal-coloured and she had teamed it up with a nut brown angora sweater which went very well with the round fur hat set jauntily on top of her dark hair. The hat had been made from an elderly stone-marten fur cape of her mother's; too good to discard completely— it looked expensive, luxurious and very becoming. She picked up her gloves and handbag and went back to the Baroness's room, smelling faintly of Madame Rochas.

The Baroness gave her an appraising look. She said gently:

'Very nice, Sappha—what a pretty girl you are,' and Antonia skipped forward to get a clearer look at the hat and said instantly:

'That hat—it's super! Rolf, I want a fur hat.'

He barely glanced at it. 'For Christmas,' he said shortly, 'if you're ready, we'll go, Sappha.'

She got into the Land Rover with the strong feeling that putting on anything more glamorous than a sack was a waste of time with Rolf. Probably he noticed what other women—women he liked—wore; she doubted if he had even a vague idea as to what she had on. She sat silently beside him, working herself up into a fine temper all the fiercer because she was forced to sup- press it. When he asked: 'Where shall we go first?' in a quite friendly voice, she replied woodenly: 'Wher- ever you wish,' and when after a further silent mile or so he remarked:

'I thought we might lunch at Invermoriston. Did you see Skye on your trip with Glover?'

She said 'No.' He persevered. 'I imagined not. We'll go down as far as Auchtertyre—there's a splendid view from there.' He glanced at his watch. 'We've plenty of time.'

Sappha said nothing to this, her bad temper was beginning to wear off; it had struck her that for the next few hours she was going to be in Rolf's company—and what was that he had said about lunch? His voice, very dry, cut into her thoughts. 'I am—er—very well aware that your feelings towards men are not very friendly at the present time. I am also aware that we agreed to a mutual dislike of each other, though I must point out that this opinion was yours—but we did agree to conceal our true feelings, did we not?' He sighed. 'I have done my best to carry on some sort of conversation with you, but really, my dear good girl, you're making no effort at all, are you?'

Sappha's breast swelled with returned temper. 'Well,' she exclaimed explosively, 'and that after two days of barely speaking to me!'

They were approaching Strome Ferry, running along the banks of Loch Carron, and before answering her he remarked upon the beauty of the scenery they were passing through. 'Do take a look around you,' he advised, 'it may help to cool your temper.'

Speechless with rage, she turned her head to stare at the view; she kept it turned while he continued: 'Of course I didn't talk to you—you terrified me.'

This outrageous statement had the effect of causing her to turn her head to stare at him. 'What complete nonsense,' she managed at last, 'you're not terrified of anything or anyone.'

'Your eyes flashed; you wore a thin coating of ice; you haven't smiled since Saturday.'

Sappha ignored the quite ridiculous way her heart was thumping; she returned to the attack. 'You took me by surprise this morning—you expected me to rush into my clothes and tear off to Inverness just because it's convenient.'

He said blandly: 'It took you exactly forty minutes to change, though I admit the result was well worth the wait—quite eye-catching, in fact. I speak in the guise of good fellowship,' he added hastily.

She said in a small, disappointment-clouded voice: 'Oh, yes, of course. I—I thought you hadn't noticed.' She was staring ahead of her and didn't see his smile.

'And we're hardly rushing to Inverness, are we? We could of course do so should you prefer that.'

She shook her head and was thankful when he began to talk about nothing in particular with a charm which she found herself responding to, so that by the time they had crossed the ferry and begun the climb through the hairpin bends of Auchtertyre Hill, her temper had evaporated once more. When they pulled up, she saw with something of a shock that it was where she and Andrew had come, and when Rolf asked: 'Is this where you stopped with Andrew?' she nodded briefly and said with careful casualness: 'We couldn't see anything, though.'

For answer he got out and helped her out too, and they stood together staring across the sea at the hills of Skye. 'So I don't suppose you did this,' he said slowly, and she shook her head. 'Or this?'

He flung a great arm around her, pulling her close to kiss her with deliberation. Sappha allowed herself a few moments of delight and then pushed against the expanse of tweed she was pressed against. He let her go at once, saying with a little laugh and no single sign of regret, 'And if I had been your Andrew I'm damned if I should have let the wind and the rain stop me from kissing my girl.'

'You've no right—' she began, breathless.

'None at all,' he replied cheerfully. 'Haven't you ever kissed someone just because you were feeling happy?'

She thought she knew what he meant then. His mother was better; likely to recover completely in time. It must have been a load of his mind to know that— probably he would have kissed anyone who had chanced to be around. She said: 'I suppose so,' and smiled a little up into his satyr's face.

'Let's cry truce just for today,' he said. 'I'll be gone tomorrow and you can forget me.'

She agreed soberly: 'Yes, I can, can't I?' and knew that she never would.

They lunched at the Glenmoriston Hotel, talking happily about a variety of subjects while they ate smoked salmon flan, steak and kidney pie, and followed these with pears stuffed with *marrons glacés* and covered with a brandy flavoured cream. Sappha, who had a healthy appetite, swallowed the last delicious morsel and said simply: 'That was delicious. How delightful Scotland is! Somehow, when one lives in London, one tends to think that there is nowhere else...'

Over their coffee, she asked a little shyly: 'Is your home anything like this—oh, I know it's flat in Holland, but is it quiet and peaceful as it is here?'

'Yes, Dokkum is a small town with a moat which gives one a curiously shut-off feeling. Everyone knows everyone else and life there is very pleasant. Groningen, where I work mostly, is big and bustling, but not to be compared with London, of course. You like London?'

She had always thought she had until now. She said uncertainly: 'Yes, but not as much as I used to,' and coloured faintly when he said:

'Naturally. Do you plan to go back there? Presumably your Andrew is waiting for you.'

She said, not looking up: 'I have no plans.' That was the second time he had referred to 'her Andrew'. She was on the point of telling him that Andrew was no longer hers and that by her own wish, when she remembered that his interest was merely the outcome of their truce. Had he not said that she could forget him tomorrow? Presumably for ever.

'You look as though you're going to cry.' His voice was gentle, quite unlike his usual faint derision; she straightened her face hastily. It would be very nice to have a good howl on his broad shoulder—after all, he must be quite used to it with four sisters. She smiled at the thought and he said: 'That's better. Shall we go? It's only half an hour or so to Inverness, that will give you a couple of hours to do your shopping.'

But when they got there it seemed that he had every intention of coming with her, for when she asked what time she should meet him he smiled down at her and took her arm. 'I'll come with you,' he said. 'I don't have to pick up Mr MacCombie until five.'

Apparently he knew Inverness rather well. They visited a couple of dress shops and several boutiques where she looked worriedly at the clothes because he hadn't mentioned prices, and in the kind of shops he had led her to, they were high. She stood uncertainly before a small elegant window, eyeing a pink angora dress which she instantly coveted. It had no price ticket, but as there was nothing else in the window but a vase of hothouse flowers and a silk scarf with an astronomical figure attached to it, she judged it to be expensive. She was about to turn away when Rolf said: 'Ah, that's it, isn't it?' and propelled her into the grey velvet interior where he said loudly: 'Go ahead, Sappha, and try it on,' which words commanded instant attention from the saleslady, so that Sappha, willy-nilly, was forced to request the removal of the dress from the window. It was a perfect fit and very becoming; she was standing before the mirror in the little fitting room at the back of the shop, wondering what to do about it, when the Baron said in a carrying voice:

'Come out here and let me have a look,' and when she complied it was to find him standing with the saleswoman, cheque-book in hand. 'Like it?' he queried nonchalantly. 'It suits you. Have it.'

Sappha liked it too, but she didn't like being told to have it. She gave him a sneaking glance and said: 'I think not—it's probably a great deal too much money.'

She turned to ask the cost and was at once frustrated by his cheerful 'I've dealt with that. Don't you like it?'

They stared at each other across the little shop and she could see that, as usual, although his face was serious, he was laughing at her. She said with dignity: 'I like it very much. I'll take it.'

Outside the shop she turned on him. 'Do you always bully people into doing what you want?' she wanted to know, to be met with a look of such innocence that she was rendered speechless.

'I?' he asked. 'Bully you? My dear good girl, don't you know that barons—the bold bad ones, that is—only bully those who are unable to look after themselves? And from what I have seen of you, you are perfectly able to do that.' His satyr's face split into a sudden grin: 'Now we will have no more nonsense and go and buy your shoes.' He took her arm again, but Sappha didn't move. She was really very angry with him, but at the same time she was enjoying every minute of his company. No wonder his mother and Antonia adored him. She remembered the truce and he was going tomorrow, anyway, and she would most probably never see him again. She said slowly:

'I'm sorry, I've been rude. I know you wouldn't bully anyone or anything I—I mean that, I'm not just saying it un-under the flag of truce.'

He stood looking down into her face; presently he nodded to himself, then said quietly: 'A remark like that needs celebrating. We'll have tea.'

He walked her briskly down the main street and presently turned into a narrow street leading from it; it was lined with old houses, some of them converted into small shops. The tea-room was halfway down its peaceful length, small, wood-panelled and cosy, with just enough people inside to make it pleasant. They found a table by the window and Sappha said:

'I should never have found this on my own. It's super.'

'It's been here for years. Mother used to bring us here when we were children. The spiced buns are to be recommended.'

They sat over their tea, for suddenly there seemed to be a great deal to talk about, and Sappha, convinced that she wasn't going to see him again, found herself telling him about her home and family, but she didn't talk about Andrew, and Rolf made no effort to ask about him.

The shoes were bought in an atmosphere of complete amiability, and the short time left was spent in the purchase of some handmade chocolates for the Baroness and a flask of Fifth Avenue toilet water for Antonia, purchased by the Baron with an assurance which could only mean that he was no stranger to shopping of that type, a fact which left Sappha a little thoughtful.

They were to pick up Mr MacCombie at his own home; Rolf drew up outside and got out. 'Stay where you are,' he commanded before he rang the bell and was admitted to the house, and Sappha stayed where she was, although it seemed to her that the two men would want to travel together, they would surely have a great deal to discuss about the Baroness for a start. But apparently she was mistaken, for within a minute or two the men came out and Mr MacCombie, after an exchange of greetings, climbed into the back of the Land Rover without a single murmur of dissent.

They travelled back to Dialach on the same road which she herself had taken when she had come from London. It was already dusk—it would soon be dark, but the Baron, who knew the road well, didn't slacken speed. Their talk was desultory and casual, and rather to her surprise, very little was said about the Baroness.

The Manse's lighted windows looked warm and welcoming as they arrived, and their own welcome was no less warm. The Baroness looked a little flushed and excited and Sappha went quickly to her room, changed into her uniform and went to find Mrs MacFee. That lady was in the kitchen putting the finishing touches to supper. She looked up with a smile as Sappha went in and said: 'Hullo, Sappha dear. Back in uniform already?'

'Yes, Mrs MacFee. The Baroness looks a bit excited— I thought if I took up her supper and did the usual evening chores and exercises it might calm her down a little. I do want her to be as well as possible when Mr Mac-Combie sees her tomorrow morning. I expect he'll see her tonight as well, but only to talk to her.'

Mrs MacFee nodded. 'Yes, dear, I'm sure you're right. It must be hard not to get excited, though. Did you have a nice day?'

Sappha was squeezing lemons at the table. 'Yes, very.'

'And did you get a pretty dress and the shoes you wanted? Those you spoilt were so very smart.'

'Yes—the dress is prettier than the one I ruined— pink angora—and the shoes are just as nice as the others. I'll let you see them later.'

She went back through the hall to go upstairs again and heard the rumble of the men's voices from the study and then the Baron's laugh. It had been a lovely day, he had been charming and generous, and most agreeable to be with. Probably when they met at supper he would be distantly polite again, and mock her with his dark eyes. She turned round and went back to the kitchen.

'Mrs MacFee, would it be an awful nuisance if I didn't come down to supper? I think I'll stay with the Baroness while she's having hers. I could get a glass of milk or something later, couldn't I?'

Mrs MacFee was tenderly removing a bubbling macaroni cheese from the oven. 'Why, of course, Sappha. We shall miss you at supper, of course, but if you think it you better to stay with the Baroness...'

It was after her patient's supper, while Sappha was arranging the room for the night, that Mr MacCombie arrived. Rolf was with him, but Sappha, busy with charts and questions, didn't look at him. It was only when the specialist had drawn up a chair to the bedside to have what he described as a little chat that the Baron came to stand beside her.

'You didn't come to supper,' he said softly.

Sappha said, equally low-voiced: 'No, your mother was a little excited—I thought it might calm her down if I stayed up here.'

He murmured: 'Ah, of course. I had imagined some other reason. Do you want me to tell you what it was?'

She said hastily: 'No' then went slowly red as he said on a laugh:

'So there was another reason.'

She swallowed her heart back to where it belonged and without answering or even looking at him, moved away to stand by the bed and presently slipped away to her own room where she stayed, doing nothing until she heard Mr MacCombie calling her. Rolf was still there, standing at the window looking out into the black evening. He didn't turn round when she went in and after one swift glance at his broad back she joined the surgeon, still sitting by the bed. Mr MacCombie said:

'Tomorrow morning, nine o'clock—is that too soon for you, Nurse? We'll get that plaster splint off before I go and take a look at the leg at the same time.' He patted his patient's hand. 'Your troubles are almost over, Baroness. A few more weeks...'

The Baroness interrupted him: 'When will it be possible for me to go home? I have plenty of help and all that sort of thing.'

She smiled coaxingly, looking exactly like her daughter, and Mr MacCombie laughed.

'Well, shall we say soon? I think Rolf and I must talk about this first, and of course Mr Devenish must be consulted—but I think I can safely say that it won't be long now.'

He and Rolf went away after that, leaving Sappha to calm down her patient once more and get her ready for the night, a lengthy business, for the Baroness wanted to talk. Sappha was reading to her when Rolf came back; she put the book down and left them together— doubtless they had a lot to say to each other. In a little while she heard him go downstairs again and went back once more to tuck her patient up for the night, then crept downstairs to the kitchen. There was some soup keeping hot on the stove; she poured a bowlful and sat spooning it up, listening to the laughing and talking going on in the drawing room. She debated with herself about going in to say goodnight, and decided that she should. There was a lull in the conversation as she opened the door and everyone looked at her. She glued her eyes to Mrs MacFee's kind face and bade the general company goodnight, then looked at Rolf.

'Thank you for a lovely day, Dr van Duyren,' she said in a polite voice which didn't sound like hers at all.

Mr MacCombie was quick the next morning. He had the plaster off and was examining the arm before the Baroness had finished wondering if it was going to hurt. The arm looked a little puny, but thanks to Sappha's efforts and the exercises, it functioned quite well.

The Baroness sat looking at it as though it wasn't her own while he examined her leg, which he did at some length, saying finally in a non-commital voice:

'Very good progress, Baroness—Rolf and I will have a little chat presently and I may possibly come back with Mr Devenish in a week or so, when I daresay we shall have some good news for you.'

With these heartening words he wished her goodbye, nodded nicely to Sappha, and went. As soon as his footsteps had died away, she said firmly: 'Breakfast first, and then you shall let yourself go.'

There seemed to be no one about downstairs. She assembled the Baroness's modest wants on to a tray and went back upstairs, to find Antonia with her mother. She turned round as Sappha went in, saying: 'There you are, Sappha. I'm saying goodbye—did you see Rolf?'

Sappha put the tray down carefully and said no while she adjusted the bedtable, and presently Antonia gave her mother a final hug and pranced across the room to plant a kiss in Sappha's cheek and say '*Tot ziens*' and then was gone. By the time Sappha had found a clean handkerchief for her patient to cry into, the sounds of parting at the front door had ceased; she got to the window just in time to see the back wheels of the Land Rover disappearing through the gate.

Chapter 5

The days seemed intolerably long and empty without the Baron, a fact made worse by Sappha's patient, who, once she had recovered from the excitement of the surgeon's visit, became increasingly depressed. Sappha, assuming a false cheerfulness she was far from feeling, tried everything she could think of to divert the Baroness's thoughts without a great deal of success. She told Gloria about it one afternoon when she had slipped out for an hour while Mrs MacFee kept her friend company.

The two girls were sitting comfortably by the sitting room fire in Gloria's cottage, a tea tray between them and a stray cat Gloria had adopted stretched at their feet.

'I don't know what to do,' mused Sappha. 'I believe she's homesick. After all, she's been here some weeks now—she was here before the op, wasn't she? And by all accounts she's been a marvellous patient—I think she should go home as soon as possible. There are another lot of tests due next week, the last batch were pretty good. Obviously her renal function is almost a hundred per cent—surely they could get her home?'

Gloria bit into some shortbread. 'You sound as though you want to get away,' she remarked sapiently. 'Are you fed up?'

Sappha bent to tickle the cat's ears so that her face was hidden.

'No, not in the least. It's a worthwhile case, isn't it? I was just wondering—I suppose they'll get some kind of help for the Baroness when she does go.'

'Lord, yes. No difficulty there. From what I've heard from Hamish they've more than enough servants who've been with them for ever—though I must say they don't behave as though they had. I don't know what they're like in their own home, but when Rolf comes here for a meal he washes up after to the manner born. He can cook too, and last year when Mrs MacFee was down with the flu and he was staying with them, he coped with quite a bit of housework as well.'

Sappha looked at her friend with round eyes. 'He did?' she asked incredulously, 'but he doesn't look as though…'

Gloria smiled. 'No, he doesn't, does he?' She ate a biscuit. 'Hamish told me that Rolf's house sounds as though it runs on oiled wheels. I must say he'll be a prize for some lucky girl.'

Sappha's heart did a double knock against her ribs. 'Oh, is he thinking of getting married?' she wanted to know in an expressionless voice.

'I haven't a clue—whoever knows what Rolf is thinking, for a start? Hamish says he's a bit of a puritan.'

Sappha gave her a startled look and she went on cheerfully. 'Not that kind of puritan, ducky—he's not above chatting up the girls, with great success, I imagine, but he once said that unless he could find the other half of himself somewhere in the world he didn't intend to marry.' She licked a finger delicately. 'What a waste!'

Sappha poured second cups. 'Antonia's a dear,' she observed, longing to continue talking about Rolf but feeling that the subject should be changed.

'Yes—Rolf has a very soft spot for her too. I suppose because she was only a little girl when their father died; he was quite a man, I believe. She twists Rolf round her little finger, you'll have noticed that for yourself, and he lets her get away with it, but he's strict with her too, for she's headstrong and gullible and as pretty as the proverbial picture, and that allied to a tidy little fortune spells trouble ahead as far as Rolf's concerned; he's got some very sound ideas about whom she shall marry.'

Sappha frowned. 'Do you mean to say he's going to tell her whom she can marry and whom she can't— why, it's archaic!'

Gloria gave her a level look. 'No, it isn't. There are plenty of heels around…are you going to make it up with your Andrew?'

Sappha's frown deepened. Here was someone else referring to Andrew as hers. She said snappishly: 'No, but no one knows that—it seems to be the accepted idea that I shall go back to London and live happily ever after. Well, I've given him up if you must know, and don't go telling anyone, will you?'

Gloria stared at her over the rim of her teacup. 'No, I won't. Tell me about the other night,' she invited.

It was a relief to talk about it; she hadn't realised until

she said it loud how bitterly disappointed and ashamed she had been feeling about Andrew's refusal to help. She remembered how nice Rolf had been about it; probably he was nice like that about everyone, even someone he didn't like, which reminded her rather painfully that he didn't like her overmuch. Her own fault of course, for he had, after all been quite right at their first meeting; she had been silly to run out of petrol and just as silly not to run the car on to the side of the road—but he had looked like some fierce brigand... She said urgently:

'He shouldn't walk about looking like a fisherman or a—a pirate!'

And it seemed quite natural for Gloria to answer at once. 'I know, so deceiving, isn't it? He looks so different. Last Hogmanay we all went up to the Lodge—the Laird gives a do then—Rolf was in a black tie, of course, and there wasn't a woman in the room who could keep her eyes off him and he was completely indifferent, if you know what I mean, and at the same time he was charming and a little bold and bad as well. It's a good thing I met Hamish first or I might have fallen for Rolf.' She turned her blue eyes upon Sappha. 'I suppose you couldn't...'

'No,' said Sappha fiercely, 'we—we don't like each other.'

Gloria digested this in silence, watching the delicate pink wash over Sappha's face and slowly fade again. She said finally in a bracing voice: 'Well, what are you going to do about the Baroness? I suppose you couldn't write; even if you don't like each other, you are his mother's nurse.'

'No,' said Sappha for the second time, 'I couldn't

do that. I'll wait another week. Uncle John said he'd be down soon—I'll ask him.'

The week took a very long time to pass. The Baroness seemed a little better; she used her arm just as she had been told to do, got up into her chair, painted and knitted and played endless games of backgammon and demon patience with Sappha, and when Rolf telephoned, which he did most nights, she chatted animatedly with him and never once brought up the subject of going home. And never once did he ask to speak to Sappha.

The evening previous to Uncle John's visit Sappha remarked cheerfully to her patient: 'Well, I wonder what Uncle John will have to say in the morning? He said he would be here about eleven o'clock; he'll stop overnight in Inverness, I suppose. I'll get you up as usual, then if he wants you back in bed I can whisk you back. Why not wear that lovely nightie Dr van Duyren sent you last week? It's such a heavenly pink.'

The Baroness agreed with a heavenly smile. 'Do you suppose it will really help?' she wanted to know, and then, 'I'm sorry, my dear, I'm an ungrateful wretch—of course you shall pretty me up.' She sighed. 'It's just that I seem to have been here for ever.'

Sappha was busying herself setting the night table to rights. 'I know, it's always the last few days which are the hardest to bear—but they are the last, I feel sure. I'm going to give you something to give you a sound night's sleep so that you look really perky tomorrow.'

Later, in her own room, sitting up in bed, hugging her knees and recalling the conversation, she had to admit that she wasn't quite as sure about things as she had made out. For one thing, there was a great deal to be thought of if the Baroness was to be allowed home. A

nurse would have to be found and the journey arranged.
She began to wonder vaguely what she herself would
do afterwards; she knew she didn't want to go back
to London. Perhaps Uncle John would know of something, or she might apply for a post in one of the Scottish hospitals. The future seemed decidedly uninviting
and she allowed her thoughts to stray to Rolf—probably
he was living it up with one of the girls Gloria seemed
to think sat around waiting for him to crook his finger.
Sappha started to cry, which, although a great relief to
her feelings, did nothing to solve her problems. After a
few minutes she blew her nose with pathetic determination, got up and washed her face and composed herself
for sleep. Time enough for her to mope about her own
sorrows when those of her patient had been resolved.

She got up very early because she hadn't slept for
more than an hour or so. She crept downstairs through
the quiet house, made tea and then went to peep at the
Baroness, who it turned out, was awake too. Sappha
went soft-footed to the bed. 'I've made some tea,' she
whispered. 'Shall I bring it up here and give you a cup
at the same time?'

The Baroness didn't answer immediately, instead
she stared at Sappha with disconcertingly bright eyes
and said in positive tones:

'You've been crying, child. Why?'

'Oh, no reason at all,' said Sappha. 'I'm going to
fetch the tea.'

She was back within five minutes with a tray which
she put on the bedside table before she drew up a chair for
herself. The fire had burned low, she poked at it gently,
put on another log to make a cheerful blaze, then, wrapping her dressing gown more closely around her, poured

the tea. They were gossiping quietly over a second cup when they heard a car draw up outside.

'The milkman,' Sappha surmised, and frowned at her watch. 'No, it can't be, it's only half past six, and it's certainly not the postman. Someone for Mr MacFee, perhaps—there's old Mr MacIndoe very ill; his wife was up here yesterday about him. I'd better go down and see.'

She crept downstairs once more and crossed the hall to the front door. The dim light in the porch was left on all night; she could see someone's shadow standing by the door. She wondered why they hadn't knocked and then remembered that they would have seen the Baroness's light. She opened the door without haste because the bolt was old and rasped a little and she didn't want to disturb the MacFees until she knew who it was. It was the Baron who stepped inside, looking larger than ever and rather sinister by reason of his bulky coat. Its collar was turned up against the early morning chill and she couldn't see his face very clearly because she hadn't bothered to put the hall light on. He said softly: 'Good girl—I didn't knock, I counted on you hearing the car.'

She stood gaping at him in utter surprise, her heart thudding. After a moment she managed to say in a strangled voice: 'Good morning, Dr van Duyren,' and was instantly caught in his arms.

'Isn't that a little formal, especially from a pretty girl in a dressing gown with her hair hanging down her back—how about this?'

He kissed her, quite roughly, on the mouth, and then again, gently this time, on top of her tousled head. When he let her go she said in a choking voice: 'Your mother is awake—she'll be glad to see you,' and turned and led the way upstairs with her heart still hammering in her ears. She had shut the Baroness's door when she had gone down; now she paused before it and turned to look at him.

'Would you like to go in? I expect you'd like something to eat and drink.' Her voice was matter-of-fact now.

He gazed down at her, his eyes snapping with laughter. 'Ah,' he said silkily, 'the mantle of friendship—or do I mean the olive branch?'

'Neither—I'm talking about tea and toast.' Her tone was astringent.

His brows described an arc. 'I expect too much,' he murmured, 'but tea and toast will do nicely for a start.'

He opened the door and went inside and Sappha flew down the stairs with the faint echo of the Baroness's excited voice pursuing her.

Ten minutes later she was back again with a tray loaded with a teapot and a plate of well-buttered toast. The Baron was sitting on his mother's bed, a fact which Sappha's strict nursing training deplored; he had thrown off his heavy coat to reveal an exquisitely tailored suit of clerical grey and a richly sombre tie; presumably he had got straight up from his consultant's desk and boarded the plane, a surprise which he confirmed as he took the tray from her.

'Is all this for me? I missed dinner and I almost missed the plane too—I have never had so many long-winded patients as I had yesterday.' He sat down again and cast his eye over the tray. 'Marmalade, too,' he observed, 'what a delightfully practical woman you are, Sappha, and so hospitable. I do believe you would feel compelled to offer any burglar foolish enough to enter a cup of tea before you laid him out with the poker. Do sit down and have some of this—yours must be cold.'

But Sappha shook her head. 'No,' she said, 'I'd finished,' which wasn't true, but she didn't care; she had to get away so that she could become as calm and quiet as he was and school herself to treat him with the same casual air as he was treating her.

She felt a good deal better by the time she was dressed. The simple act of turning herself into a nurse once more helped to steady her thoughts, so that by the time she went back to the Baroness she was, outwardly at least, cool and composed and quite prepared to answer the Baron's civil enquiries. She piled the trays neatly and started for the door, only to have them removed from her grasp and when she remonstrated all he said was: 'I've got to come downstairs to fetch one or two things from the car.' But in the kitchen he made no move to go but sat on a corner of the table watching her tidy away and stack the china in the sink.

'I'm afraid you've had rather a difficult time with Mother,' he said mildly. 'I'm sorry I could do nothing to help—it's sometimes difficult to get away. I knew you could cope.'

Sappha emptied a teapot with rather too much vigour. Flattery would get him nowhere, she told herself crossly. She said out aloud: 'Mr MacCombie and Uncle John are coming this morning.'

'Yes, I know. I telephoned Mr Devenish a day or so ago—that's why I am here.'

'The Baroness is anxious to go home. She's a marvellous patient, but I think she feels she's getting nowhere any more.'

He nodded, cut a hunk of bread from the loaf beside him on the table and began to eat it. Watching him, Sappha found the sight pathetic, which she told herself sternly, was ridiculous, the baron had enough money, presumably, to eat his breakfast at a five-star hotel should he so wish—there was no need for him to eat dry bread. All the same, she said: 'When I've taken up your mother's breakfast, I'll cook something for you.'

He smiled at her so charmingly that she turned her back quickly. He said warmly: 'Generous creature—eggs and bacon and some mushrooms if there are any and a kidney or so—on second thoughts perhaps I'd better cook them myself, you've already offered more than a fair share of the olive branch.'

Sappha dished up a poached egg with great neatness. 'You can't cook in that suit,' she said positively. 'Go and do whatever it is you want to do, I shall be about ten minutes.'

He got down off the table and came and stood beside her, an act which played havoc with her pulse rate. 'I'm overwhelmed, my dear Miss Devenish. Can it be that you have had a change of heart?'

She picked up her tray and went briskly to the door, because it seemed good sense to escape before she said something foolish. 'Ten minutes,' she reiterated.

She found her patient sitting up in bed eager to talk, something which she proceeded to do without pause for some minutes. 'I shall be going home soon,' she said with certainty, 'I must be quite well by now.'

Sappha poured the tea, for it was obvious that the Baroness had forgotten to do it for herself. 'Do let's wait and see,' she begged. 'If you get too excited your pulse rate will go up, and you know how fussy Uncle John is about that.' She whipped the cover off a plate.

'Poached eggs,' she invited, 'you know you like them. Will you eat them while I go and cook Dr van Duyren some breakfast? He says he's famished, and it's far too early to disturb Mrs MacFee. You'll be finished by then, and we can concentrate on making you glamorous.' She was interrupted by a knock on the door and Mrs MacFee, cosily dressing-gowned, came in.

'I heard voices,' she said with no sign of ill humour at being disturbed, 'and I just had to come and see…'

'Rolf's here, Ida,' said the Baroness, 'isn't it exciting? Do you suppose they'll let me go home?' This remark was made with the passionate eagerness of someone who had been inured in some dreary prison for a number of years, and was hardly one to please any hostess, however kind, but Mrs MacFee had been a lifelong friend, and far from taking umbrage, she replied with ready enthusiasm that there seemed to be a very good chance of it. Sappha saw that the two ladies were intent on discussing this possibility from every angle; she went downstairs again and fetched another cup and saucer, and wordlessly poured tea for Mrs MacFee too, inviting her to sit comfortably by the fire. This done, she felt free to go back to the kitchen where the Baron was still sitting on the table with the negligible remains of the loaf beside him. She gave him a severe look and said: 'Couldn't you wait?' At this rate she would be lucky if she got any breakfast for herself.

The Baron got off the table. 'You cook,' he said mildly, 'I'll lay the table for both of us, if you have breakfast now it will leave you free for Mother later on.'

He didn't wait for her answer but set two places, while she, admitting the good sense of this, added more eggs and bacon to the pan and when he asked 'Is there any porridge?' filled a bowl from the saucepan on the stove and put it before him, whereupon he invited her to have some too and when she refused, remarked in a friendly jeering voice: 'I suppose it makes you fat.'

'It does not...' she began furiously, then stopped because he might have said it in order to make her lose her temper. She went on sweetly: 'I have it most mornings, but I don't want it today.'

In fact, she wasn't hungry at all, although she ate what was on her plate, otherwise he would comment upon her lack of appetite. She took a small piece of toast and made it last a long time, telling herself that it was the unexpected events of the morning which had taken away her interest in her breakfast, while being aware that it was nothing of the sort. If this was being in love—besottedly in love, she amended honestly—the sooner she got herself out of it the better. She glanced up and found his eyes on her. He said in a gently ruminating voice:

'I should dearly love to know what you are thinking about to make you frown so and to make your mouth so prim. Don't you like having breakfast with me?'

His smile, coupled with the eyebrows, gave him a positively satanic look. Sappha knew better than to ignore his question; she looked down her pretty nose. 'I have no special feelings on the matter,' she observed in a cool little voice. 'More tea, Doctor?'

He passed his cup. 'How long,' he asked with interest, 'was it before you could bring yourself to call Glover—er—Andrew?'

She went a little white. 'Was it sweet enough?' she wanted to know, her voice sounded quite natural, if a bit thin. He took the cup from her without answering her question, merely spooning more sugar in with a generous hand. 'I have always thought,' he went on smoothly, 'that it should be possible to dislike some-one without making the fact too obvious; there are, after all, the conventional politenesses of everyday life—occasionally forgotten, I grant you, in times of stress—I distinctly heard you call me by name on the causeway the other night.'

He helped himself to more toast, more butter and a large quantity of marmalade. 'Call me Rolf,' he invited, 'even if only on occasion. You can go on disliking me as much as you wish.' He laughed suddenly. 'I'll be bound to put your back up whenever we meet, and if I can't think of anything unpleasant to say I can always kiss you instead; I'm sure that will have the same result.'

Sappha sat staring at him across the table. She felt be-wildered, dangerously tearful and full of a splendid rage which was too inarticulate to allow her to deliver the tell-ing reply this piece of impertinence on the Baron's part deserved. She opened and closed her charming mouth for several seconds, struggling to form her feelings into the right words and her efforts were not helped by his saying kindly:

'Don't bother to think of anything to say—I'm sure it'll come to you later. You can always write it down and commit it to memory and shoot it at me when next we meet.'

Sappha fought a sudden desire to laugh; fortunately she was able to turn it into a kind of strangled cough. She said with commendable calm:

'I think I should be attending to your mother—you'll excuse me?'

She rose from the table with tremendous dignity

which was immediately shattered by the marmalade pot which she unwittingly caught in her sleeve as she stood up. It crashed to the floor where it disintegrated into a dreadful mess of broken glass and stickiness. The Baron got to his feet and walked, without haste, round the table to join her. He stared at the floor for several moments and said at length: 'Ah, well—it's not blood, is it? And since it's my turn to show—er—friendship, I'll clear it up.' He gave her a little push in the direction of the door. 'Go on, girl, before I change my mind.'

Sappha murmured something, she had no idea what, and ran upstairs where she was kept far too busy to give the ridiculous episode another thought.

Uncle John and Mr MacCombie arrived together, both in excellent spirits and disposed to sit over their coffee, telling each other dishonest fishing stories, to the intense annoyance of Sappha who could see her patient becoming more and more nervous as each minute passed, and the obvious amusement of Rolf, who, she felt, should have made some effort to hurry them up. But when the examination finally took place, it was surprisingly short after all. The Baroness had answered their questions in a calm voice, and Sappha, even more calm, because years in hospital had trained her to a calm which allowed of no other feeling, gave her own brief, sensible replies to the more complicated questions they put to her. Finally, Uncle John said: 'Well now, shall we have Rolf back again?' and had looked at Sappha, who went down to the study where he was sitting with the minister and asked him politely if he would kindly come upstairs. He accompanied her back to his mother's room with scarcely a word and went to stand by the window, shutting out so much of the grey morning light that Sappha had leaned forward and switched the little rose-coloured lamp on. From its place on the bed side table it shed a becoming glow over the Baroness and made the room suddenly a cheerful place. Uncle John beamed at everyone and then spoke to his patient.

'Well, Baroness, we consider you fit to return home at last. No doubt Rolf will make all the arrangements, his plans are already made, I know—it's merely a question of putting them into action.'

The Baroness had gone a little pale. 'You mean I'm actually going home? I'm better?'

He nodded. 'Yes to both, but not, I must add, quite well. Several more weeks of inactivity while your leg fracture heals completely—and still pills to take, I'm afraid, and one or two small tiresome things, but I fancy the time will pass quickly enough?'

The Baroness looked across the room at her son. 'Rolf, have you really arranged for me to go home— I mean soon—today? No, not today, for I've nothing packed. Tomorrow, then?'

He crossed the room and sat down beside her and took her hands in his.

'Darling, I'm going back home today, within an hour or so, I'm afraid. I'll come back in two days' time for you. You'll have to travel by ambulance and plane to Schipol, but that's all more or less arranged.'

She smiled at him. 'What an impatient old woman I am! That will be lovely, dear.' She hesitated. 'Have you arranged for someone to look after me?'

He didn't reply but looked at Mr Devenish who was standing before the fire warming himself, but now he advanced a few steps towards the bed.

'As to that, Baroness, it seems to me that the best

thing is for Sappha to accompany you for a week or
so.' He transferred his gaze to his niece and smiled at
her gently.

Sappha had been standing quietly a little way from
the others. She gave a small startled sound and jumped
visibly. She had been taken completely by surprise, for
never once during the Baroness's frequent musings concerning her return had it been suggested that Sappha
should return with her, nor by the merest hint had either
of the doctors disclosed their views, and she couldn't
believe that Uncle John had spoken on the spur of the
moment. She studied his face now; it looked much as
usual, kind and wise, middle-aged and a shade pompous. Mr MacCombie looked much the same. The Baroness was looking at her hopefully and Rolf—Rolf was
smiling. She knew all at once that he had arranged it
all, and having arranged it, was confident that he was
going to get his own way, and a pity of it was that she
could see no way of preventing him. It would be like
slapping a happy child in the face to tell the Baroness
that she didn't want to go to Dokkum, besides, she had
to admit to herself, she did. She wanted very much to
see Rolf's home and most of all, a lot more of Rolf.

She said in a voice devoid of all expression: 'If the
Baroness would like that, I am quite willing to go with
her,' and was rewarded by the look of relief and delight
on her patient's face. She couldn't resist glancing at
the Baron too, but his back was towards the company
because he was looking out of the window, for all the
world as though he had no interest in what was being
said. Now however he turned round again and said in
a coolly pleasant voice:

'I shall be going away for ten days immediately after

we return to Dokkum.' His look was as cool as his voice had been and Sappha at once took exception to them both; obviously he was under the impression that this was what she wanted. That she had never given him reason to suppose otherwise was something she chose to forget. She said a little tartly: 'I daresay we shall manage very well,' and was about to enlarge upon this when the Baroness interrupted her. 'Sappha, you really do want to come? I wanted to tell you before this—even a hint, so that you wouldn't be unprepared, but Rolf...'

Sappha overcame a desire to look at the Baron; doubtless he was smiling in triumph over his easy victory, instead she smiled nicely at the Baroness. 'I shall like it,' she said cheerfully. 'For one thing I'll be able to see you on your feet again before I leave you, and I've never been to Holland.'

Mr Devenish coughed. 'Well, now, that's all nicely settled, is it not? I felt sure that you would agree to go, my dear. I think perhaps you should have a little talk with Rolf presently in order to settle details.' He gave another little cough. 'If you should worry about your passport, there is no need. I had occasion to telephone your mother a day or so ago and I suggested then that she should post it to you—just in case you may need it—you should receive it by tomorrow, I imagine.'

Sappha said, 'Yes, thank you, Uncle John,' which wasn't at all what she would have liked to have said, but it would be hardly fair to shock the company with the explosive words which she longed to utter. She cast the Baron a searing look, for she had no doubt at all that it was he who had thought of that too. He met it with a blandness which in no way diminished the look of satisfaction upon his face.

They had their little talk later in the morning. Sappha followed the Baron downstairs to Mr MacFee's study, feeling light-headed; a sensation possibly due to the champagne Rolf had produced for the company to drink to his mother's health; any other reason she chose to ignore. She swept past Rolf into the pleasant, shabby room and sat herself down on the same uncomfortable chair against the wall while he closed the door and went to lean against the table.

'Do unburden yourself,' he invited silkily. 'You've been swallowing back fiery words all the morning; much better to get them off your chest—besides, bad temper is so bad for the looks.'

Sappha's delightful bosom swelled with rage; she looked thunderous. It was a pity that all she could manage to say was 'Well...!'

He said to infuriate her still more: 'Oh, dear—it's worse than I had imagined—you're actually bereft of words. A pity, for you're worth watching when you're in a temper.' He frowned with sudden fierceness. 'I've no intention of apologising, you know. Certainly I arranged everything, why should I not? You are the obvious person to return with Mother, and as I was at pains to tell you, I go away the day following our return home, so you'll not need to conceal your dislike of me—and you'll be no further from Glover than you are now, so don't try and use that as an argument.'

He got up and wandered over to the window and presently said in a quite different voice: 'I had hoped that we could have achieved a more friendly footing—it seemed once or twice...'

Sappha's cheeks took on a fine glow; perhaps this was her chance to tell him that she didn't dislike him any more. She began with a hopeless incoherence: 'I—I…but I…it's not…' to be stopped by his terse:

'All right, you've no need to say anything, but at least let us be honest with each other,' so that she subsided, for what was the good of saying anything if he didn't want to know anyway? And the moment was past now, for he turned back from the window and went to sit at the desk, looking so very like his senior colleagues upstairs, that she straightened up in her chair just as she would have for their instructions.

He said now in a quiet voice: 'As regards the journey back to Dokkum, will you have Mother ready to leave in two days' time, directly after lunch. An ambulance will take you both to Inverness—I shall be driving the Land Rover and will meet you at the airport. We shall spend the night in London and fly to Schipol the following day. We shall be driving from there.' He paused, waiting for her comments, and when she said nothing, continued: 'Your mother lives in London at present, I believe—please make any arrangements you like to see her while we are there—you can talk that over with my mother if you will.'

He stood up slowly and came and stood in front of her so that she was forced to stretch her neck in order to look up into his face.

'I hope you will be happy with us,' he said formally. 'I'm sure that Tonia will be delighted to know that you are coming.'

Sappha got to her feet, for she could see that the interview was over. She replied woodenly: 'I shall be quite happy, thank you,' and walked to the door. He was ahead of her though, holding the door shut with one hand. It was a large, strong hand, it would be hopeless and rather silly to try and wrest the doorknob from him, she put her own hands behind her back and stood waiting, her eyes fixed on his tie.

When he said gently 'Sappha,' she dragged her eyes away and looked at his face. His eyes looked very dark and she thought she had caught a gleam in them before he dropped the lids so that she couldn't see clearly any more. His voice came mildly. 'We shan't be seeing a great deal of each other, and that for only a few more weeks. Do you suppose we might—er—conceal our true feelings for that time? I promise I'll not say a word or do anything to ruffle you.'

He smiled, a smile of such charm and warmth that she caught her breath and clenched her hands tightly behind her. It was a pity that she couldn't tell him how she felt and how silly she had been over Andrew, who now seemed like a misty nobody not worth remembering. She sought hastily for the right thing to say. 'Yes—that is a sensible thing to do,' she agreed in a polite voice. 'I'll—I'll try very hard...' and stopped because his eyebrows had arched themselves so violently that he looked like a satyr once more. At any moment he would laugh; he did no such thing, merely opened the door.

She didn't see him again, and he left again at teatime. The house seemed hollow without him and she found herself on the verge of ridiculous tears because he wasn't there. When she settled a jubilant baroness for the night, she retired to her own room on the pretext of writing letters and sat huddled by the fire, thinking about Rolf, which got her nowhere at all. She undressed slowly and had a bath and got into bed, where she forced herself to stop thinking about a nebulous future which wasn't going to happen anyway and concentrate on the weeks immediately ahead of her. She supposed that she would be in Holland for a month at least, although nobody had been prepared to say. All the same, it would take at least that time to get the Baroness walking with a stick. She probably wouldn't see much of Rolf during that time—had he not said that he would be away and even when he was home, his work would occupy a great deal of each day and she didn't suppose that she would be invited to join in the family's social activities. It was at this point that she realised that she could be as friendly as she wished towards Rolf; it wouldn't matter, he would merely suppose that she was fulfilling her part of their bargain. She chuckled at the idea and then burst into tears.

She went to see Gloria the next day while the Baroness, happily exhausted after a morning of planning and packing, took a nap after her lunch. Sappha, in her tweed suit and a thick sweater with a scarf tied over her hair, walked down to the harbour. It was a cold day under the great puffed-up clouds flying before the wind and she shivered as she stood looking at the grey water. She would have to telephone her mother to bring her some thicker clothing when they got to London. She shivered—again for quite a different reason as she gazed at the causeway, wondering for the hundredth time how she ever managed to scramble its treacherous length. She looked away hastily, knowing that she would face worse than its slippery danger if Rolf needed her. She wondered if Mrs MacTadd was home yet—there was a wisp of smoke from the croft, torn away by the wind as it emerged from its chimneypot. She would have to ask Gloria.

She retraced her steps to her friend's cottage and

thumped with the knocker on its stout door before going
inside. Gloria was just back from her visits and came
out of the surgery as she entered. 'Hullo,' she said, 'I
guessed you'd come—be a dear and make some tea
while I change.'

She went up the narrow stairs leading from the sitting room, still talking. 'I hear you're going the day
after tomorrow—Rolf popped in yesterday on his way
over to the MacTadds' place.'

Sappha digested this piece of information. 'Is Mrs
MacTadd back?'

'Yes—two days ago—didn't have a chance to tell
you, but I guessed Rolf would. I thought you might
have gone over with him, but he used the causeway and
I expect he remembered how you felt about that.' She
came tearing downstairs again, wearing a wool trouser
suit. 'Oh, lord, it's cold,' she observed, and pulled the
chairs close to the fire. 'I hope you've got fur-lined undies, Sappha—it'll be even colder in Dokkum, I should
think. Aren't you excited? Weren't you surprised?'

Sappha put the tea tray down, let in the cat from
the tiny back garden and sat down again. 'Yes,' she
said dryly, 'I was. Everyone seemed to know about it
but me.'

Gloria poured the tea. 'Do you mean to say that no
one told you that Rolf had arranged for you to go?'

'Yes.' Sappha bent to stroke the cat so that she didn't
have to look at her companion.

'I suppose he was afraid that you might say no—
after all, he is interfering with your love life, isn't he? I
mean, Andrew might not like it—I know you've given
him up, but if he hears about, it it might make him interested again, you know what men are. But Rolf doesn't

know you've given Andrew up, does he?' She frowned thoughtfully. 'I think you should tell him.'

'Why?' Sappha wanted to know. 'It wouldn't make the faintest difference—he has no interest in my private life.'

Gloria gave her a sharp look and said 'Um?' in a noncommittal way and helped herself to a bun. 'I'm coming your way tomorrow to say goodbye to the Baroness—will that be OK? I shall miss her, though I expect she'll be back before long for a visit.'

'When are you going to get married?' asked Sappha. 'I might not be here.'

Gloria went a faint, happy pink. 'Well, yes—we thought we might have the wedding just before Christmas. A terrible time of the year. I shall be blue with cold, but Hamish says he doesn't care if I am. I wonder where you will be, Sappha—you will come if you can, won't you? Where do you plan to go next?'

'I don't know,' Sappha replied thoughtfully, 'I shall have left the Baroness by then, don't you think? I—I suppose I'll get a job in a hospital. I think I'd like to stay in Scotland, I love it here even though it's miles from home. Mother can come up for a holiday and I'd go home for a week or two first.'

Gloria needed. 'Sounds all right. How are you going tomorrow? The village doesn't seem too sure.'

Sappha laughed and told her: 'You know, the more I think about it the more scared I become—I can't speak a word of Dutch and it sounds complete nonsense when I hear it. And I don't know what clothes to take.'

'Everything warm you can lay your hands on,' said Gloria practically, 'and some pretty things too—though

I'm sure you've got masses of those. From what I hear
the van Duyrens' life is a lot more social than it is here.'

'Maybe, but I'm the nurse, remember?' Sappha
frowned in thought. 'I'm going to telephone Mother
this evening. Dr van Duyren suggested that I might be
able to see her in London. I must get her to bring me a
thick coat and perhaps a couple of dresses.'

Gloria said quickly: 'Why do you call Rolf...' then
changed her mind and said instead: 'Something long, I
should think. What have you got?'

They spent a pleasant few minutes discussing clothes
until Sappha saw the time and jumped to her feet. 'I
must fly! The Baroness is so thrilled and excited that
she's quite capable of doing something silly like trying
to walk. See you tomorrow—why not come to tea? You
know Mrs MacFee loves you to call in.'

She bundled herself into her jacket and scarf, said a
hasty goodbye and hurried back to the house.

She found her patient just awakened from a refreshing nap and full of plans for the future. It amused Sappha a little that the Baroness had given no more than
a passing thought to the actual journey; Rolf had told
her that he would arrange everything and it seemed she
saw no reason to doubt him. Even when he telephoned
later in the evening, her talk was all of seeing her various children again and no word was said about the journey. Sappha did her own telephoning later that evening,
only to remember at the last minute that she had no idea
where they were to spend the night. She had been stupid not to ask Rolf, and the Baroness, of course, had
no idea. She arranged with her mother to telephone the
next morning before they left—surely Rolf would be
with them by then, and she could ask.

She packed the next morning, completed her patient's packing too and then went for a final walk through Dialach, saying goodbye to the friends she had made there. She would have liked to have taken a run in the Mini, but it had gone that morning—perhaps she had been silly to allow Rolf to arrange for it to be sent back to her home—it only meant that when she returned to England she would have to go and fetch it and drive all the way up again—still, she would probably have her mother with her and it didn't really matter. She walked to the edge of the causeway and stood staring along it. She would have liked to have said goodbye to Mrs MacTadd, but she knew that she couldn't possibly cross the causeway on her own and there wasn't a boat in sight. She turned her back on it and fought her way against the wind, suddenly very sad at leaving.

But she wasn't able to indulge her unhappy thoughts for long, for Gloria was at the Manse when she returned and they all had tea in the baroness's bedroom while Gloria examined over the gorgeous nighties the Baroness had given her. It was only when Meg came up to say that the minister was wanted on the telephone that the party broke up, and Gloria, clasping her present, made her final goodbyes. Sappha went to the front door with her; she was going to miss Gloria, she was gay and contented and happy—above all happy. She watched her get into her elderly Morris and nodded vigorously when Gloria shouted: 'See you at the wedding!' and, with a terrible grinding of gears, drove away.

There wasn't much to do that evening, for the MacFees spent a great part of it in the Baroness's room, making cheerful plans about future visits and remembering fresh messages every few minutes for the Bar-

oness's family. It was late when they finally left Sappha
to settle her patient for the night, and later still when
she got to bed herself. She wakened early, and because
she was far too restless to lie in bed and wait for Meg
to call her, she got up and pottered around her room.
The Baroness was still asleep; Sappha hoped she would
stay so for an hour or so yet, for the day would be long
and tiring. She opened her door and tiptoed downstairs,
made tea and sat by the stove and drank it, then presently decided that she might as well go upstairs again
and get dressed. She had her foot on the bottom step of
the stairs when there was a movement on the landing
above and she looked to see the Baron, in a dressing
gown of a startling splendour, coming downstairs two
at a time. She stepped back hastily, fearful of being run
down, but he stopped just short of her and said pleasantly: 'Hullo—you have no idea how startled you look.'

Sappha closed her open mouth. 'I am startled,' she
said reasonably. 'I didn't know you were in the house.'

He sat down on the stairs, reached up a long arm
and swept her down to sit beside him. 'No, neither did
you,' he remarked cheerfully. 'I remember now I asked
Mr MacFee not to mention that I was coming, Mother
might not have slept.'

Sappha said of course, she wouldn't have slept either,
but that was something he didn't need to know. She
went on sedately: 'Did you have a good journey?' and
tried, without success, to ignore the arm he had flung
around her shoulders.

'Yes, thanks. I slept—I mostly do, you know.' She
thought with sudden pity that he hadn't had much time
for sleep. 'What time did you get here?' she wanted to

know, and when he told her: 'Did you have something to eat?'

She felt his hand tighten on her shoulder. 'Practical Sappha—yes, I did. Mrs MacFee, bless her, left some odds and ends out for me. I'm going to make some tea—have some?'

'I made some half an hour ago, but I'll make you some fresh before I go upstairs.'

He got up, pulling her with him. 'That'll be nice, only you must have another cup with me. It's not good to drink alone.'

Sappha laughed. 'You're being ridiculous, that means strong drink.'

He opened the kitchen door. 'But I like my tea strong,' he protested as he went to fill the kettle. It was while they were drinking their tea that she remembered about meeting her mother. She told him and he said easily: 'Telephone her as soon as you like—we'll be staying at the Savoy.' He paused to stare at her. 'What's the matter? Don't you care for the place?'

Sappha shook her head and said rather faintly: 'How should I know? I've never been there, only looked at it from the outside.'

'It's comfortable,' he went on carelessly. 'I've got rooms overlooking the river. There'll be an abulance to take you there from the airport.' He looked at his watch. 'Seven o'clock, will your mother be awake?'

Sappha thought. 'Yes, she always gets up early, and her sister—my aunt, you know—sleeps like a log and never hears anything, so it wouldn't matter.'

He stood up and caught her by the hand. 'Good, we'll telephone now.'

She found herself in the study, obediently telling him

the number of her aunt's flat while he dialled it. She thought he would have gone away by then, but he sat himself on the side of the desk, quite obviously intent on hearing every word she uttered. She said cautiously: 'Mother? About tomorrow—shall I come to Aunt Caro's or will you?' but got no further, for the simple reason that Rolf had taken the receiver out of her hand, giving her a smile which made it impossible for her to do anything at all. He said quietly: 'Mrs Devenish, this is Rolf van Duyren. I wonder if you could manage to dine with us tomorrow evening at the Savoy. You could bring whatever it is Sappha wants and have time to talk. You will? Good. I'll send a taxi for you at half past seven.'

He handed Sappha back the receiver, smiled again and went out of the room. She stood gaping stupidly after him while her mother's voice came thinly over the wire: 'Sappha—Sappha! Are you still there?'

She said, a little breathless still: 'Yes, Mother, I—I...'

Her mother's voice sounded soothing. 'There, now you don't have to worry about anything. I'll see you tomorrow evening, and darling, how do you feel?'

Sappha smiled at the receiver, knowing what her mother meant. 'It's done me a lot of good being up here. Goodbye, Mother dear.'

She replaced the receiver and went back to the kitchen. She might as well take a cup of tea up to her patient. There was no sign of Rolf, but when she got to the Baroness's room, he was there, building up the fire. He gave her a half smile, said 'See you later,' and disappeared.

The Baroness was dressed and ready in her chair by ten o'clock, so that when Rolf suggested to Sappha that she should go with him to see Mrs MacTadd, there was absolutely no reason why she shouldn't. It was a little warmer than it had been and although it drizzled the wind was almost gentle. She asked anxiously: 'By boat?' and when he said yes, went to get her raincoat and scarf, knowing that if he had decided to use the causeway she would have gone just the same.

'Do you know anything about boats?' Rolf asked as they left the jetty. She shook her head. 'Almost nothing— I think I'm a bit scared of them.'

'Probably, but only because you haven't had much to do with them. I must teach you how to handle one.'

She let this pass. Where, in heaven's name, was he intending to teach her, and when? She dismissed the remark as a meaningless civility and sat gingerly, watching him row.

She found the visit not altogether successful; from her point of view at any rate, for although it was nice to see Mrs MacTadd up and about again, and to admire the baby and talk to Ian, it brought back too vivid memories of the night they had worked together—there had been no question of dislike between them for those few busy hours and it had given her some idea of how pleasant it would be to be on permanent good terms with the Baron. It was true that for the moment at least, they were on the best of terms with each other, but only because he had suggested it, and she was reminded of how precarious those terms were when, on their way back, they called in to say goodbye to Mrs MacGregor, who wanted to know if Sappha had heard from her young man. She had said no and looked at him, longing to explain and quite unable to do so because, although his expression hadn't changed, she could sense his withdrawal from the lighthearted companionship they had achieved during the morning. They walked on up to the Manse, still talking in the friendliest fashion, but now it was like speaking lines in a play. She could hear her own voice becoming more and more stilted as they went along.

There was no opportunity to speak to him during their early lunch, nor during the subsequent bustle of their departure. Only at the last minute, as she was getting into the ambulance beside the Baroness, did he look as though he was going to speak to her, but he turned away and got into the Land Rover without a word. She gave a final wave to the MacFees and then occupied herself making her patient comfortable for the first leg of their journey to Holland.

Chapter 6

The Savoy Hotel, viewed from the back window of the ambulance which had brought them from the airport, looked impressive. Sappha felt a faint prickle of excitement as the ambulance driver opened the door and invited her to get out. She did so, wishing that the Baron was there because she wasn't quite sure what she was supposed to do next. Did she march through the foyer beside the stretcher, or should she go to the desk first and discover the numbers of their rooms, in which case, surely it would be better to leave the Baroness in the comparative comfort of the ambulance while she did so. It was a pity that by the time she had reached this conclusion, the stretcher had been lifted out. She looked around, a little at a loss, and saw the Baron advancing to meet them. He said in a businesslike voice: 'Hullo, come straight up, the lift's waiting.' He saw them safely stowed into it and then disappeared again, leaving them to be carried to the next floor. Sappha didn't see him again for twenty minutes or so, by which time she had her patient sitting comfortably in an armchair by the fire while she unpacked her night things. Her own room was next door, though she had had no time to inspect it, and she had had a glimpse of another room leading from the Baroness's, where presumably Rolf was, for she had heard him talking to the ambulance men. Presently, when she had got the Baroness comfortably settled, she would take a look round; in the meantime, it was time for her patient's pills.

The Baroness, who had enjoyed a nap in the ambulance, was gently talkative. 'A pleasant journey, was it not, Sappha?' she commented happily. 'I don't care for flying, but I must admit it is far less fatiguing, and we have only a short flight tomorrow.'

'How long does it take from Schipol to Dokkum, Baroness?' asked Sappha, and was very little the wiser when that lady replied vaguely:

'Well, dear, it's all according to how fast Rolf travels and which car he will be driving.'

Sappha, biting back an enquiry as to what sort of cars Rolf usually drove, hoped that it wouldn't be a Land Rover. She knew there was a Mini because Antonia had once mentioned it, but that would be equally impossible—probably he had something more sober in the garage. She would have to wait and see. She opened the Baroness's leather beauty case and began to lay its fragrant contents on the massive dressing table. 'I don't know what time we're having dinner,' she said cheerfully, 'but would you like anything now?'

'A glass of sherry,' said the Baron's voice from the

door. 'It will help the pills down. Tio Pepe, I think, chilled. You'll join us of course, Sappha.'

He gave the order and went to sit by his mother, and Sappha, pottering busily to and fro and aware that he was watching her, thought crossly that she had had no time to do anything to her hair, which was probably hanging in wisps. She tried to remember when she had put on the last lot of lipstick—it must have been hours ago, probably her nose was shining too. Her ruminations were interrupted by Rolf saying:

'You look as though you have stepped straight out of a bandbox, whatever that is, Sappha. However do you do it? And Mother looks as fresh as a daisy too.'

His remark caused Sappha to drop a sponge in a fluster and pick it up again with great clumsiness. She mumbled: 'Oh, I don't know—you can't be looking very closely,' and was glad when the sherry arrived at that moment and saved her from uttering any more feeble commonplaces.

The room next door turned out to be a sitting room, which opened in its turn into Rolf's room and another bathroom. Sappha thought it rather an expensive way of spending the night, and some of her feelings must have shown on her face, for Rolf said: 'I thought it would be pleasant for Mother to dine with us,' and she agreed faintly, still doing sums in her head. If he chose to throw his money around it was none of her business; besides, he had spoken with a tinge of arrogance, just sufficient to remind her that he was a baron and a rich one. He went on:

'I daresay you think me extravagant,' in a voice which implied that he couldn't have cared less what she thought, so that she remained prudently silent, merely

contriving to look so meek that he burst out laughing
and the Baroness said in her light voice:

'Don't take any notice of Rolf, my dear, he's a dreadful tease, as you've no doubt discovered.'

He went away presently, leaving her to change her
patient's warm woollen dressing gown for a more glamorous one of blue quilted silk with ruffles at its neck
and wrists. While they were busy with this task she
remarked: 'I think when you get home you shall start
dressing each day. It'll be a splendid exercise for you
and you'll feel much better for it, too.' This remark led,
not unnaturally, to their discussing clothes until the
Baroness said: 'Do go and have half an hour to yourself, Sappha—did you bring anything to change into?
Though you look pretty enough...'

Sappha looked down at her tweed suit—the one she
had when she had met the Baron for the first time—and
wondered why it was that nothing that had happened
before their meeting seemed to matter any more. 'I put
in the dress I bought in Inverness,' she said slowly.

'Wear it,' commanded the Baroness instantly. 'I've
only seen it in its box—besides, you can show it to
your mother.'

Sappha nodded. It seemed a good reason for wearing
it, and she had been wanting one. She went presently to
her own equally luxurious room where she did things to
her face and hair and put on the pink angora. It looked
terrific even in her own hypercritical eyes. Even in the
eyes of such a man as the Baron, whom she suspected
of having a connoisseur's judgement in such matters,
she might pass muster. She went back to the Baroness
to receive a sufficiently flattering comment upon her
appearance as to bring a pretty colour to her cheeks,

which was still there when the Baron entered the room a few minutes later. It was a pity that he entirely failed to notice that she had the frock on—indeed, it needed prompting on his mother's part to make him aware that Sappha was in the room at all—or so it seemed to her—a slight exaggeration, she admitted later, for he had nodded at her briefly as he came in. Which, when she came to think about it, made it all much worse. However, when his mother pointed out to him that he himself had approved of the dress in Inverness, he said pleasantly enough: 'Ah, yes—very nice.' With which very masculine remark she was forced to be satisfied.

The Baroness had barely been made comfortable in the sitting room when Sappha's mother arrived. Sappha kissed her warmly, performed the introductions with unaffected grace, and went away with her mother's coat. When she returned it was to find her mother sitting by the Baroness while Rolf poured the drinks. Sappha paused in the doorway for a moment, watching her mother with a little smile. Mrs Devenish was still a very pretty woman despite her grey hair and the laughter wrinkles round her eyes. She looked up now, smiled at Sappha and said gaily:

'How well you look, Sappha dear. Scotland agreed with you,' and Sappha said yes that it had, aware that her mother was studying her to see if she had recovered from Andrew. She hadn't told her about his visit, she didn't think she would, not at present. She went and sat down on the other side of the Baroness and asked: 'Did you bring my things, Mother?'

Mrs Devenish took the glass Rolf offered her and smiled at him before she replied. 'Yes, darling—I gave the case to someone downstairs who said he'd bring it up.' She turned to the Baroness, remarking cheerfully:

'You know, Baroness, I think one of the luxuries I enjoy most is giving someone something to carry when I am quite capable of carrying it myself.' And the Baroness, who had probably never carried anything heavier than her handbag in her sheltered life, agreed fervently, which led, inevitably, to a pleasant discussion on the habits and ways of their own generation. The two ladies became entirely engrossed in the fascinating subject and after a few minutes, Rolf got up and went to sit by Sappha. He said quietly: 'Tell me about the journey. Did you have all you wanted—were you comfortable?'

Sappha was glad of his prosaic questions, for in the answering of them in her most matter-of-fact manner, her pulse rate, which had doubled at his approach, settled down to near normal. She asked a few questions of her own concerning the journey the following day and he answered her with lazy good humour, coupled with a twinkling eye which made her feel that she was being unnecessarily fussy. Presently she fell silent, looking into the glass she held between her hands, and when he took it from her she folded her hands together and looked at them instead. He said, half laughing: 'Our mothers, at least, have no need to pretend—they appear to be fast friends already.'

Which was true enough, for the two elder members of the party were so absorbed in conversation that they had apparently forgotten their companions. Sappha lifted her eyes long enough to note this fact and then allowed herself to look at Rolf. She wasn't normally a shy young woman; it was quite ridiculous that she couldn't bring herself to behave naturally when she was with him. He wasn't looking at her now, but eased himself more comfortably into his chair. 'What

are you going to do when you come back to England?'
he wanted to know.

She gave the question her serious attention, just as
though it hadn't been on her mind for days past. She
said at length: 'I haven't quite made up my mind—it
depends…'

He said smoothly: 'Upon Andrew? Of course. Did
you get a reply to the letter I posted for you?'

Sappha stared round the spacious room, seeking in-
spiration from the various articles of furniture. If she
said no, he might ask why not, and she would have to
make up some cock-and-bull story or tell him the truth.
She didn't fancy doing either. She said nothing at all and
merely tightened her lips when he said mockingly: 'Put
in my place, am I?' and then with a sudden change of
tone: 'I've ruffled your feelings, and I said I wouldn't—
I beg your pardon. Let us enjoy a calming talk about
something impersonal to us both. Ah, yes, I have it—I
will tell you the history of Dokkum.'

Under her bewildered eyes he discoursed at some
length, so that her ears rang with a great many outlandish names and a selection of dates. The doctor knew his
history well and seemed intent upon airing it, when he
broke off suddenly and said: 'You're not listening—I
thought you were an intelligent woman, thirsty for information…' She stifled a giggle. 'I think I'd rather
quarrel,' she said weakly, and broke into a laugh when
he replied instantly: 'Good—so would I. What a pity
we have no time to do so. Our parents, unless I mistake,
are wanting their dinner.'

During dinner Sappha said no more than a dozen
words to Rolf. Immediately they were seated at table, the
Baroness engaged her in conversation, leaving her mother

to get better acquainted with her host—something, Sappha was quick to notice, which that lady achieved in a remarkably short space of time. She loved her mother dearly, but with one ear strained to hear their conversation, while giving her attention to the Baroness, she was vexed to hear the illuminative replies the Baron was getting to his friendly but searching questions. She didn't feel that he really wanted to know that she had played in the school hockey team, nor that she had worn a brace on her teeth until she was twelve, still less that she had been Gold Medallist at Greggs'. She ate her way through a delicious meal, but the *Mousse de Sole au Champagne* and the *Fraises Romanoff* might just as well have been fish pie and bread and butter pudding for all the notice she took of them. It was possibly the Médoc followed by a splendid claret and topped off by the green Chartreuse with the coffee which caused the evening to become progressively enjoyable, so that by the time dinner was over, she joined in the general conversation with something like pleasure and presently found the opportunity to have a few words with her mother—casual words, it was true, because it was neither the time nor the place for anything else, and her mother, thank heaven, forbore from asking her any leading questions.

Mrs Devenish got up to go shortly after and Rolf got up too saying that he would be delighted to take her home, so that Sappha had no more opportunity to speak to her mother even if she had wanted to. She was left alone with her patient, who was more than ready for bed. Sappha wheeled the Baroness back to her own room and made short work of the evening chores.

'You won't need a sleeping pill tonight,' she said cheerfully. 'You're sleepy enough—if you wake in the night, ring your bell and I'll come and do something about it.' She smiled at the Baroness, who smiled back, looking very pretty and a little bit guileful. Sappha, while she took her pulse, studied her patient's face, and wondered why. When she removed the thermometer the Baroness said happily:

'What a delightful evening. I should like to meet your mother again—we have a great deal in common. We are both widows for a start, and she tells me that she enjoys painting too.' She cast Sappha a faintly reproachful look. 'You didn't tell me that your home was in the Cotswolds and that your mother was only staying in London.'

Sappha finished counting the pulse. She said good naturedly: 'Mother comes up for a change sometimes, but she would hate to live here. We live near Cheltenham; she can go there to shop and take the car—she wouldn't dare do that in London.'

The Baroness shuddered. 'So she was telling me. I should like to invite her to visit us—you think she might? When I'm recovered from this wretched illness, of course.'

'I should think she would love to.' Sappha tucked the sheet in firmly and switched off all but one small bedside lamp and said goodnight in her kind voice, for she could see that the Baroness was disposed to chat, and there was more travelling to do the following day. She went to the door. 'I'll leave it open,' she said with her hand on the knob, 'and come in again just before I go to bed.'

She had gone through the door when her patient called her back.

'Sappha,' she said urgently, 'you will wait up for

Rolf, won't you, just in case he wants to tell you something or give you a message from your mother.'

Sappha stood in the doorway and thought about it.
'Well,' she said at length, 'I hadn't intended to, but if
you wish me...'

'Oh, I do—please, Sappha. I'm sure he won't be
long.'

Sappha said: 'Very well, Baroness,' and walked back
into the sitting room, where she chose a comfortable
chair, picked up a magazine thoughtfully provided by
the management and began to read. She read for several
minutes without being in the least aware of what she
was reading about. She wondered how long the Baron
would be and if he would be disposed to talk—she
rather hoped so; the wine had made her a little reckless.

He came ten minutes later, casting his coat down on
a chair as he entered and exclaiming with casual surprise: 'What, still up? Surely you should be in bed by
now—tomorrow will be a long day.'

Sappha got to her feet. The effects of the wine, which
quite plainly had had no effect upon him, were wearing
off. Just for a little while they had given her the illusion
that anything might be possible. She said quietly: 'Your
mother asked me to stay up in case there was anything
you wanted to tell me about tomorrow.' She started
for the door and was glad that he couldn't see her face
when he said with a trace of impatience: 'But we have
already been over that, have we not? You should have
told her so and gone to bed.'

She had reached the door and paused long enough to
say in a smouldering voice: 'So I should, but I'm afraid
I haven't mastered your technique of doing what you
wish without regard to other people's feelings.'

Having delivered this parting shot, she went out of the room, closing the door with a snap behind her.

She had been in bed an hour or more, mulling over the evening when she heard a movement in her patient's room and was on the point of investigating it when Rolf, with a perfunctory knock on the half-open door, came in. She tugged instinctively at the bedcovers and heard him chuckle as he sat down on the end of the bed. He said softly: 'Don't worry—it's too dark for me to see anything.'

Sappha let this pass. She said urgently: 'What's the matter?'

'Nothing—Mother's asleep. I've come to apologise for being so arbitrary just now. You see, I didn't expect you to be there.'

She said 'Oh?' in a polite little voice, wondering what difference that could possibly make. She added: 'That's quite all right. Thank you for a pleasant evening. I'm sure my mother enjoyed herself.'

He moved and she felt the mattress sag a little under his weight.

'A delightful person,' he remarked. 'I look forward to seeing her again.'

She couldn't see his face clearly; it was impossible to know if he meant it or whether he was just being polite, probably the latter.

'She's marvellous,' she whispered, 'but then your mother is too.'

He agreed. 'How unpredictable life is,' he went on, showing no signs of going away. 'Our mothers are two splendid women who liked each other on sight, and yet you and I don't get on very well—those were, I believe, your words.'

He got up and the mattress sprang back with a thankful twang. 'By the way, I have been most thoughtless. I daresay you would have liked to see Glover—you could have done so easily and I should have thought of it. At least you can telephone him in the morning.'

He went soft-footed to the door and was gone; his good night reached her so faintly that she wasn't sure if she had heard it or not.

Sappha was up early, re-packing the things her mother had brought her and then, while the Baroness sipped her morning tea, packing her patient's things as well. She was rather dreading the day, partly because she wasn't sure what would be at the end of it. But the first part at least went without a hitch. The Baron had anticipated everything, so that she found herself sitting beside the Baroness in the plane with quite half the things she had been worrying about already dealt with by him with an assurance which she wholeheartedly envied. It was a pity it was such a cloudy morning, for she could see nothing of Holland as they approached its coast, and at Schipol she was occupied enough with her patient not to have time for more than a glimpse of the airport. She waited beside the Baroness's wheelchair while Rolf dealt with the Customs and luggage, feeling a little out of it because everyone was speaking Dutch, until Rolf had returned and caught sight of her face and said quickly: 'It's all a little strange, isn't it? I'm sorry you have to wait, but the car should be outside.'

It was neither a Land Rover nor a Mini, but a sleek, highly polished black Rolls-Royce. Sappha watched him lift his mother into its dove-grey interior, then got in to arrange the Baroness's various shawls and wraps and dispose cushions where they would do most good.

This done, she looked at the Baron, leaning on the door watching her. He said without asking: 'No, you're coming in front with me.'

She slipped meekly into the luxurious seat beside his while he shut the door on her and walked round the car to get in his own seat, saying as he did so: 'All right, Mother, it won't be long now.'

The big car slid forward, slowly at first, and then as they joined the motorway into Amsterdam, the Baron put an elegantly shod foot down on the accelerator and overtook everything ahead of him. He drove, Sappha noted, with the same economy of movement as he operated and with the same easy confidence. She gave an unconscious sigh of pleasure and settled back to enjoy herself. It was a grey day, inclined to rain and giving promise of a wet evening ahead, but that didn't matter. She was pleasantly tired after a long morning of attending to the Baroness, who, because she was so excited, was inclined to be more demanding than usual. But now Sappha, turning round to see how her patient was faring, saw that she had closed her eyes. 'Asleep?' queried the Baron without taking his eyes off the road.

Sappha nodded. 'I think so—she must be tired, although she wouldn't want to admit that.'

'We'll keep her in bed for a couple of days, I think— there will be plenty to occupy her, and Antonia will be at home. She's bound to want to catch up on the running of the house and so on.' He slid past a string of cars. 'We're coming into Amsterdam—we shall take the road running around the city, cross the Ij and then go more or less straight up to Den Oever. There's a map in the pocket beside you, perhaps you would like to have a look.'

They travelled in silence for five minutes or so while
Sappha picked out the route, mispronouncing the names
of the towns most abominably and then struggling to
get them right when he corrected her. She laid it aside
shortly, however, to gaze at the outskirts of the city
which she thought privately were a little dull. As though
Rolf had read her thoughts, he said: 'Don't think this
is the real Amsterdam—most of our cities are ringed
round with modern flats and houses, but their hearts
are still old and beautiful—you shall see for yourself
one day.'

They were leaving Amsterdam behind. 'Do you always come this way,' she asked, 'you must know the
road very well.'

He laughed. 'Indeed yes. This is the quickest way
and the dullest, but I want to get Mother home. There
is no reason why you shouldn't borrow the Mini and
explore for yourself while you're over here.'

Sappha thanked him nicely, though it sounded dull
on her own, but possibly Antonia would go with her
and she might even make a few friends in Dokkum.
It sounded rather as though she would have to rely on
her own resources and she reminded herself once more
that she was the nurse, primarily there to look after
her patient, then forgot all about it in the pleasure of
watching the barges chugging along a canal. Presently
a succession of windmills came into view and the next
half hour or so passed pleasantly enough while Rolf
explained their various types and how they worked.
Once or twice she had the suspicion that behind his
placid face he was laughing at her; probably he found
her company tedious. She felt suddenly out of patience

with him and herself too and said a little sharply: 'You must find it tiring—explaining everything.'

'Bored?' his voice was silky.

'No,' she sounded snappish, 'of course not, it's all new to me, but you must have travelled this way a dozen times.'

'Hundreds, I imagine,' he amended, still silky. 'But we do misunderstand each other so frequently if we become too personal, don't we? Windmills seem a safe subject; you see, you don't know anything about them, so there is no fear of you disagreeing with me.'

She gave him a quick sidelong glance. Even in profile he was wearing his most satyr-like expression. It seemed a good idea to change the subject. She said hastily: 'I expect you're glad to have finished with your journeys to Dialach.'

'Yes—my partners have had rather more than their fair share of work during the last few months, and I have had to cancel meetings and committees.'

She asked a little dryly: 'What do you do when you're not working?' and was immediately sorry that she had put the question, for he answered suavely: 'I should have thought that you would have guessed. I date the prettiest girls I can find—one at a time, of course. We tear round the country, visiting one night spot after another and—er—living it up.'

Sappha gave a snort. 'What nonsense,' she said roundly. 'I don't believe a word of it.'

'No? I felt sure you would—isn't that the sort of thing you expect me to do?'

She went pink. 'Yes—no.' She shot him a frowning look and found him smiling again. 'It was my fault for asking.'

She waited to hear what he would have to say to that; instead he observed blandly: 'We shall be crossing over the Ijsselmeer by the famous Zeedijk. It is a remarkable engineering feat of which we are very proud.' He sounded like a schoolmaster, detached and controlled, and she gave a sudden splutter of laughter. 'Oh, we can't quarrel,' she begged. 'I simply can't—my mind's still full of windmills.'

He eased the car past a bus without decreasing speed. 'I'm relieved to hear it,' he said on a laugh, 'for now I come to think about it I can't remember much about the Zeedijk—I can't think of anything to quarrel about either, can you?'

Sappha took off her gloves and then put them on again, hardly aware of what she was doing. The conversation was getting them nowhere. Rolf said quietly: 'Let's start again, shall we? I'll try and give you some idea of what I think we should do about Mother.'

He had become remote again and impersonal, but nicely so, like a family doctor. She listened carefully to what he had to say and then asked: 'Who is in charge of the Baroness? One of your partners or someone from the hospital?'

'The hospital in Groningen. She will have to have some more X-rays taken in a couple of weeks. If I'm not around perhaps you'll drive her there. We have a gardener who takes Mother to the shops and so on, but he doesn't care to go to Groningen.'

Sappha wondered what sort of man the chauffeur might be; she didn't think she cared to go to Groningen either. She asked faintly: 'Not this car?'

'Good God, girl, no. A Rover 416—you're up to driving that.'

She said with dignity: 'Of course. What is that ahead of us?'

'The sluices of the Zeedijk. Is Mother still asleep?'

Sappha had looked several times, now she looked again. 'Yes. It would be nice if she slept for the rest of the journey.'

He slowed a little as they passed the sluices. 'Probably she will. We're on the Afsluitdijk now. The Ijsselmeer is on your right, the North Sea on your left, only you can't see it. Take a good look, because I intend to make up some time.'

The car responded to the touch of his foot and Sappha watched the needle of the speedometer swing round. They didn't seem to be travelling any faster, only the land on the further side was advancing towards them at a great rate. As they flashed past the monument Rolf observed: 'There's a splendid view from the top, but it's a poor day for sight-seeing anyway. If you look hard, you can see both coasts.'

Sappha obediently turned and twisted and stared. The water looked cold and grey and empty. Only an occasional seagull, sitting on the sticks which marked the fishermen's nets, showed any sign of life. Scotland, she thought, had much more to offer, and was once more taken aback to hear Rolf say: 'You must be comparing this with Dialach, but wait until we are at our journey's end before you pass judgment. The scenery is different, but it has a charm all its own.'

They were on the mainland now, tearing past towns she would dearly have loved to stop and inspect. Franeker offered a tantalising glimpse of old houses and canals before they were once more in the open countryside. Though the afternoon was beginning to

close in now, she could see farms, standing each with its
complement of trees and fields and cows, lonely from
one another. There were churches too—wherever she
looked there were churches, and now and then a large
square house, standing as lonely as the farms. She wondered who lived in them, and tried for the hundredth
time to guess what the Baron's home would be like.

The Baroness woke up as they were going through
Leeuwarden. Much refreshed, she embarked upon a description of the country around them, begging Sappha
to look first left and then right at familiar landmarks,
which in the early dusk were now almost impossible
to see. She was glad when Rolf said: 'There's Dokkum
ahead,' and turned off the main road into a street of
modern houses, neat and orderly and a little dull, which,
once they had crossed the railway, led in its turn to a
narrow thoroughfare lined with old gabled houses which
presently opened on to a cobbled road alongside water,
running at right angles. Even in the half light Sappha
could see the old houses on the opposite side, lining the
water; she craned her neck to see more as they crossed
a bridge, where they turned to the right and drove along
by the water's edge before turning up one of the streets
leading to the centre of the town.

She turned to speak to the Baroness and so missed
the turn Rolf took down a narrow little street and over
an even narrower bridge. They were on the road which
circumvented the town now, with water on one side of
them and walled gardens on the other. She was just in
time to see a pair of wide-flung gates as they passed
between them into the grounds of a house which she
could see at the end of the curved drive, which was
short, while as far as she could see, the grounds around

them were of a moderate size, laid out with trees and shrubs and a smooth lawn. The house looked square and roomy with a gabled roof cut straight across at the top, so that it looked as though the builder had changed his mind before he had quite finished his work. Rolf had stopped the car before shallow steps leading to a heavy front door and as though this had been a signal, light blazed from the downstairs windows. Obedient to the Baron's invitation to alight, Sappha did so, removed the wraps and shawls from her patient and stood silently while Rolf lifted his mother from the car.

She had moved forward to help, but he had waved her back as an elderly man came down the steps, and after an exchange of greetings, lent his assistance, so that there was nothing more for her to do but follow the little procession into the house, across the hall and up the broad staircase. She would have liked to look around her, but the Baron's speed, even with his mother in his arms, was such that she had only a glimpse of the black and white tiled floor, the ornate plaster ceiling and wall, the panelling, the heavy carved furniture and the vast number of portraits on the walls. The stairs led to a square landing, thickly carpeted and with a variety of doors and passages leading from it, while another, smaller staircase rose steeply from one corner.

One of the doors was open as they crossed the landing and Antonia stood holding it wide, so that they could go through. She said '*Moeder!*' in an excited little voice and then, rather to Sappha's surprise, stood quietly in a corner of the room until the Baroness had been sat in a high-backed chair by the open fire. Only then did she run across the room to fling herself into her mother's arms, breaking into excited speech as she did so. Even then, when Rolf said:

'Sappha's going to put Mother to bed, Tonia. We'll leave her to do so, shall we?' she went obediently to the door with him. He flung a brotherly arm around her as they went out. Before he closed the door he said casually to Sappha: 'Ring if you need help.'

How like a man, thought Sappha sourly, to walk off without even telling her which door led to the bathroom. She flung off her coat and hat, smiled at her patient and said briskly: 'Bed, I think, don't you? I can manage your chair, it's on castors.'

She prepared the bed, a vast one with an elaborate headboard of carved oak and a fringed counterpane of rose-coloured brocaded velvet. Her patient, sitting against the big square pillows, looked small and tired and very happy. 'A wash,' suggested Sappha, 'a pretty bedjacket, supper—which I have no doubt will be something you fancy—and then an early night.' She was going round the room as she spoke, opening and shutting its several doors.

The Baroness laughed. 'Oh, you poor child! No one has told you anything. What could Rolf have been thinking of—or any of us for that matter? You must think us all very unkind and thoughtless, but I'm afraid we are excited. The bathroom's the next door on your right, Sappha, and the door over there leads to your room. The other doors are closets.'

Sappha had her hand on the bathroom door. She said soothingly:

'Of course you haven't been unkind—I can imagine how you feel and there's plenty of time for me to find my way around. The thing is to make you comfortable.'

She plunged into the bathroom—a splendid apartment, tiled in palest pink with a carpet of great depth and thickness which exactly matched the green towels, and an array of soaps, jars and bottles which merited a leisurely inspection. But her sharp eye had already discerned the jug and basin standing ready; someone had been very thoughtful. She rolled up the sleeves of her sweater and went to fill the jug.

Half an hour later the Baroness was ready. Sappha, rolling down her sleeves, asked: 'How do I let everyone know you're ready, Baroness?'

Her patient waved a hand in the direction of the fireplace. 'There's a bellrope.'

It was a handsome affair of silk cord with a great tassel at its end; a charming if old-fashioned method of summoning anyone. Sappha gave it an experimental tug and waited for something to happen. Almost immediately the door flew open and Antonia came in, followed rather more quietly by Rolf, who was followed in his turn by an elderly woman, tall and angular, with a sharp nose and pale blue eyes, carrying a champagne bucket. She put this on a table, answered the Baroness's greeting with guarded but obvious pleasure and went away again, casting a curious look at Sappha as she did so. The room had come alive—Antonia was getting glasses from a small walnut cabinet and talking at the top of her voice while the Baron and his mother carried on a calmer conversation which they constantly interrupted in order to answer her.

Just for the moment Sappha felt herself to be forgotten. It seemed an excellent chance to go to her room and do her hair and her face and perhaps unpack. She edged towards the door which she knew to be hers, her eyes on the Baron's back. He had the champagne bottle in

his hand; she judged that he would be nicely occupied
for a moment or so. She had actually reached the door
when he said without turning round: 'Where are you
going? You must have a drink.'

She opened the door and turned to face him.

'No, thank you,' she said pleasantly. 'I should like
to unpack.'

He took no notice of this. 'Has anyone shown you
your room? No, of course not—you can't have had a
moment to yourself since we arrived.' He smiled at
her. 'I'm sorry.'

'It doesn't matter in the least—I don't need anyone
to show me my room—if you would be good enough
to let me know when you would like me back…!' Sappha smiled in her turn, went through the door and shut
it quietly.

She walked straight to the window without bothering to look around her and stared out into the evening.
She had no idea which way the room faced, but she
could make out trees and a high wall and water gleaming fitfully beyond; it looked lonely and the sound of
distant traffic seemed to make it more so. Presently she
drew the curtains across; heavy silk damask curtains
of muted pinks and blues which, when she turned to
study the room, exactly matched the bedspread on the
bed—it was smaller than the Baroness's but its headboard was just as elaborate. The room was smaller than
her patient's too, but furnished with great taste. Sappha, examining everything, thought that the furniture
was probably Hepplewhite. Having taken her fill of
the furniture, she tried the doors. The first, by the bed,
opened into a fitted cupboard which could have taken
her entire wardrobe and still looked empty. The second

door gave on to the landing, the third was the one she had entered by, the fourth and last opened on to a small bathroom, pastel blue this time, with neatly piled towels in various shades of pink and a bowl of soaps in the same pleasing colour; there were jars of bath salts too. Sappha lifted their lids and sniffed appreciatively, then kicked off her shoes and began to take down her hair.

Later, as she unpacked, she wondered if she had been a little childish to refuse Rolf's offer of the champagne; she hadn't meant to be rude, but she had felt out of it. It would be better when she had met the rest of the staff, then she would feel more at home. Rolf had said that he was going away—she wondered for how long; perhaps she wouldn't see him again before she went back to England, for she still didn't know how long she was to stay in Dokkum. A cold lump of unhappiness in her chest began to spread slowly all over her body so that she actually shivered. It was a relief when there was a knock at the door and Antonia came in. She said in her prettily accented English:

'Rolf has gone to see some patients—he'll be back soon, he said if you would come to Mother now she would like to explain the house to you.'

The Baroness, looking all the better for her champagne, greeted Sappha with a smile. 'Your room is comfortable, I hope, Sappha? You have all you want? When Rolf has time he will show you the house and introduce the staff to you. They have been with us for so long, we think of them as friends and we hope you will too.' She eyed Sappha with eyes which positively sparkled. 'And now we will have a little more champagne, I think, if you will pour it, Tonia, and remember, only half a

glass for yourself—and now, I will try and tell you all
you need to know.'

The Baron came in half an hour later and although
he saw the glass still in Sappha's hand, he said nothing,
although his eyebrows rose just enough for her to be
aware that he had draw his own conclusions. She expected him to come out at any moment with some chill-
ing remark about not wanting to drink with him, but all
he said with businesslike friendliness was: 'If you've
finished your drinks and chatter, how about coming
downstairs and meeting the rest of us? You must see the
house too, but I think that will be better in the morning. I don't leave until after lunch.'

The three of them went downstairs and Sappha tried
to forget that he was going away, and answered Tonia's happy chatter in the same light tone, although
Rolf remained silent until they reached the hall when
he requested her to accompany him to the kitchen,
where she met the tall thin woman, who turned out to
be the housekeeper, and was called Annie; the elderly
chauffeur-gardener, called Jan, she had already seen
when they had arrived, a fresh-faced girl, who, Sappha
thought, could only have been described as strapping
and who had the peculiar name of Joke, and a small
round woman with white hair and bright blue eyes,
who, when they shook hands, said, 'Weel, noo, here's
a bonnie lass,' in a soft Highland voice, and laughed
at the surprise on Sappha's face. 'The young maister
said not a word about me, I'll be bound, but dinna fash
yesel', Miss Devenish, for ye can ask me ainything ye'll
need to know.'

Sappha said happily: 'Oh, how marvellous—I was
a little worried about the language, Mrs Burns.' She

turned to the Baron beside them. 'You did say Mrs Burns?'

He nodded. 'Our cook and friend for a great many years—she will tell you about meals and trays and anything else you may wish to know. I'm afraid none of the others speak English, but I'm sure you will pick up a few words and Mrs Burns or Antonia can always help you.'

He turned towards the door. 'And now come upstairs.' Which Sappha did reluctantly, partly because she disliked being told to do anything in such a forthright fashion, and partly because she would have liked time to examine the kitchen, which appeared to be a most agreeable combination of the old-fashioned and the very modern. Back in the hall, she asked: 'Why didn't you tell me about Mrs Burns?'

'I thought it would be a pleasant surprise and might cheer you up at a time when you might be feeling lonely and uncertain, as I believe you are—am I right?'

Sappha said yes rather shortly because she hadn't realised that her feelings showed like that, but he didn't appear to see her cross look, but went on in the most civil voice imaginable: 'Come and have a drink, then you shall go and see about Mother's dinner.'

He led the way across the hall and into a large room with a high ceiling bearing a great deal of plasterwork. There were three windows, tall and narrow, each curtained and elaborately pelmeted with red velvet. The floor was of polished wood upon which was a fine carpet, dim with age but still of great beauty. The furniture was for the most part Regency with a number of high-backed armchairs covered in tapestry place. The walls were white-painted, picked out in gold and almost covered with large paintings. Sappha, walking slowly

to the chair the Baron had indicated, thought it looked
very like one of the rooms in an English stately home,
only this room was lived in—there were magazines
strewn over the sofa table behind the chesterfield, some
knitting pushed into one corner of a chair, and a tabby
cat asleep in another. There were flowers everywhere
and by one of the armchairs there was a waste basket
crammed full with screwed-up paper and envelopes,
while a pile of unopened letters lay on the floor beside
it. Without doubt the Baron's chair, though he made
no attempt to sit in it but walked across to a small wall
table saying blandly: 'Am I to be snubbed if I offer you a
glass of sherry? I was disappointed in you, Sappha—we
have managed to be quite civil to each other for a day
or so, I had thought we might have kept it up until I go.'

She asked without thinking: 'Are you going for a
very long time? Will you not be back before I return
to England?'

He gave her the sherry before he answered. 'Why do
you want to know? Can you not wait to start quarrel-
ling again?' His voice mocked her.

Sappha stared at her shoes. She said loudly: 'I wish
I'd never said that!' A remark which should have been
explained, but apparently he needed none, for he said
softly: 'Ah, I have been hoping that you would discover
that for yourself.'

She lifted her eyes from her shoes and looked at him
instead. He was staring down at her, the gleam in his
eyes made them seem blacker than ever before and he
was smiling, and there was nothing of the satyr about
his face at all. It was unfair, she thought fiercely, that
he had only to smile like that for her heart to turn over

and hammer against her ribs and take her breath. She said uncertainly: 'I don't know what you mean.'

He put down his glass. 'Oh, Sappha,' he said on a laugh, 'you're saying that because you've just remembered Andrew Glover. Well, I haven't forgotten him either, though not perhaps for the same reason as you. I'll tell you now that as far as I'm concerned Andrew doesn't exist.'

Sappha's eyes were riveted on his face for the simple reason that she was unable to take them away. A wave of delight surged through her; now she could at least explain that Andrew didn't exist for her either. Her mouth was open to say so when the door opened and Antonia came in.

She said gaily: 'Hullo there, you two. I've been with Mother. She wants you, please, Sappha, right away.'

Sappha went upstairs and dealt calmly with her patient, trying not to wonder too much what Rolf might have said if Antonia hadn't come in. She busied herself with the Baroness's dinner and presently went down to have her own in a dining room as splendid, in its own way, as the drawing room, where presently they went for coffee. Rolf and Antonia were amusing company, she could have stayed with them the whole evening, but she still had to settle the Baroness. When she got up the Baron rose too and opened the door and wished her goodnight in the formal tones of a polite host which chilled her to the bone. It was still early, she had expected to be asked to return to the drawing room, but apparently this was not to be expected of her, nor, it seemed, did he wish to talk to her. She went upstairs, the lovely glow of happiness inside her turning steadily colder as she remembered what the Baroness had said about her son—that he liked his own way, especially when it came to the conquest of a pretty girl. Presumably having added herself to his collection, he had lost an interest which could never have been very great anyway; he didn't like her enough.

Chapter 7

Sappha didn't see Rolf until well after eleven o'clock. By then she had finished her morning's duties, dealt firmly but kindly with her patient's slight peevishness, due to the excitement of her homecoming, and persuaded her to stay in bed for the day in order to recover from the journey. She had gone downstairs to breakfast in a small room behind the dining room, cosily warm from the old-fashioned stove as well as the central heating which had been skilfully concealed around the house. The room overlooked the garden and was furnished with solid, comfortable Empire furniture and bright chintz curtains whose colours were echoed in the breakfast china. She had been joined after a few minutes by a rather sleepy Antonia, still in her dressing gown, who revived after her first cup of coffee and went on to make a splendid meal. She had dealt with ham, cheese and a variety of breads and was contemplating the black cherry jam and some rusks when she noticed Sappha's empty plate and exclaimed: 'Sappha, aren't you hungry? I don't believe you've eaten anything. Are you unhappy—is anything the matter?'

'No. Nothing.' Sappha answered the last question first. 'I'm just not hungry.'

Antonia eyed her across the table. 'Does your Andrew know that you are here?' she wanted to know, 'and does he mind?'

Sappha ignored the first question. 'Why should he mind?' she asked in a matter-of-fact voice. 'I really must go back upstairs. I expect we'll see each other later,' and made her escape.

She was writing up her brief report when Rolf came in. He kissed his mother, enquired how she did and said to Sappha: 'Throw that out of the window, and come round the house. I haven't much time.'

She gave him a cold glance which he countered with a twinkle.

'I know,' he said equably before she could utter, 'I order you about shamefully and if only you had the time to think of a good excuse you would doubtless offer one. Never mind, I'll be gone in an hour or so and you'll have plenty of time to think up cutting replies to blast me.'

Sappha burst out laughing, suddenly happy again. 'You really are ridiculous—you behave just as if...'

'I'm bold—bad—unscrupulous? But of course, didn't you know? I try my utmost to annoy you.'

Sappha got to her feet, avoiding the Baroness's eye. 'I'm quite ready when you are, Doctor,' she said soberly, whereupon he gave a great bellow of laughter, caught her by the arm and walked her to the door, telling his mother, as they went, that he would return Sappha within the hour.

'We'll start at the top.' He still held her arm as they crossed the landing to the little staircase she had noticed when they had arrived, where he went ahead of her, her hand still held fast in his. The steps were steep and the stair narrow, but its woodwork was old and beautiful and shining with constant care. It opened on to another landing, only a little smaller than the one below, and like it, had two windows overlooking the grounds in the front of the house. There were four doors, two on each wall, and an open arch leading to a short passage facing the windows. The doors opened on to bedrooms, with tiny, beautifully appointed bathrooms between each pair. The bedrooms were furnished with the same care and luxury as those on the floor below and when Sappha exclaimed:

'Oh, how pretty they all are!' the Baron answered: 'We use them for guests—when my nephews and nieces come to stay, we put them up here—they can make as much noise as they like and they love being on their own.' He led her through the arch and opened another door. 'This used to be the schoolroom, we were banished up here to do our homework, and the girls came up here to sew and paint—there's a pleasant view.'

Sappha followed him to the window and stood looking at the well-kept garden below; beyond the wall she could see a glimpse of water.

'The town moat,' explained Rolf, 'and from the other side of the house we can just see the river Zijl—there's a gate at the bottom of the garden leading to the path running beside the moat—if you feel energetic enough you could walk round the entire town—it's very pleasant.'

'Yes,' said Sappha, not having heard a word, for he
had put an arm around her shoulders and for the time
being at any rate, she was unaware of anything else. But
she heard him clearly when he said quietly:

'I think that you have changed your mind, Sappha,'
and she knew that he was referring to her remarks about
them not getting on well together. She didn't answer
at once, because somewhere at the back of her mind
an ugly voice was reminding her that probably he just
wanted confirmation of his conquest. When she still
hesitated he turned her round to face him and said with
a kind of desperate patience:

'Oh, we disagree, don't we?—we always shall. I
enjoy stirring up your temper to watch the splendour of
your rage. But when we've not had the leisure to argue,
haven't you noticed how well we fit? Could we not be
friends, dear girl? Let's cry quits; bury the hatchet—so
long as we are to be together.'

He put a finger under her chin so that she was forced
to look up at him. His face was grave although his eyes
gleamed. He bent his head and kissed her mouth gently.
'Kiss and be friends,' he said, 'isn't that an English saying? Or if you prefer, *absit invidia*.'

Sappha, still shaken by his kiss said weakly: 'Oh, an
absence of something or other…'

He laughed, still staring at her. 'Let there be no ill-
will.' He took his hand away from her chin and put an
arm around her shoulders again. 'Do you agree, Sappha?'

She nodded. He had said: 'So long as we are to be together,' remembering that made her sad, but she had to
say something. 'Yes, all right—but you're going away…'

She shouldn't have asked that, for he said at once: 'Yes—will you miss me?'

Sappha saw the chance to rectify her mistake. She said matter-of-factly: 'Yes, of course, just as the rest of the household will miss you.'

He looked away from her, out of the window; presently he said mildly:

'You'll learn quite a lot about me while I'm away, and that will be a good thing.' He drew her away from the window and said, his voice brisk again: 'Come and see the rest of the house.'

The rooms on the landing below were large and furnished with a collection of antiques which nonetheless gave an air of comfort and homeliness. There were silver and china and magnificent paintings too—they were mostly small and delicate landscapes, miniature family portraits and several flower studies by Bosschaert. The last room they inspected was at the back of the house with three large windows all to itself. Its walls were white picked out with gilt, and the carpet was blue, an admirable foil for the damask pink of the curtains and bedspread on the wide bed; there were a pair of bergSres in the windows, also covered in the same brocade, with a small table between them—it was round and gilded and its top was of painted porcelain. Sappha went to examine it and Rolf followed her over to explain: 'It's Louis the Fifteenth—the top is Sèvres, made by Carlin—I don't much care for it, but a very long time ago an ancestor gave it to his bride when he brought her here, and here it has been ever since.'

Sappha put a gentle finger on its intricate gildings. 'That's such a nice story it would be heartless to move it. I expect she loved it and I daresay it's rare.'

'Very.' His voice was dry and she went pink. He would think her abysmally ignorant, the whole house was full of treasures and she had had to ask about nearly all of them. She wandered over to the dressing table—chinese lacquer, at least she knew that, but its date eluded her. She turned her back on it and said too loudly: 'I know almost nothing about antiques, our furniture at home is old, but it's not—not like these.' She waved an expressive arm which the Baron was quick to possess and hold.

'But you like it?' he said pleasantly. 'I wanted to know what you thought of my home.'

She said honestly: 'It's beautiful. It must be wonderful to live here day after day in the middle of it all—only I don't know enough about it.'

She was puzzled when he said: 'That doesn't matter in the least—not if you like it—and you do like it, don't you? Come downstairs.'

She had already seen the drawing room, now she wandered round it, looking her fill at its treasures; the bracket clock by Thomas Tompion on a shelf all to itself, a collection of enamelled watches under a glass-topped table; a cabinet of marquetry in which was displayed a row of engraved goblets; a carved wooden side table with an ormolu mounted Battersea enamel casket upon it. The dining room seemed almost severe after the drawing room's richness, although it had a fine collection of silver upon its carved oak sideboard.

'You've seen the breakfast room already,' Rolf said. 'There are some rather nice pen and ink drawings and a collection of pewter there.' He had his hand on a door which he now opened. 'This is my study—if patients come to the house, I see them here. I share a surgery

in the town with my partners, of course.' As he spoke
he ushered her into a comfortably sized room with a
large cluttered desk and several comfortable chairs. The
walls here were of panelled wood and the ceiling was
elaborately plastered. The only pictures were some dark
portraits of dead and gone van Duyrens; the women
looked calmly at her from their heavy frames, the men,
she was quick to see, displayed the same handsome
dark looks as Rolf.

Rolf went before Sappha could get down to lunch.
The Baroness, still a little crotchety, had delayed her so
much that by the time she had reached the dining room
he was on the point of leaving the table. She sat down
and began on her soup, listening to his feet taking the
stairs two at a time while she turned an attentive face to
Antonia. It was only when her companion ceased speaking and looked at her enquiringly that she realised that
she hadn't heard a word. Antonia looked at her kindly.

'I expect you're tired,' she said. 'Mother's a little
cross, isn't she? What I said was, it's partly because
her dog Leo isn't coming home until this afternoon—
he's a peke and he's at the vet's having some teeth out.
Rolf's dog is there too—he's an alsatian—he went too
because Leo pines if Charlie's not with him.'

Sappha banished her thoughts of Rolf in order to consider this interesting piece of information. 'You mean to
say,' she said with some amazement, 'that Charlie has
to stay at the vet's…but he's your brother's dog, doesn't
he go around with him?'

'Of course. To the surgery each day—he sits under
Rolf's desk, and they go for a walk together early in the
morning every single day, and when Rolf goes to one
of our farms, he goes too. Rolf wondered if you would

like to come with me to fetch them this afternoon—it would be a good opportunity for you to try out the Mini. Rolf said you might.'

Sappha bristled; for two pins she would have utterly refused to drive anything while she was in Dokkum. She was about to say something to this effect when Rolf came back, with his coat over one arm and a briefcase in his hand. He stood patiently while Antonia hung round his neck, gave her a brotherly slap on that portion of her anatomy best suited to receive it, and crossed the room to where Sappha was sitting at table. She got up, for the simple reason that his elegant largeness was so close and overwhelming. She said breathlessly: 'I'll remember what you told me about your family coming and the telephone numbers and the specialist coming tomorrow—and Antonia has just told me about the dogs.'

'Did you remember anything else?' he asked quietly.

Sappha went a delicate pink. It was true she had remembered all these things, but far more vividly did she remember their conversation in the school room. She said carefully, her eyes on a level with his chin:

'I haven't forgotten anything you said.'

'Good. Think of me a little, Sappha.' He caught her hand and kissed it swiftly on its palm and went away. She heard the front door bang as she sat down to her cooling soup.

The house seemed a great deal larger and very empty when he had gone. Sappha was glad, once lunch was over and her patient tucked up for a nap, to change into a sweater and skirt and a thick tweed topcoat and go with Antonia to the garage down by the gate, where she found the Mini as well as the Rover 416. She drove the little car out of the gates under Antonia's direction and found that driving on the wrong side of the road wasn't as bad as she had imagined, probably because everyone else was doing the same thing. By the time she had negotiated the town and was heading the car northwards, she felt quite at ease. The vet lived just outside the village of Brantgum, only a few miles from Dokkum, and presently, with the dogs safely stowed in the back, Sappha drove carefully back again, feeling rather pleased with herself; besides, it had helped to pass an otherwise rather dull afternoon.

It was better with the dogs in the house. Charlie, who looked fierce and was in fact excessively good-natured, was a willing companion to any member of the household who would accept his company, but Leo stayed with the Baroness, baring what remained of his teeth to anyone who went near her, although after an hour or two of Sappha's company he seemed to realise that she was an indispensable part of the Baroness's life and contented himself with curling a lip at her.

After dinner that evening, Sappha, mindful of Rolf's instructions to her, went into his study, sat down at his desk and studied the timetable he had written out for her. The specialist would be coming the following day, and this she welcomed, for there was the chance that he might allow the Baroness to stand at least, but she was a little nervous of the following days, for the Baroness's children were coming to visit her, all at once, and although she didn't expect to see much of them she thought they might be a little overpowering—Antonia was great fun and perhaps they would all be like her, though a good deal older—all the same there would be four of them, each with husband or wife. She got up with a shake of her head at her silliness and went back upstairs to play backgammon with her patient.

The specialist from Groningen was a delightful surprise. He was a large man, and as he got out of his Mercedes, Sappha saw that he was portly as well. She and Antonia had gone down to the hall to welcome him and he had greeted them in a voice as large and exuberant as himself. He shook her hand with a strength which almost cracked her bones and boomed cheerfully: 'De Winter—and delighted to meet you, Miss Devenish.'

They all went upstairs, Mijnheer de Winter firing remarks at them in an English as English as her own. But once in the Baroness's room he lapsed into Dutch and only when he needed information from Sappha did he speak English. But even though he spoke a different language, his methods were the same as Mr MacCombie's; she thought she would have understood him in any language. The examination over, he spent another ten minutes passing the time of day with the Baroness before he said:

'Well, everything seems splendid—I must commend the work of Mr Devenish and also the good Mr Mac-Combie. I see no reason why our patient should not get on to her feet once more.' He was stopped by his patient's little shriek of delight. 'I say on to her feet, but I do not mean to walk, only to stand and do the exercises with the help of our so good Miss Devenish. When Rolf returns, he will bring you to Groningen and you shall have an X-ray—the last, I hope.' He beamed at the Baroness and then at Sappha, who smiled back at him, but not quite so broadly, because as soon as the Baroness was well again, she herself would return to England. All the same, it was a happy morning for ev-

Antonia had, but she was still very young and she hadn't been boasting—presumably they had so much of it that it wasn't important to them. She sighed without envy and went away to change back into her uniform.

Sia, Ariana and Victoria left first, Sia and her husband in a Volvo estate car. 'Clumsy great thing,' commented Antonia from the step as they watched them go, 'but they've got four children and dogs besides.'

Ariana and Bas had a Mercedes Benz convertible, although as Antonia informed an interested Sappha, they had a Fiat as well, 'Though they'll have to get a bigger car soon—they've only two children so far, but we all like large families. I daresay I shall have a great number when I marry.' She broke off to wave to Victoria and Franz who were getting into a rakish Porsche coupé, a means of transport which Sappha felt would need to be changed if Victoria shared the rest of her family's enthusiasm for children. The remaining car she supposed to be Theo's—it was a Buick GS400, beautifully kept and very fast. She liked Theo, she liked his wife too, and wondered how long they had been married; not long, she imagined, for they looked very much in love.

The evening passed pleasantly, although the Baroness was tired when at length Sappha got her to bed. She agreed willingly enough to spend the day in bed on the morrow and when Sappha said: 'I'm sure it's a good idea. I think the doctor…'

'You mean Rolf?' enquired his mother dryly. 'Yes, when he telephoned me yesterday evening he did suggest it, but he was sure that you would think of it. I would be a very stupid woman to ruin all the good work which has been put into me.' She smiled up at Sappha from her pillows. 'You like my children, I hope, Sappha?'

Sappha was pouring medicine into a glass. She corked the bottle neatly and gave the Baroness a brief sidelong glance as she did so.

'Yes, I do—very much. How proud you must be of them all.'

Her patient nodded happily. 'Indeed I am. A pity Rolf couldn't be with us—we all depend on him a great deal, you know. I have been meaning to ask you, my dear, do you still regard him as a brigand?'

Sappha was unwrapping the blood pressure apparatus. She didn't look up but said carefully: 'I'm sorry I ever said that. No, he's not a brigand. I—I think... that is, he's very... I was mistaken,' she finished inadequately.

This lame rejoinder seemed to satisfy the Baroness, who relaxed against her pillows, looking faintly smug. 'Now isn't that nice,' she murmured. 'You know, Sappha, I believe I shall sleep very well tonight.'

The days fell into a neat, tranquil pattern again, enlivened by Antonia's happy chatter when she returned from school each day. Undeterred by the amount of study she had to do, and the fact that she had to leave home soon after seven each morning, she appeared to enjoy life to the full. Sappha suspected that she did a large part of her homework on her journeys to school and back, and as her mother had told Sappha that Antonia was a brilliant scholar, it seemed that she had brains as well as beauty, she was certainly a delightful companion; Sappha began to understand why it was that Rolf was so devoted to his young sister.

By the end of the week Sappha had explored the little town thoroughly. She could have done this easily in half that time, but she had taken over the task of exercising the dogs each morning during Rolf's absence, besides which, although Dokkum was small, there was plenty to see. She had spent two afternoons in the Herformde Kerk because her guide book told her that St Boniface had built it—it was a large lofty building, with whitewashed walls and plain glass windows, which had a grandeur even when it was empty. The floor was paved with gravestones, a great many of them in Latin, a language which she had enjoyed learning at school. She had peered down, teasing her brain to remember long forgotten words and was delighted to find that hard thinking enabled her to read at least part of the inscriptions.

She discovered with a little thrill that there were van Duyrens everywhere; lying beneath her feet since the fifteenth century, while the later, more elaborate wall plaques adorned the walls. It was a pity that most of them were in Dutch, although she was able to make out the names. Rolf and Theobald occurred with monotonous frequency, as did Sia and Antonia; probably the Dutch liked to keep their names in the family from one generation to the other. She wondered which name Rolf would choose for his son when he had one, and found the thought so disturbing to her peace of mind that she walked briskly to De Posthoorn and had a cup of coffee.

She had examined the Weigh House too, and the Town Hall, where she had been left to roam around on her own. The Baroness had counselled her to view the painted wall in the Council Chamber, which she did, but found the portraits of the bygone men of Dokkum much more to her taste. They stared at her with their steadfast gaze out of magnificently painted faces, and she stared back, wanting to know more about their lives and what they had done and thought; the guide book just wasn't enough. She wished with all her heart that she could speak Dutch so that she could have asked—perhaps Rolf would have time to tell her when he returned.

She visited the museum too—it was a stone's throw from the hotel and faced the water. It had a long un-pronounceable name, and was very old, but so well restored that she was unaware of this until the cura-tor told her. He was a silent man, but when he saw that she was really interested, he did his best to answer her questions, although sometimes his English failed him, and she was forced to fall back on her own guesses, but on the whole they managed very well between them. The second time she went he allowed her to go where she wanted, for she had the place to herself; the season was over, he told her, and in any case, touring foreign-ers seldom stayed long in the little town, and even more seldom paid him a visit.

She did a little tentative shopping too, armed with her phrase book which she thrust under the nose of anyone disposed to help her, so that she had acquired a handful of useful Dutch words even though she didn't understand a word of what was being said around her.

Rolf's partners had called to see the Baroness a few days after he had gone. They were quiet men, about his age and speaking an English as faultless as his. They were on the best of terms with the Baroness and charm-ing to Sappha, offering help and advice if she should need them. When they had gone the Baroness remarked on their long friendship with Rolf. 'They were boys to-gether,' she explained, 'and even when they were little they all swore that they would be doctors and share a practice, and as you see, they have done just that.'

Sappha was massaging her patient's legs. She said, her hands still busy, 'They're nice—I suppose the practice is a large one?'

'Oh, yes. A great many patients live outside the town, but Dirk and Pieter have the lion's share because Rolf has his work in Groningen as well as his lectures which take him from home from time to time. He'll be back in a few days. It will be nice to see him again, won't it?'

Sappha said yes briefly and urged her patient to put a little more energy into her foot exercises. The Baroness gave her a thoughtful look and when she spoke again it was about something quite different.

The day before Rolf was due back was a Friday and Antonia came home early from school. Sappha, having just settled the Baroness for her afternoon rest, was on her way downstairs to give Annie a message when Antonia burst into the hall. Sappha stopped short on the staircase. 'Tonia, how did you get home? And so early.'

'A friend gave me a lift, Sappha dear. There was no class because my schoolmaster has a cold. Isn't it delightful? Now I'm free until Monday and if I do all my homework now I shall be able to spend the weekend with Rolf, unless,' she added wickedly, 'he's got some girl he wants to take out.'

Sappha said nothing to this but continued down the stairs. In the hall she stopped, eyeing Antonia closely.

'You look as though you're up to something, Antonia,' she said abruptly. 'Have you spent your allowance on something wickedly expensive?'

Antonia skipped across the space between them and put an arm in Sappha's. 'Me?' she asked innocently.

'How can I get up to anything when I have to go to that stupid school every day?' She smiled with charm at Sappha and said coaxingly: 'Don't look so suspicious—if you must know I've got plenty of my allowance left. Are you going to the kitchen? I'll come with you, for I'm famished.'

Sappha laughed, shaking the uneasy feeling away that Antonia was up to something. She was a lively girl, given to having her own way, and Rolf, who was the only person she listened to, wasn't here.

'I'm sure Mrs Burns or Annie will love to find you something to eat. Are you really going to stay home until teatime, Tonia? Because if you are I'd like to walk round the town—you know, along the path which follows the moat. It's not bad weather and I've been wanting to do it ever since...'

'Rolf told you?' finished Antonia. 'He takes the dogs every morning.' She went on without pause: 'Do you miss Andrew, Sappha? Wouldn't you like to see him?'

Sappha paused with her hand on the kitchen door handle; she didn't look at her companion. 'But how could I possibly see him? He has his work too, you know.' She went into the kitchen quickly so that Antonia shouldn't have the chance to ask any more questions.

She set off briskly half an hour later, wrapped in her tweed coat, and with her hair tied into a silk scarf, for the wind was keen. Earlier in the day it had been fine, but now the sun was fighting a losing battle with the cold looking clouds edging it from the sky. Sappha went out of the back gate, turned to her left and started along the path by the water. It was very quiet save for the rustling of the dry branches of the trees and the occasional lonely cry of some water bird. She passed a few small boys pottering, after the manner of their kind, along the water's edge, and once an old gentleman, warmly clad against the wind and smoking a pipe, which he removed in order to bid her a polite *Goeden Dag*, and which she, equally polite, replied to in her awkward Dutch.

The path was interesting, for it wandered around the edge of the town sometimes following the water which encircled it, sometimes passing over little wooden bridges or alongside a row of centuries old houses. From time to time, too, it bisected the watergates, and here Sappha lingered to catch a glimpse of the old-world roofs of the town. She inspected the windmills on their bastions, paused again to watch some barges on the water and came eventually to the Town Hall and the picturesque houses which faced it across the Zijl. The early dusk was falling by now and she slowed her steps to peer into the lighted windows of the houses as she passed them, but the sight of De Posthoorn reminded her of tea and she quickened her pace once more and turned the last corner on to the stretch of path she had started from; the house was barely five minutes walk away although she couldn't see it yet.

She was two-thirds of the distance when she heard a faint sound. She told herself, doubtfully, that it was a bird, but when she heard it for a second time she stopped to listen. It came from her right and now she knew it wasn't a bird. She walked to the bank and looked about her as well as she was able in the steadily deepening gloom. Where she stood there were no bushes or trees, but a few yards further there was a thicket and a few small trees, almost in the water; the sound came from there. She went forward cautiously, aware that the bank sloped steeply and was more mud than

grass, and bent down carefully to peer into the tangle
of branches. There was a small sack, a brick tied to the
rope which fastened its neck, but the rope had caught
in the branches of the trees overhanging the water, and
now the sack hung an inch or so above water. As Sappha watched something inside gave a convulsive wrig-
gle and she leaned forward, intent on freeing it. The
next instant she had slipped and toppled into the water.
It was cold, regrettably smelly, and she was appalled
to feel mud and weeds sucking at her boots. She had
fallen sideways so that her head and shoulders had remained free and dry, but the rest of her was up to her
waist in water and a quick look convinced her that she
was going to have an awful job to climb out.

The contents of the sack whimpered again and she
forgot her own plight in the need to rescue whatever
it was inside. She put a hand underneath to support
it and tugged at the rope, with no success at all. She
needed a knife, a pair of scissors, even a nail file—all
of which she had in the handbag she had left on the
dressing table in her room. But at least she could ease
the small creature's misery while she thought what to
do. She poked the tough strands of the sack and made
a tiny hole. When she put her finger in a small tongue
licked it gratefully. She left the finger there and talked
soothingly to the owner of the tongue while she decided
what to do. If she could scramble out she could go and
fetch Antonia or Joke—it would be a simple matter with
two. She suited the action to the thought and let the
sack go while she gripped the bank with her hands and
tried to lever herself up. Frighteningly, it didn't work—
the mud around her ankles tightened around them as
she strained to lift her feet, and the weeds, which she

had quite forgotten, felt like nylon cords. She waited a moment, aware of the numbing cold of the water, and tried again. It was no use, and what was worse, she had slipped a little further down into the mud.

The creature in the sack made a small, enquiring sound and she said, rather more loudly than she needed to because she needed cheering up as well. 'We'll have to have patience, whatever you are…' she broke off and uttered a gasp which was almost a scream as something brushed through the thicket and plopped into the water. Sappha was ready to scream properly when there was another movement in the bang above her. She looked up fearfully into the gloom and made out Charlie peering down at her with wise, friendly eyes. He gave a short bark and was joined almost immediately by his master.

Sappha didn't understand a word Rolf said. He spoke in his own language for a start and in a rough voice quite unlike his usual deep quiet tones. 'Something rude, no doubt,' she thought hazily, a trifle lightheaded with relief and fright and cold. He peeled off his top coat as he added in a subdued roar: 'What in the name of the Almighty are you doing there?'

She watched him place a large sure foot on the bank and said through chattering teeth: 'There's something in a bag—I tried to reach it and f-fell in. It's t-tied with a rope and I can't get it f-free.'

He was just above her, taking a knife from his pocket, uncaring of the water lapping his shoes. He leaned across her, cut the rope and swung the sack gently on to the top of the bank where Charlie welcomed it with gentle blowings and gruntings. Rolf had an arm round her now; without much effort he tugged her loose of the mud and weeds and heaved her unceremoniously up the bank. She landed on her hands and knees and Charlie abandoned the sack and came to blow on her instead. Seconds later Rolf was beside her, hauling her to her feet, wrapping her in his coat.

'N-no,' she essayed through chattering teeth, 'you'll ruin it.' It was, she remembered clearly, an extremely handsome and well-cut garment and must have cost a good deal of money. She pushed ineffectively against his hand fastening the buttons and he said, still roughly: 'Be quiet, do!' His voice sounded so fierce that she lapsed into miserable silence and then tears. They poured down her cheeks and she did nothing about them as it was almost dark by now and he couldn't see them. She was quite unprepared when he caught her suddenly close and touched her face with a gentle hand and spoke in his own language again. She didn't understand what he was saying, but she knew that the words were kind and tender, as was his voice. When he bent his head and kissed her wet cheek and then her mouth, the tears, the mud, the wet and cold dark melted away and for a brief moment she was in a star-spangled fairyland.

The next instant Rolf said in a perfectly ordinary voice: 'Let's see what we've got,' and took out his knife once more. It was a puppy, but what kind of puppy they would have to find out later. Rolf tucked it under his arm, caught Sappha round the shoulders, spoke briskly to Charlie who was inclined to go ratting, and walked quickly towards his home.

Minutes later they were in the kitchen, where Sappha was stripped of the Baron's coat, her own coat and boots and wrapped in a blanket which someone had produced, then told to drink the large brandy Rolf was holding out to her. She took a sip and he said equably: 'The lot, my girl, or I'll pour it down your throat for you.'

She did as she was bid, knowing that he would do exactly as he said, and felt the rich glow surge through. It made her feel instantly better so that she sat up straight and looked around her for the puppy. He was already before the fire, a thin, ugly little creature with a wizened anxious face. The anxiety turned to delight as Annie put a bowl of milk under his nose and he gave a whimper of pleasure and lowered his deplorable head, while Charlie brooded kindly beside him.

Sappha, who, what with brandy and cold and fright, was feeling peculiar, said: 'He's very ugly…'

Rolf was leaning against the table in the centre of the kitchen watching her. He said lightly: 'So would you be if you had been tied up in a sack.' He smiled very kindly at her. 'I can think of a lot of people who would have walked past and pretended they hadn't heard him. I'm glad you didn't.'

A little colour tinged her white cheeks. She unwrapped the blanket, speaking slowly because she felt peculiar. 'I'll go and have a hot bath and change.' She got to her feet and the Baron put down his glass and came across the room to her. 'You'll look after him?' she asked hazily.

His eyes looked black, a smile tugged the corners of his mouth. 'Yes, of course—he shall join the family, but I think I'll look after you first.'

He whipped her off her feet and carried her upstairs, calling over his shoulder for Joke to follow them and run the bath.

An hour later Sappha felt perfectly all right again. Antonia had rushed in while she was dressing and begged her, unsuccessfully, to stay in bed. She had the puppy under one arm, from where it peered with uncertain delight at a world which had suddenly become good to live in, and once she had been convinced that Sappha had taken no hurt from her ducking, engaged her in the interesting task of finding a name for the animal. 'You must choose it, Sappha, for you rescued him. It must have been horrid in that water—all slimy and cold and rats, I daresay.'

Sappha shuddered delicately as she pinned on her cap. 'Yes,' she said, 'and then I looked up and there was Charlie and—and the doctor.'

'Why do you call Rolf "the doctor"?' Antonia wanted to know.

'Well, he is.' Sappha tried to sound matter-of-fact. 'There, I'm ready. I'm going along to see your mother.'

'You've had no tea.'

'Never mind—I had a huge glass of brandy instead. I can miss tea.'

But she was mistaken. When they reached the top of the stairs, Rolf was in the hall. Without raising his voice, he said: 'Come down, Sappha. Mother's all right for a little while.'

She had no intention of going down. She had her hand on the Baroness's door when he said again: 'Sappha.'

She went downstairs, telling herself that she was a weak fool as she went. He came across the hall to meet her. 'You'll feel better for tea,' he said cheerfully, 'and don't glare at me in that enchanting manner or I might kiss you again.'

She went scarlet, and after one quick look at him, preceded him into the breakfast room and he shut the door as he followed her. The tea tray looked inviting. She sat down on a bergere and he sat opposite her, saying blandly as he did so: 'Don't worry, dear girl, Tonia will be here long before I can press my unwelcome attentions upon you.'

He smiled at her with lazy good humour and her scarlet cheeks faded to white. She had, for the last hour, been living in a happy, slightly hazy dream world in which his kiss had been a very real thing. Now it seemed that it was part of the dream, to be discarded with it.

She said dully: 'In that case, shall I pour out the tea?' and without waiting for him to reply, lifted the silver teapot. It was mortifying that her hand shook so badly that he leaned forward and took it from her, murmuring: 'Perhaps I had better?'

In the night, lying sleepless, she told herself that she was behaving like a fool—a lovesick fool, she amended, determined to be honest with herself. She forced herself to make plans for the future, but it was a fruitless occupation. She was still thinking about Rolf when she at last went to sleep.

Chapter 8

Rolf came in through the front door as Sappha went downstairs the following morning. He shut it behind the dogs, said good morning pleasantly enough and stood staring at her, which didn't surprise her in the least, for she was aware that after her miserable night her face looked as plain as a suet pudding. She said grumpily: 'Good morning,' and returned his stare as he removed the puppy from under his arm and set it on the floor, removed his coat, flung it in a chair and said: 'Under the weather?' He sounded as though he was speaking his thoughts out loud. 'Starting a cold, I daresay,' he cocked a crooked eyebrow at her, 'pneumonia perhaps.'

Sappha found herself on the verge of laughter despite her crossness as he said coaxingly: 'Come and say hullo to our puppy!' She crossed the hall to pick the scrap up and stroke its head. The little beast wriggled, licked her hand with a small pink tongue and barked in a shrill treble so that she said urgently: 'Oh, hush, puppy, hush!' and Rolf exclaimed: 'An excellent name—he shall be Hush from now on.'

Sappha did laugh then. 'I wonder what sort of breed— breeds—he is?' she wanted to know, and laughed again when he said:

'That I think is something we should gloss over, but it will be interesting to see what he grows into—have you had your breakfast?'

She shook her head. 'No—I've been with your mother—early morning chores. I'm just going to take her breakfast up, but if you wanted to see her...?'

He took Hush from her. 'No hurry.' He smiled at her and her heart missed a beat. She said uncertainly: 'Well, in that case...' and made her way to the kitchen. When she emerged presently with her patient's tray, he had gone and so had the dogs.

It was some twenty minutes later when she came down to her own breakfast. The Baroness was in a chatty mood, and not only did she want to know all about Sappha's health after her ducking, she wanted to know about the puppy too. She had demanded to see it the previous evening and while deploring its appearance, agreed that it must join the household. Now she wanted to know if anyone had exercised it and whether it had been fed. Sappha gave placid affirmatives to her questions, rearranged her pillows, put her letters and newspapers exactly where she wished to have them, agreed that it had turned cold overnight, explained away her own drab little face as best she might, and left her patient to her breakfast. When she entered the breakfast room a minute or so later, it was to find the Baron sitting at the table, scribbling notes in his diabolical handwriting, which she privately considered would be of no use to him at all, because he was reading the paper at the same time. He went over to the sideboard as she sat down, saying as he went:

'Scrambled eggs? Bacon? A kipper?'

She settled for the eggs, poured them both coffee and asked: 'You haven't been waiting for me, have you?'

He sat down opposite her and when he spoke his voice was silky. 'Yes—did you hope that if you delayed long enough I might be finished and gone?'

She looked at him in bewildered surprise and saw that he had become a brigand with a satyr's grin. She forced herself to answer reasonably.

'No, what a ridiculous thing to say—your mother was feeling like a chat, and I had no idea that you would be here.'

She didn't add that she had hoped that he would be. She drank some coffee and waited for an answer which she never received, for Antonia came in, dressed and ready for school. She flung herself down in a chair and grumbled: 'How lucky you two are, having time to eat your breakfast.' She looked at them enviously. 'What fun it must be, having another cup of coffee and being able to talk.' She sounded so melodramatic that Sappha hid a smile as she said soothingly:

'Never mind, Tonia—not much longer now, then you'll be able to do the same.'

The Baron looked up from his perusal of the leading article in his newspaper. He said crisply: 'You could do that now if you got yourself out of bed an hour—even half an hour—earlier in the morning.'

Antonia pouted at him and then smiled angelically

at him. 'You're an old bear,' she said fondly, 'and the trouble is no one ever tells you so or answers you back.'

She swallowed her coffee, got up, threw her arms round his neck to hug him fiercely and went to the door, where she turned. 'Actually,' she said kindly, 'you're rather nice—though I do hope your wife answers you back sometimes. Sappha does, someone like her would do very well.'

She waved airily at Sappha's startled face, blew her brother a kiss and went out, closing the door with a good deal of noise.

Sappha, aware that the Baron was watching her, fixed her eyes on her plate and because the silence became unbearable asked at last:

'Can I give you some more coffee?' and when he handed her his cup without a word, she plunged into small talk which became more and more involved and vaguer and vaguer until he cut into the jumble of senseless remarks.

'I have arranged for Mother to be X-rayed tomorrow—I shall have to go into hospital in any case, you may as well both come with me. Could you get her ready to leave the house by nine o'clock? I have a teaching round to do, but I daresay I can be free shortly after lunch, when I will bring you back.'

She took a quick peep at him. He was no longer a brigand, but detached and coolly friendly, as was his voice. She said quickly:

'Yes, of course we can be ready. I expect you will wish to tell the Baroness yourself.' She broke off as Hush, who had been sitting by the stove with the other dogs, came uncertainly across the room and made a determined effort to climb into her lap. He looked so

woebegone when he found that he couldn't quite manage it that she felt constrained to lift him up and give
him a cuddle, looking uncertainly at Rolf as she did so.
It was a relief to see a decided twinkle in his eyes as
he said blandly: 'You're quite right—I don't approve,
but like you, I feel that a little spoiling won't hurt him
for a day or two.'

Sappha gave him a grateful look and he went on:
'He slept with the cat in the kitchen, it was Mrs Burns'
idea and it seems to have worked, for when she came
down this morning they were sharing the cushion on
her chair.'

Sappha studied Hush, who was pretending to be
asleep. She said quietly:

'Thank you for taking him in, it was kind of you.
I—I wouldn't have known what to do with him...'

'No, you wouldn't, would you?' he agreed affably,
'though I daresay you would have persevered until you
had found someone foolish enough to give him a home.
How's Andrew?'

The abrupt change of topic was too much for her.
'Andrew? I—I...that is, I'm sure he's quite all right.
Why do you ask?'

He got up from the table. 'Search your memory, my
dear girl,' he advised suavely, 'then you can answer that
question for yourself.'

She hardly saw him for the rest of that day, for she
spent the morning with her patient, ironing out the
knottier points of the Baroness's clothes for the trip
to Groningen and trying gently to curb that lady's excited certainty that she would be perfectly able to walk
the moment the X-ray had been taken. Sappha ate her
lunch alone, with Joke serving her, a circumstance of

which she was glad, for it permitted her to try out her rudimentary Dutch with only Joke to laugh at her in a friendly way.

Tonia came home about four, looking so pretty and excited that Sappha's uneasy feelings returned to worry her. Had the girl got a boy-friend no one knew of—someone Rolf might not approve? Despite her pertness, Tonia was unsophisticated and so sweet-natured that she would fall an easy victim to the first plausible wolf to catch her eye. And when Rolf came home presently, Sappha was more than ever convinced that Antonia was concealing something from him. She went up to bed, wondering about Tonia, who despite her up-to-date appearance had been reared in a strict Protestant household, and Sappha had already realised that some Dutch Protestants were very strict indeed. She might have the thin veneer of a modern girl, but Sappha suspected that, under her fashionable suede jerkins, high boots, chain belts and trailing scarves, Antonia was still very young.

She was up early the following morning, because the Baroness, although one of the kindest and most sweet-natured women she had ever met, was quite incapable of being hurried. Sappha had reflected on several occasions that it was a good thing that her patient lived in comfortable circumstances and was surrounded by people who made it their business to see that her life was made as pleasant as possible—indeed, Sappha had found herself doing her utmost to smooth her patient's monotonous daily path, for although the Baroness had a great deal more than most women, she was invariably grateful for any small kindness and had shown great courage in the face of an illness which could have cost her her life.

The drive to Groningen was uneventful. Rolf had lifted his mother into the back of the car and when Sappha had got in beside her he had made no demur. It was left to the Baroness to point out the places of interest along the route, and she did this with obvious pleasure and a great number of asides as to the various castles and museums Sappha should visit.

'Menkemaborg Castle,' she mused, 'you must certainly go there—it isn't large, but it is old and some of the furniture is of great interest. If I remember aright, there are some splendid leather-covered walls in the gun room. The castle belonged at one time to a distant branch of my family.' She added as an agreeable afterthought: 'They make delicious *pannekoeken* in the restaurant there.'

Sappha, whose head was already filled with an indigestible mixture of windmills, churches, old family friends, museums and the like said rather faintly: 'Oh—how nice,' and heard Rolf laugh as he said:

'Poor Sappha—faint but pursuing. Have you had any days off yet?'

She stared at his back until she realised that he was watching her in the mirror above the windscreen. She said levelly: 'No—but I've had ample time to myself—I've explored Dokkum...'

'We'll have to do something about that.' His tone was crisply friendly. 'There's a great deal for you to see. I'll look into your free time this evening.'

She sat back a little so that he couldn't see her any more, and stared at the toes of her high brown boots, wishing she had a new coat to wear. The one she was wearing was warm, it was true, and a very good tweed, but it was last year's and she wanted to look absolutely eye-catching because she was with Rolf. She failed to realise that she looked quite a dish anyway, for the coat was a rich orange and brown and cream mixture, cut on military lines to show off her pretty figure, and her hat was of orange velvet, small and head-hugging. She looked good enough to eat, but unaware of this, she sat hankering after some dreamy spectacular outfit which would turn Rolf's head permanently in her direction, obediently turning her attractive head this way and that while the Baroness enlarged upon the geography of Groningen—and seeing none of it, because she had eyes only for Rolf, who was taking no more notice of her than he might have done of say, one of his mother's friends and according her the same polite attention. By the time they drew up in front of the hospital entrance she had almost persuaded herself that she really didn't care what he thought of her, but he smiled so delightfully at her when she got out of the car that she was forced to admit that nothing was further from the truth.

The hospital was large and put her in mind of all the other hospitals she had ever seen. There were the signposts telling you where to go—always provided you understood the language—there were the usual swing doors, the porters, the trolleys, the housemen, either in a great hurry or no hurry at all; there were the nurses too, looking like nurses all the world over, excepting for their caps, which she thought rather sweet, anyway. She turned from contemplating all these things to find a porter with a wheelchair at her elbow and the Baron on the point of lifting his mother into it. Seconds later she was walking sedately beside her patient with Rolf on the other side. She hadn't expected him to go with them and looked back over her shoulder at the Rolls, which he had left standing carelessly in the forecourt with one of its doors still open. Possibly he was something so grand on the hospital staff that he could do such things with impunity. Certainly the people they passed greeted him with respect; she wondered fleetingly if any of them had ever seen him in a sweater and old trousers, walking through Dialach, swinging fish from one hand... She wanted suddenly to be back there, walking beside him through the little town.

They reached the X-ray department presently, and were handed over to the Sister before Rolf bade them a cheerful goodbye and strode away down one of the hospital's interminable corridors. He had said nothing about seeing them again, or where they were to go when they had finished in X-ray. Sappha, at a smiling nod from Sister, removed the Baroness to a small cubicle to make her ready, and presently wheeled her out once more to meet the radiographer and Mijnheer de Winter, who wrung her hand delightedly and listened with relish while the Baroness recounted the rescue of the puppy. The radiographer enjoyed it too; they discussed the episode at some length, oblivious of Sister's impatient face peering round the door. Sappha felt sorry for her; probably the poor soul had a waiting room full of patients to be got through before lunchtime. It was a relief when the two gentlemen, having squeezed every ounce of amusement out of the Baroness's story, got down to business; straightforward business which took comparatively little time. This dealt with, the Baroness, once more dressed and in her wheelchair, was invited to take coffee with the Directrice, and since Sappha was pushing the chair, she was included in the invitation.

She sat between the two ladies in the Directrice's

comfortable office, listening to the Baroness's soft, excited voice and answering the questions put to her so shrewdly by her hostess, whose English was more than adequate to discuss hospital administration with her. The Directrice had an acquaintance with Scotland too, and presently became involved in a discussion with the Baroness, which left Sappha free to wonder what Rolf was doing. A ward round, probably—her imagination, always vivid, pictured a full complement of pretty nurses and a strikingly beautiful Ward Sister who was in love with him. So real was this picture that when the door opened and Mijnheer de Winter entered, with Rolf behind him, she stared at him as though he were a ghost, her eyes wide and her mouth open. He gave her a keen look and his eyebrows soared in enquiry, but he said nothing, merely giving her a brief nod as he took the coffee cup he was offered, leaving her to school her features as best she might; not that they mattered, for all the attention was focused upon the Baroness, who had sat up very straight and asked quickly: 'Well, I hope you have good news for me?'

Sappha looked at Mijnheer de Winter's face and decided that the news wasn't going to be quite as good as the Baroness expected. She got up casually and went and sat by her patient, who, while unlikely to burst into tears or throw a fit of hysterics, would probably be glad of a little moral support. It was a pity that Mr MacCombie hadn't been more vague when the Baroness had questioned him. He had said 'several more weeks', and they had been in Dokkum just over two weeks, and despite Sappha's gentle discouragement, the Baroness had made up her mind that today was D-Day. She watched the Baroness's face now, for Mijnheer de

Winter was speaking in Dutch and she couldn't hope
to understand a word. But she understood the expression upon her patient's face—disappointment. When
he had finished speaking, Sappha looked anxiously at
the Baron, who was standing with his back to the window, watching his mother as well. He crossed the room
at once, asking as he came:

'May I translate, de Winter? I daresay Sappha may
have some helpful ideas.' He smiled briefly at his
mother. 'Mother is naturally disappointed; Mijnheer
de Winter wants her to keep the weight off her leg for
another three weeks. He suggests a caliper to be worn
for a short period each day while Mother takes the gen-
tlest possible walking exercise.'

'I'm not sure what a caliper is,' his mother burst
out. 'It sounds horrible, and anyway, what is the use of
walking up and down my bedroom for a few minutes
at a time—I might just as well be in bed.' She blinked.
'I'm sorry to be so ill-natured.'

The Baron took her hand. 'It's not quite as bad as
that, Mother…'

Sappha interrupted him. She said energetically: 'It's
not bad at all. Why should you stay upstairs all day?
Why shouldn't you be carried down—Rolf can do it'—
she was unaware of using his name—'before he goes in
the morning—it doesn't matter how early. I can dress
you later, downstairs. You can have your friends to luncheon and tea, and can walk for five minutes in the
drawing room just as well as in your bedroom.'

She paused and the Baron interposed. 'Good girl,
Sappha, but it will make a great deal more work for
you.'

She turned on him. 'Oh, rubbish—don't you start…'

and came to an abrupt halt. Rolf's eyes were fastened on hers, the gleam in their depths could have been laughter, though his face was blank. She glanced quickly round the room. The Directrice was looking thunderstruck, Mijnheer de Winter amused, and the Baroness had such a look of deep satisfaction on her face that Sappha came to the erroneous conclusion that she hadn't heard what she had said. She meet the Baron's gaze, ignored the gleam and said woodenly: 'I'm sorry, Baron, I quite forgot we weren't alone,' and stopped for a second time, aware that she hadn't improved matters. Rolf allowed her a brief glimpse of his satyr's smile. He said with a graciousness to make her grit her teeth: 'Think nothing of it, Miss Devenish. Your idea is a good one—perhaps you have some further suggestions?'

She lifted her chin. 'As a matter of fact, I have. You suggested that I might drive a car while I was here; I could take the Baroness for drives—she could visit her friends...'

'Splendid—how do you propose to get my mother in and out of the car?'

'I shall think of something.'

'Of that I am sure.' He really was laughing at her now. 'Mother, what do you say? Shall we take advantage of Sappha's idea?' He squeezed the hand he was holding. 'Confess now, it won't be so bad after all. Another few weeks and you'll be quite well.'

His mother studied his face. 'Yes, dear. But I should like to know the reason for these extra weeks—and I am to be cured completely, or are you trying to make things easy for me?'

He laughed. 'No, dearest, you will be as good as new. The reason you must go slowly for another week or so is because the nature of your illness has made it more difficult for your bones to heal and unite.'

He looked across the room to Mijnheer de Winter, who nodded.

'Indeed, yes,' he said. 'If you will have just a little more patience, Baroness, and that shouldn't be too difficult now that your excellent nurse has made her suggestions,' he smiled kindly at Sappha, 'I think that we might have a glass of sherry to celebrate the happy ending, don't you?'

Rolf had moved nearer Sappha. 'Excuse us, will you?' he asked casually. 'I want Sappha to see something of the hospital. Come along, Sappha.'

She went with him, smiling a little uncertainly at the others as she went through the door. Outside in the corridor, Rolf took her arm.

'I've a ward round to do,' he said blandly, 'but I've asked Theatre Sister to take you to some of the wards— we'll go and collect her.'

Sappha walked beside him because there wasn't much else she could do. A dozen remarks, all unsuitable, trembled on her lips. She reminded herself just in time that there was no reason at all why he should go to the trouble of escorting her and composed her features into a pleasant smile in time to greet Theatre Sister, who was waiting for them at the end of the corridor and was, to Sappha's disgust, a raving beauty. What was more, she seemed to be on terms of the greatest possible friendliness with the Baron, who addressed her as Jan with the easy air of a very old friend. He said goodbye vaguely and disappeared up a staircase without looking back.

The hospital was large and well-equipped; despite

her unhappy feelings, Sappha couldn't help but be interested in it; besides, Jan turned out to be great fun and when she mentioned, in her excellent English, that she was leaving to get married in a week's time, Sappha felt quite a glow of friendship towards her. The morning hadn't been too successful, but at least this news cheered her up a little. They went over the theatre block thoroughly, for it was cleaning day, which meant that they could go anywhere they wished save for the one theatre kept ready for emergencies. They spent a long time in the children's ward too, and still longer in Women's Medical, and if it hadn't been for the fact that everyone was speaking a language different from her own, Sappha could have imagined herself at Greggs'.

As they went through the ward doors, Jan looked at her watch, murmured. 'It is just time, I think,' and started up the stone staircase to the floor above. Here there was another ward, its swing doors were opened wide as they approached, and Rolf, followed by his registrar, housemen, the Ward Sister and a nurse burdened with all the paraphernalia judged necessary for a consultant's round, stalked through. He stopped at the door, bade farewell to his companions with no apparent haste, and joined Sappha and her companion, who said: 'There, did I not get the time exactly right?' She smiled at them both, bade Sappha goodbye in her turn, and flew down the stairs, leaving them standing together while Rolf's recent entourage, still hanging around the ward doors, tried not to look curious. He glanced at them over his shoulder. 'Downstairs,' he said firmly, propelling her with a compelling hand down to the floor below. They passed a number of people on the way, all of whom stood back to let them pass, rather as though they had been royalty. When they reached the ground floor and were walking side by side along one of its corridors, Sappha observed nastily: 'You must be frightfully important.'

He flung open a door and she found herself in a dark brown room which could have been comfortable but wasn't. He shut the door carefully and leaned against it, facing her.

He said in a silky voice: 'Of course I'm important—just as I'm bold and bad—and what else was it?—a brigand. What did you expect? Oh, yes, Sappha, I take every possible advantage of my birth and position—a man with my deplorable character could do no less, could he? I like to be. I'm even an elder at St Martin's Church—that should make you laugh.'

She had taken the precaution of putting the width of the room between them, but now she turned away from the window and stormed across the wooden floor. She said furiously:

'I'm not amused, it's nothing to laugh about. How dare you talk like that? Of course you're an elder in the church, how could you be anything else when half the people buried there are your ancestors? You should be proud…'

She got no further, for he plucked her from the solid little table she was leaning against and caught her round the waist. 'Oh, Sappha,' he sighed, and kissed her.

'I don't think the elders would approve,' she said shakily when she had her breath back.

'In that case…' There was a knock at the door and he let her go as a young man came in—she recognised the Registrar, who smiled at her awkwardly and broke into earnest speech. Rolf listened, asked one or two questions and started for the door, taking her with him.

'Something's cropped up,' he gave her a little push in the opposite direction to the one he was taking himself. 'Fourth door on your right,' he said shortly. 'I'll see you later.'

She knocked and went inside, and was relieved to see the Baroness, still with her two companions. They all looked at her as she went in and the Baroness said: 'Back already, dear? We have had such a nice talk.' Her eyes searched Sappha's face. 'You enjoyed yourself, I hope?'

Sappha sat down on the nearest chair. 'Yes,' she replied, surprised to find herself still breathless. 'Very much, Baroness.'

She had plenty of opportunity to recover from her enjoyment during the following days. It was true that she saw Rolf each morning, for he carried his mother downstairs before he left the house. He carried her back in the evenings too, but these operations were hardly conducive to more than an exchange of commonplace remarks and he made no attempt to be alone with her. Not that she would have had much opportunity anyway, for now that the Baroness spent her days downstairs, Sappha had a great deal more to do besides the walking exercises several times a day and the massage. She rather welcomed the extra work, it kept her fully occupied and the improvement in her patient's condition was well worth the effort; besides, she still had an hour or two free in the afternoons.

On one of them she had begged the loan of the Mini and explored the flat, tranquil land around Dokkum. It had been a cold day and windy with a pale blue sky of which there seemed a great deal by reason of the horizon being so wide. She had gone to Bolwerd and watched the ferry leaving for Ameland, a few miles off the coast. It was bare and bleak on the dyke and the sea looked unfriendly. She preferred the little town, where she bought some cakes because standing on the wind-blown shore had made her hungry; she bought postcards to send home and went back to the car and wrote them before driving back again.

It wasn't until the following Sunday that Rolf appeared at breakfast. To Sappha's surprise the Baroness had expressed a wish to stay in bed for the day. She had, she declared happily, made a great deal of progress in the last few days, so she was going to write letters and read. Sappha went down to her breakfast wondering if she might suggest to her patient that she might have at least part of the day off. The morning routine wouldn't take long; Antonia and Rolf were both home and Victoria and her husband were coming to lunch. She took her place at the table, returned her companions' good mornings, and commenced her breakfast. She was buttering a roll when Rolf said formally: 'Antonia and I would be delighted if you would accompany us to church.'

Sappha stared at her knife, poised above the roll, vividly remembering her awful remarks about him being an elder. She said, with a politeness equal to his own: 'How kind—but I don't see how I can. There are things to do for the Baroness...'

Rolf said patiently: 'I am aware of that. Annie and Mrs Burns will be delighted to do them for you. Church is at ten o'clock, we will meet in the hall at ten minutes to the hour.' He got up. 'If you will excuse me?'

When he had gone Antonia observed sympathetically: 'When he comes the baron over you there's nothing much you can do about it, is there? I stop him, of course, but I don't suppose you feel you should. Still, I'm glad you're coming to church.'

Sappha helped herself to some rye bread and reached for the cheese.

'I'm coming,' she declared clearly, 'because I am interested in attending one of your church services. Not that I shall understand a word.'

The Baroness proved unexpectedly brisk. Sappha, convinced that she had done all she could for her patient's comfort, went to her own room to dress. It was a gloomy day and cold, so there was nothing for it but to wear the tweed coat again, only this time she wore a wool dress of a pleasing shade of brown beneath it. She went down the stairs at exactly ten minutes to ten and found Antonia in the hall, sitting on the arm of one of the great carved chairs, reading a letter which she stuffed hastily into her handbag when she saw Sappha coming towards her. She broke into speech at once. 'How nice you look. Here's Rolf…it's only a short walk.' She prattled on with an artlessness and speed that made Sappha wonder thoughtfully about the hastily concealed letter. There was no chance to find out, for Rolf, calmly unhurried beside her, was listening to his sister with a half smile, obviously diverted. Sappha stole a look at him as they went; he appeared immaculate and aloof in his well-cut clothes, as unlike the unshaven man she had met on her journey to Dialach as it was possible to find. He looked down suddenly and caught her staring, then smiled, and she saw how completely wrong she was. He was indeed the same man.

The church was full, which was something she had

expected. She had read a great deal about Dokkum and asked questions besides; she knew all about its religious history. Religion, she thought, was important to people of the little town, probably to the whole province. Perhaps that was why they seemed so content with their lives, and why they were friendly and good-natured, although she had the idea that any of the large, calm men around her could show a magnificent rage in a good cause.

It was a pleasant surprise to find that she knew most of the hymn tunes although she was the only person there not singing. She listened to the volume of sound rising to the roof, almost drowning the organ, and she listened to Antonia's clear treble too, and Rolf's deep, well-controlled roar.

The service wasn't so hard to follow with Tonia and Rolf to look after her. When Rolf got up to join the other elders and take the collection she didn't look up from her hymn book; not until he was standing beside their pew, holding the little black velvet bag on its long cane handle—which she might have found amusing if it hadn't been Rolf holding it—did she look up to find him gazing at her, his face grave but with a look in his eye to send the delicate pink sweeping over her face. She bent her head and kept it bent when he returned to sit beside her for the sermon, which was long, so that her thoughts began to wander. Presently, when she thought it was safe to do so, she peeped at him. In profile he looked haughty, due, no doubt, to the arrogant thrust of his domineering nose, but when he turned his head and smiled at her, he looked kind and gentle…he would smile like that at his children…

She became lost in a daydream, in which the pew

was peopled with several delightful children, with Rolf
at one end and herself at the other—or perhaps she
would be at home with the baby—no, there would probably be a nanny. He laid a gentle hand on hers and she
jumped so hard that she dropped her book. The sermon
was ended, they sang another hymn and then the con-
gregation surged out into the grey day, breaking up into
groups which disintegrated into little streams of people making their way across the square to the various
streets leading them home.

Victoria had arrived when they returned and coffee
was being served in the Baroness's bedroom; Sappha,
on some pretext or another, slipped away—the family
would want to talk, to say things that were no concern
of hers. She went to her room and tossed off her hat,
and was unbuttoning her coat when there was a knock
on the door and Rolf came in.

'Put your hat on again,' he said affably. 'You've got
the rest of the day off—we're going out.' He crossed
the room to where she was standing and rebuttoned her
coat and she said, puzzled: 'I don't understand.'

His voice was bland. 'It's quite simple and very harm-
less. We are going to Menkemaborg—remember? Where
the pancakes are. If we go now we shall have time to eat
some before we look round the castle.'

'Your sister—and her husband, they've come to
lunch…and your mother—you see so little of them all.'

'I see so little of you, Sappha.'

She started to unbutton her coat again, unaware of
what she was doing.

'Yes, but you don't need to see me.'

He sighed. 'Sappha, allow me to know what I need—

and now I have to do up your coat once more. Have you heard from Glover lately?'

It was the last thing she had expected him to say. She shook her head.

He said, frowning: 'He's not for you, Sappha—not a girl like you. If you were my sister I should take good care that he didn't get you.'

Sappha's heart, which had been thumping excitedly against her ribs did a double knock of disappointment and then began a renewed hammering when he went on: 'Not that I regard you in the light of a sister, my dear Sappha.'

She looked at him and found him smiling. 'Put on your hat,' he wheedled. 'I want you to myself.' He went to the door and opened it. 'I'll be in the hall in five minutes.'

Five minutes wasn't long; she achieved the repair of her make-up, the exact and most becoming angle of her hat, a discreet spray of *Ma Griffe* and a short visit to the Baroness's room. Her patient knew all about it, apparently, for she said: 'There you are, dear. I'm so glad you're going to Menkemaborg, I know you will love it and Rolf can answer your questions so much better than I.'

'It's very kind…' began Sappha, to be cut short by the Baroness's quick 'Nonsense—you've had no fun at all. I'm perfectly comfortable and Victoria will be here until after tea. Tonia is meeting some school friends, but Annie is in, and so is Mrs Burns, so you see, I shall be well looked after,' She gave Sappha a bright glance. 'That's a dear little hat,' she commented. 'Now run along.'

Thus dismissed, Sappha went down to the hall, to

find Rolf waiting with Charlie beside him. He smiled at her.

'Hush wanted to come too, but I think he's better in the kitchen with Moggy, don't you? She thinks he's a kitten and the mothering is doing him good. When he's a little older we'll try him on short runs.'

He opened the car door and she got in and sat silent while he fastened her seat belt and then turned away to let Charlie into the back of the car before getting in beside her. As the big car purred into life, he said: 'We'll go through Kollom and take the byroads to Munnekezijl and Ulrum, that'll cut off a corner and bring us to Warffum. We can turn off there for Uithuizen.'

Sappha nodded happily; if he had said that they would be going by way of the North Pole or the South Sea Islands, it would have made no difference to her feelings. She leaned back against the soft leather and allowed herself to forget all but the delights of the moment. Rolf looked at his watch. 'A quarter to twelve,' he remarked, 'we should take about an hour—just nice time to work up an appetite for the *spek pannekoeken*.'

'Pancakes,' and Sappha, anxious to air her Dutch, 'but haven't I seen *spek* in the butcher's?'

'Yes, it's fat pork, fried very crisp and eaten with syrup.'

She asked faintly: 'Oh, shall I like it? It sounds rather—rather...'

'Wait and see. If it revolts you you shall have something else, but I think you'll like it. What are your plans for the future—have you any?'

He had snapped his questions out so fast that she was still thinking about the pancakes; now she paused before she answered. She would have dearly loved to tell him then and there that she had no future, not with Andrew at any rate, but it seemed unfair to take advantage of his recent efforts to get on a more friendly footing with her, for she had endangered it on several occasions in the past. She had been, she realised now, far too quick to squabble, and she should have told him about Andrew. It was too late now, he so obviously thought that she and Andrew…she said now with an assumption of ease: 'No—at least, no cut and dried ones. I shall wait until I get back to London.'

'Andrew,' said Rolf pleasantly, and she echoed like a fool, 'Andrew,' letting him believe what he liked. It was strange, though, that the mention of Andrew's name seemed to clear the air before they forgot him completely. There was so much to talk about; so many questions Sappha wanted to ask, and such an exchange of views and opinions about everything under the sun, the journey passed in a flash and she noticed nothing of the country through which they passed.

Menkemaborg was a lovely surprise. She hadn't quite known what to expect—Dutch castles were a little deceptive, judging from those that had already been pointed out to her, for they resembled English country houses, but this really was a castle, not large as castles go, but old, its three wings grey-stoned and moated. Sappha wandered to the edge of the paved courtyard and studied the gardens; they were beautiful too, even in the sombre light of the chilly day. She turned round to meet Rolf, who had been dealing with Charlie's wants, and caught the sleeve of his coat to draw his attention to the swans on the moat. She said happily, forgetful of everything but the delight of his company: 'It's lovely here—the Baroness said that someone in her family lived here, a long time ago, I suppose.'

Rolf possessed himself of her hand and tucked it under his arm.

'The Albarda family—extinct, at least this branch is—that was at the turn of the century. I can't remember who inherited it, but it was given to the Province of Groningen—rather like the National Trust.'

'So no one lives here now. That's sad.'

He smiled a little. 'Yes, it is—but on the other hand it would cost a fortune to keep the place warm in winter. Come and eat that pancake.'

The restaurant was in the old barn-like building in the courtyard, there were quite a few people in it and it was gloriously warm and smelled of something freshly baked. They sat down at a red-checked covered table and drank coffee while they waited for their pancakes and when they came, Sappha exclaimed: 'But I couldn't possibly eat all that!' for they were enormous, the size of the large plates upon which they were served, and thick too. Rolf passed her the stone jar of syrup.

'At least see how far you can get.' He gave her a tolerant look that put her in mind of a good-natured, coaxing father, and when he saw the expression on her face, he asked: 'Why do you look at me like that?'

She was disconcerted that her thoughts had shown in her face and for want of anything better she said lamely: 'Nothing.'

He put his handsome head on one side. 'You are the most unconvincing liar I have ever had to do with.' His voice was light and robbed his words of any seriousness and he said nothing more, but turned away to speak to a passing waitress who presently returned with two tall glasses.

'To wash down the pancakes,' he explained, 'Pilsener beer.'

She took a sip and found it to her liking. 'Nice,' she said approvingly. 'Do you often do this?'

He was intent on adding a little more syrup to his pancake. 'Not often, it's hardly a place one would come to on one's own.'

She opened her lovely eyes wide. 'But I don't suppose you go anywhere on your own, at least, you don't need to.'

'You allude to girl-friends, am I right? Of course you have made up your mind that I have a large number—they fit nicely into my degenerate life, do they not? For your information, I have one girl-friend…' he stopped because Sappha had dropped her fork, he passed her a fresh one and went on smoothly: 'Unfortunately she happens to be someone else's girl-friend as well.'

Sappha sat looking at the food of her plate—it would be impossible to swallow any more of it because her heart was in her throat which was making breathing difficult, let alone swallowing.

'I'm sure you'd like to know her name,' Rolf went on, still smooth and she said urgently. 'No—oh, no,' in a small choking voice which he paid no attention to at all. 'Her name's Sappha,' he smiled at her as he said her name and waited, still without breath, for what he would say next. 'I thought you might like to know,' he said softly, his satyr's grin came and went. 'You see, my hands are tied until she decides who she will have. Though perhaps I should warn her that that would make no difference to me—I shall wait for her, if I have to, all my life. I have one virtue which even she must allow me—patience.'

He looked at his watch and when he spoke again it was in quite a different voice. 'If you've gone as far as you can with your pancake, shall we go—the door opens at one o'clock.'

Sappha went around the castle without seeing a thing. She gazed, when told to do so, at furniture, wallpapers, tiled floors, state beds and the like, without seeing any of them. They were in the kitchen, a large semi-basement room with tiled walls and floor, and their small sightseeing party had fanned out, the better to examine its accoutrements. Sappha studied a nappy dryer, circa seventeenth century, until she could have drawn it blindfold, and then realised that the others had gone into one of the little side rooms and she and Rolf were alone. She caught his amused eye and plunged at once into conversation which became more and more involved as she persevered with it. She had commented at least twice upon a goffering iron on the table before them, and was enlarging upon the beauties of the copper warming pans hanging on the walls when Rolf said gently, cutting her off in mid-sentence:

'Dear girl, you're not afraid of me?'

His calm calmed her too so that she said at once in a serious little voice: 'No, Rolf.'

'Then you can't make up your mind to tell me something.'

She said, still serious: 'Yes,' thinking how easy it would be to tell him that she loved him now, but she had to tell him about Andrew first and it was really rather difficult in the middle of a mediaeval kitchen with a number of people likely to rejoin them at any moment. She looked at him helplessly.

'All right, Sappha, I can wait—I'll not ask you to

pluck up courage today, tell me in your own time. And
now if you've finished examining this dull object, whatever it is, I see the guide is looking at us with every sign
of impatience.'

For the rest of the afternoon, Rolf was nothing but a
charming, agreeable companion, who talked amusingly
and knowledgeably upon a dozen topics. By the time
they were home again she was completely at her ease
once more; the evening passed pleasantly and the only
references made to their afternoon's outing had been
of a most impersonal nature. She got ready for bed in a
dreamy state which allowed of no other thoughts than
those of Rolf. He had said very little to her the whole
evening, but she hadn't minded; she wanted time to sa-
vour the happiness she had almost given up. She walked
about the pretty room, brushing her hair and finally sat
down before the delicate Louis Seize dressing table. She
was staring at her face in its mirror when there was a
light tap on the door and Antonia came in.

'I hoped you would be awake, Sappha. I want to
tell you something. It's exciting.' She smiled seraphi-
cally and flung herself down on the bed. 'You'll never
guess...'

'No, I shan't,' said Sappha with a touch of asperity,
because she wanted to be alone with her thoughts, 'unless you choose to tell me.'

'Andrew's here—in Dokkum—I went out with him
this afternoon!'

Sappha said nothing for several seconds; her forebod-
ings had been right, she felt them crowding back, shutting out her happiness. At last she said quietly: 'Why
is he here, and does your mother or—or Rolf know?'

'He's here because I wrote and asked him to come,

and no one knows, only you, and you aren't a bit thrilled, are you, Sappha? I don't believe you love him after all. I thought perhaps you didn't, but I didn't tell him that because I had to use you as an excuse to get him to come,' she paused and smiled naughtily. 'We had a lovely afternoon together; I think he likes me very much and he thinks I'm the prettiest girl he's ever met, and I told him I should have a lot of money when I'm eighteen...'

Sappha looked at her in horror. 'Tonia, you didn't!'

Antonia nodded happily. 'Yes, I did. I think he's marvellous—he said he could fall for a girl like me, and I expect I could twist him round my little finger if I wanted to.'

Sappha said gently, trying to be calm and say the right thing: 'Look, Tonia dear, you're sixteen, you'll meet lots of boys—men—in the next few years. Andrew is much older than you—of course he thinks you're pretty, you are, very, but that doesn't mean he's serious about you.'

Antonia rolled over on her back. 'If you weren't such a nice girl, Sappha, I might think you were jealous.'

Sappha let this pass, she said earnestly: 'Tonia, you must tell your mother or Rolf—promise me, you must!'

Antonia got off the bed and came across the room to fling an arm around Sappha's dressing-gowned shoulders. 'Darling Sappha, of course I'll tell.' She danced to the door where she paused. 'You won't sneak on me, Sappha—you won't tell Rolf?'

Sappha said soberly: 'No, I won't tell,' and Antonia blew her a kiss and slipped out of the room. Sappha sat for a long time, her thoughts busy as well as unhappy. Rolf was going to be furious, for he adored his young sister; on the other hand Antonia, despite her flippancy, stood a little in awe of her brother. Sappha longed to rush down to the study and tell Rolf all about it, but of course she couldn't—she had promised. Besides, she could imagine the incredulity on his face when she told him—he might even think that she was using Antonia as an excuse for Andrew's sudden visit. After all, she hadn't told Rolf that she loved him and she had told him that very afternoon that there was something she had to tell him. He would draw his own conclusions and hate her coldly for being a fickle hussy.

She got into bed at last, her thoughts chasing each other round and round inside her tired head until, from sheer weariness, she fell asleep.

Chapter 9

There was no one at breakfast when Sappha went downstairs the next morning, and when Mrs Burns, who had popped her head round the door to enquire if she had all she wanted, volunteered the information that Antonia had had breakfast with her brother and gone off early because she was going to school in a friend's car, Sappha's doubts and fears came rushing back tenfold, especially when Mrs Burns went on to say that the master and his sister hadn't been so gay for a long time. 'Laughing and joking, they were,' she chuckled, 'all about a fur hat Miss Antonia's set her heart on.' There was a great deal more in the same vein, but Sappha, while contriving to look interested, wasn't really listening. It would seem that Antonia hadn't told Rolf about Andrew. She finished her breakfast without appetite and set about the rather slow business of getting the Baroness dressed, thinking what a pity it was that she

had missed Rolf when he had gone to carry his mother
downstairs, even though she would have been able to
say nothing to him, but it would have been nice, she
thought wistfully, just to have seen him. Perhaps Antonia intended to tell him when she got back from school.
She stifled a sigh and started to strap on the Baroness's
caliper, preparatory to the morning exercises.

Sia arrived unexpectedly just before lunch, declared
her intention of staying for the meal and spending an hour
or so with her mother afterwards, and suggested that Sappha might like to go out directly the meal was over, an
offer which Sappha was only too glad to accept—a long
walk might help her think, besides there was something
she had to do. If Andrew was in Dokkum he would be
staying in one of the two hotels—probably De Posthoorn;
she would go there and see him and make him see that
the sensible thing to do would be to go back to London
before anyone else knew that he was there. Probably he
would be difficult, for Antonia had behaved very badly
and he wasn't a man to trifle with when it came to his
own dignity. Fired by this decision, Sappha pulled on her
raincoat, tied a scarf carelessly under her chin, snatched
up her gloves and made her way to the hotel.

There was no one in the warm welcoming hall, nor
was there anyone in the little bar beyond, for it was that
quiet hour after luncheon which occurs in most hotels.
She opened the door of the coffee room and that was
empty too; she was just about to explore more deeply
into the passages behind the staircase when a man and a
woman came down it, and they were speaking English, or
at least, Sappha amended, they were Americans speaking
English. The woman was middle-aged, well dressed and
still pretty, the man—her husband, almost for certain her

husband—was tall, thin and stooping. Sappha advanced
upon them and began: 'Excuse me…'

The man paused in front of her and smiled nicely. 'Why,
honey,' he observed, 'this little lady speaks English.' They
stood together, looking at her as though they had made a
delightful discovery.

'Well, I am English,' said Sappha composedly, 'and
you must forgive me for butting in like this, but I can't
find anyone to ask if Mr Glover is staying here or not,' she
added. 'My name's Devenish—Miss Sappha Devenish.'

They shook her by the hand and introduced themselves as Mr and Mrs Winkelman, and Mrs Winkelman added with a touch of pride: 'My husband's got
Dutch ancestry—and we just had to come and see where
they're from.' She smiled proudly. 'To think they came
from a little town like this! You wanted to know about
Dr Glover, my dear—yes, he's staying here—and a very
talented young man he is by all accounts—he went
away quite early this morning—he had to drive someone to Leeuwarden, wasn't it, John?'

She appealed to her husband, who said that he
thought that was the town and would Sappha like them
to give him a message when he got back?

Sappha said no, thank you in a polite voice which
successfully disguised how appalled she was at their
news, for it must surely mean that Andrew had gone
with Antonia, and even if she had gone to school, there
was still the midday break when they could have met.
She said: 'I'll come back later,' and smiled and wished
them a pleasant stay and hoped that they would meet
again, before she made her escape.

Less than an hour later, as the Winkelmans were on
their way upstairs again after a walk through the town,

Rolf pushed open the hotel door and strode down the hall to speak to the porter in the bar. Mrs Winkelman paused to look at him, for, as she was at pains to tell her husband later, he was well worth looking at. 'So tall—almost a giant, one might say—and so dark, and did you hear his voice, John? Sort of compelling.' She thought for a moment and then said with satisfaction: 'Arrogant, that's the word I want, but nice with it—I wonder what he wanted?'

Sappha had gone out of the hotel not really caring where she went just so long as she could think. She turned in the direction of the bridge, crossed the Zijl and walked briskly along its further bank, past the picturesque apothecary's shop and the smaller, just as quaint houses beyond it and presently crossed a narrow bridge which led her back into the town, where she walked up one street and down the next, not noticing where she was at all, her thoughts busy with the fact that Rolf would be home that evening. There was nothing she wanted to do more than throw herself in his arms and pour out the whole story—but that was for Antonia. She shivered, and quickened her steps, for it was cold as well as wet; she could have gone into the hotel and had some tea, but for once the idea didn't appeal to her; instead she made her way to the museum.

If the curator found it strange that this was her third visit within a fortnight, he allowed nothing of the thought to show, but opened the door wide to admit her, commented briefly in his basic English upon the weather and asked her if she wanted to see anything in particular.

She said at once: 'Oh, yes please. The first floor— those cases of ornaments and jewellery.' She added hesitantly: 'Do you have to be with me? I mean, I only want to look around for half an hour—it's so quiet here.'

He caught the gist of her remarks and smiled. 'You know your way, miss,' he smiled again, and watched while she mounted the plank staircase.

It was blissfully peaceful, with the deep quiet of aged things and she pottered slowly round, half of her mind trying to decipher the cards on the exhibits while the other half thought about Rolf. She was standing in front of a case containing the gold and silver ornaments worn by Friesian women of earlier times, when there was a murmur of voices below and a step on the stair. Sappha frowned, because it looked as though her peace was about to be disturbed, and kept her back to the staircase to discourage even the 'Good day', which was the custom even with strangers.

But this was no stranger. Rolf said from the head of the stairs:

'Hello—I should have come here first, instead of peering into every shop in town. I thought you might have been in De Posthoorn, drinking your English tea, but they said they hadn't seen you.'

She went a little pale at that—he couldn't know about Andrew then, and of course the only people to have seen her there were that nice American couple. She said faintly: 'Hello, I thought you would be working.' The white of her cheeks pinkened a little. 'That is, you usually do...'

'I took the afternoon off. What's the use of having an excellent Registrar if he can't do my work for me occasionally? Besides, I owe him one for bursting in on us the other day in the hospital.'

He crossed the creaking wood floor and stood before

her eyeing her narrowly. 'What are you looking at?' he wanted to know.

She spoke in a nervous rush. 'I like these ornaments, only I don't know what they are—I can guess some of them, but this?'

She pointed to a small silver box, embellished with scrollwork; it was oblong and only a few inches in length; it was nicely lined with velvet. When Rolf saw at what she was pointing he laughed with such genuine amusement that she asked a little sharply: 'What's so funny about it?'

'It's not funny, Sappha, only appropriate. You see, it's an engagement box—once upon a time young Friesians took such a box with them when they went courting, and when they proposed they handed it to the girl of their choice—it held the ring.'

'That's charming,' and then, although she hadn't meant to say it, 'Why is it appropriate?'

He caught her suddenly round the waist. 'Because if I had such a box, I should give it to you, dear girl.'

And when she looked up into his face he smiled at her with a tenderness to touch her heart and said: 'This will have to do instead,' and bent and kissed her with slow deliberation, then kissed her for the second time with no deliberation at all so that she was left breathless.

Neither of them had heard the footsteps on the stairs until the American exclaimed jovially: 'Why, hullo there!' Rolf loosed her slowly, tucking her arm under his as he did so. He said politely, 'Good afternoon,' and Sappha saw the American's wife pluck at his sleeve and frown, so that instead of advancing towards them as he had obviously intended to do, he said feebly: 'Well, nice to see you,' and allowed himself to be led away to the other end of the long room, where he was presently joined by the curator. Rolf murmured—and she could hear the laugh in his voice as he spoke: 'The study, I think—with the door locked!' He gave her a wicked look as they went downstairs and out through the side door which gave on to the paved path at the side of the museum. The Rolls was on the other side of the road, parked by the water, and it was only when they were both in it and Rolf had switched on the engine that he spoke again.

'We'll go through the town, Sappha, as I have to call at the surgery.' He gave her a singularly sweet smile as he put the car into gear.

They would have to turn up into the town past De Posthoorn to reach the surgery. In the midst of her happiness Sappha knew with devastating certainty that Andrew's car would be parked in front of the hotel.

It was. And what was far worse, Andrew was just getting out of it. She made a small sound, half sigh, half sob when she saw him, but it wasn't until they had almost reached the centre of the town that Rolf spoke. 'Did you know Andrew Glover was here?' His voice was silkily polite.

Sappha said miserably: 'Yes.'

'You called at the hotel this afternoon? Before I met you?'

'Yes—I...'

He interrupted her smoothly. 'Shall we talk about it later?' He had pulled up in front of the surgery. 'I shan't be many minutes.'

She sat, utterly miserable, rehearsing what she would say to him presently. Perhaps she should wait until they got home, because Antonia would be there and if she explained he would know that she herself had had no part in meeting Andrew—indeed, she thought crossly, she hadn't met him, and didn't intend to except on Antonia's behalf. Rolf got back into the car again, and began almost immediately to discuss the practice in a perfectly natural voice which nonetheless made it impossible for her to say anything about Andrew. The short ride became a nightmare which she couldn't wish over fast enough, but the nightmare didn't end when they reached the house, for they were met by Mrs Burns with the news that Antonia thought she had a wee cold and had thought it prudent to go to bed. She had taken some Disprin and hot lemon and begged that no one should disturb her.

Sappha went upstairs to change into uniform, for naturally there was no question of going to Rolf's study. He had opened its door and gone inside himself with not so much as a look in her direction. She supposed that a girl with more spirit might have said something or done something, but she felt strangely empty inside and quite dim in her wits. Probably a good thing, she thought wryly, if she was to get through the evening without making a fool of herself.

Sia was still with her mother, and as Sappha went into the room, both ladies looked at her closely, so that she felt constrained to start an animated description of Mr and Mrs Winkelman. When she had finally finished and was busying herself with her patient's medicine, the Baroness asked casually: 'Did Rolf find you, dear? I told him of all the places you usually visit.'

Sappha came across the room with a medicine glass. She said colourlessly: 'Yes, thank you—in the Museum.' Her voice faltered a little as she said it, because she remembered what had happened there. 'Shall I let the doctor know you're ready to go down, Baroness?'

'Am I, dear?' asked her patient absent-mindedly. 'Well, Sia's going now, she will no doubt want a word with Rolf as she leaves—she'll tell him.'

Sia got up without demur, kissed her mother, collected her handbag, slung her expensive fur coat over one shoulder, and with a friendly wave to Sappha went out of the door, closing it gently behind her. Scarcely had she done so when the Baroness said:

'Sappha, there's something the matter—tell me quickly.' She added wistfully: 'You were so happy...'

Sappha summoned a smile and said with forced cheerfulness:

'It's nothing, Baroness—not worth talking about.' She went on, in the same determinedly cheerful voice. 'I've been thinking, how about a drive tomorrow? You could visit some friends perhaps—I'll wrap you up warm and I promise you I'll drive carefully...' She broke off as Rolf came in and to avoid his look she turned away and made a pretence of picking up Leo, who wouldn't allow her to touch him anyway.

Listening to Rolf talking at dinner later on, Sappha began to wonder if she had dreamed that awful bit about Andrew, for she could detect no crack in the Baron's facade of cheerful friendliness, only towards the end of the meal she looked up unexpectedly and found his eyes upon her. They looked black and held no expression whatsoever.

When, finally, she had put the Baroness to bed, she went to Antonia's room, because she knew that unless she talked to Antonia she wouldn't sleep at all that night. She knocked gently, and when there was no answer, she went in.

Antonia wasn't there. If she had gone to bed as she had said, then she had got up again, and most unlikely of all, she had made her bed with Joke's incredible neatness. Sappha looked round the room. The clothes Antonia usually wore to school were cast down upon a chair—the closet door was open and it didn't take much intelligence on Sappha's part to see that the new outfit she had badgered Rolf to buy for her and which had arrived only the day before wasn't among the dresses and coats hanging there. Sappha switched out the light and went back to her room, and then, because she didn't lack courage, went downstairs to the drawing room, so that if Rolf wanted to talk to her she would be there, although she had no idea of what she was going to say to him.

At eleven o'clock Mrs Burns, coming in to put the fireguard before the fire, looked at her in surprise. 'What,' she said, 'sitting here all alone, and the house so quiet? Miss Tonia in bed, puir wee lass, and the master gone to Leeuwarden to some big reception at the Burgemeester's house. He won't be back until the small hours—there'll be those to amuse him, I've no doubt.' She took a good look at Sappha's face and said comfortably: 'Och, lassie, go to ye bed, ye're tired to death.'

Sappha obediently got to her feet, for there was no point in waiting any longer now—Rolf didn't want to talk about Andrew. Probably he would be coldly polite until she left his house, and that, she thought shrewdly, wouldn't be long if he had the arranging of it. Obviously he thought that she had been fooling him—all the same, he could have given her the chance to explain. She went tiredly upstairs under Mrs Burns' motherly eye and once in her room, went and sat by the window, her thoughts still busy. Of course Antonia would have known about Rolf going out—probably she had taken a key with her. All the same, Sappha decided to wait up and see her—she wasn't likely to be very late.

She stayed by the window, and after careful thought turned out the light. She could just see the street and there was enough light from the distant street lamps to identify any car which might stop at the gates. She dozed a little as the night wore on, and presently, fearful of falling sound asleep, she got to her feet, doing odds and ends of jobs to pass the time. It was almost three o'clock when she heard a car coming down the street. She had been busy for the last half hour or so altering one of her dresses—one she had never worn in Dokkum—a green silk jersey, a little too elaborate for the quiet life she led in Dokkum. She had been trying it on before the long mirror on the closet door and now she hastily switched off the wall light she had been using and ran to the window, pulling back the heavy curtain the better to peer through the streaming rain as Andrew's car came through the gates and pulled up before the door.

She ran from the room, flew soundlessly down the stairs and crossed the hall to the front door. There was a solitary wall light casting a soft glow over the shot bolts and heavy key in the great door's lock. It was a matter of moments to draw the bolts, for they were well oiled, as was the key, and pausing only to snatch up her umbrella from the inner porch, she slipped outside and down the steps to the car. Antonia was getting out and although it was dark for Sappha to see either of its occupants, she was aware of tension in the air, although there was no time to investigate its cause. She caught Antonia by the hand, bustled her under the shelter of the umbrella and into the house, and only then, as they reached the door, did she realise that no one had spoken a word.

She pushed the girl gently inside, shook the umbrella free of raindrops and put it back in its place before turning to close the door. She did this carefully and without haste, for although her instinct was to question Antonia immediately, she realised there would be time enough to do so when they were in one or other of the bedrooms, the thing was to get her upstairs and into bed... She was easing the final bolt gently home when she heard a gasp from her companion and turned round. The study door was open, and Rolf, leaning relaxed against it, was watching her. She stood speechless, aware that there was truth after all in that old saying about being rooted to the spot. She stood like stone, while her eyes registered the fact that Rolf, in a white tie and tails, was quite magnificent. Of course, he had been to the Burgemeester's reception, and he must have returned while she dozed; the possibility of that happening hadn't occurred to her.

He said pleasantly: 'Have I disturbed you? Naturally you would have expected me to be in bed.' He put out a deliberate hand and switched on the light, flooding them all in the brilliance of the great crystal chandelier above their heads, and looked at his watch, and then at Sappha. She caught her breath at the anger in his eyes and made a small nervous gesture with a hand to smooth her hair—to find it soaking wet, as was her dress. She had forgotten the rain, but when she darted a look at Antonia she saw that she was miraculously, and because of the umbrella, bone dry. She licked her dry lips, trying to think of something to say before Antonia gave herself away by blurting out the whole sorry business. She stalled for time. 'It's my fault—Andrew...' she began, to be interrupted by Rolf's strangely harsh voice.

'Don't bother with excuses, Sappha. I am, I believe, a tolerant man, you may do as you please with your own life, but surely you realise that to drag Antonia into your—nocturnal junketings is rather more than I can tolerate?'

He walked over to his sister and put a large comforting arm around her shoulders. His voice held icy contempt. 'Could you not have borrowed the back door key from one of the servants?'

Sappha, her mouth slightly open, listened to him. He believed that she had been the one to go out, and, meanly enough, had prevailed upon Tonia to let her in—logical enough on the face of things, for she was not drenched with circumstantial evidence, even to the kind of dress a girl might wear for an evening out with a boy-friend—and she was wet, while Antonia was most innocently dry and on top of that he had, in his arrogance, taken it for granted that she had gone to see Andrew that afternoon; if he chose to think she was capable of such behaviour after what had occurred in the museum that afternoon, then she had no intention of telling him the truth; besides, she couldn't, even if she wanted to, because of Antonia, standing there like a frightened child, terrified of being found out. Sappha, with tremendous effort, managed to smile.

'I'm sorry, Tonia, I should have known better—I hope it is quite understood that I am to blame.'

She was rewarded by such a look of gratitude from

Antonia that for the time being at any rate the lie had been worthwhile. She watched while Antonia, with a murmured good night, started up the staircase, and after a moment's hesitation, essayed to follow her, to be stopped by Rolf's cold voice.

'Perhaps you will spare a few minutes? I daresay a brief talk will make little difference to you at this hour of night—or should I say morning?' He held the door behind him wide and stood aside as she passed him and went into his study. It was lighted only by a powerful reading lamp on his desk, which was a jumble of papers and medical journals and opened letters. He shut the door quietly and walked across to his desk and sat down behind it, leaving her to stand. She lifted her chin at the slight as she waited for him to speak. Which presently he did, in a chill, remote voice which made him seem like a stranger.

'You will agree with me, will you not, that it is best that you leave my house as soon as possible?'

And Sappha, who was a reasonable girl and knew how to make allowances for people's bad temper even when her heart was breaking, agreed with him, her voice wooden with the emotion she was determined to suppress. She wasn't looking at him as she spoke and so failed to see the gleam of surprise in his eyes. Her own were fixed firmly upon an ancestral family group upon the wall before her, her whole body stiff with a strong resolve not to apologise or make excuses for her conduct in case he started asking awkward questions.

Rolf stirred in his chair, and said, still with icy politeness: 'It should be possible for you to travel tomorrow—there will be no difficulties, I imagine. Andrew should be delighted to drive you. I shall be away for the day, but I will arrange for you to be paid whatever is owing to you before you go.'

He got up slowly, and walked, just as slowly, towards her and stood staring down at the top of her head. He said in a quiet voice:

'I am indebted to you for the care you have given my mother—you are a good nurse and she has become fond of you. I should be grateful if you will say nothing of this to her. I will arrange for you to receive a telegram within the next hour or so, recalling you to England—family illness, shall we say? I'm sure you will know how to act.' His voice had an edge to it, and she thought miserably that he took it for granted that she was an expert in deceit. He paused, and the pause was so long that she felt compelled to look at him, though it was against her will. His face held no expression save a faint mockery. The desire to tell him everything was so great that she was forced to clench her teeth to prevent the words from pouring out. He spoke with a sudden fierceness to surprise her.

'This afternoon, in the Museum, I could have sworn...it meant nothing to you, did it? Probably you were amused.' His voice was bitter.

Sappha looked away. Her heart, leaping in her throat in such a ridiculous fashion, made it difficult for her to answer him, and he gave her no opportunity to do so; he was at the door, holding it open with an exaggerated politeness which was as insulting as leaving her to stand. She said: 'Goodnight, Dr van Duyren,' in a quiet little voice as she passed him.

'Not goodnight,' he answered, still pleasant. 'Goodbye.'

In her room she undressed very carefully, as though

it mattered how each garment was folded. Only when she was ready for bed did she take the green dress and bundle it up as though it were so much waste paper, and push it into the wastepaper basket, then she packed with methodical neatness, walked aimlessly around the room doing nothing at all, and finally lay down on the bed and closed her eyes. Incredibly, she slept.

She was awakened by Joke with her morning tea, and on the tray, true to his word, was Rolf's telegram. It helped enormously that Joke should linger at the door, because Sappha was able to convey to her that it contained bad news—Joke would spread the tidings, which would enable her to lie more convincingly. She was almost dressed when Antonia came in. She was in her dressing gown and her blotched, puffy face gave ample evidence of her lack of sleep. Her eyes lighted upon Sappha's packed case as she paused just inside the door and she ran across the room to cast herself in Sappha's arms and wail: 'Sappha, you're leaving. Oh, what did Rolf say to you—did he think…?'

Sappha disengaged herself gently, took the hairpins out of her mouth long enough to say: 'Now, now,' in a heartening manner, then pushed them in rather haphazardly and went on: 'Tonia, haven't you slept at all? Sit down, I'll tell you what happened.'

She did so, beginning with the telegram and working backwards, so that by the time she got to the humiliating talk with Rolf she was able to present it in a far different light to her listener. When she had finished, she sat back, quietly pleased at the good job she had made of it. She almost believed it herself. All the same, she whisked the telegram from the tray and put it safely in her pocket, so that Antonia, who had sharp eyes, wouldn't notice that its postmark was no further afield than Dokkum.

'I'll have to tell,' said Antonia. 'Rolf has a way of finding things out. Oh, Sappha, I have been a fool, haven't I?'

Sappha ignored this last obvious remark and answered the first one.

'No, you won't tell,' she said positively. 'It won't help a bit if you do. You see, dear, Rolf isn't just going to be angry if you do, he's going to be dreadfully hurt as well. He—he loves you very much, you know, he might even think he's failed you in some way, because when your father died, Rolf tried to take his place, didn't he?' She sat up straight, pierced by a sudden dreadful thought. 'Tonia, where did you go? What did you do? Andrew didn't try any…?'

Antonia interrupted her with a light-hearted giggle. 'Sappha, you sound just like Mother! No, of course not—he didn't get a chance. I may be only sixteen, but Mother and Rolf have primed me thoroughly, you know. We quarrelled, Andrew and I, and he called me a little prude. I'm not sure I know what it means, but I didn't like him any more then.' She broke off. 'Did you really love him, Sappha?' she asked. 'I can't think why.'

'Nor can I,' said Sappha simply, much struck by the fact that she had no feelings, good bad or indifferent, for Andrew any more, and at the same time sighing with relief that Antonia had fallen out of love almost as quickly as she had fallen in.

'Was Rolf cross with you?' asked Antonia. 'If he was, I shall tell him I let you take the blame last night— I was so frightened I couldn't think. Have you ever felt like that?'

Sappha smiled wryly. 'Frequently, and of course Rolf wasn't annoyed—why should he be? He knows about Andrew.'

'Yes, but he was furious when we came in—his voice was all cold like it goes when he's angry.'

Sappha got up; she didn't think she could bear to talk about Rolf any more. 'Yes, well, he wasn't,' she said positively. 'Look, I'm going to see your mother now to tell her I must go back to England. Why don't you go back to bed and I'll get someone to bring you up some breakfast—no one need know—they'll think you've got a cold.'

It was a happy thought. Within five minutes Antonia was tucked up in bed again, and she herself was free to break the news to the Baroness, not such a hard task as she had anticipated, for Joke had indeed spread the news and the Baroness was prepared for ill tidings. Sappha showed her patient the telegram, with her thumb placed strategically over the date stamp, and that, coupled with her white face, was evidence enough.

'Oh dear, and Rolf went away very early,' said the Baroness unhappily. 'Examinations or something for the first-year students—he did tell me—you must make your own arrangements, my dear. Have you enough money? And take the car if you need it. Ask for anything you want. Shall I telephone Rolf, or would you prefer to do it yourself? He'll be so upset.'

Sappha went even paler, for this was something she had forgotten. She said quickly: 'May I telephone him, Baroness? I can find out about the trains and flights and let him know and—and say goodbye at the same time.'

The Baroness turned a mournful face to her. 'Yes, dear. I can't imagine what it will be like without you—

just as I'm almost well, too. You've been like another daughter. Do you suppose you will be needed at home for very long—is there a possibility that you might come back before very long?'

She looked so wistful that Sappha gave her a heartening little hug.

'I don't see why not,' she lied cheerfully. 'I must go home and see what it's all about first, though. I'll write to you as soon as I know how things are.'

'Yes, of course, I know you will. How selfish of me to talk like that when you look worried to death. Go and get your journey arranged, dear, Annie can help me.' She smiled and wiped away a tear. 'I shall have to get used to doing without you, shan't I?'

Sappha, feeling mean, could have cried herself as she put on her outdoor clothes. She went to the kitchen and saw Annie and Mrs Burns and then left the house, glad to get away for a little while; everyone had been so kind and she felt such a fraud. She hadn't given any serious thought as to how she was going to get back to England and she had quite forgotten about Andrew; even if she had remembered, to accept a lift with him was the last thing she would have done. Now she went to the station and not without difficulty, discovered that there was a train in the late afternoon which would connect up with the boat train from Leeuwarden. She had allowed the Baroness to think that she would fly home, but there was no hurry, she might just as well go by boat. For the first time, it struck her that she had no plans and no job, she would have to go home and start looking for work, she didn't much care where, but she had to earn her living, and if she had work to do, it would fill the intolerable emptiness she saw looming ahead.

She walked back from the station, thinking she would leave Rolf's house just as soon as she could. If she left immediately after lunch, the car could take her to the station—she could leave her case there and go to De Posthoorn until it was time for her train, then if Rolf came home before his usual hour, he would suppose that she had left either with Andrew or to catch the plane. She stopped suddenly. Andrew—she had forgotten Andrew. If he hadn't already gone, it might be a good idea to go and see him and hurry him on his way, then if Rolf did find out about Antonia, it might not be quite so bad. She looked at her watch; she had time enough; she started to walk down the main street in the direction of the hotel.

There was no sign of Andrew in the coffee room—probably he was still in his rom. When the waiter brought her coffee she asked him, to learn that he had left quite early that morning. She stirred her coffee, thinking how like Andrew it was to avoid an awkward situation, but at least she could leave knowing that he wasn't likely to bother Antonia again—in a couple of weeks he would be forgotten. She drank her coffee, and got up to go, trying not to think that she would be forgotten too.

Back in the house, sitting with the Baroness in the lovely drawing room, she enlarged a little upon her journey back, telling her that she had booked on a flight which would mean her leaving immediately after lunch, and when the Baroness cried, something she hadn't done for quite some time, Sappha very nearly blurted out the whole tale from very shame.

It was after lunch, which she had eaten in the company of a silent Antonia, that Joke came in with a letter. Sappha took it from the salver, her heart leaping foolishly at the sight of Rolf's handwriting. She opened it, conscious of Antonia's look, to find nothing but a cheque inside. It was while she was folding it neatly back into the envelope that Antonia enquired of Joke: 'Is my brother home? I didn't hear him come in.'

Joke was on her way to the door; she paused and said:

'No, *Juffrouw*. He gave me this letter before he left this morning and told me to give it to Miss Devenish before she left.' Having dropped this bombshell, she left the room and before Sappha could ask what she had said, Antonia burst out: 'But that's impossible! Rolf went before you had the telegram—Mother said so, so how could he know?' She stopped and stared across the table at Sappha, who for want of anything better to do was writing aimlessly in the little notebook she had drawn from her handbag. She went on writing even though she knew that Antonia was still staring at her.

'Sappha, did Rolf tell you to go? He was angry, wasn't he?'

Sappha had no answer ready, which as it turned out, didn't matter, because Antonia didn't wait for one, but went on: 'He was—he did—I know it. It's all a botched-up story so that Mama won't know. I shall telephone him now and tell him…'

'Don't you dare!' snapped Sappha. She felt sick with unhappiness and after the things Rolf had said she told herself she didn't care any more—all she wanted to do was to get away. She said in a more reasonable voice:

'Look, Tonia, there's very little harm done—I would have been leaving in another week or two, and it's not likely that any of us will ever meet again. It's best that we should forget the whole thing, no one's come to any harm.' She got up, because if she went on talking like that she would burst into tears and spoil the whole thing. 'I'm going to say goodbye to everyone, because it's almost time to go.'

She was actually on the steps, her goodbyes said, and Jan waiting by the car, when Antonia said suddenly: 'I'm even more of a fool than I thought. You love Rolf, don't you, Sappha?'

She turned her lovely blue eyes on to Sappha's rigidly composed face; they were solemn and unhappy and ashamed.

Sappha looked away from her, across the garden to where she could see the dull gleam of water. It was a pity, she thought savagely, that she hadn't drowned when she had gone after Hush. He was cuddled in Antonia's arms now, his ugly little head, not quite as ugly as it had been, stretched to its utmost so that he should miss nothing of what was going on around him. Sappha pulled his ears gently and smiled quite naturally at Antonia. She said: 'Yes, dear. But don't let that worry you—life's not always what we want it to be, you know—things happen...'

She kissed the pretty, unhappy face. 'Goodbye, Tonia. I shan't write to you and you mustn't write to me because I don't think Rolf would like that.'

She got into the car, and as it went down the short drive, waved and smiled at the Baroness, sitting at the drawing room window. She waved to Antonia too, but Antonia had gone inside, straight to her brother's study and picked up the receiver and dialled Rolf's consulting rooms. She wasn't sure where he was, but his secretary would know.

There was no one in the coffee room when Sappha arrived at De Posthoorn. She ordered a pot of coffee, since she would have to sit there for an hour at least, and sat drinking it, her mind a merciful blank. She had begun on her second cup when Mr and Mrs Winkelman came in, ordered coffee in their turn and asked, in the nicest possible way, what she was doing there. Sappha said simply: 'I'm going home,' and when Mrs Winkelman said kindly: 'Not bad news, I hope my dear,' replied, because she was sick of lying: 'No—no, thank you. I'm going on the night boat, and I've a little time to spare before my train goes, so I thought I'd come here.'

Mr Winkelman frowned. 'The people you worked for— surely they should have sent you into Leeuwarden by car— or at least seen you to the station.'

He sounded so indignant that she hastened to explain. 'Well, they couldn't very well, you see, my patient is still very much an invalid, and Baron van Duyren is a doctor and—isn't always home.'

Mrs Winkelman leaned a little forward in her chair. 'A baron!' she breathed. 'Was he here yesterday? Tall and large and very dark?'

Sappha put down her cup. 'Yes, it sounds like him,' she admitted and tried to smile without much success. She busied herself pouring another cup of coffee so that they wouldn't be able to see her face, and Mrs Winkelman said forthrightly: 'Well, it all seems a bit sudden to me, if there's anything we can do…' She got no further. A kind of fury shook the front door of the hotel, it shook the door of the coffee room too, which flew open to admit Rolf. Sappha looked at him through her puffy, red-rimmed eyes and prepared for battle, for it was obvious that he was controlling vast feelings of some sort or another. He was also, she noticed with a sinking heart, very much a baron; it was as though he had wrapped the invisible cloak of his ancient title around himself so that he had become wholly inaccessible. Sappha sniffed back threatening tears, telling herself it didn't matter any more, she hadn't anything else to say and she wasn't going to make excuses or plead forgiveness.

He stood just inside the open door, letting all the cold air in and taking his time. His eyes lighted upon Mr and Mrs Winkelman and he wished them a good day with an icy civility which failed to dislodge them from their table in the corner. As Mrs Winkelman pointed out to her husband much later, they had every right to stay—were they not guests at the hotel, and moreover, was he not of Dutch blood with a real ancestor whose gravestone was to be seen in St Martin's church? Surely that fact alone was enough to allow them to sit tight.

As far as Sappha and Rolf were concerned, however, there was no one else in the room, or, for that matter, the world. From the still open doorway he demanded thunderously:

'Where are you going, and why are you here and where is Glover?' He had made no effort to lower his voice: it beat around Sappha's head to increase its ache, so that she said peevishly: 'Don't shout.'

He answered her with a deliberate clarity which was far worse than any roar would have been. 'I am not shouting. And I want an answer to my questions.'

'You won't get them,' said Sappha rudely, 'coming in here like a—a hurricane and shouting at me.' She didn't answer his questions either, so that when next he spoke it was in a subdued roar which had made her jump.

'Sappha, I'm waiting!'

She was plaiting the silky fringe of the Smyrna table rug, with which the Dutch, as a nation, adorn their coffee tables. She already had five little pigtails; she embarked on the sixth and said without looking at him:

'I'm going home—you told me to go, remember? Andrew went this morning, I don't know when because I haven't seen him, not at all. I'm sitting here waiting until it's time for me to catch my train to Leeuwarden, because I don't care to stay in your house a moment longer than I must.'

She had spoken in a calm, colourless voice and then spoilt the whole thing by bursting into tears, whereupon, to Mrs Winkelman's delight, Rolf crossed the room in a couple of strides to offer a very large, freshly laundered handkerchief, which Sappha snatched from him and defiantly blew her nose. She said furiously: 'I never want to see you again—never!' she repeated, as if by saying it twice she could convince herself as well as her audience. 'One minute you were…' she paused, left her sentence unfinished and tried again, 'and the next you…' She sniffed. 'You don't trust me.'

Rolf was standing very close. He said in a surprisingly mild voice:

'Did I ever say that—that I didn't trust you?'

She sniffed again, it was quite true, he hadn't. 'Well, you thought that I was meeting Andrew, and,' she declared with rising indignation, 'you told me to go back to England with him.'

'And what else was I supposed to say?' His voice was rough and had a bitter ring, 'and what the hell was I supposed to think—I'm only human, you know; bad-tempered and arrogant and God help me, jealous—one moment you were melting in my arms and five minutes later you were telling me that you'd just been to see Glover, damn him.'

Sappha stood up, pushing her chair back as she did so because he was so near. 'I'm going,' she said in a soggy voice. She would have liked to say something clever and cutting about melting in his arms, but she could think of nothing nasty enough. She went past him and he made no move to stop her, but as she reached the door he said, almost as thought it didn't matter any more: 'Antonia telephoned me—I can deal with her later, but I had to see you because I don't understand why you couldn't have told me, instead of having me to imagine that you and Glover...'

Sappha stared at the fine specimen of a Friesian clock hanging on the wall before her. 'I did—at least I tried, and you said we'd talk about it later, but you went out and then in the hall you didn't give me the chance to say anything even if I could have done, and you know I couldn't because I'd promised Tonia.' During this muddled observation her voice had risen considerably, she paused for breath and continued rather loudly. 'Why should I tell you anything, you're—you're...' What with tears and temper she was bereft of words. She went through the door and closed it quietly behind her and went out into the cold blustery late afternoon.

She wanted to hide and the only place she could think of was the Museum; at least it would be warm and dry there and it didn't close until five. She rang the bell and when the curator opened the door and saw her tear-streaked face he opened it still wider and said kindly, 'Another visit, miss?' He smiled at her kindly, pretending not to see how awful she looked. 'There's plenty of time before we close.'

She managed a tired little smile. 'Please may I go upstairs, just for a little while—it's peaceful.'

Sappha made straight for the case where the little silver box was displayed and stared at it with sad eyes. It was only a little more than twenty-four hours since she had last seen it, and then she had been so happy. She turned away at last and got out her lipstick and compact and with the aid of its little mirror did things to her miserable little face. It didn't look much better when she had finished, but at least it was the first step taken towards the new life she would have to build. She closed her bag, put her hand into her pocket and drew out Rolf's handkerchief—it was very fine linen, she saw idly, with his initials beautifully embroidered in one corner, but the sight of it was bad for her so she pushed it back again and walked over to the display case once more.

The door bell rang as she did so and she frowned because she wanted the place to herself. Sappha gave a last defiant sniff, thinking sadly that in a novel it would have been the hero ringing the bell, intent on catching up with the heroine before the last page—only there was not going to be a last page to this particular story. She put her hand in her pocket again and clutched the handkerchief because it was all she had left, and at the same time became aware that someone was coming up the stairs. She knew it was Rolf and turned round to face him as he came across the room to her. He said in a gentle voice:

'I knew you would be here, my dear—my darling Sappha,' and when she opened her mouth to speak he went on: 'No, we're not going to talk any more, my dearest love, not at present, for nothing we can say to each other can alter the fact that I love you with all my heart, and I believe that you love me.'

He caught her close and smiled down at her and kissed

her mouth and then her pale face until it pinkened and glowed with her happiness. Only then did he loosen his hold, and that just long enough to fish something out of a pocket. It was a little silver box with a beautifully engraved lid. He put it into Sappha's hand. 'Open it, my love.'

There was a ring inside, a diamond and ruby ring in an old-fashioned gold setting. Sappha looked at it and because she appeared to be about to burst into tears again, Rolf kissed her again before he spoke.

'The ring has been in my pocket for several weeks, Sappha, but the box I found this morning because I couldn't think of a better way of telling you how ashamed I was for making you unhappy.'

Sappha stared up at him, her eyes like stars. She said obscurely: 'But I wouldn't have been here.'

'I should have come after you.'

'Even if I'd been with Andrew?'

'Even if you had been with Andrew, my darling.'

'What would you have done?'

'Put the ring on your finger, of course.'

Sappha smiled. 'Please put it on now, dear Rolf,' and when he had done so she reached up and kissed him, standing within the circle of his arms. His face, she thought, studying it, was neither bold nor bad—just loving.

It was the curator who disturbed them, and that in the kindest possible fashion. He had been prowling round them for some time without either of them noticing; now he said almost apologetically: 'It's well past closing time,' and smiled at them; he was a happily married man himself and he liked to see young people happy, as these two were. He went downstairs behind them and waited patiently by the door while Sappha paused to admire her ring. He asked diffidently:

'I suppose you won't be coming any more now, miss?'

It was Rolf who answered him in Dutch. 'Oh, yes she will—when we're married and she wants a bolthole from me and our children,' and the man chuckled as he shut the door behind them.

They stopped to kiss on the steps outside; the rain had turned to snow, but neither of them noticed as they strolled down the little path.

'We'll be married in Dialach—as soon as possible, my lovely one,' said Rolf, 'because that's where we met.'

Sappha smiled at him and said meekly: 'Yes, dear.' Dialach was perhaps not an ideal place in which to have a wedding in midwinter. She said, thinking out loud: 'I shall have to be wrapped from top to toes in white fur.' She laughed at the idea and Rolf plucked her to him and kissed her with pleasure.

'And so you shall,' he promised. 'You shall have anything in the world you want, Sappha.'

She stopped and looked up at him. The snow had powdered his dark hair, making it darker than ever by contrast—his eyes looked black in the feeble light of the street lamps ahead of them. She put up a gentle finger and traced the outline of his awe inspiring nose. He looked very handsome, but it wasn't good looks she was looking for. Apparently she found what she was seeking in his face, for she smiled at him and put up her face to be kissed, knowing that she loved him dearly, just as he loved her. 'I only want you,' she said.

* * * * *

THE EDGE OF WINTER

Chapter 1

The little town was small and snug, tucked in between the Cornish hills and cliffs, and the late afternoon sun shone on its slate roofs and brightened the whitewashed walls of the cottages clustered round its small harbour, although there was a chilly wind blowing in from the sea. It was not yet five o'clock, but the October afternoon was already drawing in, and the girl climbing the path from the harbour towards the car park at the side shivered a little as she paused to look back before she rounded the corner, to thread her way through the few cars there and then follow the cliff path.

It was a little late for a walk, she reflected, but she had been playing backgammon with her father all the afternoon, sitting in the lounge of the Lobster Pot Hotel, and she had stolen frequent glances out of the old-fashioned bow window overlooking the harbour and felt envy of the intrepid yachtsmen gowling briskly out to the open sea. It would have been nice to have gone sailing, but although several of the younger men staying in the little town had scraped the beginnings of an acquaintance with her, it had come to nothing; her father and aunt had absorbed all her leisure, and quite unwittingly; they were darlings and she loved them devotedly, but they tended to forget that she was all of twenty-five with a responsible job, a life of her own, and well able to take care of herself.

She turned her back on the harbour, left the car park behind and took the path along the cliff top. Round the next great headland of grey rock was Falmouth, but it might have been a hundred miles away, for there was nothing to see but the rough grass around her and the sea below. She stopped again to watch the gulls wheeling in from the sea; the wind was freshening, but despite this there were still two or three sailing boats out to sea and she sat down for a moment on a tussock of coarse grass the better to watch them, pulling the high neck of her sweater closer and retying her long honey-coloured hair. She was a pretty girl, with large dark blue eyes fringed with honey-coloured lashes which she didn't darken and a straight little nose above a generous mouth; her long legs were encased in old slacks and when she stood up she showed herself to be a little above middle height and slim without being skinny.

The path was a narrow one, sometimes running close to the cliff edge so that she had a clear view of the sea surging amongst the rocks below, sometimes turning inland between trees and shrubs. She walked briskly, her thoughts busy. Tomorrow she would be leaving Cornwall and returning to London; to St Katherine's, where she was the Accident Room Sister, and in a way, she reflected, she wouldn't mind going back. She loved her father and Aunt Martha dearly, but they were elderly now, content to sit with a book or play cards and take a daily walk along the harbour, activities which weren't enough for her own youthful energy. But the week of doing almost nothing had done her good; she felt rested and relaxed, ready to tackle a hard day's work, and besides, there was another week's holiday to look forward to—just before Christmas, when she would go home to the pleasant little house in its small, well kept garden, tucked tidily into one of the narrow side streets of the Somerset village where she had been born and brought up. It was delightful once the summer tourists had gone, with its wide main street and Dunster Castle towering over it, and if she felt like it, she could walk down to the water to catch a glimpse of Wales on the other side of it, and if that wasn't enough, there was always Minehead a mile or so away.

The path had found its way back to the edge of the cliff once more and she slowed her pace to watch the clouds bunched angrily on the horizon. It would rain, but not yet. She had time to walk back to the hotel without fear of getting wet, and the faint sea mist beginning to creep up didn't worry her either; she had walked the path almost daily and knew it well enough.

She was on the point of turning back when her eye caught something moving far below her—something white. There was someone there, waving, and leaning precariously over the cliff face, she could hear a faint treble shout. She looked carefully round her; there was no boat within miles and certainly no other human being, and right before was an apology of a path, trickling out of sight down the rough cliff face. Someone had apparently gone down that way and was unable to get back. She could, of course, go back to the town and get help, but that would take too long; it would be dark by then and almost certainly raining. Whoever it was down there was unable to walk or climb and they would get soaked and cold. If she went down now, she and the unfortunate below would be back on the cliff top within fifteen minutes or so, and if they were injured and couldn't climb—well, all the more reason for her to go down and see what could be done.

The path was steep but perfectly safe, and she didn't find it too difficult; heights didn't bother her and she was surefooted enough. She was halfway down when she saw that it was a child on the little patch of sand between the sharp spines of rock, and she quickened her pace, for the child wasn't moving.

It was a girl, a little girl of eight or so, with a small face puffed and red with tears and one leg bent awkwardly beneath her. She was wearing shorts and it was her T-shirt which she had been waving.

She said at once in a hoarse little voice: 'I thought no one would ever come—what's your name?'

'Araminta Shaw—what's yours?' Araminta recognised that an exchange of names spelled security for the child, and smiled cheerfully at her.

'I'm Mary Rose Jenkins and I've hurt my leg—I fell…' She burst into tears, and Araminta sat down beside her and hugged her close and let her cry. Presently she wailed: 'I can't move it—I tried, but it hurts. What shall we do?' She looked round with an anxious face. 'It's getting dark.'

'Not yet, it's not,' said Araminta, and eyed the tell-tale bump, already discoloured, just above the child's thin ankle. A Pott's fracture, and how on earth was she going to find anything to splint it, and even if she found it, how were they going to get up the cliff again? Piggyback, if the child could bear the pain and she herself could manage the path with the uncertain weight of the child on her shoulders; she would tackle that problem when she came to it. Now she said cheerfully: 'Let's put that shirt back on, and then I'm going to do something about that leg of yours. You see, we must get it straight, poppet, before we climb back up that cliff path. I shall hurt you, I'm afraid, but you're a brave girl, aren't you?'

She dropped a kiss on the tangled brown hair, slid the shirt back on and studied their surroundings; surely there would be some wood lying around; an old box, a broken spar, even some cardboard. There was always flotsam and jetsam on the sea shore. 'Look, Mary Rose,' she explained, 'I want to find a piece of wood to tie to your leg—it won't hurt nearly as much then. Will you be OK while I look round? I won't go far.'

There was nothing, absolutely nothing at all. She went back to where the child waited so patiently and sat down beside her and took off the knee socks she was wearing under her slacks; they were by no means ideal, but she could tie the little girl's legs together, using the sound leg as a splint. She told Mary Rose what she was going to do, begged her to keep as still as she could, and bent to her task. In hospital, she reflected, with everything to hand, the fracture could have been reduced and the leg put in plaster with the child happily unconscious under anaesthetic; now all she dared to do was to lift the little broken leg gently until it was beside its fellow and tie her socks above and below the fracture. Mary Rose screamed all the while she was doing it, but she had to shut her ears to that; all she could do when she had finished was to hold the child close and soothe her, and presently, as the pain dulled a little, Mary Rose dozed off.

Araminta sat awkwardly, the child's small body pressed close to hers, while she debated what to do next. To go up the cliff path was going to be so difficult that it would be almost impossible; but to stay there all night was impossible too, an opinion borne out by the first few drops of rain. They became a downpour within minutes, and the wind, still freshening, sent scuds of spray on to the small stretch of sand. Really, thought Araminta, it couldn't be worse. There was no shelter, and Mary Rose had wakened and was voicing her displeasure in no uncertain manner. Araminta, who didn't quail easily, quailed now. 'This,' she declared strongly, 'is the utter end!'

Only it wasn't; a yacht was coming round the next headland, still some way off, but at least sailing in their direction. She waved, wishing she had something colourful which the people on board might see more easily in the deepening gloom, told Mary Rose the good news, laid her down carefully and then went right to the water's edge and waved again. The yacht turned a little away from them, out to sea, giving the rocky coast a wide berth; probably those on board hadn't even seen her. But she went on waving even though her arms ached; she shouted too, quite uselessly, but it made her feel better. When the yacht turned again, inland this time, she hardly dared to hope that she had been seen. She watched anxiously to see what would happen next and shouted with delight when its slender nose was pointed towards land. She waved again and then went to reassure Mary Rose, who had rolled over on to her bad leg and was screaming with pain. Araminta bent over the child, doing the best she could, and when she straightened, it was to see a rubber dinghy nosing its way slowly through the treacherous water between the outcrops of rock. She ran down to the water again, peering through the driving rain, and splashed into the surf, already so wet that she hardly noticed the water round her ankles.

'Oh, what a blessing!' she cried happily. 'I've never been so glad to see anyone in my life—I thought we'd be stuck here…'

The occupant of the dinghy cut its motor, pulled it half out of the water and stood up. He was a big, heavily built man and very tall, with dark hair greying at the temples; his hawklike good looks wore a look of extreme ill-humour as he stood looking down at her. He was just as wet as she was, his thick sweater heavy with rain and sea water, his slacks sopping. He said harshly: 'You silly little fool—don't you know that these cliffs are dangerous?' He caught sight of Mary Rose. 'And what's that?'

Araminta eyed him with disfavour; he might have come to their rescue, but he didn't need to be quite so nasty about it. She said snappily:

'That is a little girl—she's broken her leg, I certainly shouldn't have waved to you otherwise; I'm perfectly capable of climbing the cliff path.'

He smiled nastily. 'My dear good woman, I'm not in the least interested in your climbing prowess. How do you know the child's leg is broken?' He was by Mary Rose's side now, sitting on his heels, not touching anything, just looking. 'A Pott's,' he murmured, and Araminta said in a surprised voice: 'Yes, it is—how did you know?'

'I'm a doctor,' he answered her blandly as he gently undid the socks, 'and how did you know?'

'I'm a nurse.'

'You surprise me.' He ignored her gasp of annoyance, and bent to see the extent of the damage. He re-tied the socks presently, saying coolly: 'Well, at least you had the sense to leave it alone. I'll get her on board and put in at Mousehole. She can go to Falmouth by ambulance.'

'Can't you sail back to Falmouth?' Araminta wanted to know. 'It's quite close…' He gave her a withering look. 'The wind,' he explained with a frosty patience which set her teeth on edge. 'We should have to sail into it and it would take twice as long.' He bent over the child again and his dark face was lighted by a smile now. 'We're all going back home in my boat,' he told her. 'Once we are there we'll get that leg seen to.' He touched Mary Rose's brown hair with a gentle finger. 'What a brave little girl you are!' He stood up and looked out to sea to where the yacht was anchored. 'Get into the dinghy,' he ordered Araminta, 'and sit down. I'll put the child in your lap.'

She did as she was told, seething silently. Now was hardly the time to tell someone—someone who was rescuing them from an unpleasant situation—that she considered him to be the rudest man she had ever encountered. She cuddled the little girl close during the short journey, and only when they reached the yacht did she wonder how on earth they were to get on board.

She need not have worried; there was someone waiting for them, a grey-haired, thick-set elderly man with powerful arms, who reached over the boat's side and lifted Mary Rose as though she had been a feather and disappeared below with her. Araminta watched the yacht dancing in the choppy sea and wondered what she was supposed to do. 'Hold the rail,' her companion advised her, 'and pull yourself aboard—it's quite easy. Wait until I say so.'

It didn't look in the least easy, but she was beyond worrying about it; when he said 'Right,' she pulled herself up and helped by an unexpected boost from behind, landed untidily on the yacht's deck. It didn't help at all to see the man spring lightly on deck beside her without any effort at all and proceed to tie up the dinghy. 'Go below,' he said over his shoulder. And she went.

It was warm and snug in the cabin. Mary Rose was on a padded couch along one wall and the elderly man was pouring tea into four mugs. He looked up as their rescuer joined them and spoke in a language Araminta couldn't understand, and when he nodded, fetched a bottle and poured some of its contents into the mugs. 'Brandy,' said the dark man, 'and get those wet clothes off—and the child's, too.' He went to a locker and pulled out a couple of sweaters and some blankets.

'Use these.'

Araminta didn't say anything; not because she could think of nothing to say; there was a great deal she was storing up for a more suitable occasion—besides, her teeth were chattering too hard to make speech effective. She gave Mary Rose some of the hot tea and drank her own. The brandy sent a warm glow through her and she was on the point of remonstrating with their unwilling host when he urged the child to drink the rest of her tea, but he forestalled her with a quiet: 'Yes, I know what you're about to say, but we have an hour's sailing before us and the sea's choppy—she needs to sleep.'

He swallowed his own tea, spoke to the older man and went on deck, to be followed at once by his companion.

Araminta began to undress Mary Rose—luckily there was almost nothing to take off; the sweater was far too large, but it was warm and enveloped the child completely. She wrapped a blanket round her and saw with relief that she was already half asleep.

It didn't take her more than a moment to tear off her own sweater and put on the one she had been given. She was forced to turn up its sleeves to half their length, and it was so long that she debated whether to take off her slacks as well, but she decided against that; she wouldn't look dignified, and she wanted to be that at all costs. She settled for damp slacks and her dignity, plaited her damp hair and longed for a mirror. The yacht was moving now, and just as its owner had said, the sea was choppy; she supposed it was the brandy which made her feel so unconcerned about it.

Mary Rose was deeply asleep now and likely to remain so, what with fright and pain and brandy. Araminta pulled up a stool and sat by the couch, one arm over the child, and looked about her. She knew very little about yachts, but this one struck her as extremely comfortable; its furnishings were simple, but there was no lack of comfort. She fell to wondering who the owner might be and why he had spoken in a foreign tongue to the other man. She frowned a little; he had spoken fluent English to her, but now that she thought about it, there had been the faintest accent. The object of her thoughts came back at that moment, walking through the cabin without a word, to enter a cubby-hole at its end which presumably held radio equipment, for she could hear his voice speaking to someone, but when he came back it was obvious to her from his aloof expression that he had no intention of telling her anything. He said nothing, only opened a cupboard in the wall, took out a packet of sandwiches and laid them on the table beside her.

Araminta ate two of them, for she was peckish. The walk had sharpened her appetite and then there had been the climb down the cliffs and some considerable time waiting beside the child. The sandwiches were excellent—smoked salmon and very fresh brown bread; she eyed the rest of them hungrily as she wrapped them up again, but Mary Rose might wake and feel hungry too. But she didn't; not once during the rest of the rather unpleasant hour did she stir, and a good thing too, thought Araminta, for the sea was now quite rough and the wind had veered, slowing their progress. The elderly man had come below briefly to give her another mug of coffee and ask her, in his peculiar English, if she needed anything and was the little girl all right. She accepted the coffee gratefully, not moving from her stool, and wondered as she drank it if anyone had missed the child yet. Surely by now—she glanced at the clock and saw to her astonishment that it was almost half past eight; they must have been on the beach much longer than she had thought. Her father and Aunt Martha would certainly be wondering where she was, and Mary Rose's parents would be frantic... Her thoughts were interrupted once more by the dark man, who stayed just long enough to tell her that they would be entering the harbour within the next few minutes. He disappeared as quickly as he had come.

She knew almost nothing about sailing, but it seemed to her that the yacht was berthed very smoothly and in a few minutes both men came into the cabin; when the boat's owner bent to pick the little girl up, Araminta observed urgently: 'She's very sound asleep. She's all right, isn't she?'

His severe expression softened into a brief smile. 'She's a very little girl and she's had a lot of brandy.'

There was nothing she could answer to that; she picked up their damp clothes and followed him up on deck. It was raining still and very dark, and there was no sign of the wind easing. There were a few lights here and there, shining through the curtain of rain, but no one about. The three of them made their way silently down the small harbour's arm and on to the quayside, the little girl cradled in the dark man's arms, Araminta close at his heels and behind her the elderly man, walking stolidly into the rain.

Araminta skipped a step or two and caught up with the leader of the party. 'Where are we going?'

'A pub—somewhere where there are people who will know whose child this is and where we can telephone.'

'There's the Lobster Pot just along here.' She waved into the dimly lighted narrow street ahead of them, which ran round the harbour. 'They're…'

'I know—I've been here before.'

'How rude,' said Araminta severely, and went past him to open the hotel door. It was in the side wall of the hotel and led straight into the downstairs bar. There were quite a number of people in it, among them her father and aunt, in deep discussion with the hotel's owner, but they paused in mid-sentence when they saw her and her companions, and Aunt Martha, a formidable-

looking lady with severe features and a well-disciplined
hair style, made her way briskly through the throng
around her and demanded briskly: 'Araminta, where
have you been? We've been very worried—and who
are these people?'

Her sharp eyes took in the child in the man's arms
and his companion and then returned to her bedrag-
gled niece.

'Sorry you were worried, Aunt,' said Araminta,
knowing that under the rather fierce exterior was a very
nice old lady who loved her. 'I found this little girl, and
these gentlemen very kindly picked us up in their yacht
and brought us back. The child's leg is broken and this
gentleman is a doctor, so if...' she paused and looked
at him, standing silently beside her. 'If you would say
what you want us to do?' she asked him. 'A room with a
firm table—something I can use for splints, and someone to telephone for an ambulance to take the child to
hospital and to discover to whom she belongs.'

It was like being back at St Katherine's, carrying out
a consultant's orders without waste of time. 'There's an
office behind the reception desk, I'm sure the owner...'
She was already there, asking for its use and if someone would see about the ambulance. 'Two sticks,' she reminded herself aloud and heard the man chuckle; worse,
he followed it with a: 'You've more sense than I imagined.' He spoke in a faintly mocking voice which made
her grit her splendid teeth. But it was no time to consider
her own feelings, so she pushed the table into a better
position and went to fetch the variety of sticks offered
as well as a splendid collection of scarves, ties and nap-
kins to tie them with. She chose the most suitable of
them, smiled briefly at her father, standing quietly in a

corner, and went back to where Mary Rose, still merci-
fully tipsy, lay.

She admitted to herself later that the child's bony little leg had been expertly splinted, the ends of the bone
brought into alignment before the splints were put on;
probably they were in as good a position as they needed
to be before the plaster was applied. It was a pity she
would never know that; Mary Rose had been whisked
off to Falmouth in the ambulance and the dark man had
gone with her, while his companion had gone back to
the yacht. Both men had said goodbye to her, the elder
with grave courtesy, the younger with a curt brevity
which allowed her to see that he couldn't care less if
he never saw her again.

She went to bed much later, having repeated her story
a great many times for the benefit of her father and aunt,
the owner of the hotel and most of the guests staying at
the hotel. The police had come too, bringing with them
a distraught young woman who had slipped out to the
shops, thinking it was safe to leave her small daughter
alone for a little while. Araminta answered the police-
man's questions, accepted the woman's thanks awkwardly and asked if the child was safely in hospital. The
police sergeant said that yes, she was, with the leg nicely
plastered, and that the gentleman who had been such a
help us there too. Possibly, he added, Araminta herself
would see him on the following day, for he would be
returning to his yacht.

But in the morning there was no sign of him, although the yacht was still in the harbour. Araminta, put
out for no good reason, dressed in her well-cut tweed
suit, put her shining hair up in a neat coil on the top of
her pretty head, got into her elderly Mini and began the

drive back to London. Her father and aunt saw her off. Her father, as usual, had very little to say beyond wishing her a good journey and not too much work. It was Aunt Martha who said in her measured tones:

'That was an interesting man who brought you back yesterday. A pity you won't see him again, my dear.'

Araminta put a stylishly shod foot down on the accelerator. 'He was the rudest man I've ever met,' she pronounced coldly. 'The only pity is that I shan't see him to tell him so.'

Chapter 2

St Katherine's was one of the older hospitals, maintaining its proud reputation despite its out-of-date wards, its endless corridors and numerous, quite un-necessary flights of stairs. It looked particularly depressing and down-at-heel as Araminta parked the Mini in the shed reserved for the nursing staff and walked across the wide forecourt and in through the hospital's forbidding entrance. She had driven the two hundred and seventy-odd miles with only the shortest of breaks and it had taken her eight hours; she was tired and hungry and anxious to get to her small basement flat not five minutes' walk away from the hospital, but first she had to let Pamela Carr, the relief Sister who had been doing her duties for her, know that she was back, so that she wouldn't need to come on duty in the morning. She found her in the Accident Room, and for once there was

a mere handful of patients there, and none of those in
dire need. Sylvia Dawes was there too, sitting in the office, frowning over the pile of forms on the desk. She
was a small, neat girl, Junior Sister on the department
and a great friend of Araminta. She looked up as she
went in and said in a relieved voice: 'Oh, good, you're
back—now I can leave these wretched things for you.
Did you have a good time?'

Araminta perched on the edge of the desk, 'Lovely.
Quiet—rotten weather most of the time, though, but a
smashing hotel; oak beams and comfy chairs and gorgeous food.'

'No men?'

She shook her head. 'Middle-aged, and one or two
sailing enthusiasts.'

'Did you go sailing, then?'

'No—yes—well, I did, just once.'

'Was it fun?'

Araminta allowed her thoughts to dwell on the ill-
tempered giant who had rescued her and Mary Rose.
'No, not really,' she admitted, and felt regret that it
hadn't been. 'Anything happen while I was away?'

'The usual,' Sylvia told her, and Araminta nodded
her head. 'The usual' covered a multitude of things: road
accidents, small children who had fallen into the washing machine, old ladies with fractured thighs, old men
dying for lack of warmth or good food, housewives who
had fallen off chairs while hanging the curtains, youths
with broken noses and badly cut up faces, coronaries,
and distraught men and women of all ages who had taken
an overdose. She got off the desk, said: 'Oh, well—back
to work tomorrow. Pam's off in the morning, isn't she?
Are we on together at eight o'clock?'

Sylvia nodded. 'I'm off at one o'clock and then two days off—you've got Staff Nurse Getty, though, and that nice Mrs Pink as well as two students.'

Araminta nodded in her turn. 'I'm going home now—see you in the morning.' She said goodnight and went back to the Mini and drove herself back into the street, to turn into a narrow, dark thoroughfare not a stone's throw away. It was lined with grim Victorian houses, all exactly alike and all long since turned into flats. She stopped half way down the terrace, opened the squeaky area gate and descended the steps to the neatly painted door of her flat, and went inside. There was the tiniest of lobbies leading to a quite large sitting room where she cast down her handbag, wound the clock, switched on the radio and then went back to the car for her luggage before driving a few yards down the road where she had a lock up garage. The little car safely stowed, she went back to the flat, shut the door on the dark evening and went along to the minute kitchen to put on the kettle.

The little place looked pleasant enough with the lamps switched on and the gas fire burning; she went to the bedroom next and unpacked her case, then made tea and sat down to drink it, casting a housewifely eye round her as she did so. The place needed a good dust, otherwise it was as clean and tidy as she had left it; its cheerful red carpet brushed, the colourful cushions nicely plumped up, the small round table where she had her meals shining with polish. It was a very small flat and rather dark on account of it being almost a basement, but Araminta counted herself lucky to have a home of her own, and so close to her work, too.

She poured herself a second cup and looked through

her post; the electricity bill, a leaflet asking her if she had any old iron or scrap metal, and a letter or two from friends who had married and gone to live in other parts of the country. She read them all in turn and poured more tea. 'What I would really like,' she told herself out loud, 'would be a huge box of wildly expensive flowers and a note begging me to spend the evening at one of those places where the women wear real diamonds and there's a champagne bucket on very table.' She kicked off her shoes for greater comfort. 'I should have to wear that pink dress,' she mused, absorbed in her absurd daydream, 'and I'd be fetched by someone in a Rolls—the best there is—driven by...' She stopped, because the dark, bad-tempered man in the yacht had suddenly popped into her head, so clearly that there was no question of anyone else taking his place.

'Fool,' said Araminta cheerfully, and took the tray out to the kitchen.

The morning began badly with a severely burned toddler being brought in by a terrified mother. Araminta, her honey-coloured hair crowned by a frilled cap, her slim person very neat in its navy blue uniform and white apron, sent an urgent message to James Hickory, the Casualty Officer, to leave his breakfast and come at once, and began the difficult task of saving the child's life; putting up a plasma drip, assembling the equipment they would need, preparing the pain-killing drug the small screaming creature needed so urgently. It was an hour or more before Mr Hickory, the redoubtable Mrs Pink and Araminta had done everything necessary; the small, unconscious form was wheeled away to the ICU at last, and she was able to turn her attention to the less serious cases which had come in and which Staff Nurse Getty was dealing with.

The morning followed its usual pattern after that, with a steady stream of patients arriving, being treated, and dispatched, either home again or to the appropriate ward, and because there was a sudden rush at midday, Araminta didn't go to the dining room for her dinner, but gobbled a sandwich, washed down with a pot of tea, in her office. She didn't mind much; she was off duty at five o'clock; she would cook herself a meal when she got home, go to bed early and read. Viewed from the peak hour of a busy day, the prospect was delightful.

She managed to get over to the Nurses' Home for tea; the Sisters had a sitting room there, and it had long been the custom for them to foregather at four o'clock, that was if they could spare the time. There had been a break in the steady stream of patients coming into the Accident Room, and Araminta, leaving Mrs Pink—a trained nurse of wide experience—in charge, felt justified in taking her tea break.

There was quite a crowd in the sitting room, bunched round the electric fire while Sister Bates, by virtue of her seniority both in service and in years, poured out. Araminta squeezed in between a striking redhead of fragile appearance, who ruled Men's Medical with an iron hand, and a small, mousey girl who looked as though she couldn't say bo to a goose, but who nevertheless held down the exacting job of ENT Theatre Sister. They both said: 'Hi—how's work after the Cornish fleshpots?'

'Foul,' declared Araminta succinctly. 'That trachie we sent you—how's it going?' she asked the mousey girl, and the three of them talked shop for a few minutes while they drank their tea and ate toast and the remains of someone's birthday cake. 'Going out this evening?' asked Debby, the redhead.

Araminta shook her head. 'Supper round the fire, bed and a book.'

'And that will be the last time for weeks,' observed Sister Bates, who had been eavesdropping quite shamelessly. 'Who's the current admirer?'

Araminta grinned up at her from her place on the floor. 'Batesy dear, I haven't got one…'

Sister Bates frowned with mock severity. 'You've got dozens—well, all the unattached housemen for a start. I've never met such a girl!' But her blue eyes twinkled as she spoke. Araminta was so very pretty and nice with it; she never lacked for invitations although everyone knew that she never angled for them, they just dropped into her lap and she accepted them, whether they were rather grand seats at the theatre or a quick egg and chips at the little café round the corner, and not even her worst enemy—and she had none, anyway—could accuse her of going out of her way to encourage any of the men who asked her out, and she made no bones about putting them in their place if she found it necessary. Sister Bates thought of her as an old-fashioned girl, an opinion which might have annoyed Araminta if she had known about it. She had a great many friends and liked them all, men and women alike. That she got on well with men was a fact which didn't interest her greatly; one day she would meet a man she would love and, she hoped, marry, but until then she was just a pleasant girl to take out and remarkably unspoilt.

But for the next few evenings she stayed in her little flat, catching up on her letter writing, re-covering the cushions in the sitting room and painting the tiny kitchen. She made such a good job of this that she decided to paint the sitting room too, a task she began a few days later, for she had her two days off; ample time in which to finish the job. She came off duty full of enthusiasm for the idea, had a hurried meal, got into paint-smeared sweater and slacks, piled her bits and pieces of furniture into the centre of the room and started. She had just finished the door and was about to start on the wainscoting when someone banged the front door knocker and she put down her brush with a tut of impatience. It wasn't late, barely seven o'clock, but already dark, and she had no idea who it might be—true, James Hickory had wanted to take her to the cinema, but she had refused him firmly, and any of the other Sisters would have called through the letterbox. She got to her unwilling feet and opened the door, sliding the chain across as she did so. The dark giant who had rescued them from the beach was standing on the steps outside and she stood staring at him, round-eyed, for a few moments before exclaiming: 'Well, I never—however did you know that I live here?'

His eyes dropped to the chain and he smiled faintly. 'Your aunt gave me your address.'

'Aunt Martha? Why on earth should she do that?'

'I asked her for it. I thought you might like to hear about Mary Rose.'

'Oh, that's why you came. Come in.' Araminta slid back the chain and allowed him to enter. 'I'm painting my sitting room, but do sit down for a minute—I'll make some coffee.' She led the way into the muddle. 'There's a chair if you don't mind turning it right side up—I'll go...'

He filled the little room, she began to edge past him, conscious that she was glad to see him even though she didn't like him at all, and then came to a halt when he said: 'Is that the kitchen through there? Suppose I make the coffee and you can go on painting. May I take off my coat?'

'Yes, of course.' She hoped she didn't sound ungracious, but really, he had a nerve, though perhaps he only wanted to be kind. She took a quick look at his face and decided that he looked more like a robber baron than a do-gooder. She picked up the brush once more and got down on to her knees, feeling that she had rather lost her grip on the situation. 'I don't know your name,' she called through the open door, and then as he showed himself in the open doorway, 'Mind that paint, I've just done it.'

'Van Sibbelt—Crispin,' he told her, and disappeared to turn off the kettle. He was back again presently with their coffee mugs on a tray. He handed her one, offered the sugar and sat down on the wooden box she had been standing on to reach the top of the door.

'About Mary Rose,' he observed easily, 'she's doing very well, clumping round in a leg plaster.' He saw her look of enquiry and added placidly: 'I telephoned to find out.'

'I'm glad she's OK.' Araminta felt a little out of her depth. 'It was very nice of you to let me know.' She sipped her coffee. 'You live in London?'

'No.'

A not very satisfactory answer, but she tried again. 'You're not English, are you? Your name—isn't it Dutch?'

'Yes.'

She put down her mug with something of a thump.

'Look, I'm not being curious—just making polite conversation. In fact,' she added with some asperity, 'I've every right to be curious, for I can't think why you should go to the trouble of coming here. If my aunt gave you my address you could just have well sent a postcard about Mary Rose.'

He regarded her in silence, his face a little austere, then just as she was beginning to feel uncomfortable, he said: 'I wanted to see you again.'

At the very last second she thought better of asking him why, but instead she asked him, very nicely, if he would go. 'Such a pity that you should call at an awkward time, but you can see that I'm at sixes and sevens with this painting—you don't mind, do you? Do finish your coffee first, though.'

He looked as though he was going to laugh, but instead he said gravely, 'I see how busy you are. If you have a second brush I will do those bookshelves for you—half an hour's work at the most—it would help you a good deal.'

She got to her feet, which was a mistake, because he stood up too, towering over her, making her feel very small and at a disadvantage. All the same, she said a little coldly: 'It's most kind of you to offer, but I can manage all the same, thanks.'

'The brush-off,' he murmured, and grinned disarmingly, so that instead of looking like a well-dressed man of forty or so, he was a boy enjoying a splendid joke with himself.

'Men,' thought Araminta, crossly, watching him put on his coat again. Here he was, walking in and out of her life just as the fancy took him. She wished him goodbye in an austere voice and closed the door firmly on his broad back.

She went on painting until very late; the book-shelves proved awkward to do and she had to stand on the box again. The second time she fell off she was unable to refrain from wishing that she had accepted Doctor van Sibbelt's kind offer.

She finished towards evening the next day and that left her with a whole day more in which to plant spring bulbs in the troughs and pots which lined the tiny paved area outside her front door. She lingered over the task, looking up and down the street from time to time—perhaps Doctor van Sibbelt was still in London, and despite his cool reception, would come again to see her. He didn't; she went indoors, washed her hair, did her nails and watched a boring programme on TV before going to bed early.

She had been on duty barely an hour the next morning when they were all startled by an explosion, its repercussions rumbling on and on, so that even the solidly built Accident Room shook a little.

'A bomb,' said Araminta, busy at her desk, and left her papers to hurry into the department. It wasn't the first time; they all knew what to do, they were ready by the time James Hickory reached them with the news that they would be receiving the casualties. Such patients as there were were moved to one end of the receiving area with a borrowed houseman to look after them. Araminta sent a student nurse to look after him and went to answer the telephone. There would be twenty odd casualties, said an urgent voice, mostly glass wounds, but there were still some people trapped.

She relayed the information to James, telephoned for another houseman and went to cast a trained eye over the preparations. There would be more nurses coming within a few minutes and probably Debby, who wasn't on duty, but would return if she were near enough. Araminta took off her cuffs, rolled up her sleeves and went to meet the first ambulance, its sing-song wail reaching a crescendo as it stopped before the open doors.

There were two stretcher cases; the other two, both men, were walking, helped by the ambulance men. They were covered in dust and nasty little cuts from flying glass and wore the look of men who had been severely shocked. Araminta consigned them to Mrs Pink and turned her attention to the stretcher cases. They were both unconscious, badly cut about the head and face, and one of them had an arm in a rough sling. She set to work on them, with calm speed, following James' careful instructions; they had barely dealt with them and sent them up to waiting theatre, before the second ambulance arrived.

After that, time didn't matter. They kept steadily on, coping with the stream of patients, seeing that the very ill ones had priority, and Araminta had the added task of seeing that her team of nurses, now swollen by extra help sent from the wards, were deployed to their best advantage. It was fortunate that a number of the victims were only slightly injured, so that after having cuts stitched, bruises treated and a hot drink, they were able to be sent to their homes. But that still left a hard core of badly injured, and some of them she could see wouldn't be fit to be moved for a little while yet; not only were they badly injured, they were filthy dirty, with hair full of glass splinters and torn clothes which had to be carefully cut away so that they might be examined for the minute but dangerous wounds made by metal splinters and slivers of glass and wood. She was cutting away the hair from a scalp wound when another ambulance arrived and within seconds the ambulance men were coming through the door with the stretcher between them, not waiting for the porters' help. Araminta knew both the men well; solid, reliable, not easily put out, but they looked worried enough now. She handed her scissors to the student nurse who was helping her and hurried across the littered department, sweeping a trolley along with her.

'I take it it's urgent, George?' She eyed the grey face above the blanket.

'Just got 'im out, they 'ave, Sister—lorst a leg. There'll be a copper along with details—'e's in a bad way.'

She looked around her. Everyone was busy; a houseman was disappearing through a door carrying a child, the nurses were stretched to their limit, James and the house physician who had come to give a hand were bending over an elderly woman, who, not seriously hurt when she was admitted, had collapsed with a coronary. Someone would have to come. The ambulance men slid the stretcher on to the trolley and swung it into an empty bay and she lifted the blanket.

The patient, if he were to be saved, would need a blood transfusion before anything else. Araminta bade the ambulance men goodbye and picked up one of the small glass tubes lying ready on the dressing trolley; at least she could get a specimen of blood while she waited for a doctor. She was putting the cork back in when she was addressed from behind.

It was the senior consultant surgeon, Sir Donald Short.

'Ah, Sister, you appear to need help.' She had never

been so thankful to hear his rather gruff voice. 'Perhaps we could give a hand.' He had come round the foot of the trolley and was already taking off his jacket. 'I see you have taken some blood—good. Run along to the Path Lab and get it cross-matched—and look sharp about it.' He lifted the blanket in his turn. 'We must do what we can for this poor fellow.'

Araminta didn't stop to speak. There was no need to detail the man's injuries; she turned round to do as she had been told and found her way blocked by Sir Donald's companion—Doctor van Sibbelt, no less. The interesting and strangely disturbing fact registered itself upon her busy mind to be dismissed immediately; there were other, more important matters on hand.

By the time she got back with the two vacoliters of blood, the two men were hard at work with artery forceps, tying off carefully as they went. Sir Donald barely glanced at her, and Doctor van Sibbelt didn't look up at all.

'Get that up, Sister,' the consultant commanded. 'Crispin, see if you can find a vein in that arm—we'll run in the first liter as fast as we can and follow it with the second before we take him to theatre.' He paused for only a moment. 'Finished, Sister? Get hold of main theatre and tell them I want it ready in five minutes.'

He watched his companion slide the canulla into a limp vein. 'Crispin, will you give the anaesthetic? It'll relieve the pressure on the other theatres.' He added sharply: 'We need more blood, Sister.'

'It's on its way, sir,' Araminta was unflurried, 'and I'll see that it goes to theatre.'

'Good girl—let me have a pad here, then. Poor devil!'

Araminta took a blood pressure which only just registered. The face on the pillow was grey with shock; it could have belonged to an old man, although it was a mere lad lying there. She pitied him with all her warm heart but there was no time for pity; efficiency and gentleness and speed—above all, speed, came first. She could pity him later.

She sped away to telephone theatre, and saw as she went that the place was at last almost empty—there were still three or four patients waiting to be warded, and a handful of slightly injured people waiting to have stitches and anti-tetanus injections. She had a quick word with Mrs Pink and Staff Nurse Getty, then flew back to escort her patient to theatre. Sir Donald, Doctor van Sibbelt and their patient had already gone; she cleared up the mess in the bay and turned her attention to helping James. And after that there was the business of clearing up—they were quick at that, but it took time; everything had to be exactly as it was, ready for any kind of emergency once more.

The morning had gone. It was long past the nurses' dinner time, she sent them in ones and twos for their belated meal, and when Staff got back, retired to her office, where old Betsy, the department maid, had taken a tray of coffee and sandwiches. She lingered now, to receive praise from Araminta for the useful part she had played in the morning's work.

'Cups o' tea,' she declared contemptuously, 'and collecting up the dirties—that ain't much, Sister. Not when I seen you and the nurses covered in blood, mopping up and bandaging and giving them nasty jabs.'

She spoke with some relish, for although she was a dear old thing, devoted to Araminta, zealous in her cleaning operations round the department and with a heart of gold, she enjoyed any dramatic occasion.

'Go on with you, Betsy,' said Araminta. 'You know as well as I do that hot tea is one of the quickest ways of helping someone who's had a shock to feel normal again—why, if you hadn't been there with your urn, we should have had twice as much work.'

She took a sip of coffee and bit into a sandwich, and Betsy, looking pleased, pushed the sugar bowl nearer. 'That young man, 'im with the leg orf—is 'e going ter be OK?'

Araminta pushed her cap to the back of her head, allowing a good deal of her golden hair to escape untidily, she pushed that back too rather impatiently. 'I hope so, Betsy.'

Her elderly handmaiden trotted to the door, where she paused to say: 'Well, 'e ought ter get well with Sir Donald tackling 'im. And 'oo was that fine fellow with 'im?'

Araminta declared mendaciously that she didn't know, for if she had said anything else Betsy would have stayed for ever, asking questions in her cockney voice; probably the selfsame questions to which Araminta herself would have liked to know the answers. She sighed and dragged a formidable pile of Casualty cards and notes towards her, and began, between bites and gulps, to enter the morning's work into the Record Book. She had barely started when she was called away to cast an eye over an overdose which had been brought in and who Staff didn't quite like the look of. The man was indeed in a sorry state—they worked on him under James' patient directions and then coped with a sprained ankle, an old lady knocked down by a bus, a child scalded by a kettle of boiling water and a very old man found unconscious by the police, and he was followed by a baby who had swallowed a handful of plastic beads. There was a pause after that, long enough for them to stop for a welcome cup of tea while the two student nurses, back from tea, cleared up once more.

'Quite a day!' observed Araminta, 'and I've got all this wretched writing to do before I can get off duty.' She glanced at her watch. 'It's time for those two to go, anyway—Nurse Carter's on at six, isn't she? And Male Nurse Pratt—he's good; they both are. A pity Sylvia wasn't here, but we should be all right now.' She crossed her fingers hurriedly as she spoke. 'Oh, lord, I shouldn't have said that.' She poured second cups. 'Get yourself off on time, Dolly.'

'What about you, Sister?' Her faithful right hand looked worried.

'Well, I must get this done before I go, and by the time I'm ready the Night people will be on; they've been promised for an hour earlier, you know—I should get away by seven o'clock at the latest.' She added gloomily: 'Let's hope we'll be slack for a day or two so that you can all get the off-duty you're owed.'

Dolly got up and tidied the cups on to the tray and picked it up. 'That would be nice, but I don't suppose it'll work that way, do you?'

Alone, Araminta buried herself in her papers, only lifting her head to bid good night to the nurses as they came off duty and thank them for their hard work. Mrs Pink had gone at four o'clock and Dolly went last of all, putting her head round the door to tell Araminta that the two evening nurses had reported for duty and that the Accident Room was blessedly free of patients for the moment.

'Good,' said Araminta absent-mindedly. 'Night staff will be on soon now—I'll just about be ready by then.'

She was finished by the time they came, but only just, for she had been interrupted once or twice. She gave her report quickly, changed out of uniform and went thankfully out of the hospital doors. There was still some evening left; she would get into a dressing gown and have her supper round the fire—a bath first, perhaps, so that she could tumble into bed as soon as she had eaten it... Her thoughts were interrupted by Doctor van Sibbelt's quiet voice. 'Quite a day,' he commented. 'You must be tired.'

Indeed she was; it was sheer weariness which made her snap: 'Don't you know better than to creep up on someone like that? I might have screamed!'

'I'm sorry—you need your supper.' He tucked a hand under her arm and began to walk her down the shabby street. 'I'll get it while you have a bath.'

If he had given her the chance she would have stopped in order to express her opinion of this suggestion, but as it was she did the best she could while he hurried her along. 'I haven't asked you to supper, Doctor. I'm far too tired to entertain anyone—even if I had wanted to do so, and I don't.'

He gave a chuckle. 'Yes, yes,' he said soothingly, 'but I hardly expect to be entertained, merely to see that you get a good supper. Let me have your key.'

Araminta handed it over, aware that she was putting up a poor fight, but he had the advantage of her. Her head was addled with weariness and the thought that she was on duty again at eight o'clock the next morning did nothing to help. She went past him into the tiny hall, to turn sharply when he didn't follow her. Quite forgetful of her peevishness, she cried: 'Oh, you're not going away, are you?' for suddenly the idea of getting her own supper and eating it by herself seemed intolerable.

His voice came reassuringly from the dark outside. 'I'm here, fetching the food.' He came in as he spoke, carrying a large paper bag from Harrods. 'Run along now, there's a good girl, while I open a few tins.'

She had the ridiculous feeling that she had known him all her life; that to allow him—a stranger, well, almost a stranger—to get the supper while she took a bath was a perfectly normal thing to do. She giggled tiredly as, nicely refreshed, she swathed herself in her dressing gown and tied back her hair. Aunt Martha would probably die of shock if she could see her now! Come to think of it, she was a little shocked herself. Something of it must have shown on her face as she went into the sitting room, for Doctor van Sibbelt, carefully opening a bottle of wine, gave her one swift look and said in the most matter-of-fact of voices: 'I don't know about you, but I'm famished. Do you often get a day like this one?'

She sat down in the little tub chair by the fire. 'It's never as bad as today, though we're usually busy enough.'

'Nicely organised, too,' he commented. 'That young chap should be all right—Sir Donald did a splendid job on him.'

'You gave the anaesthetic...'

He put the wine down and started for the kitchen. 'Yes. I'm going to bring in the soup.'

It was delicious—bisque of shrimps. Araminta supped it up, keeping conversation to a minimum, and when he whisked the bowls away and came back with two plates of lemon chicken and a great bowl of crisps, as well as a smaller one of artichoke salad, she sighed her deep pleasure.

'I can't think why you should be so kind,' she exclaimed. 'Are you a Cordon Bleu cook or something?'

He poured their wine. 'My dear girl, I can't boil an egg. I just went along to the food counters and pointed at this and that and then warmed them up on your stove.'

She crunched a handful of crisps. 'Are you on holiday?' she asked as casually as she knew how, and was thwarted when he said carelessly: 'Shall we say combining business with pleasure?' And he had no intention of telling her more than that. His next remark took her completely by surprise: 'You don't fit into the London scene, you know—you looked more at home among the cliffs of Cornwall.'

She remembered with some indignation how austere and unfriendly he had been then and decided not to answer him. He had, after all, given her an excellent supper, even though she hadn't asked for it, and she couldn't repay his kindness with rudeness.

'You like your job?' he wanted to know.

She nibbled a crisp. 'Yes, very much, and I'm very lucky to have this flat.' She spoke with faint challenge, and he smiled a little.

'Er—I'm sure you are. I'll fetch the coffee.'

She watched him go to the kitchen. He was quite something, even though she reminded herself that she didn't care for that type—self-assured, too good-looking by far and with a nasty temper to boot. And he had this peculiar habit of turning up unexpectedly and for no reason at all—and why on earth should he have gone to the trouble of buying supper and cooking it for her? She wasn't the only one who had been overworked that day. Presently, when they had had their coffee, she would find that out, but now she contented herself with: 'Are you a physician?'

He put two lumps of sugar into her mug and four into his own. 'Yes.'

'But you don't work here—in England?' she persisted.

He sat back, crossed one long leg over the other and contemplated his shoes. 'You're very inquisitive,' he observed mildly.

'I am not,' said Araminta hotly. 'You invited yourself to supper, just like that, and—and you came the other evening, just as though we were lifelong friends, and you expect me to entertain you without knowing the first thing...you might be anyone!'

He put down his mug. 'So I might, I hadn't thought of that. I can assure you that I lead a more or less blameless life, that Sir Donald knows me very well indeed, and that I have no intention of harming you in any way.' He grinned suddenly. 'I have always favoured big dark girls with black eyes...'

Araminta snorted. 'I am not in the least interested in your tastes or habits,' she assured him untruthfully. 'And now would you mind very much if you go? You've been very kind, giving me this nice supper, and I'm most grateful,' then she added with disarming honesty: 'I don't think I like you.'

He disconcerted her by throwing back his head and laughing so loudly that she cried urgently: 'Oh, shush— do think of the neighbours!' She fetched his coat and offered it to him. 'Good night, and thank you again,' she said politely and stood while he slung the coat round his shoulders, which made him seem more enormous than he already was. At the door she asked: 'Why did you come?'

'I wanted to see you again.'

'You said that last time.'

He swooped suddenly and kissed her hard. 'I daresay I shall say it next time, too,' he assured her, and added blandly: 'I would have washed up…'

He had gone, up the area steps and into the dark street, without saying goodnight or goodbye. Araminta stood where she was, staring out into the night, her pretty tired face the picture of astonishment. Presently she went inside and cleared away the remains of their supper and washed the dishes. She did it very carelessly, breaking a mug and two plates, while she urged her tired brain to reflect upon the evening. But she gave up very soon and went to bed; she really was too weary to think straight, the morning would give her more sense. The thought that she might see the doctor again sneaked into the back of her mind and wiped everything else out of it, although she told herself that she couldn't bear him at any price—she would make that quite clear to him the next time they met.

Chapter 3

A good night's sleep worked wonders. Araminta rose at her usual hour, got her breakfast, tidied her small home and walked briskly to St Katherine's. It was a chilly, grey day and the streets looked drearier than usual, but she didn't notice that. She was wondering, in the light of early morning, how on earth she had allowed herself to be conned into inviting Doctor van Sibbelt to supper. Thinking about it, she was pretty sure that she hadn't. He had invited himself—and he had behaved very strangely; she had been kissed before, but somehow this time she had felt disturbed by it, and that was strange in itself, because she didn't like him. She would take great care to treat him with polite aloofness when next they met.

She entered the Accident Room, carrying on a mythical conversation with him in which he came off very much the worse for wear, and was brought up short by the line of people already in the waiting area. Of course, they would be some of the victims of yesterday's bomb, come for a check-up. A good number of them had been sent to their own doctors for after-care, but there had been several doubtful ones who had been asked to return. Doctor van Sibbelt's handsome features faded at once and stayed that way until she went to her dinner, leaving Sylvia to cope with the few patients who were receiving attention.

Most of her friends were there, consuming their meal with the businesslike speed of those who never have the chance to linger over their food, but they managed to get a good deal of talking done at the same time. Araminta was plied with questions and the conditions of the various patients she had dispatched to the wards the day before were discussed at some length. They were consuming their stewed fruit and custard when someone asked: 'Who was that man with Sir Donald? I saw them coming out of theatre. Didn't you say Sir was with you, Araminta?'

Araminta, her mouth full, nodded.

'And the man with him?'

She nodded again and managed: 'He's a doctor.'

'He's a smasher.' It was the same girl who spoke, one of the junior sisters on Men's Surgical, a pert, pretty girl whom nobody liked very much. 'Did you speak to him?'

'Yes,' said Araminta, 'I asked him if he was going to cut down and he said he'd have a try with a needle first.'

There was a little burst of laughter. 'Do you mean to tell me that he didn't ask you out?' asked the pert girl suspiciously.

'No,' said Araminta, and added quenchingly: 'It was hardly the time or the place, was it?'

Her questioner subsided and they got up from the table in twos and threes and went along to the sitting room in the Home for the last precious ten minutes, to drink their tea in peace before going back to their various jobs.

'I can't stand that girl!' Pamela Carr exclaimed as she and Araminta walked through the maze of passages to the main wing of the hospital, 'and just my wretched luck to be relieving on Men's Surgical while Sister West's on holiday—the creature seems to think that she knows the lot; its "Sister Carr, do this, Sister Carr, do that".' She sniffed. 'She tints her hair.'

Araminta chuckled. 'I thought she did. I didn't like her either, but cheer up, Pam, think of her face when she discovers that you've been offered Sister West's job when she retires after Christmas. The boot'll be on the other foot then.'

Pam sighed. 'It seems a long way off—ever so many things could happen…'

'Such as what?' Araminta pushed the Accident Room door open. 'You could meet a millionaire who falls for you on sight and carries you off to some gorgeous mansion…'

Her companion laughed. 'I'd like to see it happen! It sounds more like you.'

'I'm not the type. Bye for now.'

The afternoon dragged a little. The hospital had been taken off take-in for a couple of days, so that all the emergencies could go to neighbouring hospitals, leaving St Katherine's time to get back into its stride. Araminta had the time now to sit at her desk and make out the off duty for the month ahead, write the nurses' reports, harangue the laundry, the dispensary and the Admissions Office by telephone, and go on a careful inspection of her department. This was something she did regularly, for although she was on excellent terms with her staff, she allowed no slackness. She returned to her desk well satisfied; the place was pristine, she had had time to chat to each member of her staff, arranging for them to take the off duty they had missed, say a few words in the kitchen to Betsy, and go along to X-Ray to iron out one or two awkward situations which had cropped up. It was almost time for her to go to tea, but she decided against it; Dolly could go off duty an hour earlier instead. One of the student nurses had already gone, leaving herself and the junior nurse alone until Sylvia took over at five o'clock. Araminta went to find Dolly and then poked her head round the kitchen door once to ask Betsy to let her have a pot of tea when she had a minute to spare. Well satisfied that she had done her best to make everyone happy, she went along to the end bay where a junior houseman was painstakingly reducing a dislocated shoulder. He had done it very well, she noted, only now he hadn't the faintest idea what to do next. She applied the bandage for him, her unassuming manner leading him to believe that he had allowed her to do it out of the kindness of his heart because she needed the practice.

The little corner shop was still open when she went off duty, so she bought a loaf and a tin of beans and a pound of apples and went home, where, over her simple meal, she found herself wishing that the Dutch doctor was there too, bad temper and all, offering her something tasty from Harrods.

It was several days later that she overheard Sir Donald telling James that Doctor van Sibbelt was back in his own country. It was a pity that they walked away just then and she was unable to hear any more. It was fortunate, though, that that very evening she had agreed to go to the cinema with James. They had time for a cup of coffee before the film started and she led the conversation carefully round to Doctor van Sibbelt, 'What part of Holland does he come from?' she wanted to know in an off-hand way.

'No idea. I don't really know what he does—something in medicine, of course. He comes over here quite a bit, so I hear. His English is pretty good, isn't it?'

'I—yes, I suppose so...'

James rambled on. 'He's rather a splendid-looking chap, I thought—made a great impression on the girls...' He chuckled to himself. 'Not bad, seeing that he's reaching for forty.' The way he said it made it sound like eighty, and Araminta said sharply: 'That's not even middle-aged,' and then hurried on because James had given her a mildly enquiring look: 'Ought we to be going? I'd hate to miss any of the film.'

And that was the last of Doctor van Sibbelt. Or so she told herself.

She went home the following weekend, driving herself in the Mini. It was a splendid morning, although there was a nip in the air which warned her that winter wasn't so very far away. She left early, before the morning traffic piled up, so that she was out of London and on to the M4 while the roads were still fairly quiet. She drove fast, stopping briefly for coffee before turning off the motorway to go across country to Bridgewater. She was a good driver, but if she went through Bristol she would be held up for hours and she knew the quieter country roads very well. At Bridgewater she took the Minehead road and slowed down to enjoy the scenery, and Dunster, when she reached it, was delightfully quiet. She entered the little town on a sigh of pleasure, past the Luttrell Arms and the smalls shops lining the broad main street, with a glimpse of the castle at the end of it, and then past the church and into a narrow lane where the houses, although small, were well kept. At the end of the row, standing a little apart, was her home, just the same as all the others but with a small garden before it. Araminta pulled the Mini into the side of the road and jumped out, running up the path like a small girl to fling herself into Aunt Martha's arms and then embrace her father. And there was Toby to hug too, an elderly nondescript cat who had walked in one day years ago and had been a close member of the household ever since. He sat on her lap, purring, while she drank the coffee her aunt insisted she needed before they had their lunch, and presently she went upstairs to her small, rather dark, room, with its shelves full of china ornaments and the bits and pieces she had collected since she was a very small girl, and its narrow bed with its faded eiderdown. She tidied herself slowly, savouring the quiet and the delicious smells coming from the kitchen. Aunt Martha might look like a straightlaced dowager, but she was a dream of a cook.

It was after lunch, when they had washed up and were sitting round the fire, her aunt with her knitting, her father with his pipe and a massive book at his elbow and Araminta sitting between them with Toby in her lap once more, that the name of Doctor van Sibbelt cropped up. They had been talking about their holiday and it was

Aunt Martha who remarked on his charm of manner as she went on to say: 'And did he go to see you, child? I gave him your address; he seemed anxious to let you know about that little girl—Mary Rose.'

'Oh, yes—he called one evening.' Araminta had her voice casual.

'Very thoughtful of him—a kind, considerate man,' pronounced her aunt. 'You agreed with me, William?'

Mr Shaw nodded. 'A first-class sailor, too.' He smiled at his daughter, and as they both expected her to contribute her share of his praises, she said: 'Yes, well... As a matter of fact, he's a doctor. I daresay you know. He lives in Holland—he went back...'

She hadn't meant to mention that fact. Now they would ask any number of questions, bless them. But she need not have worried, for her father exclaimed: 'Good heavens, that reminds me, I had a long letter from your cousin Thomas this very morning. My elder sister's boy, if you remember, my dear. He's been married some years now and he must be ten years or more older than you—more,' he paused to think. 'I can't quite remember in which year he was born...'

'That doesn't matter,' interrupted Aunt Martha firmly. 'Tell her about the letter.'

'Ah, yes. He went into the Civil Service and has been living for several years in Amsterdam—something to do with the Common Market. There's a boy, he must be about ten years old.' He paused again, this time to relight his pipe while his listeners waited with outward patience. 'Thelma, his wife—perhaps you remember her?—is very ill; leukaemia, and it seems she can't live long, poor girl. Thomas asks if you would go over to Amsterdam and look after her and run the house. It would be a question of a month or so—even weeks. Thelma doesn't speak the language very well and doesn't want anyone in the house. Thomas thought of you.' He looked at Araminta over his spectacles. 'I daresay he doesn't know that you have a very good job; after all, we don't correspond very much. I daresay you don't remember him at all...'

'Oh, yes I do, Father. Not very tall and going a little bald and he was pompous—poor little man.' She returned her father's look steadily. 'You'd like me to go, wouldn't you, Father?'

He smiled. 'His mother was my favourite sister and we were very close, though I can't say I ever took to Thomas. I leave it to you, my dear, but it would be very nice if you could get leave from the hospital. He doesn't mention paying you and I suppose if you could get leave it would be unpaid? There is such an arrangement?'

'I think so, but I'm not sure for how long I could go. If I got a couple of weeks, would that help? Just long enough for Thomas to make some other arrangement? If Thelma is very ill she might have to go into hospital, or if she's able, be brought back to England.'

'Now that's an idea,' agreed Aunt Martha, 'and perhaps if you were there with her, you could persuade her. Does she really have to go into hospital?'

'When she becomes very ill, yes, although she could get worse suddenly before she could be moved. I don't know anything about it, but if she's fit enough and the doctors there would agree to it, I could bring her back— has she got any family?'

'None,' said her father, 'more's the pity.'

'And the boy?'

'Well, they've been there three years or more and of

course he goes to a Dutch school—probably Thomas wouldn't want to take him away.'

Araminta was aware that she was being looked at intently. Her father and her aunt were both sweeties, but they still lived in a different age. They had made sacrifices in their youth; probably done a great many things they hadn't wanted to do because it had been their duty, and they couldn't conceive of anyone doing other than that. Probably, she thought wryly, they thought that she wouldn't mind jeopardizing her job—her future, even, in order to do her duty by the family. Any minute now they would remind her that blood was thicker than water. She said quietly: 'I'll go and see about it when I get back—will that be time enough? I'm sure something could be arranged.'

She was rewarded by their relieved smiles.

The weekend went far too quickly. Araminta went to church on Sunday morning and then stood about in the churchyard, talking to the people she had known all her life, and in the afternoon, her elderly relations nicely settled by the fire, she put on an old tweed coat, tied a scarf over her hair and walked briskly through the village and down to the water. The weather was still clear and sunny, Wales seemed very close with only the Bristol Channel between them. She walked along the rough sand, kicking up the stones, her hands in her pockets, and thought about going to Holland. It would be fun to see another country; true, she had been to France several times, but Holland seemed more foreign, probably because she knew very little about it— not that she would get much time to herself to explore, she thought gloomily; running Thomas's house, looking after Thelma and keeping an eye on the boy would surely keep her fully occupied.

She turned for home and found herself wondering whereabouts Doctor van Sibbelt lived—Holland was such a very small country, they might bump into each other. She stopped to throw stones into the water, frowning. She seemed to remember reading somewhere that Holland was very densely populated, which made their chance of meeting amongst the teeming millions even less likely.

She went to the office when she got back on Tuesday morning. The Accident Room was busy, but not so busy that Staff Nurse Getty couldn't manage very well for half an hour; besides, since the bomb, she had been sent two extra nurses. Miss Best, the Principal Nursing Officer, heard her out without interruption and then sat frowning down at the papers before her. At length she said: 'Well, Sister Shaw, I won't deny that your request comes at a very awkward time—just when we need every nurse we have, and you are invaluable to us, you know, but I don't see how I can refuse you. I suggest that you have three weeks unpaid leave and if circumstances allow you will return within that time, and if for any reason you are unable to do so, then we must review the situation. When do you wish to go?'

Araminta thought. 'I have to write to my cousin and find out when he wants me—imagine that will take a day or so. If I am prepared to go in three days' time— just in case he telephones—and go on working until I hear for certain. Would that do?'

Miss Best nodded a majestic head. 'That seems a sensible idea,' she agreed. 'You will of course return as soon as possible, Sister Shaw?'

'Yes, of course, Miss Best—only supposing my cousin's wife should need me longer than the three weeks—I mean, for a much longer period?'

Miss Best eyed her morosely across the desk. 'Then I shall have no choice but to fill your post—you see, I cannot afford to hold it open, much though I should regret having to replace you, my dear.' She added bracingly: 'But I trust that this won't occur, and if it should, I shall do my utmost to help you, you may depend on that.' Her severe face broke into a smile. 'Let us look on the bright side and hope that you will return very shortly.'

And that was all very well, thought Araminta confusedly, but it might not be the bright side for Thelma. She made a suitable reply and went back to the Accident Room, which, in her absence, had become a hive of industry, so that it was impossible to tell anyone that she would be going away very shortly. She wrote to her father during her delayed dinner time, and wrote to Thomas too, thinking as she did so that she wasn't going to enjoy his company very much, but if Thelma was very ill, she wouldn't have much time to spend with him. Besides, there was the boy whose name she had forgotten to ask. She sighed as she stuck on the stamps. She might have made her father and Aunt Martha happy, and possibly Thomas, but she certainly hadn't followed her own inclinations. She went back to her work, and when there was a breathing space, told Dolly and Mrs Pink, who promptly offered to increase her hours of duty while she was away—a kind gesture, seeing that she had a husband and two children to look after as well as doing her work as a staff nurse at the hospital.

She received a pompously worded telegram two days

later, urging her to leave for Amsterdam at the earliest moment, and the following morning, with the good wishes of her friends ringing in her ears, she was on her way. She had decided to fly to Holland, though it would have been nicer to have taken the Mini, but the chance to get out on her own would be slight and it would have been a waste of money and effort. Besides, it was only for a week or two, sooner than that perhaps, if she could persuade the doctors to let Thelma return to England.

She followed the other passengers off the KLM plane at Schiphol and hoped that there would be someone to meet her. There wasn't, so she stood around for a little while until it became evident that Thomas hadn't been able to get to the airport, and in all fairness to him, she hadn't asked to be met, merely said at what time she would arrive, so she went outside and got on a bus, in which she was whisked to the city in a very short space of time, and found herself outside the KLM offices where she got herself a taxi, showed Thomas's address to the driver, and then sat back to enjoy the ride. For the first ten minutes or so she gazed enchanted from the taxi window, trying to look at everything at once—the tall, gabled houses, the bustling streets and the glimpses of steel grey water as they crossed the canals. But presently they turned away from the city's heart, driving now through narrow streets lined with blocks of modern flats, red brick and functional. Araminta hoped fervently that Thomas didn't live in one of them, and breathed a sigh of relief when the street merged into a wide thoroughfare with a broad canal running alongside it, and the other taken up by more flats—but they weren't as high as the previous ones, and they had wide windows filled with flowers and handsome entrances as well as grass lawns between the blocks, laid out with trees and shrubs which, even at the end of autumn, looked pleasant enough. Perhaps Thomas and his family lived in one of these.

It seemed that he did; the taxi-driver slithered to a halt before the entrance to a block half way down the street, got out, carried her case into the hall for her, waited patiently while she found the right money, and bade her a cheerful goodbye. She felt a little lost without him; she quite understood that Thomas might not have been able to meet her at Schiphol, but surely he could have been on the look-out for her arrival? She stood looking around her. The hall was square with a staircase in one corner and two lifts, side by side, and it was very quiet. For all she knew the building might have been empty. She went over to the lifts and tried, with no success at all, to decipher the notices beside them, and muttering crossly because she couldn't understand a word of them, got into one and pressed the button for the third floor. Thomas's number was one hundred and thirty-five, and she had to start somewhere. The third floor landing looked very like the entrance hall and was just as silent; the flat numbers went no higher than one hundred. Araminta got back into the lift again and pressed the button to the fifth floor, and this time she was lucky; the flat was at the end of a long corridor, well carpeted and very clean. When she rang the bell, the door was opened by a small boy who stared at her for a long moment and then said in an accusing way: 'You're Araminta—we've been expecting you.'

It was on the tip of her tongue to point out that it didn't look much like it to her, but she smiled instead, wishing she knew his name, and contented herself with a cheerful 'Hullo.'

'Father's waiting for you in his study,' the boy told her. 'He's stayed home until you got here.'

She bit back the words teetering on her tongue. It would never do to start off on the wrong foot; probably Thomas was beside himself with worry and anxiety. But when she was ushered into a small dark room facing the front door, to find Thomas sitting behind a desk much too large for him and looking incredibly pompous, she was inclined to change her mind about that. He didn't look anxious about anything, only annoyed and impatient. And his greeting was hardly what she had expected, for he pushed aside some papers before him and without bothering to get out of his chair, said: 'Bertram saw your taxi arrive. If I had had the time to write to you, I should have told you to take the bus, it would have cost far less—as it is, you've taken a good deal longer than I should have thought necessary.'

Araminta chose a chair and sat down. She said in a calm, cool voice which hid her rage very well indeed: 'It seems that you've changed your mind, Thomas. From your telegram I gathered that you wanted me to come and help Thelma—probably you've made other plans and no longer wish me to stay with you.'

He looked so astonished and dismayed that she almost laughed. 'Why should you say that?' he demanded.

'You don't appear to be at all pleased to see me. You knew what time I was arriving at the airport, but I hardly expected you to meet me there. I thought you would be looking after Thelma—and really, the least you could have done, when Bertram saw my taxi arriving, was to have come down and met me. Instead of which you sit there as though you were interviewing a new maid—perhaps it's living in Holland,' she added reflectively.

Thomas looked as though he would choke; his face went a rich plum colour and he gobbled. He got up from his chair and came round the desk, a short, stout man, not even middle-aged. But he was, she decided judicially, a man who had never been anything else... 'I'm sorry,' he said stiffly. 'I have a great deal of work on my mind—an important job, you understand; extra time on committees, and so on...'

'And Thelma?' prompted Araminta.

'Naturally, although I fancy that she takes advantage of her sickly disposition. I'm aware that she's ill, but she's still a young woman—to resign herself to the life of an invalid seems to me to be quite unnecessary.'

'Well...!' Araminta breathed deeply, biting off the words she had been about to utter and contenting herself with a fervent: 'I'm glad I came.'

She was misunderstood, for Thomas said graciously: 'Amsterdam is a splendid city in which to live, and as you see, I have an excellent flat. And I own a Mercedes.' He allowed himself a smile. 'I venture to think that my work is by no means unimportant here.'

'Where's Thelma?' asked Araminta, her patience at such a low ebb that she very nearly reached and thumped her cousin.

'She's probably in the bedroom.'

'Then since I'm here—at your request, Thomas—to do what I can for her, I'll go and meet her.'

He preceded her to the door. 'Splendid—now that you're here, Cousin Araminta, I shall leave for my office.'

She paused outside the door. 'You come home to lunch?'

'No—Thelma usually gets herself a little something.'

'And Bertram?'

'He has a midday snack with the children of a colleague of mine, and returns home about four o'clock.'

'And you? When do you get back?'

He smiled thinly. 'Dear me, what an inquisition I usually return about six o'clock—I have various people to meet...'

She cut him short mercilessly. 'And who cooks the evening meal and does the shopping for it?'

'Thelma is quite able...and there's a woman who comes in to clean—she'll shop if she's asked.'

Araminta gave him such a ferocious look that he took a step backwards and then hastily opened a door in the hall, saying as he did so: 'Here's Cousin Araminta, my dear. I'll leave you to renew your acquaintance and go to the office, I've already missed several hours' work,' he sounded accusing. 'I'll take Bertram with me and drop him off at school, it's very nearly time for his midday break.'

He had gone before Araminta could say anything more, closing the door behind him, and leaving her to cross the large, expensively furnished room to the chair by one of the windows where Thelma sat.

During her years in hospital Araminta had learned to school her pretty features into a smiling calmness, however horrifying or shocking the sights she had met with. She was glad of that now, for Thelma shocked her. She hadn't seen her for more than ten years, it was true, but this white-faced, thin woman, sitting so tiredly, wasn't anything like the Thelma she had known. She bent and kissed her gently, saying cheerfully: 'Heavens, what ages since we last met, and what a great deal we have to talk about. Look, I'm going to put my things in my room and make us a drink.'

Thelma smiled then. 'You didn't mind me not coming to meet you? I get tired, you know, it's this anaemia, I suppose. Thomas said he would see to everything—he's shown you your room, I expect?' She paused and added hesitantly: 'He was angry when the doctor said I ought to have someone to help me around the house and be with me when I go out—I'm afraid to go alone, you see—so silly, but sometimes I feel faint. Wasn't it lucky that Thomas remembered that you were a nurse? I was so glad when I heard that you were coming—I'm a great expense, you see; he said if you didn't come I should have to manage, for he couldn't afford to pay anyone.'

Araminta went on smiling while she boiled with rage. Her cousin's meanness made her feel sick, and that he should actually be a member of the family made her feel even sicker. She managed a cheerful reply and went in search of her room—small and overfurnished with the same expensive modern furniture—and then went to inspect the kitchen, where she made a large pot of tea, buttered some toast, and carried the tray back to the bedroom. Tomorrow, she promised herself, things would be different.

Over their tea, Thelma began to talk. She got tired and breathless doing it, but it was obviously such a relief that Araminta didn't interrupt her. She had this anaemia, she explained, and she had gone to the hospital once or twice, besides having a very good doctor who gave her pills, only despite these she felt so tired, and then Thomas was so easily annoyed. 'He thinks there's no need for me to go to the hospital, the last twice he rang up and cancelled the appointment—you see, he has so little time to take me. He has a car, but he needs it for the office, and besides that he's on several committees and goes out a good deal in the evenings.' She added wistfully: 'I should like to go out sometimes—with Bertram, you know, he's getting a big boy and I sometimes think…' She paused. 'Thomas has no time…'

Araminta sniffed delicately. Thomas, in her opinion, was just about the worst husband in the world. 'When do you go to the hospital for your next check-up?' she wanted to know.

'In four days' time—Thomas asked them to put it off for two weeks. I can't manage to go there by myself, you see, and it wasn't convenient for him to take me. He told them that I was quite well. You see, he'd just remembered you and hoped you would be here to take me.' Thelma's eyes filled with tears. 'I'm such a nuisance,' she whispered.

'Oh, no, you're not,' declared Araminta vigorously. 'What's more, you're going to feel better in no time at all—I don't think you've been eating enough for a start, and there's no reason why we shouldn't take a short walk every day—the doctor won't know you when he sees you at the hospital.'

And that was true enough, for sadly, unless she was very much mistaken, Thelma was very ill indeed.

She tackled Thomas about it that evening. She had spent the rest of the day helping Thelma to dress and then sit her comfortably in the living room while she took stock of the kitchen once more. Apparently she was expected to get an evening meal ready as well as cut sandwiches for Bertram, who came back from school famished. He wasn't a nice boy, she decided, for a ten-year-old he was far too precocious. She had told him off roundly for coming in with muddy boots and sent him to take them off and put on slippers and wash his hands besides, and his surprise had been quite ludicrous. Evidently he had been doing more or less what he liked around the place, and he treated his mother with an off-hand casualness which annoyed her very much.

After they had all had tea together, Araminta had suggested that he got on with his homework, and very much at a loss as to how to treat her, he had done so meekly enough, leaving her free to prepare a meal for the evening and resume conversation with Thelma.

Thomas had come home about six o'clock, greeted his wife with a brief peck on her cheek, nodded to Araminta, remarking that she had probably had an enjoyable day, and retired to his study, whence she followed him without delay. Determined to keep her temper at all costs, she said urgently: 'Thomas, you do realize that Thelma is very ill?'

He fussed with the papers on his desk and muttered: 'I'm a very busy man—some other time…'

'Now,' said Araminta, 'and don't talk a lot of rot about being busy, because you're not. And while I'm here I'll make one or two things clear. I came because you sent for me urgently, not to be an unpaid housekeeper while you sit behind that desk doing nothing, but to look after Thelma, who heaven knows needs all the care she can get. I'd imagined that you would be beside yourself with worry about her,' she went on, 'but you're not. But that's not my business, though it is my business to see that she gets good food, proper rest and gentle exercise, which means that you'll have to hire a

taxi every afternoon to take us to the nearest park and
back again. And she needs things to make her feel better, even if she isn't—champagne, and not just half a
bottle, but each day—flowers in her room, anything
she fancies to eat…'

He was plum coloured again. 'My dear Cousin Araminta, the expense!'

Her voice trembled with her effort to keep it matter-
of-fact. 'You've got me for nothing, think what you're
saving on a nurse's fees, besides,' she added soberly, 'it
won't be for long, you know.'

She turned for the door and paused there. 'And another thing, why did you cancel her appointment at the
hospital? Don't you know it's vital that she should be
seen regularly?'

He didn't look at her. 'It's difficult for me to get
enough time—she wasn't ill, only tired and a bit pale.'

'I suppose you told the doctor that she was doing
fine.'

'I said she was feeling much better…'

'Pah!' snapped Araminta, and went out, leaving the
door open. There was a great deal she longed to say,
but there was Thelma to think of.

She lay awake that night, wondering if she had been
too hasty in her judgement of Thomas. She had been
tired and uncertain of what she would find and intoler-
ant because of it—she would apologise in the morning.
She slept fitfully on the thought.

She was roused just before six o'clock by Thomas.
Thelma had been sick after a bad night, and perhaps
Araminta would go and freshen her up. 'I need my
sleep,' he explained grumpily. 'I shall go to the spare
room—don't call me until eight o'clock.'

Araminta, looking like a sleepy angel, gave him a non-angelic look. 'I shan't call you at all,' she assured him coldly, 'and don't expect me to get your breakfast, either—it's Thelma I'm looking after.' She sailed past him, her beautiful little nose lifted, and went into Thelma's room and closed the door.

She was as good as her word. She attended to her patient's wants, stayed with her until she fell into exhausted sleep, and then went back to her own room and dozed until the banging of the front door roused her. Thomas had gone, taking Bertram with him and leaving chaos in the kitchen. Despite that, she and Thelma spent a pleasant day together, and Araminta, who could cook quite nicely when she had a mind to, was delighted to see the invalid eat at least some of the dainty lunch she had prepared, and in the afternoon, nicely rested, Thelma, warmly wrapped against the wintry wind, and with Araminta's arm to support her, went for a short taxi ride and an even shorter walk in the neighbouring park before returning home to tea and toast before Bertram got home. Araminta was pleased to see that he wiped his boots carefully as he came in, although his manner towards his mother left a lot to be desired.

Thomas was, if possible, even more pompous than before when he got home. Araminta ignored this, however, merely asking him if he had remembered to bring the champagne and reminding him that he owed her the taxi fare from their afternoon's outing. He paid up with ill grace and muttered something about the champagne which she didn't quite hear. 'I can always telephone an order for it and have the bill sent here,' said Araminta sweetly.

The next two days followed the same pattern. By

the fourth morning Araminta told herself that Thelma had improved just a little. She was eating—not nearly enough, but it was a start, and she was certainly brighter in herself, even talking about a few hours' shopping, and Araminta had entered into her plans wholeheartedly. Probably their day at the shops would never materialise, but Thelma was enjoying the prospect of it. It seemed only too evident that she had had very little pleasure in the last few months.

They arrived in good time for Thelma's eleven o'clock appointment, so that there was time to look around them while they waited. The hospital was old, but the outpatients' department had been modernised and made very comfortable in the process. It was, naturally enough, packed, but Araminta would have been surprised if it had been otherwise. There seemed to be plenty of nurses too. She watched them with interest as they went about their work, quite unaware of the glances she was attracting to her own person, and even if she had been she would have thought little of it. She had accepted her honey-coloured hair as something a little out of the common at which other people stared, years ago. She turned to smile at Thelma, already tiring, but cheerful still.

'Not much longer, I think—you're all right?'

'I'm fine, and I don't mind waiting, it's nice to see so many people. I've loved these last few days—it's been such fun with you here.' Thelma smiled slowly. 'You do look nice in that suit.' She studied Araminta's outfit, and indeed it was worth a look; its russet brown, flecked with tawny orange and complemented by Araminta's best leather handbag and gloves, was decidedly eye-catching, as were her elegant brogue shoes.

'You don't look so bad yourself,' countered Araminta. 'I like that blue coat. When we go shopping let's look for a dress to match it—corduroy perhaps, or fine wool...' She launched into an undemanding chat about clothes which filled in the time nicely until their turn came at last. But when the nurse called Thelma's name and came towards them, Thelma said urgently: 'Araminta, you must come with me—I can't... I...'

'Why not?' asked Araminta matter-of-factly, and tucked a firm hand under her arm, glancing at the nurse as she did so. The nurse smiled and nodded and led the way past the rows of other patients to one of the doors facing them, and opened it.

The man behind the desk was young still, with a serious face and a quiet voice. He wished Thelma a sober good morning and looked enquiringly at Araminta, who said quickly: 'I hope you don't mind, Mrs Shaw asked me to come in with her.'

He nodded. 'You are of her family?'

'I'm her husband's cousin—I'm staying with her for a little while.'

He nodded again and bent to read the papers before him. 'You should have come two weeks ago,' he stated, and listened while Thelma explained, not very clearly. When she had finished, he said: 'I should like to examine you, Mrs Shaw, and take a blood test, for that is long overdue. We will do that first.'

He took his time with her and Araminta liked the way he put his questions, careful not to allow Thelma to guess how ill she was. He was still writing notes when the nurse came back with the path lab results of the blood count. The doctor read it with the expressionless face Araminta had come to know so well, and laid it on one side. It was only after he had written another line or two that he said casually: 'Well, I think it's time the professor saw you again, Mrs Shaw—it's, let me see, two months since you saw him, isn't it? I'll see if he can spare a minute or two.'

He gathered up his notes, nodded to the nurse and disappeared, and Thelma said worriedly: 'Oh, dear, why do I have to see the specialist? Am I worse?'

'Of course not,' said Araminta soothingly. 'It's just a routine thing, love. You see, you're under this consultant, whoever he is, but he can't see all his patients every week. He sees them the first time, decides what's to be done for them, tells his registrars the treatment he wants done and then casts his eye over them every month or so.'

She turned round as the door opened, to admit the doctor who had been examining Thelma. With him was Doctor van Sibbelt.

Chapter 4

Araminta sat with her head over one shoulder, staring at him, her mouth very slightly open, feeling she had just travelled downwards in a lift very fast. She had wondered if she would ever see him again, and had even admitted to herself that it would be rather exciting to do so; only this was more than exciting. She closed her mouth and eyed him in silence.

Doctor van Sibbelt wished Thelma a pleasant good morning, said briefly and disappointingly: 'So we meet again, Miss Shaw,' and glanced at the notes he was carrying. After a moment he went on: 'Mrs Shaw, I think that, as you are here, it would be a good idea for you to have a blood transfusion—you won't object to that?' He paused to smile at her with great charm. 'It would save you coming back this afternoon, would it not? And it will take only a short time. After an hour's rest you will be able to go home.'

Thelma looked worried. 'Oh—must I really? Thomas doesn't know—shall I feel all right afterwards?' She added uncertainly: 'I thought that those pills I've been taking…wouldn't they do as well?'

His voice was reassuringly calm and decidedly soothing. 'They have done you a great deal of good, but if you have this transfusion, it will do the work of any number of pills in a fraction of the time. You will feel the benefit almost immediately.' He smiled again and questioned gently: 'You are becoming a little tired lately?'

'Well, yes.'

'I can promise you that you will have a great deal more energy, Mrs Shaw. If you would go with Nurse— just across the passage. Miss Shaw can wait for you.'

His manner was quiet but compelling. Thelma cast a look at Araminta, who smiled and nodded encouragingly, and followed the nurse from the room. The door had barely closed behind them when Doctor van Sibbelt muttered something to the registrar, who went out too. Only then did he sit himself down.

'Perhaps you can explain why Mrs Shaw hasn't been for her check-ups?' he observed coldly. 'I see that she has missed the last two, and over the period she has been coming to us she has missed several more—and this last one,' he picked up the path lab form and waved it at her, 'her haemoglobin is thirty-two per cent. We'll give her a transfusion and that will keep her on her feet a little longer, but she will need another in a few days' time, and then another and another…a rapid deterioration.' He sighed. 'Didn't you see? You are a nurse…'

'Of course I saw! I arrived four days ago and found her sitting in a chair in her room, too tired to dress

herself. My cousin, her husband, refuses to admit that
she's ill. She's been managing somehow, but she hasn't
bothered to eat and she hadn't been out for weeks...'

'They are poor people?'

'Certainly not—Thomas runs a Mercedes and the
flat is in the Berestraat, which is quite a good neigh-
bourhood, so I'm told, and it's stuffed with expensive
furniture.'

'She should have a companion or daily nurse—we
advised that some time ago, I cannot think why...' He
paused at Araminta's impatient little snort, and then:
'Start at the beginning and tell me all about it,' he invited.

She hesitated, but only for a moment. The ill-tempered
man who had rescued her in Cornwall had been wholly
swallowed up by this quiet, well-dressed man who was so
sure of himself. She could think of no one to whom she
would rather unburden herself. She drew a deep breath
and plunged into her sorry tale. When she had finished
she made a small choking sound and declared furiously:
'Men!'

Her listener hadn't interrupted her once, but now he
said with the faintest of smiles. 'We aren't all Thomases,
my dear girl.' His tone became brisk. 'We have to think
what is best for Mrs Shaw—I think you should take her
home presently and put her to bed and give her her supper there. In the morning she will feel very much better,
but as you know, that isn't going to last long, but while it
does, I suggest that you get her out as much as she feels
she can manage—let her feel she's leading a normal life
as far as it's possible. I'll arrange for her to come in for
another transfusion on—let me see—two days' time,
and in the meantime I'll get my secretary to make an

appointment for her husband to see me.' He got up and crossed the room and stood looking down at her. 'I'm afraid Mrs Shaw's days are numbered,' he said gently.

Araminta nodded, not looking at him. 'Yes, I—I guessed that. I'm glad I came.'

He stared down at her downbent head. 'So am I, although it was inevitable.' He didn't attempt to explain this remark but looked at his watch. 'Mrs Shaw won't be ready for almost two hours,' he paused for so long that she looked questioningly at him. 'I have two more patients to see and in rather less than that time I have a lecture to give. Will you have something to eat with me presently? If you like to go back to the waiting room?'

She was surprised to find how pleased she was at his invitation, but all the same she hesitated. 'It's very kind of you, but I'm sure you have a great deal to do, and I don't in the least mind just sitting and waiting for Thelma.' Araminta hoped her voice sounded more convinced of this than she felt; apparently it didn't, for he took no notice of this at all, merely opening the door for her and repeating: 'About twenty minutes, then,' in such bland certainty that she found herself saying yes quite meekly.

The waiting room had emptied of the morning clinics and was rapidly filling again for the afternoon session. She sat quietly, taking stock of all that was going on around her, telling herself that she was really very foolish to feel so excited at the prospect of an hour of Doctor van Sibbelt's company, especially as she didn't like him. Being an honest girl, she had to admit to herself that that wasn't true any more; she wouldn't quite admit to liking him, but she did admit to a lively interest in him. Perhaps she would have the chance to ask a few pertinent questions over their meal—where he lived, whether he was married—surely he would be?—if he had children... Her reflections were interrupted by his arrival, and she watched him covertly as he came without haste across the vast room, trying to discover in this distinguished-looking man some remnant of the arrogant, faintly mocking giant who had offered to paint her bookshelves for her, and most surprisingly, cooked supper for her, too. But there was no trace. He greeted her casually, led her through OPD and out into the chilly grey day, and walked her down a narrow side street and into a small coffee shop, already half full. It wasn't at all what she had expected, for somehow he fitted into her daydreams of hothouse flowers, Rolls-Royces and champagne, but she was content enough to sit down on a high stool at the counter and cast a hungry eye over the menu.

'Coffee?' he suggested, and when she nodded, 'And how about a *kaas broodje* and a salad?' and when she nodded again, gave the order to the girl behind the counter and sat himself down beside her. He took up a great deal of room; what with a wall on one side of her and him on the other, Araminta was sadly squashed, but somehow she didn't mind at all.

'This is a splendid place in which to talk,' observed her companion, 'it's so noisy and everyone is in a hurry—now tell me about yourself.'

Their coffee had arrived. Araminta poured cream into it and stirred in the sugar before she said: 'There's nothing more to tell.'

'You left a great many gaps,' he pointed out. 'Let's fill them in: do you intend to go back to St Katherine's?'

'Well, I've been given unpaid leave for three weeks—I've had almost a week of that.' She took a bite of her roll and munched contentedly.

'And after that?' prompted her companion.

'My post will be filled.'

'I see—probably I could arrange for a nurse to take care of Mrs Shaw if you want to return before then.'

She took another bite and said with her mouth full: 'Oh, I couldn't do that! Thomas wouldn't pay for anyone, you know.'

'He doesn't—forgive me—pay you?'

'Heavens, no. So you see I must stay now I'm here, especially as Thelma... I can always get another job.' She made her voice cheerful, although the idea of packing up her little flat and finding fresh work wasn't a pleasing one.

'You would miss your friends there, and your work.' He smiled at her, his face very close so that she could see how dark his eyes were. 'Have another roll and some more coffee?'

'Please.' She watched him give the order, admiring his good looks.

'As I was saying, you will miss your friends—I daresay you went out a great deal?'

'Well, yes—I suppose I did.'

'Dinner at the Savoy, orchids and a Rolls to take you there?' he asked with faint mockery, coming too close to her daydreams.

She poured more cream into the fresh cup of coffee he had just handed her. 'Don't be silly—housemen haven't that kind of money. It was mostly egg and chips and very nice too.'

He grinned. 'And did you expect orchids and champagne and quantities of red plush today?'

Araminta put down her roll and gave him a direct look; she was nothing if not honest, it had never occurred to her to be anything else with him. 'Yes, I did—oh, not the orchids, but perhaps a little red plush. You don't—that is, one doesn't expect a consultant to nip across the road for a roll and coffee.' She frowned quite fiercely. 'But before you say something scathing, let me tell you that I'm not in the least disappointed—it's the company, not the food.'

The mocking smile was back again. 'You've stolen my lines, Araminta.'

She went a bright and very becoming pink. 'You're extremely rude! I was actually beginning to like you, but I see now that you're exactly the same as you were when we met...'

'Do tell me.' He sounded amused and not in the least repentant.

'Bad-tempered and impatient and laughing at me.' She drank the rest of her coffee and said in a small, polite voice: 'Thank you for my lunch,' and put out a hand to pick up her purse, but his own large one came down, very gently, on to it.

'I'm all those things, and more,' he told her quietly, 'but could you not like me a little despite them?'

She sat looking at his hand; it felt cool and strong, cherishing hers in its grasp—the hand of someone who would help her if ever she needed it. She said uncertainly: 'I don't understand you, or know anything about you, but I do like you.'

The hand tightened just a little. 'Good,' said the doctor, 'and you're not feeling hurt because you had coffee and *Kaas broodjes* instead of champagne and red plush?'

She tugged at her hand and found it fast held. 'Of course I'm not hurt, and if I had been you I wouldn't have wasted my money on an expensive lunch with someone I hardly knew—you could put it to better use for your wife and children.'

His eyes danced with amusement, although he answered gravely; 'But I have no wife and as far as I know, no children.'

'Oh, well—aren't you even engaged?'

'No, and I think that when I do marry I shan't want to waste time over an engagement.'

'That's arrogant of you—why, the girl might not like that at all.'

'Ah, but the girl I intend to marry will.'

It was strange how deflated Araminta felt at the thought of him marrying, silly too, she told herself sharply, and suggested that it was time for her to fetch Thelma. The deflation was completed by his readiness to go back to the hospital immediately. They parted in OPD and she thanked him once more for her lunch, to be utterly disconcerted when he remarked blandly: 'What a very pretty girl you are—I really think we must have the orchids and red plush together, don't you?'

For some reason his words infuriated her. He was adding her to his list of casual girl-friends, was he? And what about the poor girl he presumably intended marrying? 'How kind,' she told him haughtily, 'but I don't think I want to, thanks.'

He smiled down at her, not in the least put out. 'You

are a very unusual girl, and of course you don't like me quite enough yet, do you?'

He walked away and was at once immersed in conversation with a harassed nurse bearing an armful of notes. Araminta watched him look at the clock and then stride through the swing doors. He didn't look round, but she hadn't really expected him to, so that the disappointment she felt was really rather silly.

Thelma, more animated than she had been since Araminta's arrival, and with faintly pink cheeks which made her look much younger, was just ready. Araminta took her home, joining in her companion's gay chatter with a cheerfulness which hid the knowledge that within a very short time Thelma would feel as ill as she had done previously, but at least she could enjoy herself while she felt able to. Rather recklessly, Araminta told the taxi driver to take them as near as he could to the Kalverstraat and wait for them there. Vroom and Dreesman, a large department store, was at the very end of the shopping street; they would only need to walk a very few yards to reach it. The driver was an obliging man, he got out of his cab and gave Thelma an arm across the street and they gained the shop without trouble. It took Thelma only fifteen minutes to find and choose the blue dress she had set her heart on; they were back in the taxi and on the way home in no time at all, and once indoors, Araminta lost no time in putting her to bed with a cup of tea and the injunction to have a nap while she prepared the evening meal before Thomas got home.

Actually, it was he who looked in need of her care when she presented him with the bill for the day's activities. He went an alarming puce, and was in fact so incensed with her wanton spending of his money that he had no time or inclination to worry about Thelma. Araminta saw that it would be hopeless to try and make him understand; perhaps Doctor van Sibbelt would be able to do that. He ate his dinner in a stony silence, declared that he had a committee meeting to attend, and left the house, leaving Araminta to urge Bertram to his bed and then spend a cosy half hour with Thelma, until the invalid dozed off, happier than she had been for a long time.

She stayed happy for the next two days, although on the third morning, when she was due at the hospital again, she was noticeably tired. She answered the sober-faced young doctor's careful questioning cheerfully enough, submitted her finger for the routine prick, and then went off with the nurse to have her second transfusion. When she had gone Araminta got up to go too, but the doctor stopped her.

'The professor wishes that I should tell you how Mrs Shaw progresses. I am afraid that today's results are not good—twenty-nine per cent, despite her previous blood transfusion. She is now gravely ill, but I think that she must not be told of this.' He looked earnestly at her. 'You agree?'

'Yes, I do. She's been very happy—she thinks she's getting better...' Araminta stopped to steady her voice. 'Only I can't make her husband understand.'

'That has been the difficulty with us. The professor tells me that he is seeing Mr Shaw today, perhaps he will be able to explain. In the meantime, Mrs Shaw must lead a quiet life, you understand that? Let her sit up, if she wishes, but that must be all. There will be another transfusion very shortly, but she will be fetched by ambulance. The professor will arrange with Mr Shaw that he is to call his own doctor should Mrs Shaw become worse, and he will be asked to give a report by telephone each day. The end sometimes comes suddenly.' He gave her a kindly smile. 'You have met their house doctor? Doctor de Vos.'

'I've never seen him, although I seem to remember my cousin talking to a doctor on the telephone.'

Araminta spent the next two hours in the waiting room, telling herself that Thelma might want her, and hoping that she might see Doctor van Sibbelt again. But there was no sign of him. She took Thelma home presently, feeling strangely let down.

The next few days passed quietly. If Thomas had seen Doctor van Sibbelt, he gave no sign, and Araminta could detect no change in his bullying attitude towards his wife. His impatient intolerance of her weariness was only too apparent, and he did little or nothing to curb Bertram's tiresome demands to have this or that done for him. Araminta, sending the boy sulkily to his bed long after he should have been there, found herself speculating as to what would happen when Thomas was left on his own to cope with the boy.

It was the following morning when Thelma, sitting dressing-gowned in the living room while Araminta vacuumed, collapsed. She did it so quietly that Araminta, who had her back to her, heard no sound; only when she turned round did she see Thelma sagging in an untidy heap in her chair.

It was something she had dreaded and half expected. She switched off the vacuum cleaner, laid the unconscious girl back in her chair, took an almost imperceptible pulse and flew to the telephone. It didn't occur to her to ring anyone else but Doctor van Sibbelt at the hospital, and when she heard his voice very calm in her ear, she told him what had happened without wasting words. And nor did he. His: 'I'll be with you in less than ten minutes, and see that the front door is open,' was all she needed to hear. She went back to Thelma, and was still trying to revive her when he arrived.

He said without preamble: 'I'll carry her into the bedroom,' and stooped to pick up the inanimate form while Araminta went ahead of him opening doors and turning back the bed covers, then sped back to the living room for his bag. It was only when he was busy with phial and syringe that he asked: 'How did it happen?'

She told him with concise brevity and he nodded. 'It was to be expected. There was nothing to worry you until she collapsed?'

'No—she's been very bright for the last day or so, although very tired. I asked Thomas to mention that to the doctor.'

He bent over his patient. 'Telephone Mr Shaw and tell him to come now. When does the boy get home?'

'Not until almost four o'clock.' She was already half way to the door.

Thomas wasn't available, said a brisk voice at the other end of the line; he had given instructions that he was on no account to be disturbed.

'Tell him it concerns his wife,' said Arainta, 'and kindly look sharp about it.'

There was an annoyed gasp and the brisk voice said: 'There is no need...'

'Oh, yes, there is—this is urgent, life and death urgent.'

She cut Thomas ruthlessly short when she heard him prosily telling her not to disturb him with hysterical messages. 'You'd better come home—now—Thomas. Thelma's collapsed. The doctor's with her; she's unconscious.'

She didn't wait to hear his reply, but slammed down the receiver and darted back to the bedroom to meet Doctor van Sibbelt's steady eye. He moved away from the bed and said softly: 'A few minutes at the most, I'm afraid—she isn't responding at all.' He bent and took off Thelma's shoes and laid them neatly on the floor. Not looking at Araminta, he went on: 'This is the best way, you know. There was no chance at all.'

'Yes, I know. Is there anything I can do?'

He shook his head. 'Nothing at all.' He crossed the room and took her hands in his. 'Don't look like that.'

She said soberly: 'She's only thirty-five, you know— it's very young…' she had been going to say 'to die', but she choked on the words.

He tucked a hand under her arm and drew her back to the bed and they waited quietly side-by-side. Presently he leaned down and took Thelma's pulse, then straightened himself. 'A truly peaceful end,' he said, and added something in Dutch.

'You don't think she knew?'

'She would have known nothing.' He paused as the flat door was opened and Thomas's deliberate tread crossed the hall. He began to speak before he reached the bedroom, in a blustering, aggrieved voice: 'Araminta, what is all this? I really cannot have you sending hysterical messages…' He broke off, standing in the doorway while his rather high colour faded slowly. 'Why wasn't I told sooner?' he wanted to know.

The doctor looked at him with distaste. 'Your wife died rather less than five minutes ago,' he said evenly. 'We will leave you for a little while—we can talk presently.'

He walked to the door, sweeping Araminta with him, passed Thomas and closed the door on him. In the hall he said: 'An unpleasant man. I find it hard to remember that he is a relation of yours, Araminta.'

'So do I! He always was awful—now he's older he's much worse. What do we do next?'

'Doctor de Vos should be here at any minute, I told someone to telephone him from the hospital.' The doctor's face assumed such a ferocious expression that she drew a quick breath and decided prudently not to ask any more questions for the moment. It was fortunate that the silence which followed was quickly broken by the arrival of Doctor de Vos. He was a thin, stooping man with a harassed expression, whom Doctor van Sibbelt introduced briefly before walking him up and down the hall, while they conferred together in muttered undertones. Araminta, watching them, decided that they had forgotten her and went off to the kitchen. It would have to be coffee, she decided resignedly; the Dutch took their cups of coffee as seriously as the British took their tea, and she was in the minority. She had the percolator going and cups and saucers on a tray when she heard the bedroom door open and Thomas's voice calling her, and the moment she poked her pretty nose round the door he began irritably: 'I should like to know…'

He wasn't allowed to finish. Doctor van Sibbelt interrupted him with a suavity which barely concealed the ferociousness she had observed earlier. 'Ah, Mr Shaw, but first Doctor de Vos and I would like to know why it is that you told him that there was no need for him to call and see your wife. If you remember, I asked you to telephone him each day—something you did not do— and when he contacted you, you gave him to understand that he was not to visit as Mrs Shaw's condition was very satisfactory, and this after Miss Shaw had asked you to let Doctor de Vos know that your wife was becoming increasingly tired.'

He was standing very close to Thomas now, towering over him, showing him a bland face, although Araminta sensed his fine rage as she waited to hear what Thomas would say.

Thomas blustered again. The two doctors heard him out gravely with impassive faces and slightly raised eyebrows, and presently he realized that he was getting nowhere and fell silent, looking round him until his eyes lighted upon Araminta, which caused him to say: 'You should have told me—after all, you came here to look after Thelma. You're a nurse.'

He was interrupted once more. 'No possible blame can be laid at Miss Shaw's door,' said Doctor van Sibbelt in a cold voice, 'and you are, I imagine, aware of that. I thought that I had spoken plainly enough to you the other day, but apparently you are one of those people who knows better than everyone else.' He added with quiet authority: 'Be good enough to show me where I may sign the necessary papers.'

Araminta went silently into the bedroom and fetched his bag, and he took it from her with a brief word of thanks, then disappeared into the dinning room and sat down at the table. Doctor de Vos followed him, and so, presently, did Thomas. Araminta went back to the kitchen and took the coffee off the stove and sat down. She supposed that Thomas would expect her to do a great many things when the doctors had gone. She didn't want to do them, but she couldn't refuse him, but afterwards she would pack her bag and leave as early as she could in the morning. She would be able to return to St Katherine's after all, although perhaps she should stay for the funeral...

Her thoughts were interrupted by Doctor van Sibbelt who paused in the doorway, remote and professionally impersonal, to say that he had been given to understand that they would be going to a hotel for the night.

'We have advised Mr Shaw to make all the necessary arrangements and he has done so; everything will be attended to and there should be nothing further for you to do. The boy is to go straight to friends after school, and his father will go there presently and meet him.' He glanced at his watch. 'You'll be all right! I'm afraid I must return to the hospital.'

'I'll be fine,' she assured him sturdily, 'and thank you for coming so quickly.' She looked at him in sudden consternation. 'Heavens, I suppose I shouldn't have telephoned you, but you were the first person I thought of. You must have been taking a clinic...'

'A teaching round,' he corrected her, 'but that doesn't matter, I'm glad that...' He didn't finish what he had started to say. 'Goodbye.'

Doctor de Vos went shortly after and Thomas came into the kitchen, saying stiffly: 'I shall have to stay here until they've taken Thelma away.'

'Then we'd better have coffee, Thomas. I'll bring it into the living room.'

They drank it in almost total silence and presently when the door bell rang, Thomas went away, leaving

Araminta to sit listening to the murmur of voices and the slow tread of feet in the hall. When everything was quiet again she went in search of him. He was putting things into an overnight bag and when she said at once: 'Oh, shall I look out some of Bertram's things for you? Are we going now?'

He didn't quite meet her eyes, but fussed with the lock of the bag. 'I've already packed all he needs. I shall go now, but I must ask you to stay here until five o'clock or thereabouts—the office may telephone with some urgent message for me, and you can see for yourself that I must go and break the news to Bertram.'

She agreed reluctantly. To sit in the flat alone for several hours was an uninviting prospect, but it was true that Thomas had had no time in which to make any arrangements about his work. He had shown no grief at Thelma's death, but she would have to give him the benefit of the doubt. Perhaps he was suffering from shock.

He went to the door. 'I'll telephone you from my friend's house,' he told her. 'As you've nothing to do this afternoon, you could start clearing out Thelma's things.'

She looked at him with something like horror. Even allowing for shock, he was being horribly indifferent. 'No,' she forced herself to speak quietly, 'I can't do that, Thomas, she was your wife—although listening to you, I find that hard to believe. I shall pack my own things, though, and be ready to leave tomorrow.'

He stared at her in disbelief. 'But what am I to do—and what about Bertram?'

'I came here to look after Thelma. She doesn't need me any more and you haven't liked me being here, have you? Besides, I have a job to go back to, or perhaps you'd forgotten that? You must get a housekeeper,

Thomas. And as for Bertram, he can't bear the sight of me, anyway.'

'You're a hard young woman,' Thomas pronounced, but she shook her head.

'No, Thomas, I'm not, but you're a hard man, and a hypocrite as well.'

He gave her a look of dislike as he opened the door and walked away without saying goodbye.

The flat was terribly quiet. Araminta packed her things, tidied the flat, drank the coffee pot dry, sitting lonely in the kitchen, then wandered into the sitting room. She felt lost and said; she hadn't known Thelma well, but she grieved for her death, and she felt guilty too because she could find no sympathy for Thomas even though he deserved none. It would be a good thing for her to get back to St Katherine's and her work once more and put the whole sad little episode out of her mind.

The unwilling thought that she wasn't going to find it easy to put Doctor van Sibbelt out of her mind, too, disturbed her a little and to dispel her thoughts she went to the window and looked out. The early November afternoon was already fading and a steady wind was whirling the fallen leaves into untidy spirals and forcing the people walking in the street below to lower their heads against its chilly strength. It was a pity she wouldn't see more of Amsterdam; only this modern corner of it and a brief glimpse of its older streets on their trips to and from the hospital. The nearby churches tinkled out their four o'clock carillons and Araminta went to the kitchen, made some tea, and turned on the radio. She turned on the living room lights too, as well as the hideous glass lamp hanging in the hall.

It was better with the lights on. She drank her tea slowly and when the clocks chimed the hour again, tidied the tea things away, made sure that she had all she needed packed for the night and sat down again to wait for Thomas to telephone, wondering idly which hotel they would be going to. He hadn't mentioned it, now that she came to think about it, it had been Doctor van Sibbelt... Thomas hadn't told her his friend's name either, or where he lived. As her watch ticked steadily on towards six o'clock, she began to feel uneasy, especially as she wasn't sure of the name of his office or where it was. Surely he had had ample time in which to break the news to Bertram, make arrangements for them all that night, and telephone her? He had been gone for almost four hours. On the other hand, he might have encountered all sorts of difficulties which had prevented her hearing from him.

She went through the flat, switching on lights in every room but Thelma's, and found a book which she painstakingly read until she heard the clocks strike once more. It was very dark outside now, but she had left the curtains undrawn and she wandered from window to window, peering out, wondering what to do. She could of course pick up her overnight bag and go and find herself a hotel, leaving a note for Thomas, but on the other hand, if he and Bertram were to come back to the empty flat she would feel pretty mean. Perhaps his friend's address, or even his office, would be in his study. She went along to see and found that although the door was open, everything else was locked; the only information on show was the calendar on his desk. She stood staring at it, wondering what to do. She wasn't a nervous girl, but the idea of staying alone in the flat was daunting. She could of course try one of the other flats on the floor, but she had never seen any of the occupants, and supposing they couldn't understand English? And she had no key. She spent ten minutes looking for one without success and had gone back into the hall when the door bell rang, sounding very loud in the quiet, so that she jumped with fright. It rang again almost immediately—whoever it was was very impatient. Araminta walked slowly to the door and opened it, and Doctor van Sibbelt walked in.

He stood just inside the door, immaculate and calm and reassuringly large. 'I was passing,' he observed, 'and noticed that all the lights were on. I couldn't imagine that Mr Shaw would allow such an extravagance, so I came up to see what was happening.' He lifted his dark gaze from her face and looked around him. 'You're alone?'

She had had no idea that she was going to cry. The tears trickled down her cheeks and she gave a loud sniff, quite unable to say anything. The doctor drew her close, one arm round her shoulders; it held her gently, although his voice was by no means gentle. 'Cousin Thomas hasn't been back? Do you know where he is?'

She shook her head, sniffed again and said: 'He—he was going to telephone about five o'clock. He said he had to go and fetch Bertram and I'd have to stay here in case his office telephoned.'

'And did anyone telephone?'

She shook her head again, sniffed for the third time and looked at him. 'I have no idea what to do, but I'm not usually so poor-spirited—I think I'm a little tired, and it's lonely here.'

He didn't answer but took a very white handkerchief from a pocket and offered it to her. 'I should have thought of this,' he told her, 'but no matter, it can be sorted out in no time.'

She eyed him from behind the handkerchief. 'Oh—you know where Thomas is?'

'Lord, no, my dear, nor do I intend to find out. You shall come with me.'

'Oh, but I…' She was interrupted by the ringing of the telephone. 'The telephone!' she exclaimed superfluously, and hurried to answer it.

It was Thomas. Araminta listened wide-eyed to what he had to say and then spoke herself with some spirit. 'I'll do no such thing!' she declared. 'Have you no feelings at all, Thomas? I'll not stay…'

The receiver was taken from her grasp and her companion spoke: 'Doctor van Sibbelt here—am I right in supposing that you expect Araminta to remain here alone tonight?'

She could hear Thomas's querulous voice at the other end, and when the doctor said levelly: 'I think you should take care of what you are saying, Mr Shaw,' she looked at him enquiringly and asked: 'What did he say—why do you look so angry?'

'Nothing of importance. If you have your things packed, we'll go.'

'Where?'

'To my house.'

'Oh, I can't do that!' She stood a little way from him, looking out of a window.

'Afraid of your reputation, Araminta?' She could hear the mockery in his voice.

'Well, no,' she told him, considering the question carefully. 'I was really thinking of yours.'

He chuckled. 'Good of you, but quite wasted on me,

I'm afraid. I have a very old aunt living with me. Her moral standards haven't altered since the turn of the century and I imagine that she is more than capable of preserving the conventions.'

'But I still can't—I mean, foist myself upon you like this. If you would be obliging enough to take me to a small hotel, I shall be quite all right.'

'No, you won't—you will sit and brood all night. Besides, surely you know by now that I only oblige myself, never anyone else? Go and put on your coat.'

It was a relief to be told what to do, and she certainly didn't want to stay alone in the flat. How mean Thomas was... She pulled on her coat without much attention to her appearance, tied a scarf over her bright hair, caught up her handbag and gloves and pronounced herself to be ready, so that it only remained for the doctor to pick up her case, turn out the lights, usher her out of the door and shut it behind them.

They saw no one on the way down and the street outside was deserted. Drawn up to the curb was a silver grey Jensen convertible; the doctor unlocked its door, urged her to get in, cast her case on to the back seat and got in beside her, taking up a good deal more than his fair share of space. Araminta, taken aback at the car's splendour, and still wondering if she was doing the right thing, had fallen silent, and it was left to her companion to say placidly: 'You must be hungry—I know I am. I missed my lunch.'

He turned the car and slid down the street, ready to turn into the main road beyond. 'Let's hope there's something nice for supper.'

This normal remark, made in a normal voice, restored her considerably. She relaxed against the comfort of the leather seat, too tired to think of anything much, aware at the same time that she no longer felt lost or lonely.

Chapter 5

The car's elegant nose was pointed towards the city's centre, and although the traffic was heavy, Doctor van Sibbelt drove with the apparent nonchalance of a cyclist in a deserted country lane. He made no attempt to talk, so that Araminta occupied herself in looking at the lighted streets, trying to guess where they were. They left the main road presently and he swept the Jensen through a succession of narrow streets lined with old houses and intercepted by small hump-backed bridges with wrought iron railings, which spanned the dark waters of any number of canals. The houses now were rather splendid, with lights shining from their wide windows, so that she could catch a glimpse of the rooms beyond as they went past. For her the drive could have gone on for the rest of the evening, but the doctor wanted his supper and it surely couldn't be much farther.

It wasn't. The doctor slowed down to cross yet another bridge where two canals met, and instead of going straight on, slid across the cobbled street and stopped before an imposing corner house.

Araminta peered out of her window at its handsome façade and asked doubtfully: 'Do you live here? Are they flats?'

'God forbid! An ancestor of mine built it a long time ago and no one has wanted to change it since—least of all myself.'

'It's very large.'

'Have you forgotten that I intend to take a wife?' He turned to look at her, half smiling.

'You'll still rattle round like two peas in a pod,' she pointed out.

'Not for long. Just lately I have felt a strong urge to become a family man.'

She gave him a shocked look. 'That's no reason for taking a wife.' She added with some warmth: 'Poor thing!'

He laughed, but there was no mockery in the sound. 'It won't be like that—my wife will be the most important thing in my life and I shall never give her the chance to think otherwise.' He got out of the car and opened the door for her. 'Welcome to my home, Araminta.'

The great front door was opened as they reached it—by the elderly man who had been on the yacht—and Araminta exclaimed: 'Oh, how nice to see you again!' She smiled widely at him, her own troubles forgotten for the moment, feeling almost carefree. Doctor van Sibbelt had taken charge of her for the moment, and now here was another old friend. She held out a hand and he said gravely 'It is for me a great pleasure also, miss,' and then looked questioningly at the doctor.

'A long story, Jos. I'll tell you later.'

They had been standing in the vestibule and now Jos threw open the inner door to disclose a long, wide hall with a branched staircase at the far end of it. The doctor threw off his coat and flung it into a great carved chair. 'My aunt has dined, Jos? Will you ask Frone to find some food for us? We're both hungry. Miss Shaw will be staying the night, so see that someone gets a room ready for her, would you. Frone can take her up presently.'

Jos murmured and went away and Araminta said: 'He's the butler, I suppose.'

'Yes—he's also a family friend of long standing. He taught me to swim and sail and skate—we still sail together.'

'He's nice...'

The doctor smiled down at her. 'Indeed he is, and I'd trust him with my life.'

She smiled back rather shyly. 'I expect he feels the same about you.'

'I like to think so. Let me have that coat—someone will take you up to your room presently, but come and meet Tante Maybella first.'

Araminta stared about her unashamedly. The hall was very imposing with its marble floor and silk rugs and lighted by an enormous chandelier and a number of wall sconces, set between a collection of large and somewhat gloomy portraits. She would have liked the opportunity to have examined them at her leisure as she allowed herself to be led across the hall, through a double-arched doorway, into a room not less impos-

ing but having a pleasantly homely air about it, partly
due to the cheerful fire burning in the wide hearth and
the very ordinary tabby cat spread out before it. There
was a dog too, a long-haired Alsatian, who advanced to
greet them with welcoming barks and an obvious desire
to put his front paws on their shoulders and look into
their faces. The doctor fended him off with a cheerful:
'Manners, Rikki!' and crossed the room with Araminta
held firmly by the arm.

The old lady sitting in the small upright chair by
the fire was very small and frail, and this was empha-
sized by the black silk gown she wore and the quantity
of gold chains which hung round her high frilled collar. She smiled at them as they stopped before her and
said something to the doctor in a high, tinkling voice.
Araminta could understand none of it, although she was
very conscious of a pair of sharp blue eyes studying her
as the old lady talked. She had the uneasy feeling that
she wasn't welcome, but it must have been imagination,
for when the doctor introduced her—in English, to her
relief—his aunt smiled charmingly.

'You must tell me all about yourself,' she cried in
an English as good as her nephew. 'I'm a lonely old
woman, you see—if it weren't for Crispin's kindness I
should be living quite by myself.'

The doctor laughed gently. 'You naughty old thing,'
he chided her, 'you know as well as I do that you have
a perfectly good home of your own—two, in fact, and
you won't live in either of them. Besides, what should
I do without you? But you shall have your gossip with
Araminta presently, but first she wants to go to her room
and tidy herself for supper.'

'You are staying the night?' The old lady sounded apprehensive.

Araminta smiled at her. 'The doctor kindly brought me here, because I had nowhere to go…' She was interrupted by the entrance of a large, stout woman, very neatly dressed, who spoke to the doctor and then nodded and smiled at her.

'This is Frone, Jos's wife—she will take you upstairs. She can't speak a word of English, but I have no doubt you will be able to understand each other.'

Araminta, with Frone beside her, wished once more that she could be allowed the leisure to look at everything as they went through the hall and up the stairs to a wide corridor. The room she was shown into was half way down it, a fair-sized, lofty apartment, deliciously warm and furnished with delicate Regency pieces and a great deal of pastel chintz. Her case was already there, unpacked; moreover there was a small bathroom leading from it, with everything in it that a girl could wish for. Araminta inspected it with a delighted eye. It was a charming room; she pictured it occupied by the daughter of the house and sighed without knowing it as she attended to the business of doing her face and hair.

They had drinks when she went down to the drawing room again, and then left the old lady in her chair while they traversed the hall once more to enter a small, softly lighted room with a round table at its centre, laid with a white cloth, sparkling glass and gleaming silver. Araminta had supposed that supper would be a simple meal of soup and perhaps an omelette, but she couldn't have been more mistaken. There was soup, certainly— french onion soup, served in brown earthenware pipkins, and lavishly sprinkled with cheese, but that was followed by poached turbot and lobster sauce, accompanied by a salad. There was a Charlotte Russe to follow these dainties, and all of them helped along nicely by the hock which the doctor poured for them both, so that Araminta's pale face got back some of the healthy pink it had lost.

All the while they ate, the doctor kept up a smooth flow of talk about nothing in particular, so that presently she began to forget her unhappy day, and by the time they went back to the drawing room for coffee with old Mevrouw van Sibbelt, she was nicely relaxed and had no difficulty in answering that lady's numerous questions for the next hour or so, and when the old lady went to bed, she got to her feet too, with the intention of doing the same thing. But her host had other ideas. He ushered his aged relative to the door, kissed her cheek, then closed it firmly before Araminta was anywhere near it. 'A little talk?' he suggested. 'I know you're tired and you've had a wretched day, but it's barely ten o'clock—I think we should make a few arrangements for tomorrow, don't you? You said you wished to go back to England—would you like me to get you a seat on a morning flight?'

He sounded a little remote and disinterested, but then, Araminta told herself, why should he be anything else? He had been kind and helpful, but probably he would be glad to see the back of her. He had gone to sit by the fire again, with Rikki beside him, and it struck her with the most unexpected suddenness that it would be nothing short of happiness to sit opposite him for the rest of her life. He would probably be a difficult husband, but she saw no reason why she couldn't manage him. She remembered with a pang of pure sorrow that he had already told her that he had plans to marry…

'You're wearing a sad look. Why?' he asked.

She had no intention of telling him, instead she said briskly: 'I don't think I had better go home—not just yet. I can't, you know. I can't stand Thomas—or Bertram—but they'll need someone for a day or two, just until the funeral is over and he can find a housekeeper. Father and Aunt Martha would expect me to do that.'

He smiled faintly. 'I expected you to do that too, Araminta. I'll take you back in the morning, if you like, I don't need to be at the hospital until nine o'clock—will that be too early for you? Have you a key?'

She shook her head. 'No, but surely Thomas will be there? He said something about someone coming in the morning.'

'We'll go and see, and if there is no one there, I'll bring you back here.'

'Thank you, but I shall be quite all right.'

He didn't dispute this, only smiled again. 'Would you like to telephone your father?' he asked.

'Oh, yes, please!'

'And the hospital?'

Araminta hesitated. St Katherine's was the last place she wanted to see; once she got back there, the doctor would be someone to forget about as quickly as possible, and she didn't want to do that, not yet. While she stayed in Amsterdam she had a chance of seeing something of him, and while she knew it was a futile thing to do, she couldn't bring herself to do anything else. 'I had three weeks' unpaid leave,' she told him a little breathlessly.

'So you did,' he agreed gravely. 'Will Thomas be glad to see you?'

'No, but I think he'll be glad to have someone to cook and look after the flat for a day or two.'

'He might want you to stay indefinitely.'

She shook her head. 'Oh, no, he wouldn't; he'd have to pay me a salary, and that would seem like a waste of money to him—paying a cousin.'

Her companion stretched his long legs and lounged back in his chair. 'You're a very pretty girl,' he observed matter-of-factly, 'hasn't anyone wanted to marry you?'

She flushed a little but answered with a total lack of conceit: 'Oh, yes.'

'And you've always said no?'

She nodded, looking away from him. How surprised he would be if she told him that if he cared to ask her she would say yes at once. He didn't, of course, but went on half mockingly: 'Don't tell me that you're a dedicated nurse?'

'Certainly not. I like nursing very much and I have to earn my living.' She didn't want to talk about it any more; she cast around for a suitable topic of conversation and came up with: 'Is there a shortage of nurses in Holland?'

There was a spark of amusement in his eyes, but he followed her cue and they discussed nursing and hospitals and the newest theatre equipment until Araminta finally said good night and escaped to bed. Any other girl, she thought dispiritedly, would have turned an hour of the doctor's company to her own advantage. All she had done was to illustrate to him what a dull creature she was, making stilted conversation about her work. He had probably been bored stiff. It only surprised her that he hadn't said so; he hadn't struck her as a man to suffer fools gladly.

Despite her troubled thoughts she fell asleep in her comfortable bed at once and didn't wake until she was roused by a strapping girl with pink cheeks and blue eyes, bearing her morning tea. As soon as the girl had gone, Araminta got out of bed and padded across the thick carpet to peer out of the window. It was another grey day, with rain dripping from the rooftops and the early morning traffic making its way through wet streets. It matched her mood; Thomas and Bertram loomed large on her horizon, and larger still was the thought that after the doctor had deposited her at her cousin's flat in an hour or two's time, she might not see him again.

But mooning around being sorry for herself would do no good. She bathed and dressed and went downstairs, to find her host in the hall going through his post. The sight of him sent her heart thudding, but despite that she achieved a good morning in an ordinary enough voice as she bent to pat Rikki's great head.

The doctor made a cheerful good morning in reply, adding: 'My name's Crispin. Tante Maybella doesn't come down to breakfast, so you must excuse her, and I, I regret to say, have formed the bad habit of reading my letters while I eat—that's what comes of being a bachelor. You won't mind?' He smiled charmingly. 'I have so little time.'

'I don't mind at all,' she declared with earnest mendacity. 'I have a great deal to think about, anyway.'

So breakfast was an almost silent meal, relieved only by Jos's solemn greeting and their own polite exchanges concerning more coffee, more toast and the expression of mutual agreement over the pleasure of hot croissants for breakfast. And the drive to Thomas's flat was almost as silent. The doctor looked thoughtful, as he drove and Araminta, imagining him to be concentrating upon the day's work ahead of him, held her tongue. She was a little pale as they went up the stairs together, though, for she had just realised that she had made no plans in the event of no one being home.

But someone was there. In answer to the doctor's firm knock, and for good measure, his finger on the bell, Bertram opened the door.

He grinned slyly at Araminta, and without bothering to say hullo declared: 'Father said you'd be back. He told me to wait until you came—he's gone to work. There's a list of things he wants you to do on the dining room table.'

His two listeners observed him with astonishment, Araminta burning with rage at the cool assumption that she would go back and cope. Instructions, indeed! She was about to make herself very plain on that point when Bertram remarked carelessly: 'I'm going to my friend's now. I don't have to go to school—not till the funeral's over.' He smirked. 'Three days' holiday!'

Araminta's hand itched to box his ears. 'Why, you horrid, unnatural…' and was drowned in the subdued thunder of the doctor's voice.

'Get inside, boy! You'll stay here until you have done everything Araminta wishes you to do and go only when she says so.' He looked and sounded so fierce that the boy backed away, staring at him. 'And be sure,' continued the doctor, 'that I shall know if you do otherwise. Be good enough to carry your cousin's bag to her room.'

It was Bertram's turn to look amazed. He picked up the case meekly enough, though, and took it along to Araminta's room. Then Doctor van Sibbelt said: 'I must go, I'm afraid—you know where I am if you want me.' He bent and kissed her swiftly and started on his way down the stairs, not looking back once.

Araminta, once she had stifled the urge to run after the doctor, plunged into the numerous tasks Thomas had seen fit to leave her, but she took care to see that Bertram helped her. He did it ungraciously, but at least he did the small jobs she gave him to do while she started on the pile of washing in the little laundry room off the kitchen. Poor Thelma had obviously got very behind with the laundry. Araminta had done everything she could lay her hands on when she had first arrived, but this lot must have been hidden away somewhere. She got the first batch out on the line on the kitchen balcony and went to look in the fridge. There was food enough. She put the coffee on and went back to her washing. Once that was out of the way she would have time to unpack her things. The flat didn't look too bad—true, Thomas had left the breakfast things on the table, but she prevailed upon Bertram to clear them away.

The washing out of the way, she poured coffee for them both and sat down to drink it. Bertram was sulking. She suspected that he had had things very much his own way while Thelma had been ill, and looking at him now, she could see no sign of grief on his face.

'Will you mind having a housekeeper here?' she asked him.

He shrugged. 'What do I care who comes? Anyway, Father says you'll stay.'

Her fine eyes sparkled. 'Did he now? But you see, Bertram, I'm not going to stay, only until the funeral.'

'I'm not going!' he told her loudly.

'Well, I hardly thought you would,' she agreed, and

added gently: 'Will you miss your mother very much, Bertram?'

'Miss her? No—she was always ill. Father says she didn't think about us, only thought about herself.'

Araminta felt the tears prick her eyelids. 'That's not true! Your mother thought about you both—she was ill, and it seems to me that neither of you cared.' And when he shrugged: 'You'd better go to your friend's house, Bertram.'

She got up and walked out of the kitchen, anxious to be free of his company. It was better when he had gone. She dusted and mopped and got herself some lunch which she didn't eat after all, then went to the kitchen to get the supper ready. Thomas would be home, presumably about six. There were pork chops in the fridge and a carton of custard. If she got the vegetables done now she would have the afternoon to herself. But that wasn't very satisfactory, as it turned out, for she sat doing nothing, tired from all the washing, allowing her mind to wander. Which it did, but always back to Crispin. Such a waste of time, she told herself crossly, and went to see if the clothes were dry.

She had supper almost ready when Thomas came in. He had Bertram with him and it was obvious that the boy had been telling tales, for his father, greeting him with his usual pomposity, added: 'I'm told that you made Bertram do a great many chores this morning—I don't care for your attitude towards him, Araminta.'

'Well, you expect me to do a great many chores, don't you, Thomas? And I don't care for your attitude towards me, either.' Araminta's pretty face went pink. 'And if you think I came back because I wanted to,' she snapped, 'you're very much mistaken. I came back because of Thelma.'

He had the grace to look uncomfortable, but only for a moment. 'I shall work for half an hour in my study,' he announced, 'and supper promptly at seven o'clock.' He gave her a frowning glance. 'I've had a busy day, arranging for the funeral and so on, and of course my normal work must be done at all costs.'

She wished he wouldn't talk as though the world would crumble unless he did a day's work in the office. She muttered something and went back to the kitchen.

At five to the hour the front door bell rang, and at its second peal, knowing that no one would answer it unless she did, Araminta went, not in the best of tempers, to open it. Crispin was leaning against the wall outside.

'You took your time,' he observed. 'You look as though you've been slaving over a hot stove, too.'

'Well, I have,' she told him testily, aware that the apron she had put on did nothing for her at all and that her hair was no longer neat. She had been thinking about him all day, and now that he was here, he was making unkind remarks! Self-pity tied itself in a knot in her throat as she glared at him, to be instantly disarmed by his placid:

'Well, it suits you—there's nothing like an apron to give a girl that little extra something.'

She laughed then and he said cheerfully: 'That's better! Now do take it off, there's a dear girl, and put on a coat. We're going out to dinner.'

'But the chops—' she told him worriedly.

He peered past her into the gloomy hall. 'Anyone home? Yes? Surely they don't need your help in dishing them up and eating them?' He edged past her, took the door handle out of her hand and closed the door behind him, and said: 'Ten minutes?'

Her self-pity and bad temper had disappeared. She nodded happily and skipped down the hall to her room, she had the door open when Thomas came out of his study. 'Who…?' he began, and stopped as his eyes fell on the doctor, who wished him good evening in a frosty voice and added:

'I'm taking Araminta out to dinner.' Thomas made a gobbling noise and the doctor walked past him to where Araminta was still standing, pushed her gently into the room and closed the door. 'You have no objection?' he wanted to know silkily.

'Going out to dinner and Thelma dead barely a day?' said Thomas in a righteous voice.

Doctor van Sibbelt smiled nastily, his dark face quite menacing. 'Will you be going without your dinner?' he asked. 'I should be careful what you say, Mr Shaw.' His voice was as nasty as his smile, so that Thomas subsided, his face very red, and muttering that he supposed he would have to see to the supper himself, went loftily to the kitchen.

Araminta, happily unaware of this brief conversation, whipped out of her slacks and sweater and took a doubtful look at her scanty wardrobe. She had worn the suit yesterday, which left her with the jersey dress and her winter coat. She changed rapidly, did her face, put up her golden hair, snatched up handbag and gloves and went back into the hall, where she found the doctor standing gazing at nothing. But his abstracted air left him when he saw her. 'Do you still have a key?' he asked.

She nodded. 'Thomas left me one this morning—

so that I could do the shopping.' She went along to the kitchen to say good night to Thomas and found him dishing up the chops. He threw her a sulky look.

'You're a poor housekeeper,' he observed in a patronising tone which led her to suggest that he got himself a good one at the earliest possible moment. 'I shall advertise tomorrow,' he assured her. 'After a year of Thelma's slapdash ways and now you...a man needs to be looked after.'

Araminta didn't trust herself to reply, for her pent-up emotions were almost choking her, so that when she rejoined the doctor he observed mildly: 'You've had your feathers ruffled again, I see. We had better go quickly before I do your cousin some injury.'

On the stairs she said uncertainly: 'I feel mean—I ought to feel sorry for Thomas and Bertram...'

Crispin caught her by the arm so that she was forced to stand still and look at him. 'Was he sorry for his wife?' he demanded. 'I don't believe in an eye for an eye, but can't you see that pity is quite wasted on a man like that?' He kept his hand on her arm and hurried her down the rest of the stairs and out to where the Jensen was parked.

He took her to Dikker and Thijs in the Leidsestraat, where they were shown to a discreet corner table. Araminta couldn't help but notice that her companion was well-known at the restaurant, and she found herself speculating as to who he brought there. The sharp prick of jealousy confused her so much that he had to ask her twice what she would like to drink.

Thinking about it later, she wasn't quite sure what she had had to eat, only that everything tasted delicious, served in elegant peace and quiet, and that her companion had been an amusing and thoughtful host. There were so many facets to his character; the ill-tempered yachtsman, the suave doctor, and now the perfect host. She found herself wondering which was the real Crispin. Not that it mattered, she loved him whatever he chose to be.

He hadn't taken her back to the flat after their leisurely meal, but had driven to his home, where Jos had quite obviously been glad to see her, and just as obviously Tante Maybella hadn't. The old lady had had friends to dinner, but they had been gone some time before Araminta and the doctor returned, and she complained in her high, sweet little voice that she had been lonely and had given Araminta a look which gave her plainly to understand that she had been the cause of it. Which was probably why she remained in the drawing room talking animatedly until Crispin had suggested that it was long past her usual bedtime, when she observed gently: 'But, my dears, I have been waiting up so that I might wish Araminta good-bye.' Which seemed such a strong hint to Araminta that she said at once that she hadn't realised that it was so late and got up to go.

Crispin had said nothing at all, only smiled faintly and the hope that he would protest died almost before she was aware of it. Araminta said her goodbyes nicely, quite understanding that the old lady was jealous of her, although she wasn't sure why—surely Mevrouw van Sibbelt wasn't jealous of all the doctor's friends? And surely he entertained them when he chose? After all, it was his house.

He had driven her back to the flat without any attempt to dally on the way, and she wished him good night and thanked him quickly as he drew up outside the entrance. The evening, she felt, hadn't been all that satisfactory. Dinner had been delightful, she had relaxed and enjoyed every minute of it, but sitting between him and his aged aunt in his magnificent drawing room hadn't been very successful. Perhaps she wasn't cut out for the restrained opulence in which he lived.

She got out of the car and found that he had got out too, to walk upstairs with her, not hurrying at all, talking of their evening just as though it had been a smash hit. Outside Thomas's door he put his hands on her shoulders and said: 'You found Tante Maybella hard going, didn't you? Have patience with her, dear girl. She can't help but love you in time, but she has to get used to you—the idea of you.'

He caught her close and kissed her, a gentle, tender kiss, and then had taken the key from her hand and opened the door for her. 'Good night, dear Araminta!' She had closed the door on her own whispered good night.

She had ample time to think about it all the next day, once she had got Thomas off to the office and Bertram away to his friend's house. In the light of a cold November day it seemed clear to her that she was allowing her own feelings to run away with her. Just because she was in love with Crispin there was no good reason for supposing that he was in love with her—on the contrary, he was being kind, in the same way as he would be kind to a lost puppy who had thrown itself on his mercy, or an old lady who had lost her purse. For he was a kind man, despite his mocking manner upon occasion and his black looks. She allowed her thoughts to become daydreams while she did the housework.

Crispin had said nothing about seeing her again.

There was a chicken in the fridge, so she prepared it
for the evening meal, peeled potatoes, opened a can of
peas and found another carton of custard, chocolate
this time. An uninspired meal, but shopping was still
something of a closed book to her and Thomas hadn't
even bothered to tell her where the nearest food shops
were. She filled in the afternoon with the ironing, put
the chicken in the oven and went to lay the table. One
more day, she promised herself, and she would be able
to go home with an easy conscience; Thomas would
just have to find himself a housekeeper. When he got
home she would have a talk with him and ask at the
same time what arrangements had been made for the
following day. The funeral was to be in the morning,
and as Thelma had no relatives and very few friends,
presumably no one would come back to the flat.

Araminta went to baste the bird and then answer
the telephone. It was Crispin. 'I'll be round about eight
o'clock,' he told her, for all the world as though he had
already told her he would be coming. 'We'll have dinner
at home, shall we?' he asked her. 'I'm going to be held
up this evening, but I won't be later than that.'

'I've a chicken in the oven,' Araminta told him.

'What a busy little housewife you are! Thomas and
Bertram will enjoy it. *Tot ziens.*'

Thomas wasn't too pleased when she told him, but
he had really nothing to complain about, for the meal
was ready for him to eat, and what was more, there
was ample time for her to wash up before she went to
get ready. She would have had even more time if one
or other of them had helped her, but all the same, she
was ready and waiting when the doctor arrived. They
left the flat together after the most casual of greet-

ings on Crispin's part, and Araminta kept quiet during their brief drive, for he looked tired and preoccupied, so much so that before they entered the house she asked hastily: 'You are sure you want me to come? I'll quite understand...you've been busy, haven't you? I daresay all you want to do is sit down by the fire with a drink and the papers.'

'I'll settle for you instead of the papers,' he said, half laughing. 'I've had a heavy day, but I would rather be with you than with anyone else, Araminta.' He opened the door and ushered her inside. 'You seem to have grown on me.'

Such an awkward observation to answer, she decided, and said nothing at all, concluding that he wasn't expecting one. Jos, advancing upon them from the back of the hall, took his master's coat, wished them both a good evening, indicated that Araminta might wish to go upstairs to tidy herself, and retired again.

'Do you really need to go upstairs?' asked the doctor. 'You look perfectly all right to me. There's a mirror if you want to look at your face—women usually do.'

'Just for that, I shan't look,' said Araminta crisply, and was whirled round to be kissed swiftly.

'Such a lovely girl,' declared Crispin thoughtfully. 'She never minces her words, cooks chickens to a turn, knows what to do when a bomb goes off, and always looks dishy. I shall have to do something about it.'

Araminta longed to ask what, but didn't. For one thing she felt sure that he was teasing her, and as she couldn't think of anything gay or clever to say, it seemed wise to remain silent. She smiled rather uncertainly at him and watched his features become placid again.

'Drinks,' he suggested cheerfully, and led the way

to the drawing room where Tante Maybella was await-
ing them.

The old lady greeted her warmly, so that Araminta
decided that she had been quite mistaken on the previous evening and enjoyed her dinner very much in
consequence, with Mevrouw van Sibbelt regaling her
companions with tales of her youth and the people she
had known. Her gaiety had tired her, though, for shortly
after they returned to the drawing room, she declared
that she would go to bed and wished Araminta as warm
a good night as her welcome had been before trotting
off with Crispin to escort her to the stairs.

He was back in a very short time to ask her: 'Would
you like to see something of the house? There are some
rather nice pictures and some silver and porcelain.'

They were housed in the library, a vast apartment,
its walls lined with books, its polished floor covered
with a Persian carpet. There were comfortable chairs
arranged in groups round mahogany tables, and a bright
fire burning below the magnificently carved chimney
piece. They went slowly from one display cabinet to the
next, while the doctor explained about Tiger ware, of
which he had several specimens, and then pointed out
the beauties of the *nef* which took pride of place in his
collection—it was a salt, made in the shape of a ship,
and was, he declared, early sixteenth century. Araminta
admired it dutifully, although she very much preferred
a George the Second shell pattern sugar box, which,
while neither so old nor so rare, she considered to be a
great deal prettier.

The glass was exquisite, too, housed in a great bow-
fronted cabinet lined with blue velvet, and she pored
long minutes over a goblet by Verzelini before enquiring

how it came into the doctor's hands. 'Elizabethan, isn't it?' she essayed. 'Were the English and Dutch friendly then?'

'On and off. One of my ancestors married an English-woman and that was part of her dowry. One of the daughters of the marriage married an Englishman in her turn and their son gave my family the diamond-pinched *roemer,* just behind the goblet. Personally, I like the Beilby goblets—and there's that truly priceless *doppelpokal* on the top shelf. I feel guilty every time I see it because I dislike it so much.'

Araminta laughed. 'You ought to be bloated with the pride of possession,' she told him as they crossed the room to a smaller cabinet housing a collection of dainty china—a hand-painted tea-set, violets on the thinnest of porcelain. Araminta exclaimed: 'I like this best of all…'

'My father gave it to my mother when they were first married. He had it specially made for her because she loved violets. I like it too.' He gave her a brief glance. 'She died when I was thirty, almost ten years ago, and my father died two years before her; he was a good deal older. They were devoted.'

'Have you any brothers or sisters?'

'Oh, yes. A young brother in Canada and two sisters, both married. One lives in Groningen, the other travels a good deal; her husband builds bridges.' He grinned suddenly. 'All I have left is Tante Maybella.'

'Oh, you really must do something about it,' cried Araminta, quite carried away by pity for his loneliness and not stopping to think what she was saying.

Crispin had come to stand very close to her and now he took her hands in his and asked unexpectedly: 'When do you return to St Katherine's?'

She was quite unable to answer immediately; surprise had her tongue, and a half-felt disappointment, too. She stared up at him, her dark blue eyes wide. 'The day after tomorrow. It's—it's the funeral tomorrow morning, you know, and I told Thomas I wouldn't stay any longer.'

His hands moved a little on hers, holding them closer. 'When you get back, will you resign?'

Shock took her breath. 'Resign? Whatever for? I haven't another job.'

He ignored that. 'And during that time—before you leave—will you think of me?'

Her eyes hadn't left his face. 'Yes.'

'Good—you see, I want to be very sure, Araminta, you've seen me at my best and almost at my worst. I'm not an easy man, you know that, but I'm prepared to wait—you are young and not very worldly.' He smiled, and when she would have spoken: 'No, don't say anything, dear girl, not now.' He bent to kiss her. 'I'll take you back to the flat now.'

Chapter 6

Araminta, naturally enough, spent a great deal of the night deep in thought, a circumstance hardly likely to improve her day, which, when it came, was far worse than anything she could have imagined. Bertram had been fetched after breakfast, to spend yet another day at his friend's home, and that had left Thomas and herself. She had cleared up while he gloomed round the flat, making no effort to help her, and it wasn't until she was almost finished that he disclosed the fact that a dozen or so people would be coming back after the funeral.

Araminta paused in her carpet sweeping. 'Thomas, you never said a word! Will they want coffee and sandwiches? There's no time…'

'Naturally I shall offer my friends refreshment,' he told her. 'I've arranged for sandwiches to be sent in, all that's required of you is to make and serve the coffee.'

He was hateful! She felt her temper rising and tried to subdue it so that she could answer him in a normal voice. 'I'll do my best—and Thomas, I've had no chance to tell you, but you must have guessed, anyway. I'm going back to St Katherine's tomorrow—an early morning flight.' That wasn't quite true, but he might argue with her unless she was quite definite. She would have to make arrangements later on; she didn't want to stay any longer now, she had done all she could, and a thankless task it had been, too. She listened, not very attentively, to his prosy voice going on and on about her lack of loyalty, her selfishness and the impossibility of coping with the flat, the shopping, Bertram and above all, his work. When he paused for breath she observed sensibly: 'Well, Thomas, you've had two or three days in which to find a housekeeper, and surely your friends will rally round—they always do, you know.'

'Naturally they will,' he said stiffly, 'but I'm more than surprised that you should bring up the subject of leaving today of all days.'

She turned to face him, very pink. 'But today isn't any different from any other for you, is it? You aren't grieved about Thelma, are you, so why pretend?'

She had gone to the kitchen and started banging the cups and saucers on to the trays, longing for the day to be over.

Four hours later, listening to the church bells ringing out one o'clock, she realised that there was still a lot of the day left. Thomas's friends had come back with them, and sat around drinking the coffee she handed round, and the sandwiches—not nearly enough—had all been eaten up so that she had had to go to the kitchen and cut more. They had talked in loud, high voices, commiserating with Thomas while they cast accusing looks at Araminta. Thomas had obviously got them all on his side—and no one mentioned Thelma. Araminta disappeared into the kitchen as soon as she could and began on the piles of crockery. She had no wish to wash up, but it would be something to do, and it would be better to clean the cups and saucers than throw them around the kitchen, an action which would have suited her mood exactly. She was half was through her task when the door bell rang; no one would hear it in the living room, judging from the hubbub of talk going on there, so she wiped her hands down the front of her apron and went to see who it was.

Crispin slid his bulk round the door, and the mere sight of him sent such a wave of happiness through her that she had much ado not to clasp her soapy hands round his neck.

He closed the door gently behind him and surveyed her slowly before observing: 'You look like Cinderella—why are you covered in an apron?'

'I'm washing up—Thomas's friends came back here…' she choked suddenly and felt his arm on her shoulder.

'Go and take that thing off and put on a coat and something on your head, for it's cold—we're going out.'

'Out?' she repeated foolishly. 'What about the hospital—your patients—it's only a little past one o'clock…'

'What a girl you are for keeping my nose to the grindstone! Occasionally I give myself a half day—I'm having one now. Go and get your coat.'

'Thomas?'

He smiled, looking all at once forbidding and quite

frighteningly remote. 'Leave Thomas to me,' he advised her blandly.

Going downstairs with him five minutes later she asked apprehensively: 'Was he angry?'

'So-so, my dear, so-so. At what time do you leave tomorrow?'

She stopped on the landing the better to explain. 'Though it doesn't really matter, just as long as I can get away from here early. There must be dozens of flights—anyway, there are boats too,' she added vaguely.

'Leave it to me. I'll telephone presently and get you a morning flight, if that's what you want. Have you telephoned the hospital?'

Araminta's lovely eyes grew round. 'Oh, no, I quite forgot—there's still time?'

'Of course there is, goose. Have you enough money?'

It seemed the most natural thing in the world that he should ask her that, so she answered him matter-of-factly: 'Yes, thank you. I took a single ticket when I came because I didn't know how long I'd be here.'

Crispin took her arm and they went out into the bleak afternoon and crossed the pavement to where a Rolls-Royce Camargue was parked. When the doctor unlocked its door and invited her to enter, she hesitated. 'But where's the Jensen?' she wanted to know.

He went round the beautiful bonnet and got in beside her. 'At home. When I take a long trip I use this one.' He turned to smile at her. 'I hope it makes up for the *kaas broodje*.'

'I've never been in a Rolls before,' she confided, and then remembered what he had just said. 'You were saying a long trip...'

'Not so very long; to the sea to blow some colour

into that white face of yours and then up to Friesland and back through the Veluwe—that's one of the prettiest parts of Holland, although it will be dark long before we get there—all the same, you'll see a little of the country.'

'How lovely.' Her eyes sparkled. 'The day's been beastly, and now it's marvellous!'

She didn't see the gleam in his eyes as he allowed the Rolls to slide into the traffic. They didn't talk much as he drove through the city and out of it again on to the motorway to den Haag. Here there was room and to spare on the broad road even though the traffic was heavy. The car shot forward into a silent speed and the doctor asked abruptly: 'Do you want to talk about this morning? It will help, you know.'

Araminta drew a deep breath. 'Oh, may I? Just—just to get it off my chest.'

'Quite—talk on, my dear.'

She wasn't his dear—at least she didn't think so. He liked her, it had been wonderful to discover that, but it was just possible that he wanted her to go away so that he could discover if he did more than like her. Falling in love, she reflected, must come in a number of ways. It had hit her on the head; a great thump from which she was still recovering, but perhaps for some people it was a slow process and they weren't quite sure about it for a considerable time.

'I'm listening,' said Crispin patiently, and she abandoned her thoughts and plunged into an account of the morning. She paused a good deal and started any number of sentences she never finished, but she knew that she had her companion's attention. She petered out finally and he said in a kind voice: 'That's better, isn't it?

We're just coming into den Haag; we'll go on to Scheveningen and take a quick walk by the sea, that should blow the last unhappy thoughts from your head.'

He began to point out the places which he thought might interest her as they edged their way through the crowded streets and then picked up speed again for the last mile or two to the coast.

It was hardly the day for a walk. There was a howling gale blowing into their faces and great grey clouds sweeping in from the sea to smother the colourless sky above them. Araminta, with the doctor's arm through hers, stepped out briskly into the teeth of the wind, her gorgeous hair streaming from beneath her scarf, her eyes watering, and with barely enough breath to breathe with, let alone talk. But it made her feel wonderful, and when they turned back, bowling along now at a fine pace, she cried: 'This is great!'

Crispin came to a halt and turned her round to look at her. 'Pink cheeks,' he observed, 'and a pink nose too.' He bent to kiss it lightly and walked on, sweeping her along with him.

'Tea?' he suggested when they reached the car.

She could think of nothing nicer, and then clapped her hand to her head. 'But I can't; not like this—my hair's all over the place.'

'Put it back where it belongs then.' He sat patiently, holding pins and comb and anything else she thrust at him, assuring her finally that she looked very nice as she tied her scarf back on.

They had tea at Maison Krul, in a delightful atmosphere redolent of Queen Victoria. It was still early in the afternoon and there were few customers. Araminta, eating some of the richest cakes she had ever seen in her life, suspected that Crispin had brought her there because it was exactly the kind of teashop a girl would like, a thought which triggered off another, not so pleasant idea. Perhaps he was in the habit of bringing all his girl-friends here. She frowned so fiercely that he wanted to know what ailed her. 'Nothing,' she declared hastily, and added ingenuously: 'What do you usually do when you have a free afternoon?'

She had asked for it—that mocking little smile, that pleasantly snubbing voice: 'Why, Araminta, exactly what I am doing now, of course, taking the prettiest girl I know out to tea.'

She bent her head over her plate, feeling a fool. And yet he had hinted at all kinds of things—or hadn't he? Had she been indulging in wishful thinking? After a moment she said in a cold voice: 'I'm sure they must enjoy that very much.'

Crispin seemed bent on needling her. 'I enjoy it too.' He grinned at her across the little round table. 'Have another of these cakes.'

'No, thank you.' She wondered how many other girls he had said just those words to, and as though he had read her thoughts, he said quietly—and there was no mockery now: 'You're not just a pretty girl I'm taking out to tea, Araminta.'

On the road once more they travelled fast, bypassing Leiden, which, the doctor pointed out, needed several days in order to explore it properly, and then racing up the motorway to Alkmaar, to turn off across the rather bare countryside along the road leading to the Afsluit-dijk. The afternoon was clearer now, with a watery sun getting low in the sky, and it was still possible to see something of the country around them. The doctor kept up a running commentary and Araminta, wishing to miss nothing, peered from side to side, asking endless questions, which he answered with remarkable patience.

They seemed to flash across the Afsluitdijk and once on the mainland of Friesland, they skirted Harlingen to turn off on to a minor road so that she might see something of Franeker and its splendid town hall. Leeuwarden, when they reached it soon after, was already brightly lighted, its streets bustling with shoppers, for it was getting dark now, but the Rolls' powerful headlamps lighted the road ahead of them as they took the road south, through Heereveen and Steenwijk and Meppel and on to Deventer. Araminta couldn't see much now, but the soundless speed of the car was very soothing; she could have gone on for ever and she had lost count of the time. It was only when Crispin observed: 'We're going to have a meal soon, just a few miles the other side of Amersfoort,' that she realised how hungry she was.

They left the motorway at Amersfoort and took a country road to Scherpenzeel, a large village where Crispin parked the car outside an old country inn with which Araminta instantly fell in love. The food matched its attractive appearance, too; she ate with a good appetite, her cheeks still nicely pink, her eyes sparkling. They didn't hurry over their meal; the restaurant was almost empty and no one seemed impatient for them to go. Araminta, her tongue loosened by the warmth and good food, had quite a lot to say, more than she had intended perhaps, led gently on by her companion's quiet comments and questions. She forgot the time completely, and it wasn't until they were in the car again, driving the last thirty odd miles back to Amsterdam that she looked at the clock and exclaimed in a bemused voice: 'It's after nine o'clock! I had no idea—we must have driven miles…'

He flashed her a smile. 'About three hundred miles.'

'It seemed… I've forgotten this morning,' she confessed.

'That is what I hoped.'

'I haven't done anything about my seat on the plane—it's too late.'

'I think not. We'll call in at the house and telephone Schiphol.'

She relaxed again. It was lovely to be taken care of, not to have to make plans and worry about times and flights and cooking meals. She closed her eyes in a happy daze and presently her tired head slid sideways on to Crispin's shoulder.

He wakened her gently when they reached the house, and she apologised, feeling foolish, until he told her: 'Your head fitted very nicely into my shoulder—I enjoyed the experience.' He smiled at her and her heart jumped a little. It was a good thing that Jos opened the door then and they went inside, into the softly lighted hall and thence to the cosy little room at the back of the house, where Araminta was told to sit down while the doctor telephoned. Jos appeared seconds later with coffee, and Crispin broke off his conversation to ask her to pour out, something she did very carefully from the beautiful silver coffee pot. She handed him a fragile porcelain cup and said: 'I ought to be at the flat—it's late.'

He only smiled as he sat down opposite her. 'I've booked a seat for you on the midday flight tomorrow, I have to be at the hospital, but Jos will call for you and drive you to Schiphol.' And when she protested. 'No, Araminta, don't argue.'

She stammered a little. 'It's very kind of you,' she began awkwardly.

'There's something more than kindness between us,' he told her quietly.

Her cup rattled in the saucer as she set it down, and she said quickly for something to say: 'It will be awfully strange working in hospital again—it seems like another life.'

'But not for long. I'll make no promises about seeing you again, Araminta, because it isn't easy for me to make plans and keep to them. You understand that?'

'Yes, of course.' She smiled brightly, but her mouth had gone dry. Did he mean that he didn't intend them to meet again? she wondered—perhaps it would be as well if she believed that. She went on, her voice stiff with her efforts to keep it casual: 'Thank you for being so helpful—I don't know what I should have done without you. It was strange that we should have met again, wasn't it?'

'Not strange at all,' he corrected her. 'These things are meant. Do you know your Tennyson? Doesn't he say something about: "Ask me no more: thy fate and mine are sealed..."' He stared at her for a long moment. 'You're twenty-five, Araminta, and I am almost forty. Fifteen years is a big difference—not for me, perhaps, but for you, with those great blue eyes and golden hair.' He sighed, and she sought for words to tell him that the years didn't matter at all, that she was quite sure, but before she could speak Crispin had got to his feet. 'Don't say anything,' he begged her. 'When you're back in England, whatever you feel now, you will probably forget me.'

A remark so unjust that she almost cried out in protest. But he gave her no chance to speak, but caught her by the arm and marched her to the door for all the world as though he wanted to be rid of her. All of a sudden he had become remote and ill-humoured—she knew that whatever she said, she wouldn't be able to reach him. She allowed herself to be driven back to the flat, chattering in a meaningless fashion as they went, desperate that he shouldn't see that she was hurt and bewildered as well as angry. She had been given no chance...

He took the key from her at the flat door and opened it for her. 'Jos will be here at half past ten,' he told her. He was the casual, kind-hearted friend again; his kiss was light and quick and meant nothing at all. He was whistling as he went back down the stairs.

Araminta went to bed and cried herself to sleep. How could a girl tell a man she loved him when he didn't want to be told? She woke up in the morning with a fearful headache, and the knotty problem, returning the moment she opened her eyes, made it even worse.

It was raining when she opened the door of her little flat, and she put on all the lights and turned on the gas fire before she took off her coat. The place looked more cheerful then. A cup of tea, she told herself resolutely, fighting an overpowering loneliness, and then she would telephone her father and let him know that she was home again. She went through to the bedroom with her case; she would unpack presently, it was still early afternoon and there was nothing for her to do for the rest of the day. She shied away from the thought. It was a good thing that she was going on duty in the morning;

there was nothing like hard work to make the days go quickly. She sat down to drink her tea and think about her journey. It had been easy; Jos had arrived at the flat in good time to drive her to Schiphol. Thomas had gone to work by then, bidding her a grudging goodbye and an even more grudging thanks, so that Jos's appearance had cheered her up a little. He wasn't a chatty man, but he answered her small talk with respectful monosyllables, saw to her luggage and her ticket, and bought her a pile of magazines before seeing her off in a fatherly manner, waiting until she was aboard the plane. She had turned to look for him at the last moment and had seen him in the distance and waved goodbye. Not just to him, but to a great many other things as well. She refused to put them into coherent thought.

She got up at last, washed the tea things and went to unpack. She would have to go to the shops, for there was nothing in the house to eat and she would never have time to shop in the morning; she would have to go and see Miss Best too. She sighed. The prospect of returning to St Katherine's had suddenly become dull and uninteresting. Perhaps a change of job? Another part of the country, or a week or so at Dunster? She toyed with the idea and rejected it just as the door bell rang.

It might be Sylvia, or one or her many friends, off duty and come to see how she was getting on. But it wasn't anyone she knew but a messenger boy, thrusting a long rush basket at her.

'For me?' Araminta asked, surprised.

'Miss Shaw, ain't yer?' And when she nodded: 'Sign 'ere, miss.'

She signed, found her purse and gave him something for his trouble and carried the basket into the sitting room. It was packed with roses, red and pink, cream and white; two dozen at least, and here was a card with them, inscribed disappointingly: 'Araminta, instead of goodbye. C.v.S.'

She arranged them in all the vases she possessed while she ruminated on the words. They could mean several things, and taking all in all, the most likely seemed to her that Crispin had sent the roses as a nice way of letting her know that he had thought better of it; that although he had liked her—more than liked, perhaps—it hadn't been enough… She wept a little into the sweet-smelling flowers, then blew her nose vigorously, arranged the vases round the room, and went out shopping. But it was no use. Crispin filled her head to the exclusion of all else. She had been a fool not to have shouted him down when he had bidden her to say nothing. The arrogance of the man, she fumed, telling her what to do and what not to do and then sending her roses, so that her state of uncertainty was worse now than it had ever been. She banged and thumped her possessions in her little home in a very fury of exasperation, cooked herself a deplorable meal, which she didn't eat, and went early to bed.

She was instantly plunged into work the next morning. The Accident Room filled up as fast as it was emptied, and it was with difficulty that Araminta managed to get away to see Miss Best; a purely formal interview, with that lady expressing her sympathy at Thelma's death and at the same time declaring her satisfaction at Araminta being back at her post once more. She added a rider to the effect that the department had been very busy during her absence, and Araminta, remembering the queue waiting for attention in the Accident Room,

made a suitable rejoinder and got herself back on duty,
to be kept fully occupied for the rest of that day.

Two days slid by, nasty, dark November days, not
quite winter yet, but bleak enough. Araminta, caught
up in a vast amount of paper work, was thankful to have
every minute of her time filled, so that by the time she
went off duty each evening she was too tired to do more
than cook herself a meal, do a few household chores
and go to bed, but on her fourth morning back James
stopped her as she was going to lunch, hurrying down
the long passage which could lead her eventually to the
nurses dining room. She would have passed him with a
word of greeting, for they saw each other often enough
during their working hours, but he stopped her.

'I never have the chance to talk to you,' he complained, 'and I know this is short notice, but will you
come along to the Butterfly'—a favourite café frequented by the hospital staff—'this evening?' He looked
suddenly rather shy. 'I've got engaged—you don't know
her, but I'd like you to meet. There'll be quite a few
there—you know them all. It's by way of being a cel-
ebration.'

She beamed at him. 'James, you dark horse, and how
splendid! Of course I'll come. What time?'

'Seven o'clock. Come back here to the main entrance—
several of us will be going at the same time, there'll be
plenty of room for you in one of the cars. Mary has to
come from Woolwich, so her father is going to run her
up here.'

'It sounds fun. I'll be there on the dot of seven
o'clock.'

She very nearly wasn't, though; an R.T.A. came in
at five o'clock and it took all of the next hour to get the

three people involved examined, X-rayed, tidied up and sent to their appropriate wards. Araminta cleared away with Dolly's help, made sure that the two student nurses were getting everything ready for anything else which might come in, handed over the keys to her faithful staff nurse and tore back to her flat, where, after a hasty cup of tea, she set about getting herself ready for the evening's outing. The other girls had decided to wear long dresses, so she put on the russet velvet pinafore with a chiffon blouse beneath it, piled her hair, did her face in record time, flung on the black velvet coat she had had for years, and walked briskly back to the hospital. It wanted five minutes to the hour as she went through the main doors, but James was there, looking nervous in his best suit.

His face cleared when he saw her. 'The others went on. I thought you might be a bit late—you must have moved like lightning.'

Araminta was still some way from him, so that she raised her voice to answer. 'I did—I was in a panic that I'd never make it in time. I've been looking forward to our evening all day.' She started towards him and then paused to look back over her shoulder because the doors had swung open behind her.

Crispin had come in. She forgot James and his party, she forgot where she was; her pretty face glowed with her delight at the sight of him. She choked on all the things she wanted to say; all she managed was: 'Oh, it's you!'

'Indeed, it is I.' His voice was bland and icy and she saw that his face was dark with rage, so that she faltered in her headlong rush towards him. He continued nastily: 'I'm delighted to see that you are enjoying yourself, Araminta. Don't let me keep you.' His dark eyes flickered towards James and he nodded carelessly.

'Oh, but it doesn't matter,' declared Araminta, light-headed with her joy still and choosing her words badly. 'James won't mind…'

'How accommodating of him.' The doctor's hand-some mouth was touched by an unpleasant smile. 'I had no idea that you were so fickle, Araminta.'

The smile became so ferocious that she blinked, quite bereft of words. By the time she had thought of something to say to this, he had gone. She watched his broad back disappear down the corridor leading to the con-sultants' room and the look on her face prompted the kindly James to ask: 'Shall I go after him, Araminta? I think he misunderstood…'

'Of course he misunderstood,' she said fierily, 'and I wouldn't go after him for all the money in the Bank of England.' She tossed her head so defiantly that her topknot looked to be in danger of coming down. 'Let's go,' she said in a bright voice which nicely disguised her wish to burst into tears.

James gave her an anxious look. 'I say, would you rather not come? I mean, he'll be back presently—he's bound to come this way.'

The very words needed to stoke up Araminta's tem-per. 'And find me waiting?' she demanded in a high voice. Her lovely eyes flashed. 'You're mistaken, James, I wasn't expecting Doctor van Sibbelt, you know—I had no idea that he was in England. We—we met in Amster-dam.' With a considerably heightened colour she cried: 'Oh, do let's go. Your Mary will think you've cried off, and that would never do.' She laughed so gaily at this witticism that James, who was a nice young man, laughed with her out of politeness.

Araminta got through the evening very credibly. She laughed and talked and toasted James and Mary, contributing her share of the gaiety of the occasion, and only when it was over and one of the house doctors had taken her back to her flat and she was alone again did she allow herself to think. It was already after midnight, but she sat straight down, still in her velvet coat and without even bothering to put on the gas fire, for at the back of her head was the foolish thought that Crispin might come. She waited patiently, occupying the time in trying out suitable explanations to offer him, wondering at the same time if she should have swallowed her pride and waited for him there in the hall until his return, but when she heard the clock strike one she knew that he wouldn't come and she went to bed, to lie awake for a long time, trying to make up her mind if she should write to him. Perhaps he was still in London. She would ask old Charlie, the head porter, in the morning. He might even seek her out…she slept on the happy thought.

She had no chance to see Charlie until the morning was well advanced. Staff Getty had a day off, leaving them short-handed. Charlie heard her out and then shook his bald head. 'He's gorn, Sister—spent the night and went 'arf n'hour ago. I seen 'im leave.' He eyed her with some curiosity. 'Oo wants 'im?'

'No one, Charlie,' Araminta said hastily. 'It's just that Doctor Hickory saw him yesterday evening and wondered why he was here.' She turned away and then paused. 'Any messages for me, Charlie?' she asked casually.

He looked across at the row of pigeonholes behind him. 'No, Sister.'

Araminta hurried back to the Accident Room to find a merciful lull in the work, so that she was able to go to her office and get the daily book up to date, make up the list of instruments for repair, engage in a slight altercation with the CSU, and embark on the off duty lists for the next two weeks. She didn't get far with this, however, for her thoughts turned to Crispin. She wasn't a conceited girl, she didn't think it likely that he had come to London for the express purpose of seeing her, but at least he could have made some effort to see her—even a note or a telephone call. Surely if a man sent roses to a girl, he would, given the chance, at least pass the time of day with her? He had been in a filthy temper, too.

She squashed a rising desire to telephone him then and there and find out exactly what was the matter. A hare-brained idea, for she hadn't a clue where he might be. Not that he would tell her; she could imagine his mouth, set like a rat trap in his dark face. She paused to draw a not very good likeness of him on her blotting pad; on second thoughts, there was nothing really wrong with a rat trap, and most of the time his mouth was rather nice, with a quirk at the corners as though he were on the point of smiling. Her reflections were interrupted here by one of the student nurses with the news that there was another overdose coming in. Araminta closed her books and started to roll up her sleeves. 'They always come just when we're due to go to dinner,' she said testily, and sailed away to check that everything was in readiness.

Thinking about it afterwards, she had no idea when

the preposterous idea first entered her head; she only knew that it was there, taking shape during the afternoon, so that by the time she went to tea she knew exactly what she was going to do.

She did it the following morning as soon as Miss Best was available, and that lady heard her out with outward calm at least.

'You have some other job in mind, Sister Shaw?' she asked finally.

'No,' said Araminta, 'it's just that I want to leave London for a time—perhaps for always—I don't know yet.'

Miss Best looked mystified, but said gamely: 'Very well, if your mind is quite made up, Sister. You have three weeks' holiday due to you, have you not? Would you prefer to work the full month and receive a salary for those weeks, or leave—let me see—in five days' time?'

'Five days' time,' said Araminta quickly before Miss Best could think better of her offer.

Her superior blinked. 'Sister Dawes is capable of taking over your work permanently?' And when Araminta said yes: 'And do you consider Staff Nurse Getty suitable for the post of Junior Sister in her place?'

'Oh, rather,' Araminta agreed. 'She's jolly good at her job.'

At least Sylvia and Dolly would be happy, especially Dolly, who had been such a faithful right hand and longed, without making a thing of it, to get her Sister's blue. Dismissed by Miss Best, she went back to the department and when the opportunity occurred, invited her two colleagues into the office and over their morning coffee broke the news. It surprised her that they really minded her going, even though it would mean their own promotion, and James, when he was told, was flatteringly put out. Araminta had always been popular, now she was a little shattered to find how many of her friends were sorry to see her go. Of course they wanted to know why she should suddenly want to leave for no reason at all, and she had no answer for them, indeed she wasn't sure of the answer herself. Only she had an instant need to get away from St Katherine's and London, because if she stayed, sooner or later she might meet Crispin, and if he was going to smile at her like that again and call her fickle she wouldn't be able to bear it. She couldn't bear it now, just thinking about it.

She lived through the five days in a state of nerves in case he should appear suddenly once more, but he didn't. She said goodbye to her friends, handed over the key to her flat to Sylvia, who had begged to take it over, promised Miss Best that if she should reconsider her decision to give up nursing, she would let her know, got into the Mini and drove herself down to Somerset.

Chapter 7

Araminta had warned her father and Aunt Martha of her plans, but she strongly suspected that they hadn't believed her to be serious about them. A week or so at home, Aunt Martha had said over the telephone, would do her a great deal of good—dear Thelma's death had upset her; they would have a nice little talk about everything when she got home. Araminta, driving out of London, frowned uneasily. She had told her elderly relations very little about Thomas and now she wondered just how much she had better say about him.

She stopped for lunch on the way, for she had planned to arrive just before tea; talking over a meal was always easier and her father and aunt would both be rested after their afternoon nap. The road was surprisingly empty and she didn't hurry, but when she reached Dunster she felt her delight at seeing it again, its street almost empty, although the shops were cheerfully lighted. There were lights shining from her home too and the front door was opened as she stopped the car. She could see her aunt in the doorway; she got out of the Mini and ran to meet her.

They were glad to have her, too, they made that plain, but they were also mystified as to why she should give up a perfectly good job apparently on impulse. Over their leisurely tea she told them a good deal about her stay in Amsterdam, taking care not to dwell too much on Thomas. Just the same, when she had finished, her father observed: 'I never liked him—I told you that, did I not? But I'm glad you went, my dear, you must have been a joy to Thelma. You say you went with her to the hospital. Could the doctors there do nothing to help—with Thomas, I mean?'

'Oh, yes—they did all they could; talked to him and advised him, but you see, he wouldn't take any notice of them.'

'Were they nice? The doctors, I mean?' asked Aunt Martha.

'Very nice—and so kind. Thelma liked them all.'

'I suppose you didn't see that nice man who rescued you at Mousehole?'

Araminta took some cake she didn't want because it gave her time to think up a casual answer. 'As a matter of fact,' she told her listeners, 'he was the consultant in charge of Thelma's case.'

'Now there's a coincidence,' declared her aunt happily. 'Talk about the world being small! I expect he was very glad to see you again.'

'He didn't say,' said Araminta truthfully. 'He was very kind to Thelma.' There was a short silence while they both looked at her. Presently Aunt Martha said briskly: 'A holiday will do you good, child. You look tired—and you couldn't have come at a better time, with Christmas only six weeks away and the puddings and mincemeat to make, I shall be glad of your help.'

Araminta expressed an entirely false pleasure at her aunt's suggestion. Six weeks to Christmas and she had no job—her own silly fault—and no future without Crispin. Oh, she would make all the puddings and pies Aunt Martha could wish for and cut out the interesting bits in *The Times* for her father so that he could paste them in his reference books, and in a little while, because they really did expect it of her, she would go away and find herself another job exactly like the last one, and in a year or two her hair would lose its brightness and instead of being slim she would be bony, and bad-tempered with it.

'You look melancholy, my dear,' her aunt said sharply, so that she hastily rearranged her features into a light-hearted smile, while strongly denying any feeling other than that of pleasure at being home again.

And it was a pleasure. The calm routine of the small household was very soothing. She found herself, after the first two days, absorbed into it without any effort at all, helping with the small chores, doing the shopping, painstakingly cutting up the fruit for Aunt Martha's puddings. It was on the third morning after her arrival, with her father and aunt in Minehead, visiting the tailor and the dentist, and Araminta busy in the kitchen, that she went to answer the thud of the old-fashioned door-knocker. The baker, she supposed, not bothering to take off the old-fashioned pinny she was wearing.

It was Crispin, large and elegant, with the faintest of

smiles twitching the corners of his mouth; not at all the kind of smile he had given her in the entrance hall of St Katherine's—She frowned at the awful memory of it, even while her very bones melted at the sight of him.

'Good morning,' she said coldly, steeling her loving heart.

The doctor eased himself nearer the door. 'I've come to apologise,' he said, quite humbly for him, 'if necessary on bended knee—er—perhaps a length of sackcloth and a few ashes if you have them handy?' He peered over her shoulder into the narrow hall beyond. 'If I might come in?'

Araminta had perforce to give way before his bulk, standing on one side as he passed her, saying peevishly to him: 'Oh, all right, but you'll have to come into the kitchen—I'm cooking.'

'Ah, yes—the apron. Lunch, dear girl? I didn't stop on the way down.'

She turned round sharply, which was a mistake, for he was right behind her and she found her nose in his waistcoat. 'Your car,' she said with dignity. 'You can't leave it in the street, it's too narrow.'

'I didn't—the grocer on the corner very kindly allowed me to park beside his shop.'

They had reached the kitchen and she went to the stove to peer in her saucepans and open the oven door. The doctor's splendid nose flared. 'Roast beef?' he enquired hopefully.

'Baked potatoes, Yorkshire pudding, sprouts,' Araminta recited, shutting the oven door on the delicious aroma and going to the table. She didn't look at him, but picked up a rolling pin and attacked the pastry before her.

'Apple pie for afters?' went on the doctor, still hopeful, 'with thick cream?' He sighed in a dramatic way. 'I'm hungry.' He leaned over and picked up a pastry crumb and ate it. 'Of course it wouldn't do for you to invite me to lunch, would it? Not until we're on speaking terms again, and if I apologise now, you, being you, my dear, will probably think that I have done so merely in order to get a good wholesome meal.'

Araminta giggled; she hadn't meant to, it sent her dignity crumbling as she peeped at him sideways. 'Oh, Crispin,' she uttered, torn between exasperation and amusement, 'you're incorrigible!' She might have said a good deal more, only he had taken the rolling pin from her hand and put his arms around her, floury hands and all.

'I was abominable to you,' he said quietly, not smiling now. 'I had no right to speak to you like that, and none of it was true. But there you were, apparently on the point of spending a cosy evening with another man—a young man, too, and I'd come hell for leather to see you.'

She glowed at the words, although she answered him soberly enough. 'I was going to James' engagement party, he was giving me a lift.' She went on slowly: 'I spent a miserable evening—I hope you did, too.'

'Vixen—of course I did.' He swooped and kissed her lingeringly. 'You looked so young, my dearest girl, and I felt so very middle-aged. Just for a little while I made up my mind that I would never see you again, and then I found that I couldn't do it—you are so exactly what I want—have always wanted.' He tilted her chin and looked into her eyes. 'But am I right for you, I wonder?

Set in my ways and used to doing exactly what I like with my life, and ill-tempered to boot.'

'I don't care…' began Araminta, but he stopped her.

'No, don't say it, not yet, my dear. Do you know why I came?'

'To see me?' she asked anxiously.

'That, yes, but also to ask you to come back with me and stay in my house, so that you may get to know me.'

'But I know you already,' she protested strongly. 'Crispin, I'm not a child…'

His smile was tender. 'No, perhaps not, only a green girl. Will you do as I ask? No ties, no strings, I promise you. Tante Maybella will love to have your company and we will be together as often as I can arrange it. And when you are sure that you can be happy with me, I shall ask you to marry me, and if you aren't sure, then you shall come home again and everything will be as it was before we met.' He let her go and the smile changed to a grin. 'May I stay to lunch?' he asked.

She said: 'Yes, of course,' in what she hoped was a normal voice, while she swallowed disappointment. A cleverer girl than she would have known how to make him marry her out of hand. She had done her best to tell him that she loved him, but he hadn't let her say it. Perhaps he didn't want her to, and he hadn't said that he loved her. She said steadily: 'I'd like to come very much. I expect you know that I've given up my job at St Katherine's—I was going to have a few weeks here and then look for something else.'

She finished rolling the pastry and laid it neatly over the apples lying in the dish, and the doctor went to sit on the edge of the table beside her. 'Well, you can spend a few weeks with us instead,' he assured her comfortably. His voice was very placid; he could have been an old family friend, having a chat about the weather.

It was all arranged very easily. To Araminta's surprise neither her father nor her aunt raised even the faintest of objections, but then it would have been difficult for them to have done so, for Crispin, when she had introduced him, had said calmly: 'It is delightful to meet you again. You must wonder why I am here, Mr Shaw. I have asked Araminta to come back to Amsterdam with me and stay with us—my aunt and myself. I want to marry her, but she has had very little opportunity of knowing me. I should like her to have that opportunity before I ask her.'

He had taken her hand in his while he had been speaking and held it fast, and she had stifled the thought that he still hadn't told her that he loved her. Perhaps he took it for granted that if he said that he wanted to marry her, it would mean that he loved her too.

Later on, when they were alone together, she had wanted to ask him that, but in the face of his placid friendliness, she had found it impossible.

They went, all four of them, to the Luttrell Arms for dinner that evening, and it was obvious before the evening was out that Aunt Martha was as wax in Crispin's hands, and that Mr Shaw, while saying little, took it for granted that they would marry. Indeed, when they were back home again and Crispin had left them to return to the hotel, he made the observation that Crispin was a man of intellect and good sense and one whom he would gladly welcome as a son-in-law. It was a pity, he added, that more young couples didn't get to know each other in such a sensible fashion before marrying— a view to which Araminta couldn't subscribe. Surely, her heart argued, if you loved someone, that was all that mattered? Crispin had called her a green girl, but she was twenty-five, a grown woman, and if he imagined that she was just infatuated, he was quite mistaken. She thought about it, upstairs in her bedroom, getting ready for bed; she had never been more sure of anything in her life before—it was a pity that Crispin couldn't be made to see that. Perhaps things would be easier once she was staying in the house in Amsterdam—there might be opportunities. She lay in bed, sleepily thinking up a few.

Crispin came after breakfast, wished her good morning and accepted her father's invitation to glance at some interesting documents concerning the history of the village. Araminta watched the two men disappear with mixed feelings. True, Crispin had kissed her, but it had been a very ordinary, quick kiss which meant nothing; perhaps he was a man who didn't like to be demonstrative. It struck her that he had been quite right, she really knew very little about him.

She made the beds, dusted the sitting room and went to make the coffee, while her aunt arranged the best cups and saucers and rubbed up the silver spoons—proof, if further proof were needed, that she entirely approved of Crispin.

Mr Shaw continued to discourse on local history while they drank their coffee, to the exclusion of all else, so that his daughter viewed him with a jaundiced eye and wished that he would stop, and her humour was hardly improved by the sight of Crispin, apparently enjoying every word of it. It was Aunt Martha who broke in firmly, reminding her brother that if Araminta didn't go to the shops there would be no lunch that day, and since Crispin was interested in the village, what better opportunity of his seeing it for himself while accompanying Araminta.

This sensible remark had the desired effect. Araminta whipped up to her room to put on her coat, and when she got down again, Crispin had his coat on too and was in the hall, holding the shopping basket.

She felt a little shy at first, going in and out of the butcher's and the baker's; choosing cauliflowers and apples and grapes at the greengrocers, but her companion appeared perfectly at home in his new role and when they had delivered the basket to Aunt Martha, suggested that a walk might be pleasant. It was a splendid morning, cold and windy, but the sun was shining as they bent their steps towards the church, where they wandered round while Araminta called to mind all she knew of the Luttrell family and the monks who had lived in Dunster so long ago. 'They were in the hotel, you know,' she told him. 'It's really very old. The village is lovely, isn't it, and so is the church.'

He took her hand and slowed her walk to a halt. 'Would you wish to marry here, Araminta?'

She had had her dreams like any other girl. 'Well, yes, though I don't think it matters where you marry, as long as you love each other.'

He only smiled faintly. 'I expect you're right. Where do we go next?'

He wasn't going to let her say that she loved him; she wondered fleetingly if he was afraid that she might regret it. With an effort she kept her voice friendly and nothing more. 'We can go through the castle grounds, if you like—they're not open to the public, but no one minds if the village people take the short cut through the wood to the main road.'

It was pretty amongst the trees. Far in front of them they could hear the traffic on the main road between Minehead and Bridgewater, but here it was quiet except for the wind whistling and moaning between the leafless branches. The path was narrow, and Araminta, who knew it like the palm of her hand, went in front, pausing every now and again to explain some part of the terrain when it came into view, but when they reached the edge of the wood and paused to look beyond the road to the grey, wind-tossed water of the Bristol Channel, Crispin put an arm across her shoulders and drew her close.

'Will you be ready to come back with me tomorrow?' he asked.

'Tomorrow?' She turned to look up into his face. 'But Father might…'

'He assured me that he could see no possible objection; it is for you to say, my dear.'

She smiled at him. 'It was just that I'm surprised—everything's happening so quickly. What time do you want to leave?'

'In the early afternoon—we'll go from Harwich.' He turned her round to face him. 'Your second visit to Amsterdam will be quite different from your first,' he promised, and kissed her with a gentleness which sent the tears to her eyes, so that she had to look away quickly in case he should see. 'I'm looking forward to it,' she told him quietly, and then: 'We've time to go down to the water, we only have to cross the road at the bottom of the hill and go down that lane.'

They walked fast, arm-in-arm into the wind, talking about a great many things, and Araminta was glad to discover that they agreed about most of them. They got back to the house just in time to drink their sherry before lunch, and when it was eaten, Crispin washed up in the manner of someone who did so every day of his life, something which Araminta doubted very much, before saying that he had one or two matters to attend to and might he come back for tea? She had no idea what the matters might be and he didn't enlighten her, but he looked remarkably pleased with himself when he returned.

He took her out to dinner again that evening and she wore the dress she had most fortuitously seen in the smart little boutique in the main street. It was very pretty; of crêpe, its colour a shade darker than her hair. It fell in tiny pleats from a high-necked yoke and its wide belt made her slim waist seem even slimmer.

'Very pretty,' observed Crispin when she joined him, and she wasn't sure if he meant her person or her dress, but it was a good beginning to an evening which became better and better as its hours slipped away. They took their time over dinner, for at this time of year there were few guests at the hotel. The food was superb and the dining room warm and softly lighted, and when they had finished they crossed the narrow, flagstoned hall to the coffee lounge, happily empty, and had coffee before the blazing log fire while they talked comfortably about nothing in particular. It seemed to Araminta that she was discovering a number of aspects of Crispin's character she had never considered before. She had, until now, thought of him as a doctor first and as a man—a rather remote, ill-tempered man—second; now he was letting her catch glimpses of the man and she had liked what she had seen very much—and that, she reminded herself, had nothing to do with loving him.

They set off the next day, with one of Aunt Martha's

excellent lunches inside them and Araminta's largest
case in the boot. She hadn't been sure what to pack, so
in the end she had taken an armful of sweaters, some
slacks, her newish tweed suit, her thick coat and the jersey dress, and naturally she had added the new crêpe;
anything else she would have to buy while she was in
Amsterdam; she had sufficient money for that.

She settled into the comfort of the Rolls' front seat
with a sigh of pleasure and only the faintest twinge of
anxiety that things might not work out right, after all.
She buoyed herself up with the promise that it wouldn't
be her fault if they didn't and decided wisely not to
allow her mind to dwell on it too much. She waved
to her family, gave Crispin a small, loving smile and
gave herself over to the pleasure of a long journey in
his company.

By the time they had reached Harwich and were
safely on board, she felt as though she had known him
all her life. She told him so before going below to her
cabin and his answering smile had been charming, although he had given her a searching look. 'That's the
object of the exercise,' he reminded her blandly. 'Sleep
well.'

Surprisingly, she did, and even the darkness of the
six o'clock morning couldn't damp her good spirits.
It was only just getting light by the time they reached
Amsterdam, fifty miles away, but there were already
lights shining from the windows of Crispin's home, and
Jos, with Rikki beside him, was there to welcome them.

'Breakfast,' said the doctor. 'Can we have it in ten
minutes, Jos? I expect Miss Shaw would like to go to
her room first.' He turned to look at her. 'Will that suit
you, Araminta?'

She said shyly that it would, and followed Frone upstairs to the same room as she had had before. There
were fresh flowers there, even English magazines and
a newspaper, and everything she could possibly need
in the bathroom. She looked at everything in a happy
daze, tidied her hair in a perfunctory fashion and went
downstairs again and found Crispin waiting for her in
the hall. As they went into the pleasant little room where
they had breakfasted together before, she asked: 'Do
you have to go to the hospital today?'

'Not until the afternoon, but I've some patients to
see privately this morning.' She handed him his coffee
and he asked: 'Forgive me if I run through my letters?'

She sat like a mouse, drinking cup after cup of delicious coffee and eating her croissant while she watched
him. He looked as though he had slept the night through
and had had all the leisure in the world to achieve the
impeccable appearance he now presented. Araminta
suspected that he had what Aunt Martha would call
an iron constitution, able to do without sleep and food
and still present a calm, elegant front to the world; a
resourceful man too, but once roused, of a very nasty
temper. She loved every inch of him.

He looked up suddenly and caught her staring. 'I'm
abominably rude,' he told her, and stacked his letters
neatly. 'I'll be back about six o'clock this evening. If
you're not too tired, shall we go out after dinner? The
shops will be shut, but they'll be lighted, and you might
enjoy looking at them.'

'Oh, I'd love that—but wouldn't it bore you?'

He answered her gravely: 'When I'm with you I'm
never bored, Araminta. Tante Maybella will be down
at about half past ten—get her to show you the house,

there's nothing she enjoys more, and you might find it interesting.'

Araminta beamed at him. 'Crispin, you're such a nice man!' She added worriedly: 'I do hope I fit in…'

He got out of his chair and came round the table and bent to kiss her cheek as he said laughingly: 'You fit in quite perfectly.' He dropped a second kiss on top of her head, said *'Tot ziens,'* and was gone.

She unpacked first and then had a bath, made fragrant by Madame Rochas, put on a skirt and sweater, did her hair and face very carefully, then went downstairs. She was crossing the hall slowly, wondering where she should go, when Jos appeared.

'There is a fire in the small sitting room,' he informed her, and ushered her into a room—not small at all, according to her standards, with a large bow window overlooking the garden at the back of the house. It was furnished very comfortably with a number of armchairs and sofas, a richly piled carpet upon the floor, and a profusion of paintings upon its walls. Araminta rather liked it, and so apparently did Rikki, who in company with the tabby cat was stretched out before the fire.

'Shall I take the dog, miss?' asked Jos.

'Oh, no—please don't, she's such good company.' She smiled and received an answering smile from the craggy face.

'Then I'll bring you some coffee, miss; Mevrouw van Sibbelt will be down any minute now.'

The old lady arrived with the coffee tray. She was still wearing black, but this morning her dress was of a fine wool, with a little white pleated frill round the high collar. She was wearing her gold chains, though, and a small enamelled watch fastened by a brooch to

the tucked bodice. She looked like a small porcelain doll
with her beautifully dressed hair and pink and white
complexion.

Araminta was a little surprised at the warmth of her
welcome, for she still had some fleeting doubts as to her
hostess's true feelings towards her, but now she began to
think that she must have imagined them, for the morning was passed delightfully, chatting over coffee, and
then by an inspection of the house. Mevrouw van Sibbelt, surprisingly nimble for her eighty-odd years, led
the way in and out of rooms which Araminta found surprisingly beautiful; they were seldom used, explained
her guide, only when Crispin gave a party, or invited his
numerous cousins, aunts and uncles to visit him on the
Feast of Sint Nicolaas, or to stay over Christmas and the
New Year. 'New Year is the most enjoyable,' declared
Mevrouw van Sibbelt, 'for the house looks so splendid
and every room is in use, there are so many people...'

'You act as hostess?' asked Araminta gently.

'Indeed I do—a task I thoroughly enjoy.' The old
lady paused to enjoy a reverie of her own and then said
brightly: 'You will like the ballroom, it is along there—
if you would open those double doors, Araminta...'

It was a splendid apartment, very formal, with its
gilded pillars and silk-panelled walls. It was at the back
of the house, reached by a short passage over-looking
one side of the garden. Araminta twirled on its polished floor, imagining herself in a really super dress,
dancing with Crispin—apricot chiffon would do very
nicely, with some really beautiful embroidery. She gave
a final twirl and came to a laughing halt in front of her
companion, and was shocked by the expression she surprised on the old face—not hate, exactly, not even dis-

like, but a look of speculation tinged with fear, and what could Mevrouw van Sibbelt, living in the lap of luxury in her nephew's house, have to be afraid of? Araminta stopped in mid-twirl and asked anxiously: 'Is anything the matter, Mevrouw?'

The look had gone even as she spoke; it was just an elderly face once more, gently smiling at her. 'Of course not, my dear, just a twinge in my bones, I expect— natural enough at my age, is it not? It's a little frightening to grow old. One becomes useless...'

Araminta took a small, beringed hand in hers. 'You are certainly not useless, Mevrouw van Sibbelt, and you have no need to be frightened. You have Crispin and he loves you very much.' She would have liked to have added 'And you will have me too,' but it seemed presumptuous to say that.

Mevrouw van Sibbelt smiled then. 'You're a nice child,' she declared, 'and not at all like any of the others.'

Araminta didn't ask who the others were. Her companion was obviously speaking about the other girls whom Crispin must have brought to his home from time to time. And why not? she asked herself stoutly. He had been free to do as he liked and have the friends he chose, had he not? It was a pity that this charitable sentiment should have been entirely swamped by a great wave of jealousy; she hated herself for it.

'It takes all kinds to make a world,' she pronounced in a bright voice. 'Where do we go next, or would you like to rest for a little while?'

'The first floor, I think.' Mevrouw van Sibbelt was looking at her with faint disappointment. 'For a young girl you have very little curiosity,' she said tartly, and when Araminta didn't answer, went on: 'After lunch I shall take my little rest, perhaps you would like to explore the rest of the house then. Let us go back the way we came and go up the main staircase.'

By the time they had reached the head of the stairs, her little flash of ill humour had vanished and they spent the next hour wandering through the rooms which led off the gallery which ran round three sides of the hall. They didn't go into all of them; Mevrow van Sibbelt paused before the arched door with its swags of fruit and flowers carved above it and which dominated one side of the gallery and explained that it was the principal bedroom of the house and not in use. 'It will be a different matter when Crispin marries,' she said, and peered sideways at Araminta. 'It is a very a lovely room.'

She led the way to another door and opened that instead. 'This is one of the guest rooms—charming, is it not?'

Araminta looked around her. The room was certainly that, with its heavy Beidermeier furniture and the pale pastel silk of the curtains and bedspread. She began to wonder, a little uneasily, just how rich a man Crispin was; much richer than she had imagined, she realised that now as they continued their inspection of one room after the other, each perfection and all apparently ready for instant occupation. Presently they went down to lunch together in the small room in which she had breakfasted, and over their omelettes and fruit, discussed the house and its treasures, and the old lady, quite forgetting her nap, lingered long after they were finished, talking of her youth and the balls she had attended and telling of the family's history. Araminta sat enthralled; anything to do with Crispin interested her, and this was his home and his family... She watched her companion mount the staircase for her long delayed rest with a feeling of real regret.

But there was the second floor, and when she reached it presently it was to find that it was almost exactly similar to the one below, save that here, at the back of the house, there was a nursery wing. A large, high-ceilinged room, overlooking the garden and beyond that, a canal and an interesting vista of gabled rooftops. A smaller room led from it, as did a bathroom, tiny kitchen and two much smaller rooms. 'Enough for six children,' commented Araminta, aloud, 'with a couple of nurse-maids thrown in.'

There was a cupboard along one wall and after a moment's hesitation she opened it, to spend an enraptured half hour looking at the toys stacked neatly away on its shelves. Some of them were very old; dolls with china heads and flaxen hair and most beautifully dressed, clockwork toys, a magnificent dolls' house, small wooden horses on wheels, a whole Noah's Ark— she inspected them all, wondering which of them had belonged to Crispin when he was a little boy and imagining the delight of future inhabitants of the nursery when they opened the cupboard doors. She heaved an unconscious sigh and went down to the drawing room and had a solitary tea, for Mevrouw van Sibbelt hadn't reappeared, before getting her coat and going into the garden to play ball with Rikki until it was dark.

Crispin was home when she went to the drawing room an hour later after changing into the jersey dress, and over their drinks engaged her in a pleasant desultory conversation, wanting to know how she had spent her day, which naturally enough led to talk of the house and its history, talk which became general when his aunt joined them, and which stayed so throughout dinner. It was after they had had their coffee and Crispin had suggested that she should get her coat that Araminta feared that the old lady was going to complain at being left alone, but he reminded her kindly that an old friend of hers would be arriving shortly. 'You won't miss us at all,' he told her, laughing. 'Besides, we shan't be late back—I've a busy day tomorrow.'

Their outing was an unqualified success. True, it had begun to drizzle with a cold rain and the wind was blowing, as Araminta had discovered it did in Holland, round every corner, but she hardly noticed it as they walked briskly through the wet streets, stopping here and there to admire the dark outline of some small bridge or a particularly impressive gable, until they reached the Kalverstraat, where Crispin obligingly shortened his stride so that she might peer into the shop windows. There were quite a lot of people strolling around, despite the weather, doing exactly as they were doing, and when she remarked on it, he said half laughing: 'I expect they're couples setting up house together, deciding what they want to buy for their homes.'

'You're got everything already,' she pointed out.

'I haven't got you, Araminta—not yet.'

It was on the tip of her tongue to tell him then and there that he had got her—had had her for quite some time, but if she did he might think her too eager. He had said that she was to stay at his home and get to know him and she had been there barely twenty-four hours; he would remind her of that if she said anything, so she kept a prudent silence, albeit with difficulty. Here was a man, she knew that now, who refused to be hurried—

or rather, refused to hurry her. She swallowed everything she so longed to tell him and said gaily: 'This is fun! Most men hate looking at shops—Father would rather run a mile.'

'Well, I don't make a habit of it, Araminta, but I must admit that I'm enjoying it very much with you. Shall we have a cup of coffee somewhere?'

They were home again before Tante Maybella's visitor had gone. Araminta was introduced to the lady, a large, rather plain-faced woman with an overwhelming bosom and an air of consequence. She smiled kindly at Araminta, engaged her in conversation in excellent English, addressed a few laughing remarks to Crispin and took her leave, and very shortly afterwards, Mevrouw van Sibbelt went to her bed.

'I think I'll go to bed too,' said Araminta. 'I daresay you've got some work or something or other to read.'

The doctor looked up from tickling Rikki's ear. 'Indeed I have—why not come and keep me company while I do it? There's a stove in the study and you can curl up in a chair and read too, if you have a mind to do so.'

'I won't be in your way?'

He shook his head. 'No.' He straightened up and crossed the room to stand before her. 'Do you know, I am just beginning to realise how lonely I've been?' He took her hand in his. 'It's the room next to the small sitting room—did you see it this morning?'

She shook her head. 'Your aunt said that she never went in there.'

He laughed. 'You don't find her tiresome, I hope? She is very difficult sometimes, but then she is an old lady now—I remember her when I was a little boy and she was my favourite aunt.' He added thoughtfully: 'She was always so kind…'

Araminta looked up into his dark face. 'You're a kind man yourself,' she told him gravely.

The study was warm, smelled of leather and tobacco and was furnished with a giant-sized desk and chair and several comfortable armchairs drawn up to the stove. The desk, she noted, was piled high with a conglomeration of papers, notes, letters and a book or two, and once Crispin had settled her in a chair with a copy of *The Lancet* to amuse her, he sat down contentedly to work. She didn't read but watched his dark head, the silver in it showing up strongly in the lamp's light, while he wrote, occasionally telephoned, and then read his letters. She was quite startled when he said: 'It's like having a friendly mouse in the room. Rikki always comes with me, of course, but he isn't the same as a pretty girl.'

'You called me a mouse!'

He chuckled. 'A restful mouse as well as a pretty one.' He cast down the last of the letters on his desk. 'Thank you for bearing me company, Araminta.' He shot a quick look at her. 'You didn't find it too dull?'

'No, of course not, I like being here with you.'

'You enchant me,' he told her as they crossed the hall, 'but that's no reason for keeping you out of your bed.' He gave her a gentle push in the direction of the staircase. 'Good night, dear girl.'

Araminta found that the days passed quickly, although she did very little. She spent a good deal of time in Mevrouw van Sibbelt's company, ventured out by herself in the afternoons and spent her evenings with Crispin, walking Rikki in Vondelpark, driving to

Schevingenen to dine and then walk along the boulevard in the cold dark, or visiting the Concertgebouw.

On the fourth afternoon after her arrival she had gone shopping, for it was obvious that her wardrobe fell far short of her requirements. She had liked the look of Krause en Vogelzang when they had been window-shopping, so now she ventured inside its elegant doors, to emerge a good while later, much lighter in the purse but deeply content with her purchase—a silk jersey dress in a soft sage green, its long sleeves gathered into deep cuffs and having a demure neckline ornamented by a chiffon bow under her chin. Just in case Crispin should find the time to take her dancing, as he had hinted the evening before, she had bought an evening dress too, of blue velvet which matched her eyes exactly, its deep neckline outlined with tiny silk frills. She counted herself fortunate in matching it exactly with velvet slippers and a velvet stole which just happened to catch her eye.

She had the opportunity to wear this charming outfit two evenings later. Crispin had telephoned during the afternoon to tell her that he had booked a table at the Amstel Hotel for dinner and dancing; he endeared himself still further to her by asking, in the nicest possible way, if she wanted a new dress for the occasion, because if so she had only to say so and he would instruct his bank.

'What a dear you are!' she exclaimed warmly, and heard his chuckle. 'As a matter of fact, I saw a dress I liked and bought it...'

She found the Amstel Hotel quietly impressive, solidly comfortable to the point of luxury and a most fitting background for the velvet dress, and it was delightful to discover that their table overlooked the Amstel River. Even on a near winter's evening, it was a pleasant sight, with the lights of countless barges and boats twinkling on its black water. Araminta turned away from watching them to find Crispin's eyes on her. 'You look delightful,' he told her. 'That's a pretty dress, and a pretty girl inside it.'

She pinkened. 'Thank you, Crispin. I—I hoped you'd like it.' She smiled shyly. 'Don't look at me like that.'

'Like what?' he asked blandly.

'Like that. Did you have a busy day?'

His eyes gleamed with amusement. 'Yes, I did. Araminta, you're shy.' His smile enfolded her, so that she smiled back at him, suddenly at her ease.

'What shall we eat?' he went on matter-of-factly. 'Shall we order now and then dance?'

They finished their drinks and danced—they danced a great deal. Araminta hardly noticed what they ate and it wasn't until her glass was being refilled that she remarked dreamily: 'It's champagne, isn't it?' which made Crispin laugh and urge her to drink up so that they could dance again. It was towards the end of the evening as they were circling the room to 'Let's dance the old-fashioned way' that he said softly: 'I couldn't agree more with this song; it's how I'd like to dance with you always, darling.' And when the music stopped, he said: 'Let's go home. I want to talk to you.'

Araminta had the pleasant sensation that she was dreaming and then waking up to find it was real. 'Yes, of course,' she agreed in a voice which trembled just a little and sped to get her wrap.

It had begun to freeze outside and she wrapped the soft velvet close as they went out to the car. They hardly spoke on the way home and she was aware of a mounting excitement as the doctor drove through the narrow streets. There were still lights showing in the house, and Jos came from the back of the hall to enquire if they would like coffee, then went away to fetch it.

Araminta allowed the doctor to take her wrap and then her hand as they went into the drawing room. It looked quite beautiful in the firelight and the soft glow of a solitary lamp; Araminta looked lovely too. Crispin eyed her with satisfaction and told her so before he kissed her soundly. 'I had no idea I was so impatient a man,' he observed. 'Will you marry me, Araminta?'

She stood within the circle of his arms, looking up at him. He was a handsome man, if one happened to like dark, beaky-nosed faces and dark, heavy-lidded eyes, and she did. They were smiling at her now in such a way that she could hardly wait to say yes, and it was a good thing that she hadn't hesitated, for she had barely uttered when the telephone rang and with an impatient word Crispin went to answer it.

Such a pity, she thought, when there was so much to say between them, and listening to his urgent, low-voiced questions. She could see that it was some knotty medical problem, that just for the moment had swept her right out of his head. It didn't surprise her in the least when he put down the receiver and said: 'There's an emergency which presents several problems. Go to bed, my dear, we'll talk tomorrow.'

He kissed her briefly, his mind already grappling with whatever awaited him at the hospital, and she, understanding very well, said quietly: 'Yes, dear? I hope it isn't anything too bad,' and stood where she was until she heard the heavy thud of the front door. Only when Jos came to take away the coffee tray did she wish him good night and make her way up to bed, still very happy; unwilling to come out of her lovely dreamlike world.

When she got down in the morning, it was to find that Crispin had been home, slept for a couple of hours, breakfasted and returned to the hospital. He hoped to be back, said Jos, in the early afternoon, but there was a possibility that it might be considerably later than that. Araminta ate her breakfast, had a brisk session with Rikki in the garden and came indoors to find Mevrouw van Sibbelt in the little sitting room. The old lady seemed pleased to see her, and they spent an hour together chatting until it was suggested that Araminta might like to take a walk before their lunch. It was colder than it had been for some days, but she walked briskly, coming back with glowing cheeks and bright eyes. The glow evaporated a little when Jos met her with the news that the doctor didn't expect to get home before evening, a piece of news which took away her appetite, something which the old lady remarked upon while they were having their coffee after lunch.

'You are excited, my dear,' she smiled across the room. 'I think perhaps it is because Crispin has asked you to marry him. Am I right?'

'Well, yes, he has,' admitted Araminta, and was a little taken aback when her companion murmured: 'You are so suitable...'

'Suitable?' she echoed, rather at a loss.

The old lady smiled gently. 'You are young and strong and like children, do you not? And you find this house to your taste—Crispin would never marry a girl who would want to alter his home in any way. You

are a pretty young woman too and have nice manners—
and quite different from Nelissa.'

'And who is Nelissa?' asked Araminta, aware that
her voice was too sharp.

'You do not know about her? She is the girl whom
Crispin loved—still loves—and can never marry.'

Araminta felt an icy hand move slowly up her spine.
'Crispin will tell me about her if he wants to,' she said
stoutly, and heard the hateful shake in her voice as she
spoke.

The old lady peeped at her over her old-fashioned
gold-rimmed spectacles. 'My dear, as you grow older
you will learn that there are some things about which
a man never speaks.'

'You mean I mustn't ask him?'

Her companion nodded.

'But why not? He—he wants to marry me, Mevrouw
van Sibbelt.'

'Crispin is forty years old, Araminta, he knows that
he must marry soon if he wishes for a son to carry on
the family name, and believe me, he does wish that.'
The silvery voice was decisive. 'You should count yourself fortunate he has chosen you. There are several suitable girls who would be only too glad to step into your
shoes.'

'But it was me he asked,' said Araminta flatly.

'And I am glad, child—his strong feelings of pity for
you in the first place, when he discovered you slaving
for that cousin of yours, more than tipped the balance
in your favour.' She met Araminta's outraged eye with
a smile and asked in a sympathetic voice: 'Has he ever
said that he loves, you, my dear?'

He never had. Araminta admitted that in a proud little voice which disdained sympathy. 'This Nelissa,' she asked in a voice as calm as she could make it, 'you said that Crispin would marry her if he could—why doesn't he?'

'There are circumstances...' said her companion mysteriously, and paused. 'A few days ago—you remember that he went away unexpectedly? I must say no more than that, only—if he had not already had an understanding with you...but he had. He made that clear when he came back from your home in England, and he is not a man to go back on his word, whatever the cost to himself.'

'So I'm standing in the way of his happiness,' said Araminta. She sat staring at the old lady, sitting there tearing her lovely dreams apart in that silvery voice. Of course the dear soul didn't realise what she was doing, and that was a good thing really, because there was still time to do something about it—only she would have to look sharp; she felt strangely numb, but her brain was clear enough and already busy with a plan. And after all, it was easy enough. Mevrouw van Sibbelt was making preparations to go upstairs for her nap and she wouldn't come down again until tea time or later, and Crispin wouldn't be back until the evening. Araminta could be miles away by then. She went upstairs with the old lady with the remark that she would get her coat and go for a walk.

In the room she snatched up her jacket and put it on, found her overnight bag, stuffed it with whatever caught her distracted eye, picked up her gloves and handbag and hurried through the quiet house and out of its door. She still felt very peculiar and her mind wasn't as clear as it should have been, which was probably why, when she reached the station and joined the ticket-buying queue, she discovered that she had left her wallet and almost all her money, as well as her passport, behind. She could go back, but the risk of encountering Jos was great and she would never be able to think up a plausible story as to why she had gone out with an overnight bag.

The woman in front of her bought a ticket to Valkenburg, and Araminta bought one too, because she remembered that it was a long way from Amsterdam, and that was important… Her state of mind didn't allow her to realise that her ticket had cost her considerably more than half the money she had with her.

Chapter 8

Araminta was aware that the time spent sitting in the train should be put to good use deciding what to do next, but her mind refused to work. She stared out of the window at the unfamiliar scenery, her head empty of anything but deep misery, and when she saw the woman who had been in front of her in the queue gather up her bags, took her own small bag from the rack, guessing that they would be nearing Valkenburg. When the train came to a halt in the well-kept station, she followed her out on to the platform, gave up her ticket and walked out into the street.

It was already dusk and the wind was decidedly fresh. She thanked heaven that she was wearing her tweed suit and a wool jumper under it, took a reassuring grip of her paltry luggage, and looked around her.

There were several hotels across the quiet street—she dismissed two of them at once; that they were

spotlessly clean she had no doubt, but their black net
curtains and purple lighting proclaimed them as ultra-
modern and frequented by those addicted to pop music.
The third hotel was large, brilliantly lighted and quite
obviously much too expensive. The thought of the very
small sum she had in her purse sent a shiver down her
already cold spine, although it didn't weaken her resolu-
tion. Telling herself that there would be any number of
small, suitably cheap hotels in a town given over almost
entirely to the summer tourist trade, she started briskly
for the end of the street. It led in its turn into a wider,
busier thoroughfare filled with a fair amount of traffic
and lined with more hotels, all regrettably closed for
the winter, and so it proved with all the smaller hotels.

Araminta walked, not quite so fast now, round the
main streets of the compact little town, with its ruined
castle brooding over it. There were several bars open
now, filled with cheerful, noisy groups, mostly men, but
she was tired and the idea of wrestling with enquiries
about a room which might cost too much money, and
the difficulty of explaining that she could only afford
a certain amount, and that before a crowd of strangers
who would probably not understand a word she said,
made even her stout heart quail. She retraced her steps,
out of the town's centre, up the hill once more and over
the level crossing by the station, feeling a little desperate. She had been a fool to leave Crispin's house without making sensible plans; without taking sufficient
money with her...even as she thought that she knew that
she couldn't have stayed another minute, even though
it had been the silliest thing she had ever done in her
whole life.

She blinked back tears, gave a defiant sniff, and

looked about her. There were a few shops in the street and a number of hotels and guest-houses, all closed, but at the top of the hill there were welcoming lights. Recklessly Araminta walked towards them, longing only for a place in which to put her head for the night. They streamed invitingly from a large hotel standing back from the road; a pleasant place, surrounded by trees and flower beds. It looked warm and cheerful, and without stopping to think she made for its entrance—at least she could have a cup of coffee there.

It was delightfully warm inside and the faint clatter of knives and forks reminded her of her hunger. A little lightheaded at the thought of a meal, she went to the desk and asked if they had a room.

They had, and its cost would take all but a couple of gulden of her money, but she really didn't care any more. She filled in the form she was offered, took the key and followed the receptionist through the foyer, past the dining room and into a quiet hall, where she was advised to mount the staircase at its centre. 'Number fifty-five,' said the receptionist, and left her.

The room was small but well-furnished and warm. Araminta took out the meagre contents of her overnight bag and laid them on the bed: a nightgown, a change of undies, writing paper and envelopes—she wondered why she had put those in—a brush and comb and a bag of hastily collected toilet articles, and that was the lot. She stared at them at though by doing so she could turn them all into the things she had left behind, then picked them up despondently and arranged them on the washstand and in a drawer of the dressing table. Even for one uncertain night, one should remain tidy. Then she combed her hair, put her jacket back on again and went downstairs and out into the street. She had noticed a *potat frites* stall in the town—chips would be filling and only fifty cents a portion, which would leave her enough to buy a cup of coffee at the hotel before she went to bed, pay her bill and still have almost a gulden over—sufficient for a glass of milk, perhaps... She would worry about that in the morning; a good night's sleep and breakfast would give her back her usual resourcefulness and energy.

She found the stall, bought her paper poke of chips and walked along munching them. She had never eaten chips from a paper bag before and perhaps it wasn't very good manners, but they hardly mattered now; there was no one to see her, and even if there had been, she didn't care; the chips were crisp and their warmth was decidedly heartening. She polished off the last crumb and started back to the hotel, feeling much better.

She hadn't realised that there were quite so many people staying there; middle-aged and downright elderly, they sat at the small round tables covered with Persian rugs, the men drinking beer or gin, the women sipping glasses of wine. There was a band in one corner of the foyer, too; a man at the piano and another younger one, sitting in the centre of an assortment of instruments, with an accordion on his knee, and when the waitress brought her coffee she told Araminta in a mixture of Dutch and English that there was to be an evening's music for the benefit of the old people's club staying at the hotel on their annual outing.

Araminta sipped her coffee, making it last, and bent her mind to her problems, but not for long. The band, making up for its lack of size by its enthusiasm, burst into a gay tune which had everyone round her stamping and clapping and presently singing too. The noise was overpowering, but it drowned her sad, frightened thoughts while she sat on, long after her coffee cup had been drained, glad that thinking had become an impossibility.

But presently, despite her determination to stay where she was in such cheerful surroundings, her eye lids began to droop and she made her way up to her room. A good night's sleep was what she needed; she was tired and headachy and she would need a clear head in the morning. She got ready for bed, laid her head on the pillow and was instantly asleep.

She wakened in less than an hour, her mind crystal clear, ready to tackle all and every problem. Hours later, listening to a chorus of clocks chiming seven, she was forced to the conclusion that none of her problems were surmountable; ideas had raced round and round inside her weary head with all the energy of mice in a wheel, and none of them had been of any use to her at all. She got up and made a slow toilet, unable to do much to her poor white face, for she had only her powder compact and lipstick with her, then she rammed her miserable bits and pieces back into her overnight bag, and went down to breakfast.

The old people's club were making an early start for home. The more active members were already hatted and coated and waiting for the bus which would take them back to Amsterdam, while the laggards finished their breakfast. Araminta sat down for her own breakfast at a small table in a corner of the dining room and eyed the basket of assorted breads upon it with hungry pleasure. Despite her headache, she made a good breakfast, washed down by the milkless tea the waiter fetched for her, and felt all the better for it, so that when she had paid her bill and carefully counted the handful of coins which was all she had now, she still felt quite able to cope with whatever the day might bring.

During breakfast the half-formed notion that she might hitchhike her way to Rotterdam and there borrow her fare home from the British Consul had been taking shape in her mind. She had never thumbed a lift in her life, but thousands did, and if they could, so could she. She buttoned her jacket, wishing for a scarf to tie over her head, pulled on her gloves, and pot-valiant from her breakfast, left the hotel. The road north ran past the hotel. She walked along it for a mile or more until she was quite clear of the town and took up her position.

For a little while cars streamed past her, but none of them stopped. She walked on, stopping every few yards to lift her hand at a passing motorist, but her stops became less frequent, for the sky, which had been a cold, unfriendly grey since early morning, had become darker, the clouds whipped up by a mean wind. She had no idea what the time was; she had left her watch behind too—like a fool, she told herself fiercely—and she was on a stretch of road now with no houses in sight and almost no traffic. She had thought innocently enough that she had only to stand by the side of the road and lift a hand for someone to stop. That her appearance was spoiling her chances was something she hadn't guessed at; a well-dressed young woman, with neat hair and gloved hands holding a smart overnight bag, was so unlike the usual type of lifter that the majority of drivers hardly noticed her, and once or twice, when she had stepped into the road to attract attention, the irate drivers had merely shaken their fists at her.

She stood irresolutely, trying to make up her mind what to do; she could walk on and hope that sooner or later someone would stop, but supposing they didn't? She might be better off in the town, after all, and a few drops of icy rain decided her. She retraced her footsteps, making plans as she went. She would go to the police station and ask someone there to lend her enough money to get to Rotterdam… She frowned; they would want to know why she wanted the money in the first place, and when she explained, why she had left Crispin's house in such a hurry, and they would certainly want to know why she had come to Valkenburg, which was, after all, miles away from Amsterdam. If only she had gone to Rotterdam—with enough money—and gone down to the Hoek and got on a boat to Harwich, but she hadn't, and on second thoughts the police would be no good, they might even clap her in prison. She didn't know anything about Dutch Law, perhaps it was the same as France where one was sent to prison until one could prove one's innocence.

She was back in town by now and surprised to find that it was already past two o'clock. She fingered her purse. The thirty-five cents in it weren't enough for a cup of coffee, but they would be sufficient for a roll or a small bar of chocolate. Araminta settled for the roll, counting the money carefully into one hand as she crossed one of the little bridges over the narrow river which ran through the town between the shopping streets. It was sheer ill-chance that a passer-by in a hurry should bump into her so that she lost her balance, clutched at the bridge railing to keep her feet, and let every single coin in her handfall into the water below.

Araminta stared down at the sluggish little river, and

being a girl of some spirit, voiced her thoughts aloud, which, while relieving her pent-up feelings, did nothing to help her. She was now quite penniless, and the sensation wasn't a pleasant one. She thought of the roll she had been going to buy with passionate longing and told herself in a loud, cross voice because there was no one to hear her: 'This is the last straw!'

But it wasn't. The very last straw of all came in the form of more icy rain; it had been falling in a desultory fashion on and off for the last hour, and now it became a sudden torrential downpour, soaking her within seconds.

There was no shelter on the bridge, but at its end she could see what appeared to be an old castle set in a small enclosure of trees and shrubs which would afford some shelter at least, she lost no time in making for it.

It was indeed a castle, half hidden by ivy and bushes against its walls, and although it was small, its vast front door stood open with steps leading down to a second door, firmly shut. But it gave some shelter. Araminta perched gingerly on the bottom step, and presently, with her bag beside her to lean her head on, she went to sleep.

It was still light when she woke up, although the doorway was considerably darkened by Crispin, whose bulk was blocking it. She couldn't see his face properly, but his voice, icy with rage, set her shivering.

'You silly little fool,' he said with suppressed violence, and she remembered in a bemused way that the very first time they had met on the patch of sand below the Cornish cliffs, he had said just that.

He leaned down and plucked her to her feet and caught up her bag. Her empty purse fell to the ground as he did so, and he picked that up too and turned it over in his gloved hand. There was no expression on his face now and she couldn't understand what he said, but it sounded violent and not quite nice, and even though she wasn't sure if she were awake or dreaming she said tartly: 'Don't you swear your beastly Dutch oaths at me!'

He gave a crack of laughter. 'Had you no money at all?' His voice still held that icy anger to make her shiver again; Araminta felt defeated and so unhappy that she had no anger left. She told him in a dreary little voice: 'I had thirty-five cents, but someone bumped into me on a bridge…it was in my hand and it fell into the water.'

She waited for him to laugh, but he only sighed deeply and said: 'The car's in the Dekkerstraat, just over the bridge. Come along.'

'No,' said Araminta—a waste of breath, for he took no notice at all, but caught her by the arm and marched her back the way she had come, back over the bridge and across the covered pavement to where the Rolls stood. He opened the door, tossed her on to the front seat and said curtly: 'Get that wet jacket off—and your shoes.'

Not her shoes, she warned herself silently. She couldn't run away without shoes, and she would have to do that somehow or other; to go back to Crispin's house with him was unthinkable. She fought with the buttons of her jacket with numb fingers while the idea of getting money from him in some way or other crept into her tired head, until the doctor took her hands from the buttons and undid them for her in an impatient manner, then tossed her jacket on to the back seat in very much the same way as he had tossed her on to the front one, then he took off her shoes and reached behind him for a mohair rug, into which he wrapped her with impersonal care before unscrewing a small silver flask.

'Drink this,' he commanded her in a no-nonsense voice, and when she said: 'No, I won't,' went on, still in the same icy rage: 'If you don't, I shall pour it down your throat.'

Araminta opened her mouth then and gulped and spluttered and coughed, and by the time she had her breath Crispin was in the car beside her and the engine was purring gently. The brandy spread its warmth around her insides, creeping into her arms and legs; it also made her feel very peculiar. She made an effort to think clearly, for undoubtedly she would have to have it out with Crispin, and what better time than now? She was wide awake now and not quite as cold as she had been, and she was curious to know just how he had found her. Once they were clear of the town she would ask him to stop and they could each say what they had to say... She essayed to tell him so, gave a small hiccup, and went to sleep.

Her companion made a small sound which might have been a laugh, slowed the car long enough to draw her close so that her head rested against his shoulder, and then sent the Rolls scything its way through a fresh downpour of rain. It was pitch dark now and the curtain of water made it difficult to see, but Crispin didn't slacken speed. They had joined the motorway now, going north to Eindhoven, and there was almost no traffic. Presently the rain became torrential and far ahead of them there was a flicker of lightning. The doctor glanced at the dashboard clock and then at Araminta curled up beside him, dead to the world, and pulled into the next parking bay.

It took a few minutes to waken her and even then she wasn't in full possession of her wits. 'When did you eat last?' he wanted to know.

Araminta opened her eyes unwillingly. 'Breakfast.'

'Supper before that?'

She shook her head, and shook it again when he asked: 'And did you sleep at all last night?' and then feeling that she wasn't being polite, she mumbled 'No,' before her head tumbled sideways against him again.

The doctor started the car once more, driving slowly now, looking for the signpost he sought. Presently he turned off the motorway into a narrow country lane, awash with water, which led through a small village and then beyond it, curving through fields until it made a final bend into a much larger village with a cobbled street with high walls on either side of it. Its centre was taken up by a church, dimly lighted by a few street lamps, and facing it a row of houses showing a lighted window here and there. Crispin stopped the car and got out into the downpour, to cross the road and inspect the largest of the buildings which bore the appearance of an hotel—which it was, but empty and dark and closed for the winter months. He muttered something under his breath and was about to retrace his steps when he noticed that a few doors down the street there was an inn, its lighted windows revealed it to be small and distinctly cosy, with lace curtains at its windows. Someone inside was playing an accordion and there was a good deal of cheerful noise besides.

The doctor pushed open the door and looked around him, nodding a civil good evening to the half dozen people sitting in the coffee room—a distinctly old-fashioned apartment, its dark panelled walls hung with heavily framed pictures, a huge stove, crowned with an ornate metal cap, jutted out into the room from under an overmantel bristling with old pistols and pewter tankards, and the tables and chairs were arranged with almost military precision around its walls. At the farther end there was a bar, very old-fashioned and massive too, with an enormous mirror behind it, freely ornamented with fretwork shelves and an elaborately carved frame. Crispin took in these antiquated features in one all-embracing glance, he also took lightning stock of the pleasant-faced, elderly woman watching him from behind the bar. Without further hesitation he crossed the room and addressed himself to her.

Araminta woke up again as the doctor lifted her from the car and asked in a panicky voice: 'Where are we? What are you doing?'

Crispin didn't pause on his way over the cobbles back to the inn door, and since it was still teeming with rain, she could hardly have blamed him. He kicked the door open with a foot, set her down at a table nearby and observed: 'We're in the village of Thorn—south of Eindhoven. The weather is too bad to go on; besides, you need a meal and a night's sleep. Sit there while I find somewhere to put the car, and don't let us have any nonsense about running away—you have no shoes and we are both much too tired to splash around in this confounded weather. Drink your coffee when it comes and don't worry about speaking to anyone—I told the landlady that you're English.'

She peered at him, her tired, unmade-up face framed by the soft wool of the rug. 'Are you still angry?' she wanted to know.

He didn't answer her, only smiled a little and went

away, and a moment later a young girl came with a tray
of coffee. It was hot and creamy and sweet and there
were little biscuits in the saucers. Araminta ate hers at
once, aware that she was famished, then sipped the coffee slowly, her hungry eyes on the biscuit in the other
saucer—presently she ate that one too.

Crispin was taking a long time, she thought uneasily.
Supposing he had driven off and left her? The preposterous idea took root in her muddled head and swelled
out of all proportions, to disappear like a pricked bal-
loon when he opened the door and came in, sat down
opposite her and put her jacket, shoes and bag on the
chair between them.

The woman from behind the bar came with fresh
coffee and the menu card, and Araminta said apologetically: 'I ate your biscuit...'

The doctor gave her a quick glance and picked up the
card. 'Soup?' he asked her, and there was no hint of rage
in his face now. '*Echte soup,* I think—there's not much
choice, I'm afraid, but there are *gehakt balletjes* and
pommes frites. What would you like to drink? I doubt
if they serve tea—how about more coffee?'

He gave the order, hung his Burberry on the old-
fashioned coat stand by the door and sat down again
to sip his coffee, his face still blandly impassive. Araminta, feeling better after the coffee, eyed him doubtfully. Perhaps this wasn't quite the place in which to
have a serious discussion, but provided they both kept
their tempers... She began in a carefully polite voice:
'How did you know where I was? I thought Valkenburg
was a long way away...'

'Not far enough, Araminta.' His eyes glinted beneath
their lids. 'I was fortunate enough to find the clerk who

sold you your ticket—he remembered you.' He didn't mention how long it had taken him to do that, or how many clerks he had searched out and asked before he had been successful.

'Oh, I should have thought of that—my Dutch...'

'Your pretty face, Araminta,' he corrected her gently.

She decided to ignore that. 'But you didn't know where I was in Valkenburg.'

He shrugged. 'It's not a very large town. The hotel at which you stayed was the third one I visited. They didn't know where you were, but one of the waiters had seen you walking back into the town—it was just a question of looking.'

She said 'Oh,' again, at a loss for words, but presently she said: 'It was very kind of you to come after me, but unnecessary—I'm perfectly all right, you know, and I—I knew exactly what I was doing.'

His stern mouth curved just a little. 'Yes.' He might have added more, but just then the soup arrived and instead of speaking he watched Araminta's delightful nose twitch at its appetising smell. He passed her the salt and enquired in an off-hand manner: 'What did you have instead of supper last night?'

She didn't look at him. 'Well, I—I wasn't hungry. I bought a bag of chips and then I had coffee at the hotel.' She picked up her spoon then and he forbore from asking any more questions, leaving her to enjoy her meal.

The *gehakt balletjes,* richly brown and crisp, tasted like heaven. Araminta ate them slowly and the chips and *appelmoes* besides, thankful that her companion was leaving her in peace. The thought reminded her that even though he might wish to remain silent, there were several things she must say. She accepted yet more coffee and when he offered her brandy to go with it, prudently refused. 'The brandy you gave me to drink,' she reminded him coldly, 'was very strong; it sent me to sleep.'

His eyes gleamed with laughter. 'It does have that effect on an empty stomach, and I neglected to ask you whether yours was empty or not. I'm sorry.' He smiled properly for the first time and she said quickly: 'But you wanted that, didn't you, so that I would go with you without a fuss—how very unfair!'

'Everything's fair in love and war, Araminta.'

She put down her coffee cup, noticing that her hand was shaking. He must be very anxious to be rid of her— Tante Maybella had been right, and nothing was turning out as she had planned. She had meant to disappear without a fuss and write a letter—a dignified letter, betraying none of her feelings—when she got home to Dunster, instead of which she had merely given him a great deal of trouble of leaving him free to go to his Nelissa with a clear conscience. She wondered briefly if Nelissa was a nice girl and said meekly: 'I'm sorry I've been such a nuisance. Everything went wrong—I should have stopped and packed some things and made sure that I had my notecase with me…but you see I thought that if I could get away before you got home…'

The doctor eyed her narrowly across the table, but she wasn't looking at him. 'I should like to talk…' she began once more.

He interrupted her very firmly. 'And so should I; I fancy we have a great deal to say to each other, Araminta, but not now. You are too tired, and so, for that matter, am I. Tomorrow will be time enough. Now you will go to bed and sleep.'

He got up as he spoke and she got to her feet reluctantly, for she had screwed up her courage and now it was oozing out of her again, but he was right, of course. So bade him good night without another word and followed the young girl up a narrow uncarpeted flight of stairs and into a small, very clean bedroom, where she was made to understand that she was to let her guide have her damp skirt. She supposed that that too was to be cleaned, together with her jacket and shoes, which, Crispin had already told her, would be returned to her in the morning.

He had been as good as his word. Not only were they returned to her dry and pressed and the shoes shining, but the girl brought her a tray of tea in the morning, as well. True, the tea was in a glass and there was no milk, but it was a nice normal way in which to start the day, although whether the day itself was going to be normal remained to be seen. There was a note under the miniature teapot, too, in Crispin's wellnigh unreadable scrawl: 'I imagine you might not get up without your tea. Breakfast is in half an hour.'

'Orders, orders!' muttered Araminta pettishly, and swept the hair out of her eyes and drank her tea, then got out of her comfortable bed and dressed herself, taking a defiant extra five minutes over her exquisitely neat hair-do. But if she had hoped to annoy the doctor by this, she was disappointed, for he merely put down his paper, got to his feet, wished her an austere good morning and hoped that she had slept well. He then asked her if she would like coffee with her breakfast, sat down again and resumed his reading. There was no one else in the coffee room, so it was an excellent opportunity to state her case, even borrow some money from him so that she might carry out her still nebulous plans to run away again, but somehow it was difficult to address herself to an upheld newspaper.

When their breakfast came, Araminta ate and drank mechanically, rehearsing what she would say when she had the chance, and presently, when he lowered his newspaper, the chance came. Even then, she found it difficult to begin, for he made some matter-of-fact remark about the weather which quite put her off her stroke, although she did finally achieve: 'You said we might talk…'

He was looking over the bill the landlady had just presented, but he put it down so that he might give her his full attention. 'Ah, yes—and so we will, but not, I think, until we have Tante Maybella with us. It would only be a waste of time and we should be at loggerheads.'

'We shan't… I won't come back with you, I won't… can't you see?' Her voice rose a little.

'No, I don't see,' he told her, 'but I believe I can guess… afraid to come back?'

'Of course not—it's simply that there's no point… I don't know why you pretended to…' She stopped, for she was making no headway at all, and Crispin must have shared her view, for he said gravely: 'You know, you haven't finished a single sentence since we started this conversation—I think it would be better if we waited.'

His manner was pleasant, faintly amused now, and wholly impersonal; it was impossible to imagine that this was the same man who had called her his darling, although it wasn't very wise to remember that now.

'If you had told me about her—right at the beginning,' said Araminta wistfully.

His eyes were steady on her face. 'About her?' he queried softly.

'Nelissa.'

He said sharply, 'Ah—Aunt Maybella *has* been talking to you.'

'Yes.'

He didn't say anything for a minute or two but got to his feet. 'We will go home now,' he told her. 'There is a great deal to say to you, but I prefer to wait until we are there. If when we have had our—er—discussion, you still wish to go back to Dunster, you have only to say so and I will arrange for you to go immediately.'

It was a handsome offer and she could see that there was no alternative; he would stop her if she tried to make off, and if he couldn't stop her he would come after her. 'Purely from a sense of duty,' she reminded herself sadly. So she said: 'Very well, I'll get my bag,' in a wooden voice and went back to her little room to fetch it. But when she reached it she sat down on the little bed to think. Things weren't turning out the way she had wanted them to; Crispin was determined to take her back with him; perhaps his sense of hospitality had been outraged and he wished to make amends. He had liked her even if he hadn't loved her; possibly, if Nelissa hadn't suddenly become available, they might have been quite happily married. She sighed; she would have been, anyway.

She got up and went to look at her face in the very small looking-glass which was all the hotel allowed its guests as a concession to their vanity; she looked awful, no wonder Crispin hadn't bothered to look at her during breakfast. She picked up her bag and went downstairs to find the Rolls, polished and gleaming from some hard-working, invisible hand, standing before the inn door. There was no sign of Crispin, and she looked around in a sudden absurd state of panic, quite forgetful of her brave resolve to run away if she had the chance, aware that it was ridiculous to feel utterly lost just because he wasn't there. After all, she was going to have to manage without him for the rest of her life, wasn't she?

She didn't hear him come up behind her. 'I've been listening to the weather report,' he observed mildly. 'More bad weather on the way, I'm afraid, but we should be home in time for lunch.'

He ushered her into the car, talking about the village as he did so—a small feudal town, he told her, owned by one family for a very long time, hence its pristine appearance, its cobbled streets and its air of not belonging to modern times. Araminta listened with half an ear, her mind already kilometres away, in Amsterdam, trying to think what she should do, and say, when they got there. She observed politely that the information was fascinating, and the doctor, who had passed on to some mundane remark about the state of the road, hid a smile as he started the car.

He talked for a good part of their journey, seemingly oblivious of the fact that her replies were distrait to say the least, and when they reached s'Hertogenbosch, he left the motorway briefly and took her to the Chalet Royal for coffee. The leaden sky which had been brooding over them since they had left Thorn dissolved into a torrent of rain while they were drinking it, made worse by the strong wind which came from nowhere to toss the bare branches of the trees and turn hastily opened umbrellas inside out. Araminta gazed out of the window and shuddered despite the luxurious warmth of the restaurant. What would she have done and where would she have gone if Crispin hadn't found her? Something of her feelings must have shown on her face, for he leaned forward to say: 'Don't think about it now, Araminta. Shall we go? It's only another sixty miles.' And at the entrance: 'Wait here while I get the car, there's no need for us both to get wet.'

He was kind, she thought, watching his broad back in its enveloping Burberry weave its way through the other cars to where the Rolls stood. He would be kind to anyone—he could also be, she reminded herself, the nastiest-tempered man she had ever met. Moreover, he liked his own way, he was overbearing too... She saw him get out of the car and walk towards her, unmindful of the rain. A prudent man would have stayed where he was behind the wheel and beckoned... Her heart rocked at the sight of him; he could be as nasty as he chose and marry his Nelissa and forget all about her, but he would be the only man she could ever love. She sloshed through the rain, trying not to notice the grip of his hand on her arm.

The rain turned to sleet as they neared Utrecht and then almost imperceptibly to snow, but the Rolls speeded along the straight ribbon of highway ahead of them, cutting the slowly whitening fields on either side of them in two.

'It's winter,' said Araminta.

'The edge of winter—the first uncertain days of cold and snow and wind. The seasons have their uncertainties as well as us, you know.'

'I'm not in the least uncertain,' she assured him, too quickly.

'Good. Neither am I.' He slowed the car to edge it into the Amsterdam lane and presently they were in the outskirts and then the heart of the city. She had had hours in which to think, thought Araminta, and she had wasted them; she had used her wits to no good purpose and her mind was most regrettably blank. She saw the familiar *grachten,* veiled in snow now and quite beautiful, and in no time at all Crispin was stopping before the house, hurrying her across the pavement and up the steps and in through the door, and there was Jos coming to meet them across the hall. His 'Good morning, doctor, good morning, Miss Shaw' was very correct, although he did allow the faint flicker of a satisfied smile to cross his blunt features.

Araminta gave him a shy smile and stood uncertainly. A ridiculous, vague idea of flight, back through the solid door behind her and into the icy street, had taken possession of her once again. 'I shouldn't,' said the doctor, so that she jumped and went pink. 'I must say you're a very persistent girl. Go upstairs and comb your hair,' he suggested. 'Lunch will be ready.'

She stood her ground. 'You said we could talk...'

He looked shocked. 'My dear girl, on an empty stomach? Unthinkable! Now make haste, do.'

Chapter 9

Her room looked exactly as it had done when she had left it, although when she looked round she saw that the bed had been made up with fresh linen, there were violets and baby cyclamen in the cloisonné bowl on the bedside table and a fresh stock of magazines and English newspapers, and in the bathroom there was a pile of fluffy pink towels and a fresh assortment of soaps, for all the world as though someone had known that she would be returning. Had Crispin been so certain of finding her that he had given orders for her room to be got ready? She took off her jacket and wandered over to the window and stared out. When someone tapped on the door she said 'Come in' without thinking.

It was Crispin. He said at once and gently: 'Now stop mooning about, Araminta. You're on the wrong tack, and the more you puzzle the more wrong you'll get. Come along—you'll feel better when you've had a meal.'

He crossed the room and took her hand, and when she protested that she hadn't tidied herself, said in the same gentle voice: 'Never mind, you look very nice,' and bent to kiss her surprised mouth.

'Oh!' exclaimed Araminta, and went on quite fiercely: 'Why didn't you tell me about Nelissa?' she paused to swallow tears. 'It was unfair—if I'd known about her and you I'd never have come, and if I'd been told after we got here I'd have gone back home, and now, when I'm trying to put things right, you're making it as difficult as possible.'

Crispin was staring at her, standing very still. He said slowly: 'I wonder just what Tante Maybella told you…'

'Well, it doesn't matter, does it, and if she hadn't, I wouldn't have know…'

'I'm not sure about that. Araminta, Nelissa died sixteen years ago.' He went to the door and held it open. 'Shall we go down?'

Araminta had gone rather pale, but she didn't move an inch. 'I should like to know…' she began just a little shrilly.

'All in good time.' He smiled at her, a smile to turn her heart over and take her breath. 'My darling girl,' he said as she went past him.

They lunched in the little sitting room at the back of the house with the animals for company and Jos to wait on them. He urged Araminta in a low, fatherly voice to try the excellent soup Frone had made especially for her, and when she had obediently supped it up, he begged her to try the turbot, backed up by Crispin's: 'You had better do so, my girl, or you will offend Frone. Jos, I suppose you and she put your heads together over the sweet?'

'Indeed, yes—Miss Shaw's favourite—vacherin.'

'Splendid—will you tell Frone that lunch is delicious?'

After that, Araminta had no option but to accept whatever was put on her plate and eat it, and indeed she had to admit that she felt the better for it, and the wine Crispin had poured for her made her feel better still. All the same, she refused a second glass with a look at him which made him chuckle.

'Keeping a clear head, Araminta?' he wanted to know.

Her head hadn't been clear for some time, not since he had called her his darling girl and told her that Nelissa was dead, but she was given no chance to brood over this, for Crispin kept up a gentle flow of talk which required little or no answer but required her attention at the same, so that although she still felt very muddled and bewildered by the time they went into the drawing room she was much more in command of herself. The coffee tray had already been carried in and Crispin turned back to say something to Jos, who went upstairs.

'Tante Maybella is to join us for coffee,' said Crispin, 'she has already lunched in her room.'

Araminta had sat down, but she got up again as the old lady came into the room. She looked very small and fragile and frightened, even when Crispin had kissed her with his usual kindness and settled her in her usual chair by the fire and invited her to pour the coffee.

'You see that I have brought Araminta back home again,' he remarked cheerfully as he dispensed the coffee cups, and Mevrouw van Sibbelt darted a glance at him, looking more alarmed than ever and most dreadfully unhappy. 'We shall be married quite soon,' he went on, taking no notice at all of Araminta's astounded gasp. 'She will find it wonderful to have you here, teaching her how to run the house and care for its treasures, and I hope to love them, just as you do, my dear.'

'Oh, Crispin, I never meant to… I've been a wicked old woman…you want me to stay? To live here after you are married?' The old, anxious face puckered. 'I thought that if you married, you wouldn't want me…'

Crispin was standing with his back to the fire. 'Is that why you told Araminta about Nelissa, Tante Maybella? Allowing her to think…well, never mind that now, but there was no need. How could you have thought such a thing of me? Home wouldn't be home without you. Isn't that true, Araminta?'

Thus addressed, Araminta made shift to close her mouth which had been hanging open in surprise and then murmur something or other. The nerve, the colossal nerve, taking it for granted that she would accept the situation like a lamb! So she was to marry him now, was she, without a word of explanation? Her bosom heaved with her strong emotions and the doctor's eye lingered lovingly on her. Her own eyes kindled with temper as she prepared to tell him just what she thought of him. Love him with all her heart she might, but he could annoy her more than anyone she knew. Only, on the point of embarking on impassioned speech, her gaze fell upon Mevrouw van Sibbelt and at the sight of that small, unhappy face, her own unhappy ill feelings disappeared entirely. She flew across the room and cast herself down on her knees beside the old lady's chair.

'Of course it's true,' she declared strongly, 'and how could I possibly manage to run a great house like this without you to guide me? I'd be lost, I would indeed.' She put her arms round the thin shoulders and kissed the delicately made-up cheek. 'Oh, you must forget that you ever thought such a thing of us...'

'You're not angry? I am very fond of you, Araminta dear—I don't know what came over me. It was very wrong of me, I have known that, but I'm old, you see, and I was afraid. The old aren't always wanted, you know. And I didn't mean to tell you a lie, exactly, but you made it very easy. I have been very unhappy, for I never thought that you would go away. You're quite sure...'

'Quite, quite sure. Now will you not drink your coffee?'

Tante Maybella accepted the fragile cup and sipped daintily. 'There is a great deal I can teach you, my dear, and so much to tell you about this house, although I suppose Crispin has already told you a great deal.' Her voice faltered a little. 'You are not angry, Crispin?'

'No, my dear.' His voice was very kind, so was his smile. 'How could I be angry with someone to whom I am devoted?'

His aunt put down her cup. 'There, now I am happy again; it is such a relief, and now I think I should like to go to my room and sit quietly. I have a great deal to think about, and the wedding to consider.'

She kissed Araminta and took Crispin's arm. 'You will be very happy, just like your dear father and mother.' She trotted to the door, her arm in his. 'It will be delightful to have children in the house,' she observed happily as he ushered her out of the room.

There was silence after she had gone. Crispin closed the door and leaned against it, his hands in his pockets, and Araminta, aware that he was watching her intently, fidgeted with her coffee cup, then put it down and fell to examining her nails. At last he said: 'I expected a torrent of abuse.'

'Well, I can't think of anything to say.' Whereupon she burst into speech. 'I don't know why you couldn't have told me—you had only to say…at Valkenburg or that funny little inn, and all you could say was that we must wait for your aunt.' Her voice rose a little. 'I can't understand at all. Besides that, you made it very awkward for me, having to tell Mevrouw van Sibbelt…' She added with elaborate casualness: 'Who was Nelissa?'

Crispin was across the room and she found herself wrapped tenderly in his arms. 'That's better,' he spoke on a laugh. 'What would have been the use of telling you anything, my darling love? Would you have believed a word of it? In any case, when I found you you were in no fit state to listen, were you? I should have told you before; I was going to tell you, but the telephone rang and I had to go—remember? And I had no idea why you had run away. I only knew that I had to get you back.' He kissed her swiftly. 'I haven't thought of Nelissa for a long time now. Sixteen years is a long time, my darling, and I haven't thought of anything or anyone but you since I first saw you standing defiantly below those Cornish cliffs.'

'You were very rude,' said Araminta.

'I was thunderstruck—to come across my dream girl in such an unlikely place. I wanted to kiss you…which reminds me…'

This time his kiss wasn't gentle or brief; it was entirely satisfying. Araminta sighed happily. 'I thought—all this time—that you weren't sure about loving me.'

'I've never been more sure of anything in my life, my dearest, but I had to give you time to be sure.'

'I didn't need any time.' She stretched up to kiss him.

'Good—so you won't need any time to think about marrying me. Never mind about clothes and so on, we'll get those later. I arranged about the licence when I was in Dunster.'

She looked at him with loving admiration. 'Since you've gone to so much trouble,' she told him, 'the least I can do is to fall in with your plans.'

* * * * *

*Can Chase McCabe help Mitzy Martin with matters
of business when the beautiful single mother has him
thinking of matters of the heart?*

Read on for a sneak preview of
The Texas Cowboy's Quadruplets,
the third book in Cathy Gillen Thacker's heartfelt series
Texas Legends: The McCabes.

"So, the boot is finally on the other foot."

Mitzy Martin stared at the indomitable CEO standing on
the other side of her front door, looking more rancher than
businessman in nice-fitting jeans, boots and a tan Western
shirt. Ignoring the skittering of her heart, she heaved a sigh
to convey just how unwelcome he was. "What's your point,
cowboy?"

Mischief gleaming in his smoky-blue eyes, Chase looked
her up and down in a way that made her insides flutter. "Just
that you've been a social worker in Laramie County for
what…ten years now?"

Electricity sparked between them with all the danger of
a downed power line. "Eleven," Mitzy corrected. And it had
been slightly longer than that. Since she'd abruptly ended
their engagement…

"My guess is, very few people are happy to see you
coming up their front walk. Now you seem to be feeling
that," he continued with an ornery grin, "seeing *me* at your
door."

Mitzy drew a breath, ignoring the considerable physical
awareness that never failed to materialize between them.

She gave him a long, level look to show him he was *not* going to get to her. Even if his square jaw and chiseled features, sandy-brown hair and incredibly buff physique were permanently imprinted on her brain. She smiled sweetly. "Well, when people get to know me and realize I'm there to help, they usually become quite warm and friendly."

He surveyed her pleasantly. "That's exactly what I hope will happen between you and me. Now that we're older and wiser, that is."

Mitzy glared. She and Chase had crashed and burned once—spectacularly. There was no way she was doing it again.

He stepped closer, inundating her with his wildly intoxicating scent. "Mitzy, come on. You've been ducking my calls for weeks now."

So what? "I know it's hard for a carefree bachelor like you to understand, but I've been 'a little busy' since giving birth to quadruplets."

He shrugged. "Word around town is you've had *plenty* of volunteer help. Plus the high-end nannies your mother sent from Dallas."

Mitzy groaned and clapped a hand across her forehead.

"Didn't work out?"

"No," she bit out. "Just like this lobbying effort on your part won't work, either."

"Look, I know you'd rather not do business with me," he said, even more gently. "But at least hear me out."

Don't miss
The Texas Cowboy's Quadruplets
by Cathy Gillen Thacker.

Available October 2018 wherever
Harlequin® Special Edition books and ebooks are sold.

www.Harlequin.com

HARLEQUIN®
SPECIAL EDITION

Life, Love and Family

Save **$1.00**

on the purchase of ANY
Harlequin® Special Edition book.

Available wherever books are sold,
including most bookstores, supermarkets,
drugstores and discount stores.

Save $1.00

on the purchase of any Harlequin® Special Edition book.

Coupon valid until December 31, 2018.
Redeemable at participating outlets in the U.S. and Canada only.
Limit one coupon per customer.

52615971

Canadian Retailers: Harlequin Enterprises Limited will pay the face value of this coupon plus 10.25¢ if submitted by customer for this product only. Any other use constitutes fraud. Coupon is nonassignable. Void if taxed, prohibited or restricted by law. Consumer must pay any government taxes. Void if copied. Inmar Promotional Services ("IPS") customers submit coupons and proof of sales to Harlequin Enterprises Limited, P.O. Box 31000, Scarborough, ON M1R 0E7, Canada. Non-IPS retailer—for reimbursement submit coupons and proof of sales directly to Harlequin Enterprises Limited, Retail Marketing Department, Bay Adelaide Centre, East Tower, 22 Adelaide Street West, 40th Floor, Toronto, Ontario M5H 4E3, Canada.

5 65373 00076 2 (8100)0 12386

U.S. Retailers: Harlequin Enterprises Limited will pay the face value of this coupon plus 8¢ if submitted by customer for this product only. Any other use constitutes fraud. Coupon is nonassignable. Void if taxed, prohibited or restricted by law. Consumer must pay any government taxes. Void if copied. For reimbursement submit coupons and proof of sales directly to Harlequin Enterprises, Ltd 482, NCH Marketing Services, P.O. Box 880001, El Paso, TX 88588-0001, U.S.A. Cash value 1/100 cents.

® and ™ are trademarks owned and used by the trademark owner and/or its licensee.

© 2018 Harlequin Enterprises Limited

HSECOUP04505

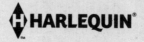